MAKO BAY

OTAGO WATERS - BOOK 1

STEPHANIE RUTH

TĪ Kōuka

PUBLISHING

ISBN 978-1-7386059-8-9 (Paperback)

ISBN 978-0-473-59007-9 (Paperback POD)

ISBN 978-0-473-59008-6 (Epub)

ISBN 978-0-473-59009-3 (Kindle)

ISBN 978-0-473-59010-9 (Digital Audiobook)

Cover design by Tī Kōuka Publishing.

 Formatted with Vellum

CONTENTS

For Aaron,
to the dinosaurs and back again.

And in recognition of Kiwi musicians, both living and gone, who gifted us
the soundtrack of our lives.

Ngā mihi nui. Aroha nui.

TE REO MĀORI – MĀORI LANGUAGE GLOSSARY

Ākarana - Auckland (loan from English)
Aotearoa - New Zealand
Āraiteuru - (also *Araiteuru*) ancestral canoe of legend, originating in Hawaiki
Aroha - love
E hoa - friend, partner, spouse
E hoa wahine - female friend, wife
Haere mai - come here
He waka eke noa - we're in this boat together
Kaihana - cousin (loan from English)
Ka pai - good, good job
Karakia - prayer, chant, incantation
Kaumātua - elder, person of status
Kia ora - hello, good wishes, thank you
Kiwi - flightless bird, New Zealander
Kōrero tuku iho - history, stories of the past, oral tradition
Koru - coil, curled shoot
Ko ___ te tau o taku ate - ___ is my sweetheart, I have great affection for ___
Ko ___ toku ingoa - ____ is my name
Ko ___ toku matua - ____ is my father
Māori - indigenous people/person of Aotearoa
Māui - legendary demigod
Mako - common shark

Manaakitanga - hospitality, kindness, generosity, support
Mana whenua - territorial rights, power from the land
Marae - courtyard, complex surrounding wharenui
Marama - moon
Matau - fish hook
Matua - father, parent, uncle
Mere - flat weapon made of stone
Mihi - speech of greeting, tribute
Miri - rub, twist, shortened form of Miriama
Miriama - Miriam (loan from English)
Moana - ocean, sea, large body of water
Moeraki - small township and tourist attraction: eastern coast of Te Waipounamu
Moko - tattoo
Mōrena - good morning (loan from English)
Nau mai - welcome
Ngaio - small indigenous tree, poisonous leaves and berries
Ngā mihi - acknowledgements
Nui - big
Ōtautahi - Christchurch city, largest city in Te Waipounamu
Ōtepoti - Dunedin city, largest city in Otago
Otago - southeast area of South Island. Originally *Ōtākou* denoting the marae
Pākeha - New Zealander of European descent
Pāua - rainbow abalone
Pīwakawaka - fantail, indigenous bird
Pōhutukawa - indigenous tree, red flowers
Pounamu - greenstone, jade
Rā - sun, day
Rimu - red pine
Tāmaki Makau Rau/Tāmaki-makau-rau - Auckland city, land desired by many
Tāngata - people
Taka - to range, roam
Tēnā koe - hello (to one)
Te tau o tāku ate - my sweetheart
Te Reo - the language
Te Waipounamu/Te Wāhi Pounamu - The South Island, otherwise

known as *Te Waka-o-Māui* or in more ancient times *Te Waka-o-Aoraki*

Te Whanganui-a-Tara - Wellington city, the capital of Aotearoa

Tipuna/tīpuna - ancestor/ancestors

Tuahine/tūahine - sister/sisters, female cousin(s)

Tuakana - older sister (to a female), older brother (to a male)

Wānaka - lake and township in central Otago

Wahine/wāhine - woman/women

Waka - boat, vehicle

Whaea/whāea - mother/mothers, aunt/aunts

Whakapapa - genealogy, lineage, descent

Whānau - family

Wharenui - large meeting house

Whenua - land, country

For an extensive Te Reo dictionary, with audio examples, go to Te Aka, at maoridictionary.co.nz.

SVENSKA SPRÅKET – SWEDISH
LANGUAGE GLOSSARY

Älskling - loved one, darling, honey
Fredslilja - peace lily
Hej - hello, hi
Hej min älskling - hi honey
Hur går det - how are you
Jag älskar dig - I love you
Lilla flicka - little girl
Morfar - grandfather (maternal)
Mormor - grandmother (maternal)

MAKO BAY

What's a crush among friends?

Fashion designer Shal Hoffner's back in Ōtepoti after eight years of self-imposed exile. Setting up a satellite boutique and juggling bridesmaid duties for her best friend's upcoming wedding, she's determined to forget her ripped-up past, soulless love-life, and the guy who broke her heart.

She should've known it wouldn't be that simple.

Assuming the proximity of Cameron Dante—builder, guitarist, surf-buddy, and ex-flatmate—the least of her worries? Big mistake. Huge. Because there's more to the past than Shal knows, on a collision course with her immediate future, and if she can't stick to friends-with-benefits there's a chance she might snap, just like before.

'No promises, no commitment, and no exclusive rights...' Shal's mantra is fast losing traction, and it's all Cam's fault. He's not the shy surfer-down-the-hall he once was, and he's out to prove something, no matter the cost. He's been in love with Shal forever, so what's he got to lose?

His newfound roots, his music career, his heart and soul...

Pretty much everything, actually.

.

NOTE FROM THE AUTHOR

This novel deals with the trauma of a past car accident, parental infidelity, and past partner infidelity (historical). Please read at your own discretion.

Winner of the Daphne Clair de Jong First Kiss award and finalist in the Koru Best First Book award, MAKO BAY is the first story in the Otago Waters series, set in the beautiful South Island of Aotearoa, New Zealand. Each book stands alone, but reading them in order provides a deeper experience. Intended for readers who enjoy their slow-burn, feel-good romance on the steamy side, with the promise of a happily ever after.

1
———

Listening to…
Welcome Home - Dave Dobbyn
From the album: Available Light

Two digits and six letters in all.

She'd memorised the simple address, but Shal Hoffner checked her phone to make doubly sure before leaning across the dashboard to peer up at the brickwork.

Definitely the one.

Fumbling with her keys and handbag in her haste to get out of the car, she had to push herself back against the door when a bus rumbled past.

Shitsticks.

Her hatchback was in dire need of a wash after the long drive, and now her jeans were too. Shal brushed at the dark denim with agitated fingers, wanting to be here, yet not.

She'd studied briefly in this southern university town, and though it seemed like a lifetime ago, the lessons the place had taught were deeply scored. Etched indelible.

Knowing the campus had to be somewhere nearby, Shal scanned her surroundings to get her bearings. Cam's directions had engulfed her in downtown Ōtepoti, where Victorian villas and Edwardian townhouses crowded around her like disapproving great-aunts.

Her ex-flatmate's latest doer-upper stood proud amongst them, brick firewalls separating it from the single-storey neighbours. The window frames had been repainted, white sills fresh against the terracotta, and it wasn't the only tarted-up house on the street.

The overall atmosphere of the area was moving towards city chic, which was a bit of a surprise. When Shal had flatted nearby eight years ago it'd been strictly student grunge—slack bellied sofas on front porches with peeling paint, hiked up rents, cold rooms, and noisy neighbours.

Perhaps parts of the city were moving on and moving up?

Shal took the short path and rapped on the front door, trying to convince herself it was excitement, not dread, fisting in her stomach.

She *was* excited about returning—about being Katie's bridesmaid and pushing forward with the southern boutique. But darker emotions weren't so easily shoved aside now she'd actually arrived.

Cupping her hands up to her eyes like blinkers, she tried to peep through the stained-glass panel.

Still no answer.

Shal rummaged through her handbag for her cell phone, but a shadow appeared behind the glass before she'd had time to place a call, evaporating her tension like a curl of steam off a welcome cup of tea.

Cam.

God, she was a sight for sore eyes.

Shal stole Cam's breath away. Always had, and probably always would. She stood on the front path exuding an easy elegance—even in worn blue jeans.

His old flatmate's coat was looped over her arm and she wore calf-hugging boots and an oversized scarf. Obviously more prepared for the southern weather this time, she was layered up to stay warm.

Eight years ago it had been a different story.

Glossy dark hair was twisted into some sort of tie at the back, but a few wayward tendrils had escaped to frame Shal's oval face, softening the strictness. Ocean eyes startled against her olive complexion and right now those beauties were crinkled up at the corners.

Her smile was infectious.

"Cam!" Shal held both arms wide, inviting a hug.

What was a man to do? He swung her into a quick embrace.

Shal laughed, so maybe she didn't mind a week's worth of whiskers as he smacked a kiss on her cheek and placed her carefully away from himself.

"Nau mai, haere mai. Welcome, e hoa."

"Thank you. It's been too long! You smell like wood… Pine?"

"Ah, sawdust." He brushed at his T-shirt. "Sorry," he added with a grimace, eyeing the soft and probably expensive weave of Shal's scarf. "Forgot I was covered in it."

And he'd planned to have a shave, too.

"Don't be an idiot." Shal reached one hand up, stopping just before touching his hair, which was getting too long. "Dreads are gone," she said with a wry little twist to her mouth.

"Long gone." He ran his fingers through his rough mop with a faint sense of disquiet, feeling Shal's non-touch more acutely than if she'd grabbed a handful and yanked on it.

"You look different."

"Yeah? Well you look just the same. A little warmer maybe. Your lips aren't blue," he teased, tugging on the corner of her scarf. "But otherwise just the same."

Gorgeous.

"You know it's still summer, right?" he continued to hassle, gesturing towards her winter get-up.

"*Almost* autumn. But you can't ever be sure of the season in Arctic Otago."

"Hm." Cam didn't bite at the old taunt. He'd been thinking about her all day, inching ever closer on the southern highway. "Good drive?"

"Beautiful. I finally got to see the boulders."

"Moeraki? Worth the wait?"

"Amazing. Monumental, in fact," Shal enthused. "I was half expecting one to hatch."

3

"Yeah, I know what you mean."

Forged out of concreted marine mud, the orbs emerged like giant eggs from the soft cliffs to the north.

The legend of Āraiteuru had been one of his father's favourite stories, and Cam had heard many renditions of how his ancestral waka had run to ground on the reef, spilling its cargo. The boulders were crosshatched with calcite-crystal fissures, and it wasn't hard to imagine them as fishing nets, fossilised full of the day's catch. Or enormous eel baskets, washed overboard in stormy seas.

They'd been planning to go to Moeraki as a group long ago, but the time had never come.

Cam studied Shal surreptitiously as they talked. She still exuded an exotic quality, though there had been a few subtle changes. Like all of them, she'd done some growing up. Confidence seemed to sit easier on her shoulders now, diminishing the underlying fragility of before.

"Get some shots?"

Shal had rarely been without her camera as a student.

"Plenty," she returned with a soft smile, looking up through her lashes.

Like sunshine breaking through the clouds.

Cam swallowed. "Sound a bit husky too. I'd say you've been singing."

"Yep. All the way. You know me too well!"

Laughter made Shal's face light up, eyes sparkling like polished pāua.

Endearing in its pure lack of pretence, Cam was relieved Shal's snort and chuckle remained every inch the same. For all her spit and polish, she'd always had an incredibly geeky laugh.

Not just gorgeous, not just sunshine, she completely undid him.

Cam cleared his throat and brought one hand up to rub the back of his neck.

"Bags? Board?" Realising he'd been staring, he shook off the old, all too familiar feeling. It was a bit of a shock to have it back full force, seemingly undiluted by distance or time.

"I didn't bring a board, but I've got plenty of other stuff. This one's mine." Shal gestured to the late model hatchback parked out front, and Cam ragged her about not bringing surfing gear to arguably the best breaks in the world as he followed her towards her car in his work socks.

———

"Hells bells," Cam whistled. "How long did you say you were staying again?" He nodded towards Shal's luggage, and she reassessed the heap.

True, quite a lot.

She'd folded the seats down to double the boot space when she'd left Te Whanganui-a-Tara, then stuffed it full of suitcases and black zip-up hanger bags.

"It's mostly samples for Jac and Katie," she justified, pointing towards the clothing bags before pressing the same finger to her top lip, realising belatedly she hadn't labelled which was for whom.

"Okay. Let's haul, then." Cam nodded, his jaw locked in a resigned line.

"The big suitcase is all yours." Shal was quick to delegate, having struggled with the damn thing at the other end. "It's bloody heavy."

Cam tested its weight and pulled a comical face.

She'd really missed his easy manner—missed having him around to laugh with. No matter how long they stretched time between seeing each other, with Cam there was always the comfortable hum of being with a friend who accepted her as she was.

His scruffy, handsome face was smiling right back at her.

Scrap that last bit. Best to remove it from the equation. Attraction wasn't a complication she needed.

Though Cam *was* good looking, and always had been in a boy-down-the-hall kind of way, he called her e hoa—friend, and that's what they'd been to each other since the beginning.

Unshaven, his caramel hair shaggy without the signature dreadlocks, she mightn't have recognised her old flatmate if she hadn't kept up with him online. Except for those cocoa-and-honey eyes, they were just as she remembered.

He'd filled out, too. His well-used T-shirt showed off the

muscular arms and solid chest of a man who obviously worked with his hands.

Cam took the two larger suitcases and returned for the smaller ones as Shal ferried piles of hanger bags into the hall, studying the place with great interest. The period features remained in the moulded ceiling medallions, while the paintwork was all soft-tone white, making it feel light and airy.

"Wow, this is really lovely. I wasn't expecting it to be so complete. I thought your place was still a work in progress?"

"No. This one's nearly done. Actually, it was supposed to be signed off last week." Cam ran a palm over the back of his head again, making him look boyish, younger—more like the guy she remembered. "Touch wood, the tradies should be out of your hair by Wednesday." He rapped his knuckles on the bannister then angled a look at her, returning back from wherever his thoughts had just taken him.

His frown eased off.

It was kind of him, giving her a place to stay for a couple of weeks till Katie and Rue's wedding.

"So nice to see you," she murmured.

"Yeah, nice to see you too."

Shal noted the laughter lines at the corners of Cam's eyes, more than he'd ever had before, and the deep fissure dimples forming down his cheeks as his grin grew to match hers.

He smiled with his whole face, the one errant eye-tooth that refused to stand in line endearingly familiar.

She lifted a hand to wipe a smudge of finely powdered sawdust off Cam's forehead, not thinking about the intimacy of the gesture until she was half way through executing it.

They'd been so close once, living in each other's pockets, but that was a lifetime ago.

Shal dropped her hand self-consciously. "So, show me around?"

Cam cleared his throat. "Sure. Right."

Cam took Shal through the ground floor of the restored townhouse, satisfied it was almost complete.

Dundas Street was one in a chain of purchases he'd made since starting out five years ago with his business partner, Jonno. They were gradually pulling together a portfolio of properties—some for rental, some for clients, and the occasional one to on-sell.

A renovation with major concessions to the cold winters this far south, the team had been stripping and refitting the old brick two-storey since Jonno had bought it—just before Christmas. The timing had been perfect to outfit it with basic furniture for friends and family to use.

Well, almost perfect.

With his cousin's March wedding fast approaching, whānau needed places to stay. Only two weeks left until the main event, and Dundas Street had presented itself as an indirect wedding present to Katie.

Free accomodation for her bridesmaids.

Thompson & Dante would lose money on the delay in property turnover, but it was a worthwhile cause.

"Downstairs bedroom is pegged for Aroha and Links." Cam hefted the largest of the suitcases and began to lead Shal up the wide staircase. "Otherwise, you're first in, so first served."

"Which one's your...?"

Turning back, he shook his head, noting the sudden stiffness in Shal's posture when she cottoned on.

"You don't *live* here?" she squeaked. "I thought..." Confusion made her eyes appear even bigger.

Cam sighed, re-bracing his stance against both the weight of the suitcase and his decision to move out.

"I did while we refitted it, but as soon as the next job's up and running I move in and live onsite." A half-truth... "Like a hobo, my mother kindly informs me." That bit was the whole truth. "I'm just a couple of blocks away up on Park Street."

Cam knew damn well he could've stayed on until the others needed the beds, or even camped in the lounge. It definitely would've been a more comfortable option. But he'd lived with Shal before, and knew from experience how hard it was have her on the home front, without ever actually having her. Two weeks within her general vicinity was going to be awkward enough.

Park Street wasn't exactly fit for habitation yet, but he'd make do.

"Oh. I see." Shal was still blinking at him, her knuckles white on the bannister. "Well, it was really kind of you to invite me to stay here, either way. Thank you." She attempted to mask her bewilderment politely, but he could still read her, loud and clear.

"No worries. I hope you know you're welcome anytime." Cam could still feel Shal's eyes still on him as he turned and continued up the stairs, and for the first time that day, considered the clothes he'd thrown on for work. Paint-stained jeans and a holey Wild Foods T-shirt might come across as a tad on the shabby side to an award-winning clothing designer.

He reached the landing and took some pleasure in dumping Shal's case down for a breather.

"Disclaimer. Don't tell her I said so, but Mum's not entirely wrong. I tend to live like a tramp on whatever worksite I have on the go." Best to get that straight from the get-go. "Three bedrooms up here." He pointed to the corresponding doors. "One with an ensuite. This is the shared bathroom. Not quite finished yet, sorry about that. The tilers…" he trailed off, grimacing.

Shal didn't need to hear about the screwed up tile order and ensuing delays.

"So, you're alone here until my brother turns up sometime this week, then Aroha and Links arrive the following Thursday. Adele's somewhere in the middle, I think." Katie's sister lived in Oz, but would be flying over soon-ish. This week? Cam had a scratch at the back of his head, but it didn't jog the memory. "Katie's got it all written down."

"I've never met your brother. He's not staying with your mum?"

Cam laughed. "Māui couldn't drag him there. Not when all Mum's sisters are descending for the wedding."

"They don't get on?"

"Like a house on fire, with dynamite under the floorboards. Inflammatory comments get biffed his way until eventually he explodes. It's entertaining to watch. From a distance. Like an extreme sport."

"Dante D," Shal said a little too dreamily for Cam's liking. He turned to look at her sharply, hands riding low on his hips.

It was years ago now, but his older brother would probably never lose the nickname. Daniel had been dubbed 'Dante D' when he'd rocketed into the spotlight as first-five for the prestigious provincial rugby team. The name had stuck, and gained momentum when he'd made the national line-up two seasons running. He'd been young for the team, but ready. Even now, and even if you didn't follow rugby, everyone knew who Dante D was.

Cam was used to the hype, though it was nothing compared to the fever-pitched intensity it'd reached when his brother was still playing. Before his catastrophic knee injury.

Cam hefted up Shal's suitcase again, shaking off his faint unease at her reaction. "So, the house is yours for two weeks until the wedding, and however long you want to stay after, but the others aren't coming until closer to crunch-time."

"High-noon."

"What?"

"Call it high-noon, not *crunch*-time, it sounds less... I don't know... Ominous."

"Less ominous? Okay. High-noon," Cam conceded. "No, let me think. I'm sure I can come up with a better one. I know! Do or die time," he teased. "Sink or swim time?"

With her arms full, he knew Shal couldn't throw a punch his way. She tried to kick his butt instead, but he evaded easily, anticipating the move.

"The point of no *retuuuuurn*!" Cam hammed it up like he was doing the voice-over for a movie trailer, bugging his eyes out and using a deep, spooky tone. He was gifted a light snort and a goofy grin from Shal for his trouble.

"Idiot."

Their views on marriage and commitment were poles apart, but he'd rather make light of it than have a serious discussion on the subject. Over the past few years Shal had flitted in and out of so many relationships, Cam was hard pressed to keep track. The only thing he was sure about was none of them were particularly long-term. Six months seemed to be Shal's own version of crunch-time.

Carrying on down the hall to the room overlooking the back courtyard, Cam nudged the door open with his shoulder.

"If I were you, I'd definitely lay claim to the biggest, sunniest

9

room with the ensuite—the *only* working bathroom at present. Besides…" He flicked a nod towards the large suitcase in his hand with a slow grin. "It's got the biggest wardrobe."

"Sold!" Shal walked in and her jaw dropped almost comically. "Oooh. I *love* this room." Dumping her clothing bags on the white linen duvet, she popped her head into the walk-in wardrobe. "God, Cam. It's beautiful."

"You mean the wardrobe?" he joked, vaguely uncomfortable with the level of admiration Shal was oozing.

"No. I mean all of it."

The master had come up really well. Two large sash windows, bordered in a heavily lined satin, overlooked the greenery beyond and threw a ton of light into the generous space. The plain carpet and walls were a blank canvas for the sparsely furnished deep blue and teal scheme.

Acting as both bedhead and feature wall, the wall-hung Turkish rug behind the bed was huge. An undeniable focal point, with the aquatic colours repeated in the throw cushions on the simple chaise between the windows.

Shal cocked her head to one side, walking over to touch the hand-woven wall rug. "These are my favourite colours," she said softly, almost under her breath.

"I'm glad you like it."

It was a marginally better line than 'I know,' which of course he did.

Shal looked like part of the overall design standing there in her blue jeans. In fact the room hadn't seemed quite complete until she'd walked into it.

Following Shal towards the white-tiled ensuite, Cam caught sight of the gift bag he'd left in the centre of the vanity bench.

"This bathroom's good to go." Thank the gods. "And there's a goodie bag from Katie." He reached in with one arm, not wanting to crowd Shal in the small space, and handed her the string-handled bag.

"Oh, she spoils me!" She was immediately rummaging within. "Smell this. *So* good." Removing a bar of fig and honey soap, Shal waved it under his nose before moving back to the main bedroom and spinning with her arms outstretched to encompass the space.

The gift bag circled her like a ring around Saturn. "Did you do all of this?"

"The interiors? Yeah. There's a team of us on building and reno, though. Jonno's registered, so the building-to-code stuff falls to him. We contract out for the tiling, some of the painting, plumbing, electrics…"

After bouncing on the bed, Shal went over to try out the chaise as well. Like a kid in a candy shop she seemed to need to touch everything, stroking the teal velvet before reaching up to rub curtain fabric between her fingers.

Cam had picked up the 1960's chaise at auction, then had it restored and reupholstered. The chair and the antique Turkish rug were worth more than the rest of the upstairs furnishings combined.

He'd had Shal in mind when he'd finished this room.

He'd had her in mind a lot recently.

Who the hell was he trying to kid? He never really managed to get her fully out of his head.

"Make yourself at home and I'll bring the rest of your stuff up." Cam removed himself from Shal's bedroom, asap.

He found her a while later, downstairs in the kitchen.

"I've boiled the kettle and I'm looking for…?" she started to query when Cam came in from packing away decking supplies in the courtyard. "Oh!" she exclaimed on spotting the arrangement of flowers in his hand. "Are those for me?"

"A welcome back gift." Cam shifted his weight uneasily, stopping himself a split second before welcoming Shal 'home.'

He'd grown up in Ōtepoti, but for Shal it'd been under a year, and with all that had gone on, it'd taken her the best part of a decade to venture back this far south.

He offered the flowers forward a little awkwardly. On getting them out of the ute, he'd begun to second-guess himself. Purposefully avoiding traditionally romantic flowers, he'd chosen a cluster of brightly coloured daisies with sunny faces instead.

"Thank you! They're gorgeous."

As Shal turned to put the flowers on the counter, adding more water to the oasis foam, Cam let out the breath he hadn't realised he'd been holding.

Given as a friend, accepted as a friend—all smooth sailing.

"Joining me?" Shal brushed against him as she reached around to pick out two cups, and once again his ex-flatmate was much too close, and achingly familiar.

"No, thanks. I'd better get on with... Ah, work stuff." He took a step sideways, pulling open the top drawer and handing Shal the unopened box of her go-to Dilmah, before edging towards the wooden bi-fold doors.

"Are you coming to Katie's for dinner? Do you want to share a ride?"

"Tonight?" Of course, his cousin would be eager to see Shal. The two women had remained close since university. Ever since Shal moved into Cam's flat to live with her boyfriend. "No. I've got plans I can't get out of." Suddenly remembering the spare set of house keys, he dug in his pocket and laid them on the bench. "I might be able to drop by later, though."

Katie hadn't specifically invited him, but she had an open-door policy when it came to family.

"Great. Organic oat milk? Yum." Shal had her head in the fridge, and her jeans fitted every bloody curve of her legs and butt, leaving nothing to his imagination.

Yum. The word reverberated around in Cam's head unhelpfully.

"Katie chose it." He reached into his back pocket and double-checked the time on his phone, giving himself something else to gawk at. "I'd better fly."

Stepping outside and easing into his waiting work-boots, Cam was edging the door closed before he remembered. "I've told the team to come in after nine a.m. tomorrow. I hope that's not too early? I realise you're on holiday." And not exactly a morning person.

"Working holiday," Shal corrected him. "No, that's fine. I'm meeting Jac at the boutique at nine, so I'll be out of their way."

Cam was familiar with Shal's business partner, and knew if Jac had arranged a nine-a.m. meeting at the boutique, the builder onsite would potentially be in for an earful. He wondered briefly if he should warn Jonno, then smothered a grin as he decided against it.

Let the big man put out that particular fire on his own.

Shal squeezed out her teabag with a spoon—as always, too

impatient to wait for it to steep. She added plenty of oat milk before taking a large swig, arching her neck first one way, then the other.

Driving tension in her shoulders, no doubt. He could offer to rub those knots out.

Cam dug his fists into his front pockets instead.

"Okay. I'll let them know to use the tradie keys."

"Maybe see you later tonight, then." Shal smiled. "And Cam?"

"Yep?"

"Thanks again for letting me stay here. It's beautiful, and I really appreciate it. No, *really*," she insisted as he tried to shrug off her unwanted gratitude. "It's *so* much nicer than a hotel."

Placing her cup back on the bench, she slid over to give him a quick hug in the doorframe. The crest of her dark head rested just under his nose.

"Ah… Sure." Her hair smelled like vanilla and peaches, and a hunger that had nothing to do with food shafted through him. "Don't forget to lock the door after me," he cautioned gruffly, stepping back.

"Yes, *Grandad*." Shal nodded with mock earnestness.

"Will you be okay here by yourself?" The empty house suddenly seemed like an unfriendly place to leave her, and for the first time, Cam was conflicted about staying somewhere else.

He remembered how much trouble she used to have sleeping.

The nightmares.

"Don't be silly. I live on my own in Te Whanganui-a-Tara." Shal smiled, but the light didn't quite reach her eyes.

2

Listening to…
Love Your Ways - Salmonella Dub
From the album: Inside The Dub Plates

Like an emerald brooch on a muddy sweater, Roseneath emerged as surprisingly pretty. Clasped to the silt bay by a saddle of lower-lying land, the peninsula was small and robust, and heavily bejewelled with both trees and houses. It would've been easy to miss the turnoff; the hidden pathway to Katie and Rue's secret hideaway, but Shal had been given detailed directions.

She arrived on time, no longer in the city but not yet in the port, and cried fat tears when Katie squeezed her extra tight on the front porch of the restored bungalow.

It'd been a full six months since Katie's last trip to Te Whanganui-a-Tara, where Shal was now based. Possibly their longest spell apart since they'd met. They'd had a fabulous girls' weekend to celebrate Katie's twenty-eighth birthday, and filled it with wine and food, talk and chatter, bridal boutiques and plans for the wedding.

Katie's fiancé, Rupert, stood a little back in the shadows of the panelled hall, eventually moving forward to give Shal a chaste kiss on the cheek. It was a refined greeting, but the tall, softly spoken Englishman appeared sincere in his welcome.

"You have *such* a lovely home." Shal moved into the open-plan living area, where traditional gave way to a light-filled, modern interior. "And I can't fault your view, either."

Dove-grey water took on the muted purple of the evening sky, and the hills of Otago Peninsula folded into shadow on the other side of the harbour.

"Yeah. I feel a bit like the cat with the cream." Katie's grin was Cheshire-wide.

"You *look* a bit like the cat with the cream."

"What?" Katie's hand instantly moved to her belly.

"No, dingbat!" Shal laughed, hugging her friend again and fluffing up her short, auburn hair. "Not *that*. Happy. You look really happy."

Katie began to laugh too.

"Call me Bridezilla. I'm so stressed about fitting into my dress, the thought of cream makes me jumpy. Shoot me if I start talking weight loss."

"I *will* shoot you if you start talking weight loss. You look fantastic, as always." Katie had curves rather than height, and a prettily rounded face with wide-spaced eyes.

"Nobody's shooting anybody," Rue objected. "It would be a decidedly macabre affair if the bride was topped by a bridesmaid a few weeks before the wedding."

"*Two* weeks," corrected Katie and Shal at exactly the same moment. They turned to grin at each other and link pinkie fingers.

"Jinx! *Duplo* jinx! *Triad* jinx! *Quad bike* jinx!" They chanted the childish litany in unison, then fell together, choking with laughter.

"Separated at birth, were you?" Rue looked a little bemused.

"Mmm. Something like that," Katie agreed, catching Shal's eye.

A fleeting sadness passed between them, and Shal knew they were thinking the same thing.

Not birth. Death.

Death had wedged eight years and eight hundred kilometres between them.

The two had first met as students, when Katie had come around to the flat to borrow a surfboard off her cousin. Shal had been unpacking her single meagre suitcase in the cold, cavernous room she was supposed to be sharing with Mason—her boyfriend at the time—and Katie had sneaked her a few of Cam's coat hangers to cheer her up.

The straight-up, tell-it-like-it-is Ōtepotiite had earned Shal's loyalty from that moment forward.

Shal had relied on Katie, loving her almost immediately—never considering whether their friendship was a mutually beneficial one until much later on.

Perhaps Katie had needed to nurture Shal as much as she'd needed to be mothered?

Highly doubtful.

It was just in the redhead's practical nature to pick up and dust off those who fell by the wayside, setting them back on their feet with a clear direction in sight.

Katie had energy in spades, an infectious laugh, and knew her way around a kitchen. She managed to conjure a simple lamb roast into a mouth-watering, restaurant-worthy dish with a handful of spices and fresh herbs.

Rue was mashing salt and butter into the steaming potatoes, and it smelled divine. "Is Shal a shortened version of Sheldon, or Michelle, or…?" He let the question hang for a moment in the warm kitchen. "Something else?"

An unwelcome burst of heat crept up Shal's cheeks.

"Something else, actually. People usually assume it's a hippy love-child thing. Seashell. But I was named Shalom as a nod to my Jewish heritage. I've always disliked it." Possibly the understatement of the decade. "My father's the only one who calls me that, now."

"I know shalom as a greeting. Hebrew, isn't it?"

"Yes. Meaning peace. I have a running joke with the Swedish side of my family. My parents should've called me 'G'day,' or 'Kia ora,' and been done with it. Much more Kiwi." Shal grimaced. "In Sweden *hej* means hello, so my cousins had a field day with that, too." She paused, remembering the warmth behind the teasing.

Rue had a red biro propped behind one of his ears, and Katie smiled as she gently removed it.

He blinked first at his fiancée, then at Shal before replying, "Whereas, I was named after a bear in a children's story. I'm rather grateful it wasn't Paddington."

"Or Pooh," Katie added, smirking.

Catch up—what a strange idiom. It felt more like filling up. The easy domesticity and laughter between Rue and Katie topped up Shal's contentment, and she began to relax.

The two women were opposites in many ways. Where Katie had creamy skin and pretty constellations of freckles passed down by her Scottish ancestors, Shal's own complexion gave the illusion of a spray tan enthusiast. Katie was straight-up and open, family oriented and giving. Shal knew she came across as a lot more closed and insulating of herself—perhaps the upshot of being an only child.

It was tricky opening your inner self to expose less likeable traits, and hard to estimate how much to share, when other's reactions were impossible to predict. But with Katie it had always been easy, because she accepted Shal totally unvarnished.

"Do you feel okay being here?" Katie's question caught Shal off guard.

They'd finished their meal and stacked the dishes off to the side, but remained seated at the table, wine easing ever lower in their glasses.

They'd been discussing their mutual friends, Aroha and Links, and whether the couple would stay in Ōutautahi or return to Otago. The earthquake that had rocked their adopted hometown a few years ago couldn't exactly be called out of the blue, but no one had expected an aftershock with such disastrous results.

"Okay about being at your place?"

"No. Okay about being back in Ōtepoti." Katie had a look that cut cleanly through bullshit, and she was wearing that expression now; leaning forward and fixing Shal with a stare.

Glancing across at Rue, Shal mutely sought for a way out of this particular conversation. But the Englishman didn't lift a finger to bail her out. Instead he appeared to take their fleeting eye contact as his cue to leave, winking at Katie as he picked up the pile of dishes and blatantly left the women alone to talk.

"You had your own personal disaster down here. Not an earthquake, exactly, but a really good shake." Katie's voice was laced with regret. "I know you didn't ever want to come back."

Feeling the pinch of her friend's admission, Shal reached both hands across the table, capturing one of Katie's. "You're wrong. I wanted to come back. I *needed* to." She met Katie's gaze, trying to answer as honestly as possible. "I'm not saying I haven't been avoiding it, but I feel..."

What, exactly?

Removed? Disconnected?

"I'm separate from that now. It happened, but it's gone." Shal gave the hand in hers a quick squeeze. "I want to concentrate on now. I'm so excited about your wedding, and the new boutique ices the cake for me."

Turning purposefully, Shal looked over her shoulder at the serene view. The hills of the peninsula both welcomed and taunted her with memories. She'd been holding the sense of loss at bay, but the nostalgia brought on by being in Ōtepoti was forcing her to be a bit more honest with herself.

"When Links gets here... I feel a bit more conflicted about that. He lost so much."

"Not his life."

"No. Not his life." Shal swung back to blink across the table at her friend, who perhaps knew her just a little too well.

"Are you planning to go out to the memorial?" Never one to pussyfoot around, Katie laid the burning question on the table.

"I was thinking about it." Shal swallowed a faint bubble of panic.

"Promise me something? Don't go alone, okay? I'll come out with you. Or Cam would take you."

Katie was clearly nervous. The aftermath of the accident and how it had affected them all was still fresh enough, eight years on.

Shal took her own rising fear and mentally pushed it back down to stillness. "I promise." Giving Katie's hand a final pat, she picked up her water glass and deliberately changed the subject. "I drove to St. Clair today, straight off the motorway."

St. Clair had always been her favourite spot, and she'd found herself drawn inexorably to where the Pacific Ocean slammed into the coast.

"Figures. Goofy bird. Catch a few waves, then?"

"No, I didn't bring my board. It was stunning though. I've missed it."

"Did you head on up to Poppy's?" Mid-way up the hill, Cam's mother's house had magnificent views of the bay.

"No. I thought about it, but didn't have time." Shal would need to put a couple of hours aside to visit Poppy—to fully catch up and debrief.

And if she was honest with herself, she didn't have the emotional reserves to deal with that right now.

"I dropped her a text to let her know I'm around."

"Oh, don't you worry, she *knows* you're around. I swear my Aunt Poppy's third eye is permanently tooth-picked open."

Though she laughed along with Katie at the spot-on depiction, Shal was actually looking forward to seeing Cam's mum again. The woman had an expansive heart and loved conversation, though being one of five sisters she always seemed to be besieged by company.

Shal coped better with one-on-ones.

"I guess we should all do lunch," she murmured, wondering vaguely just how many people that would involve. "And speaking of food, I wanted to thank you for the groceries at Dundas Street. That was lovely of you."

There was a brief silence.

"Yeah, I could take the credit for that, but the food thing was Cam's idea," Katie admitted.

"But he said—"

"He asked me to write a list of what you liked. I guess he wanted you to feel at home," Katie interrupted gently. "So, you've caught up with him, then?"

"Oh! Yes. He was at the Dundas Street house to give me the keys and show me around. It's beautiful, isn't it?"

"Mm. You should've seen the state it was in when they bought it. That's their specialty though. Ruins to riches. I haven't seen the kitchen finished on that one. How did it look?"

"Dreamy." Shal rested her chin in her hands, elbows on the table.

"Really? *Dreamy*?" Katie laughed. "I'll have to pass that on to Cam and Jonno."

"He gave me flowers."

"Who, Jonno?" Katie's tone went sharp.

"No, Cam." Surprised by the snappy reaction, Shal turned to stare. "I haven't met Jonno face-to-face yet. Is he nice?"

The tension in Katie eased a little.

"*Urgh*, he's alright. Bit of a lad, but he and Cam seem to get on well. They make a good team."

Something in Katie's demeanour hinted she was hiding something.

"And?"

"And nothing. They like to give each other a hard time, that's all. I thought Jonno might've… Well, he's a bit of a ladies' man," Katie grumbled.

"You thought he might've put the moves on me already?" Shal deduced.

"Obviously missed the memo that the hottest chick this side of the Southern Alps was in town." Katie grinned, and Shal snorted. "So, flowers then?"

"A bouquet of gerberas. He's so sweet."

"Ha! Sweet…" Katie mumbled something else under her breath, her smile skidding off to be replaced by a twitchy frown.

"It really was in a mess," Shal decided aloud, studying the before-and-after photo album of the fire damage at Roseneath. Rue was leaning in, pointing out interesting details.

"After we bought the place, Cam invited one of his father's relatives. An uncle? I've forgotten the Māori word for his position. One of the elders. Held in high esteem." Rue looked at her expectantly.

"Kaumātua?"

"Yes! Kau-*mā*-tua," Rue rolled the unfamiliar word around his tongue and turned the pages until he came to the blessing. A solid man with a shock of white hair held an ornately carved walking stick. Flanked by two middle-aged women, he wore regular clothes —suit pants and a blazer—but the elder's pounamu was a large and seemingly old piece, the jade so dark it appeared black against his light tie.

"Matua Teddie." Though he was older, Cam's great uncle was very distinctive.

"Oh, you've met him?"

"Just the once." At a funeral. Shal swallowed hard.

"He blessed the land. Spoke about his ancestors and the gods of the earth, sky, and sea. Cleansed it, I suppose. Removed the shadow of the fire. When the women sang, it was haunting." Rue rubbed his arms. "Gives me the chills just thinking about it. It's hard to explain, but that's when I knew for sure it was the right place for us. I felt welcome."

"Lucky, considering we'd already bought it." Katie had returned from answering the phone. "That was Cam, exhibiting the impeccable timing of a hungry kaihana." When Shal looked up in askance, Katie smiled. "I was just about to serve dessert, so he's invited himself over. More wine?"

"Not for me, thanks." Not when she was driving home. She was borderline obsessive about it. Better to be safe than immeasurably sorry.

"Okay, more for me." Katie eyed Shal shrewdly as she nodded, no doubt guessing exactly where Shal's mind had crept. "He's bringing some music printouts for the wedding."

While Rue went to find plates and Katie got dessert ready, Shal continued to pour over the photo book. The bungalow was a true transformation story, from fire-damaged auction to the pristine home she was sitting in right now. Every image attested to the mammoth task undertaken.

Shal was about to turn the page when one of the smaller snapshots caught her eye.

Holy *hell*.

She dragged the album closer.

Cam had obviously been working on the roof in the heat, and the picture had been taken from ground level, looking up at his smiling face. He'd taken his T-shirt off and it was hanging out of his back pocket, revealing a slim trail of dark hair that disappeared into a low-slung builder's belt and well-worn jeans. He looked sweaty, bronzed, and muscular, with his familiar pounamu settled close around his neck and a shabby Otago cap shading his eyes.

Shal stared, blinked, then flushed a little before turning the page. She hadn't finished with that particular picture, but neither was she willing to get caught perving.

"So much work." She swallowed, closing the book and tapping the cover when Rue set a plate and fork to her right.

"I kept out of it for the most part. Tits on a bull, me."

Shal laughed at Rue's farming turn of phrase. It sounded so comical in his clipped English accent.

Reaching out, she played with the simple white daisies in the centre of the table and was reminded of her grandmother in New York, who always kept freshly cut flowers in the house. Snapping a single bloom off she stroked its soft golden heart, still a little off-kilter from the warmth Cam's picture had stirred up.

"You fronted up with half of the dosh though, which makes you pretty indispensable." Katie approached, sliding behind Shal's chair.

Shal could relate the money side of things to her Nana as well.

"And if he hadn't been so damn calm about it every time I changed my mind...?" Katie set down a serving bowl of fresh whipped cream. "Things could have gotten a whole lot more stressful."

Having stolen the flower from between Shal's slack fingers, Katie repositioned it behind her friend's ear.

Pointedly avoiding a certain page, Shal reopened the photo album and flicked back to some of the images she'd skimmed over earlier. There was a shot where Katie's clear happiness was caught mid-laugh, Rue's arm slung over her shoulder.

"This is one of my favourites. I was so bummed I couldn't make your housewarming party." Shal had been in the States, mixing business with a long overdue visit to her father's side of the family. She motioned to the next snapshot. "Dante D?"

"Yes. Daniel. Unmistakable, isn't he?" Katie's laugh had a brittle edge as she bent to study her cousin's not-exactly-smiling face. "I'd forgotten that picture was there."

"And his girlfriend?" Shal's finger hovered under the cool

blonde who stood next to the well known rugby player, raising her champagne glass to his beer bottle in a coy 'cheers' for the camera.

"No." Katie looked at her strangely. "That's Cam's ex. I thought you'd met Jody before?"

"Oh, right. I thought she looked familiar. Yes. We met at Links and Aroha's once, in Ōtautahi. She really is stunning, isn't she?"

"She's a piece of work alright," Katie muttered.

3
———————

Listening to...
Fallen - Lauren Wood
From the album: Cat Trick

Homemade pumpkin pie was Shal's absolute favourite. By the time Cam arrived, bringing a rush of cool harbour air and the scent of the evening inside with him, Katie had dessert all laid out on the dining table.

"Not for me, thanks love." Rue bowed out, patting his stomach. "I'm done."

"You're turning down Katie's pumpkin pie?" Cam called through from the kitchen, where he was washing his hands. "Nutter."

"Yeah, but *so* damn cute with it." Katie reached a hand out to pat Rue's butt as he passed, and he grinned, softening up all his serious features.

New York Nana made pumpkin pie whenever Shal was in the States, and though she was careful never to express disloyalty in so many words, Shal much preferred Katie's version. What was not to like about freshly roasted pumpkin? The crust was a beautiful honey-brown, and the filling a rich, dense orange. Her mouth was watering in anticipation well before Katie plonked her share in front of her.

"How's the recording going?" Katie passed the second plate to Cam as he settled at the table, before serving herself a very small sliver.

Remembering her friend's earlier instructions regarding weight loss, Shal formed a gun out of two fingers, sighted Katie up, and mimed the shot.

The redhead grinned. "Calm down. I'm having some, aren't I?"

"It's coming along. I didn't stay to hear the final mix tonight, but they're sounding clean. Fresh." Cam dumped a generous spoonful of freshly whipped cream next to his slice of pie.

"What recording?" Shal laid down her imaginary gun and looked from one cousin to the other.

"Cam didn't tell you? He's doing some session work for Pieta."

Shal's jaw dropped. "What? Pieta as in... *Pieta*?" Her brain stalled, then raced on ahead. Pieta was a relatively new sound on the Kiwi music scene, but her first EP had been so well received the title song popped up practically every time you turned on the radio.

"Yep." Katie gave her cousin a slow-mo punch on the arm. "Best damn guitar player this side of the straight, isn't that right, Rue?" Rue grunted in the affirmative from the sofa, his face partially hidden behind a newspaper. "Not to mention best *looking*. Old Pieta knows what side her bread's buttered on."

Pieta wasn't old, she was young and pretty.

The singer was also a talented songwriter, with a voice that evoked angelic comparison. Already the sweetheart of the national media, Pieta was beginning to get recognition on the international stage, too.

The woman was seriously going places.

"Well, *shit*. That's amazing! She's recording down here? She's from Otago?" Shal swivelled to aim her questions at Cam, who was sitting diagonally across from her.

"Cromwell, originally." Cam shovelled another forkful of pie in. "Man, Katie." He rolled his eyes. "That's *so* good. You should go into the pie business."

Shal huffed at him impatiently as he leaned back in his chair.

"What? It's delicious. She studied at Otago, but years later than me," Cam explained. "I met her through Davis."

One of Cam's old music degree mates was a sound engineer, working out of what was little more than a soundproofed double garage. Locally known as The Den, the studio had become a hive of indie music over the past decade.

"Pieta's original guitarist turned out to be a bit of an asshole." Cutting off a chunk of pie-crust with the side of his fork, Cam dragged it through his whipped cream ever-so-slowly. "So, I agreed to step in."

"Super-Cam to the rescue." Shal's voice sounded a little sarcastic; snarky even to her own ears.

She busied herself with her water, embarrassed at herself. She was *jealous*, she realised, choking on the liquid instead of swallowing it.

Cam raised an eyebrow and cocked his head to one side, waiting till she'd finished her coughing fit before replying, "I'm not doing it for superhero status."

Shal felt the heat rise on her face, and wondered if she was as see-through as she felt.

"I'm getting paid," he stated matter-of-factly.

"Of course you're getting paid!" Katie interjected. "You're incredibly talented, and she's lucky to have your amazing-ness anywhere *near* her album."

"Thanks, Kit-Kat. Since I'm so *uhh*-mazing, can I take some of this pie home?"

"Sure." Katie looked from one to the other before getting up to join Rue on the sofa. "You can wrestle Shal for it. Best I don't have the leftovers taunting me from the fridge come breakfast time."

"Gonna fight me for it?" Cam challenged Shal across the table, those long dimples on show again.

"Goes without saying," she returned snootily.

"But I missed dinner," Cam lamented, all puppy-dog eyes.

"Not my problem." Shal attempted to keep a straight face, but failed.

"Go halves with you?"

"Honestly? I'd be happy with one slice." As Cam's grin widened, Shal quickly began to add stipulations. "A *big* slice. On the

26

proviso you scratch together a wetsuit and board for me this week and take me to St Clair, the rest is all yours."

"Done." Cam half stood, reaching a hand across the table to shake on it.

"I'm a little envious," Shal blurted, finding it strangely disconcerting to be holding Cam's hand, even under the guise of a handshake. Especially when he was looking at her so intently like that. His palm was work-rough and strong, enveloping hers in heat. "*I* want to be recording with Pieta."

But it wasn't the entire truth. Shal was feeling more jealous of Pieta now she was basking in the beam of those amused, honey-brown eyes.

A warm curl of awareness flickered alight near the base of her belly, and the image of Cam shirtless came back to her, clear as day.

Hell, no. Just friends, as they always had been.

Shal removed her hand hurriedly.

Cam brought out a sheaf of song printouts after dessert, resigned to the fact he'd have to spend some close-up time with Shal and suffer for it.

"Katie and Rue chose the music. I just put them in the key I thought would be suited to your voice."

Shal, who had the lyrics splayed over the coffee table, looked up, her eyebrows drawn together.

"You used to sit comfortably as an alto," Cam reiterated, reaching over to pluck two song sheets from the group. "We can easily change the key if we need to." He handed the lyrics over. "Lauren Wood, *Fallen*. We did it once as a cover, remember?" He tapped the top of the second page. "And, *There's Something in the Water*, Brooke Fraser. I haven't heard you sing any of her stuff but it got a lot of airplay, so you'll know it."

"My favourite," Katie called from her spot on the sofa somewhat dopily. Rue had laid down the newsprint and was rubbing her socked feet.

Shal's vocals had always appealed because she was unstudied. Imperfect. But Cam wasn't about to tell her that. Raw emotion came through in every lyric, every run. Sometimes that got studied out of a person.

Shal ignored the offered papers. Motionless beside the coffee table, she knelt with her hands pressed between her knees.

"You're nervous." Cam could see it—recognise the tightness.

Shal looked almost childlike with her hair out, glossy and dark, a white daisy tucked behind her ear.

Cam refocused on the lyric sheet. It was wordy, and that had sometimes been Shal's downfall. Stage fright had swallowed up the familiar lyrics and left her standing mute.

"Yes."

"Shal was always sick with nerves before a performance," Katie turned to Rue to confide. "And I mean *sick*. Then she'd get up on stage and knock it for six." Her demeanour lost all hint of humour as she angled herself back towards Shal—concern obvious, and probably well warranted. "Look, I know you said yes to this, but I don't want you to feel pressured into it, or feel bad about pulling out. Cam can fly solo. Right, cuz?"

"Absolutely."

"No. I really want to. It's just…" Shal looked across at Katie with a touch of desperation. "Cam's been recording with *Pieta*, for God's sake. I'm just an amateur. I could so easily screw this up—"

A cushion lobbed from the sofa flew across and walloped Shal on the side of the head, knocking her sideways into Cam and cutting off her self-doubt, mid-stream.

"Amateur, my ass," Katie followed up sardonically. "That's my *bridesmaid* you're dissing. I didn't ask frickin' Pieta, because I didn't *want* frickin' Pieta."

Grins built slowly, until the two women were laughing at each other across the carpeted room. Shal's hair was all mussed up across flushed cheeks, and Katie gripped a second cushion, threatening to biff that too.

"Well. When you put it like *that*." Shal blew hair out of her eye. "It would be my honour to sing for you both."

"Plus a hundred or so of their closest friends," Cam muttered.

He picked up the bruised daisy, knocked to the floor by the cushion, missing the fact Katie had re-aimed the second missile at his own head. The closest cousin to him in age, she had always jumped at any excuse to knock him down a peg.

She was also a damn good shot.

Shal smiled hopefully at Cam as he righted himself, flicking his hair out of his eyes and shoving the offending cushion under his knees. In another time and space Katie would've received that cushion back with interest, prompting all-out war.

Shal was clutching the Brooke Fraser lyrics to her chest. "Maybe I just do backing vocals for you on this one?" she whispered.

She'd probably need to barf up her nerves before she performed, backing vocal or not. Katie wasn't the only one who'd held Shal's hair back on occasion… but they could stress about that later.

Shal's tension had been beginning to ease, but when Cam casually invited her to run through the new song with him, she suddenly felt all kinds of awkward again.

"No. Let me get familiar with it first." She hadn't forgotten who Cam had just been in a studio with.

In the process of getting his acoustic guitar out of its hard case, Cam stopped, narrowing his eyes at her across Katie's living room.

"Cold feet?"

"No!" she blustered, suspecting Katie was only *pretending* to read the article Rue had handed her, and was actually listening keenly. "Of course not."

Getting up and strolling nonchalantly over to where Cam was kneeling on the far side of the room, instrument half in and half out of its case, Shal lowered her voice as she reached down to touch the hand holding the neck of the acoustic. "But I *do* want it to sound good when Katie first hears it, so I need to practice on my own first."

Cam's face was close now, and she could follow his expression as it changed from askance to humour—watch the smile spread. From the first eye twinkle, right down the long dimples tugging generous lips upward.

"Right. Belt it out in the shower a few rounds before airing it in public. I forgot about that."

"Exactly." She smiled, glad Cam understood.

He knew her so well, she rarely had to explain herself.

Cam had actually managed wipe those overheard moments from his memory. How was that possible?

Shal had always scuttled off to be alone when learning a new track—alone on the water, in the shower, or simply with her head thrust out the car window—she'd burst into song. Not always with the correct lyrics though. Cam would catch her out, then bait her by calling out corrections like, 'Elephant in the room, not elephant of *doom*.'

They'd argue about it, sometimes for days, until he'd finally rustle up a copy of the lyrics and plant them in front of her face.

Shal hadn't always been gracious about the heads-up, either.

Cam had a million more memories of his ex-flatmate crowding around, anxious to be aired after such long suppression. Shal's hand still covered his, and her cool fingers moved to stroke his forearm absently before dropping to her thigh, silver bracelets jangling.

It'd take a million years to wipe those goddamn million memories.

"If you play both songs solo tonight, I'll record you on my phone," she cajoled.

He was a sucker for her big ocean eyes. Always had been. Something shifted in him when she looked down at him like that.

"Sure." He got up to put some distance between them. The soft timbre of Shal's voice and the smell of her so close was intoxicating, and he found it hard to think straight. There was a tendril of hair brushing her cheek, begging him to tuck it back behind her ear.

It seemed like a mammoth task to keep his hands to himself.

Gripping his guitar, Cam collected the lyric sheets and moved towards the back deck, needing to be in the open air. "Out here?"

"Oh." Shal sounded dubious. "Won't you need a jacket?"

"No." He laughed. "But you'd better bring yours."

By the time Shal joined Cam on the harbour-facing deck, coat firmly buttoned and phone in hand, he had the outdoor gas heater going and was sitting off to the side, strumming. He'd left her the seat directly under the heat, and she was grateful. The evening was cool off the ocean, moonlight dipping the water in pewter.

The setting seemed both wildly open, and strangely intimate.

"So stunning." Shal breathed in the briny tang of the bay. The view across to the shadowy peninsula was dreamlike in its calmness, with small lights twinkling from faraway windows.

"Sure is." But Cam wasn't looking at the view, he was looking at her, his face partly in darkness so she couldn't read his expression.

"I suppose you built this deck too?" Shal surveyed the wooden expanse—wide steps leading down to the garden. She knew without turning to look that this was the portion of roof Cam had been photographed standing on, directly above the French doors.

Cameron Dante had carved a solid niche for himself, constructing monuments to good living. All these beautiful, practical things he built and restored with his own hands.

"I had some help." Cam had his head to one side as he watched her pace around, and she tried to pinpoint why the familiar action made her feel so unsettled.

It was as if he could see straight through her, while he himself hid in the shadows.

"How did you end up as a builder, when you have a music degree?" she wondered aloud.

Cam shrugged. "The two aren't mutually exclusive. I had some collateral from working the cruise ships, started as Jonno's lackey, and learnt fast on my feet. Dad was a carpenter, so it runs in the family. You can't expect to make ends meet as a full-time muso in Aotearoa."

No. Though it seemed like an almighty waste of talent.

When Shal had first heard Cam play guitar in their old shared flat, the hair on the back of her neck had risen with the pure, soulful beauty of it. And years later, on a deck in Roseneath, it was incredibly disconcerting to find her body reacting in exactly the same way.

But something was different this time. It wasn't the guy she'd known in the past whose fingers slid and flew over the strings.

There was a nuance of confidence—a practiced grace in how Cam paced out the underlying emotion of the piece.

Shal shivered, the familiar music yanking at her memories and turning her inside out, and upside down.

Fallen. She hadn't heard this song for years. Not since Mason.

The thought brought a sudden rawness to her throat.

Oh, God. Don't cry.

Mason was *long* gone, and Shal was well past holding onto his memory with any semblance of grief. It was ridiculous to miss him when he'd gambled with her emotions, the truth, his life.

He'd lost that final idiotic game of chance, and with it, his beautiful, glowing spark.

The sheer wastefulness of it clamped her windpipe shut.

She could almost see him, eyes closed as if in sleep. But for the stillness of his lungs, no longer breathing. But for the silence of his heart, no longer beating.

Mason had died instantly. That's what they said, though how could anyone know for sure? Shal had wondered vaguely at the time, and forever after, if those words were just a fallback they used to anaesthetise the ones left behind after a horrific accident.

If he'd died instantly, there wouldn't have been any pain. If he'd died instantly, he wouldn't have heard Links screaming as the bones in his lower legs were shattered and mangled by the impact.

If Mason had died instantly, he would never have had to face the enormity of what he'd done.

Shal could hear the vocal lead coming up.

"You sing it," she whispered. Cam looked up from the strings but didn't miss a beat. One side of his face was tawny in the intense light from the heater, the other in deep shadow as he sang the opening line.

Shal scrambled to record him, catching a glimpse of the innermost self he rarely allowed to show—the level of emotion he usually hid from view. Once again, it made her wonder how deep the iceberg went.

Just how much of Cameron Dante remained unseen?

4

Listening to...
Maxine - Sharon O'Neill
From the album: Foreign Affairs

Shal had arranged to meet Jac at nine a.m., but found herself wide awake at sunrise with the past on her mind. She tried rolling over and snuggling back into her pillow, but the soft promise of dawn was already creeping around the corners of the heavy curtains, calling her to the ocean.

She had more than enough time spare to skip down to the beach at St Clair before her meeting, if only to blow the cobwebs out.

Ōtepoti had put Mason on Shal's mind, and there was a discomfort in having her old boyfriend back, slinking around in her thoughts. His baby-blues had always melted her best intentions, and hidden the biggest untruths.

She scooted out of bed and headed for the heavenly shower.

From her vantage point on the esplanade, Shal took in the wide arc of sand and high dunes reaching toward the northern lookout. The gulls flew a lazy circle around the bay and back out to White Island, lamenting the imminent change in season.

A platoon of blue gum piles still rose from the ancient groyne; soldiers sent out to wage battle with the tides. But it appeared the ocean had already won. Once covered in golden sand, the boulders below the esplanade were now open and exposed, foundations of the high sea wall swallowed by the ebb tide.

Shal shuddered, turning her eyes away, but the hollowness still niggled, too closely resembling the loss she felt. Where would that sand find a home now? Argentina? She squinted at the far horizon.

Mason had met Cam surfing, drawn away from the halls of residence by the offer to take up Cam's brother's place on the lease in the all-male flat.

Links, Cam, and Mason had all gotten on, so he'd chosen to stay for another year, despite his mother's increasingly desperate demands he transfer back to Tāmaki-makau-rau to graduate.

Maybe Lynette Knox had sensed something sinister in the air?

Shal hadn't been able to join him until his final year, but the affection she'd discovered within Mason's group of friends in just under twelve months had quickly grown into something akin to family, inclusive of extreme highs and lows.

Her mind skipped naturally to Links, who'd soon be here for the wedding, and unease resurfaced. Her old flatmate wouldn't thank her for guilt or distress on his behalf, but her response was an unconscious one—gut based.

Links' partner, Aroha, would be travelling with him too, and Shal had always found her a bit prickly.

In a spot sheltered from the wind, Shal watched the early morning surfers out back, weaving and racing down the line. It had been too long since she'd been out on the water herself, and she longed for the peace it brought.

Unconsciously, she'd picked a favourite. Female? Hard to make out from this distance, but compact, with a high ponytail and a leading right leg. The surfer rode low, with quick turns and snaps off the top of the wave.

A goofy rider, like herself.

Out of the four in the group who surfed, Katie and Cam had been the only two with any real skill, and the close cousins had known the local breaks well. Agile, quick-witted, and highly competitive, both had seemed impervious to the cold, and were forever throwing challenges and goads back and forth.

Trying to keep up with them had been a waste of time, but Shal had taken mental notes and wasn't too proud to ask for pointers.

She dug deep into the pockets of her overcoat while strolling back to the car, trying to pick out Cam's childhood home on the hillside... Maybe the one half-obscured by the southern pohutukawa?

Another day, Shal promised herself silently as she climbed back behind the wheel and headed into the city.

Ditching her warm outer layer and grabbing her purse, Shal checked her lippy in the mirror before sliding out of the car.

Jac always showed up dressed immaculately, and Shal wasn't about to let the team down.

Playing up the corporate look, she'd chosen deceptively simple tailored black pants and a short, fitted jacket in charcoal wool. The Venetian blue-glass choker encasing her neck would be what caught the eye, as it was the only real colour in her outfit.

The charm of the tree-lined street was more familiar than she'd been expecting, and she experienced another minor tremor in her equilibrium. Maybe a little hasty believing she could dump the past so easily?

She'd done a quick drive-by yesterday on her way to Roseneath, but daylight highlighted the great bones of the boutique. Even crawling with tradesmen, it looked amazing. Jonno had been sending formal progress reports, and Jac was in charge of interior photos, merchandising catalogues, and a heavily laden Pin-board link. None of that came close to the experience of standing in front of the pretty brick facade, though.

In the centre of the store's whited-out window hung an ornate wooden frame with the scripted lettering:

Soon to be opened
Award winning New Zealand Designers

Pressing her palms together and bringing her fingertips to her lips, Shal was glad she was alone when tears began to smart.

If her twenty-year-old self could only see a glimpse of this. Award winning!

She'd never tire of reading acknowledgements next to the 2-PEAS logo. Imposter Syndrome still reared its ugly fin at times, but Shal and Jac had worked bloody hard to paddle to the crest of this wave, and they both knew they'd have to continue to work their tails off just to stay afloat.

When Shal had been accepted into fashion design school in Ōutautahi eight years ago, it'd been a means of escape from Ōtepoti and the memory of Mason as much as it had been a new start.

Anonymity was a finely woven cloak, and Shal had gratefully wrapped herself in it. Starting fresh, those around her had no idea what had just been cast off, and she'd almost managed to convince herself the lack of connection was the lesser of two evils.

Her incomplete English degree still niggled though, like an unfinished garment left on the cutting table.

Shal's ankle boots had enough height to bring her eye-level with the more senior of the two painters, who jumped to open the door for her when he realised she was planning to enter the boutique.

"Kia ora! Top of the mornin' to ya."

"Mōrena," she returned, sharing a smile with the chipper tradie. "Is Jac in?"

"Sure is." The man's leather-like face split even wider into a wicked grin. "In fine form, too."

Shal had no doubt. She'd never seen Jac in anything but 'fine form.'

"Speak of the devil," she murmured.

The horns and pitchfork connotation suited, as Jac entered from the back corridor in hot tones. Fire-engine red from her boudoir curls right down to the tips of her four-inch peep toe wedges, and just as inflammatory. The short tulip skirt was hemmed well above the knees, showing pale satin legs to full advantage.

"Shal!" She was enveloped in a quick, uncharacteristic hug, then kissed lightly on each cheek by the shorter woman, whose signature scent was deep and spicy.

Shal had missed the vibrant life, love, and drama of working with Jac, who'd lived through a train-wreck of a childhood and still managed to pop out the other side like a shiny new button. The Te Whanganui-a-Tara store had been distinctly lacking in colour without her co-designer swanning in and out over the past month.

It was Jac who had originally stumbled across the Ōtepoti site—a dilapidated second-hand clothing shop—and overseen the refit. Shal had co-signed the five-year lease, but opted to stay in their flagship North Island store as long as possible, running sales and finalising the delivery and showing of the upcoming winter line. Now she'd run out of excuses to stay away, both designers were deep in the heart of Otago.

Shal hoped their instincts were right on this one. They'd worked so hard to see their second boutique come to fruition, and the refurb costs were already creeping well past budget.

Upstairs, in the apartment above the boutique, there was a rock number Shal didn't recognise belting from a room off the hall. Someone knew the lyrics, but whoever was singing with more gusto than tune was out of her direct line of vision.

A painter was working on the walls of the small atrium above the stairwell, and going by the sheen on the paint, he hadn't long finished the ceiling. He turned, noticing the two women as they neared the top of the stairs.

He wasn't much more than a kid, long hair pulled back into a topknot, and visibly coloured when he clocked Jac. She was all but poured into her fitted business suit, with ample cleavage on display.

"Ah…" The boy cleared his throat. "Wāhine on board!" he yelled through the open door, wiping his face on his shirt-sleeve. "Mornin.' " The offered greeting was much quieter, without any attempt to establish eye contact. His shyness appeared to have swallowed everything else.

"What the actual fuck?" The expletive came from the other room, and though the previously singing male muttered the words, his frustration was clearly discernible.

The voice belonged to a builder. He emerged with his tool belt slung low, in a grubby T-shirt, cargo shorts, and work boots. With a muscular tension more weight-lifter than carpenter, the tradesman had short-cropped hair and an old vertical scar delineating his forehead, giving him an air of asymmetry.

There was no smile, and from the depth of his frown Shal surmised there wouldn't be one coming.

"*Jesus*, Jessica. We're working here."

"Good morning to you too, Jonno," Jac countered coolly. "Mind your manners, this is Shal."

Jonno's hand came out to shake Shal's firmly, and although hers was promptly swallowed, she was aware he was trying to be gentle. His steely blues didn't miss a trick though, and she felt the scan as clearly as if he'd run his big hand over her.

"Don't touch anything. Paint's wet," he grumbled.

"You'll have to excuse the Neanderthal. What he means is, 'Welcome to Ōtepoti. I hope you like what we're doing to the place, since you're *paying* for it.' " Jac brushed past them both, a mere hairsbreadth from the freshly painted door jam and into the room.

Jonno sucked in a hiss of breath.

Turning back toward the builder, Jac eyed him coolly, as you would a misbehaving dog. And just as staunchly he returned the stare, seemingly unperturbed.

Intrigued, Shal looked from one to the other. The tension between these two was molasses-thick, and just as sticky.

Shal followed Jonno into the bare room with a lot more care than her co-designer, shimmying sideways through the door frame and drawing on the Hoffner charm as she picked her way over paint speckled drop-sheets. "It's looking fabulous! I hope you don't mind if we have a look through?"

"Actually—" Jonno began.

"Of course Jonno doesn't *mind*," Jac interrupted, again with more than her usual quota of arrogance.

"Have a look through, but don't touch." Jonno appeared resigned to Jac's snarky tone, which seemed to rile the designer up even further. Her fisted hands were locked to her hips.

"Sage advice." Jac was the ice queen. "Don't *touch*, Shal." And there was a world of meaning behind her words.

After ferrying the sample bags back to Jac's hotel, Shal spread them out on the bed. The clothing was for the spring line, though they hadn't even entered autumn, and jewel colours shone vibrant against the plain coverlet.

The new sustainable line would have to be signed off this week if the fabric print runs and production was to be finalised in time.

Jac's designs were quirky, on point, and astute, and Shal thanked her lucky stars once more for the other woman's skill. It'd taken the co-designers one look across the classroom that first day in Tech to size each other up, just from what the other had thrown together to wear.

It could've been all out war, and knowing Jac's competitive side intimately now, Shal was forever surprised it hadn't been. Instead, they'd pushed each other to be bolder and more cutting-edge in their designs.

Shal valued Jac's professional opinion above all others. Not because their tastes were the same, they absolutely weren't, but it had seemed like a natural progression to work together after graduation. They hadn't been expecting instant recognition, or even steady success to start with, yet that's what had come. Selling their brand 2-PEAS out of a well-established Te Whanganui-a-Tara boutique in their first year, they'd been hard pressed to keep up with stock demands. Even so, they couldn't have opened their own small boutique two years later without an injection of cash from Shal's trust fund.

Jac referred to any Hoffner money as 'The Bank of David,' in reference to Shal's father. Not because he deserved her respect, but because he wielded that all-elusive commodity—*available funds*.

In the soulless hotel room, the co-designers worked steadily through the successful pieces and changes for their projected spring collection. Shal modelled the finals for Jac, and they rehashed again, tweaking silhouettes, hemlines and details. They argued over buttons, accessories and fabric weights, and debated the best colour-way combinations.

Both Jac and Shal checked, then ignored, multiple phone interruptions throughout the morning, but Shal scrambled to answer Cam's call when it came through.

"Hey, Cam." She turned her shoulder in a muted attempt to gain a smidgen of privacy, causing Jac to sling a hand on her hip and send her *that* look.

"Hey, yourself," Cam's voice was low and inviting, making Shal smile despite attempting to maintain a business-like expression for Jac's benefit. "Practice tonight?"

"Five?"

"Yep. Five works. Your place?"

"Sounds good. See you then."

Jac was still eyeing her shrewdly when she hung up.

"Full of surprises, aren't you?"

"I don't know what you're talking about," Shal hedged, tossing her phone on the small side table and picking up an off-the-shoulder sweater in garnet tones.

"What's happening with hunky Cam at five?" Jac demanded.

"How come he's hunky, and Jonno's been branded a Neanderthal? "

Jac raised an eyebrow in mock incredulity. "You'd better tell *me*, Shal. I had a suspicion I was sharing a room with Lauren Bacall for a moment there... *Hey, Caaam*," she mimicked in a breathy tone, her ensuing chuckle betraying unapologetic delight in Shal's embarrassment. "And you didn't answer my question. Romantic meeting at five?"

"*No*. Friendly music practice at five. Why? Are you interested?" Shal was unsure why that particular thought rattled her quite so much.

Jac threw back her head and laughed. "If I was interested in that sweet honey of man, Shal, I'd have had my scent all over him well before you showed up."

"You're stuck on the other one?" Shal surmised slyly.

"Urgh! The one who insists on calling me 'Jessica' for no apparent reason? Wash your mouth out!" Jac negated with way too much heat. "There's no telling *where* he's been."

The usually un-rattle-able Jacqueline was definitely shaken and stirred, and Shal smiled, pleased to discover the heat was once again off herself.

Shal experienced an empty echo as she walked the three blocks back to her car.

Jac would be returning to Te Whanganui-a-Tara on tomorrow's red-eye flight, and Shal wouldn't see her workmate for almost two weeks due to the timing of Katie's wedding. An unfamiliar loneliness nipped at her, and she dug her chin deeper into her cashmere scarf and strode a little quicker to keep warm.

Originally from the subtropical 'burbs of northern Tāmaki-makau-rau, Shal had struggled with the more defined seasons in Otago the year she'd lived down here.

Eight years ago, now. Had it really been that long?

She hadn't possessed nearly enough clothes to ward off the cold back then. No coat, just a denim jacket. No boots, scarves, nor gloves. Not even a beanie to her name. She'd arrived in all her naïvety at the tail-end of summer, thinking she was prepared for March to arrive with a suitcase stuffed full of light beachwear.

The warmest item of clothing she'd possessed was a brand-new winter wetsuit. Not something you could comfortably turn up to lectures in, though she'd been sorely tempted at times.

Second hand clothing had been a godsend as Ōtepoti had eased into a golden autumn, with frosty mornings and crisp days. Katie had introduced Shal to the joys of op-shopping, though more often than not her new layers of pre-loved clothing had needed alterations to fit.

Borrowing a sewing machine from one of the girls in her English Lit class, she'd moved from small nips, darts and buttonholes onto full transformations—surprising even herself. By the time the October ball season was upon them, she'd bought her own second-hand Bernina and was re-designing and putting together one-offs that were helping pay the rent. An uncanny knack of surmising the most flattering styles for different body types recompensed her well, and word got around fast.

But all that had all gone belly-up in Mason's aftermath.

He'd cheated. More than once. Shal could call Aroha many things, but dishonest wasn't one of them. Links' girlfriend could be straight-up to the point of cruel, and the hard-nosed brunette had thrust hard evidence in the form of grainy video footage under Shal's nose. There hadn't been any point in denying it was Mason draped over yet another random girl at a bar, this time with his tongue down her throat.

So, Shal had moved out, and less than a month later Mason was dead.

Raising her white flag in defeat, she'd left her English degree hanging out to dry after the accident. Thank God for Poppy's dogged insistence, pushing her to apply for her doctor's certificate and subsequent aegrotat pass that November, or a whole year of study would've been wiped.

Shal slipped back into her car and drove back to Dundas Street. As always, carefully, and probably overly defensively. She still had a couple of hours before Cam was due, but forgot there'd be tradesmen in the house until she pulled up to park behind a plumber's van.

Bugger. Well, at least the background noise would help fill the trough of regret she'd found herself wallowing in.

Grateful the work was complete in the master suite, Shal shut herself in and listened to the two recordings she'd made of Cam the night before. He had an easy confidence when he played, not to mention a beautiful voice.

There was something soul-destroying about a guy who could sing.

Shal remembered Cam holding her hand across the table yesterday, Katie baking her favourite pumpkin pie, and Poppy texting an invitation to lunch later in the week. Her black mood began to loosen its heavy hold.

There were people here who cared about her here.

During the second play through, both the lyrics and the melody began to sink in for the Brooke Fraser song. Perhaps if she sang a harmony over Cam for the chorus, then whistled the refrain?

She tried it again. It was a little different from the original, but had potential.

By the time she heard the knock on the front door she was alone in the house again, and super buzzed about going over Katie's wedding songs with Cam. She took the stairs four at a time in her haste to let him in.

5

Listening to...
Something in the Water - Brooke Fraser
From the album: Flags

Manoeuvring his guitar inside the front door of Dundas Street, Cam was set upon by a very enthusiastic Shal. He handed her a percussion bag as a means of self-preservation before she could get all up in his face and kiss him hello.

"Hi! Why are you knocking? Don't you have a key? I've got some harmony ideas for the Brooke Fraser song," Shal announced, her eyes sparkling with possibilities.

"I thought you might." He smiled. She was like a puppy with a new toy. "I've got till seven, so let's squeeze as much time as we can on that one."

Shal practically danced upstairs to the master, where she must've set up with her gear. Cam looked up after her and sighed.

Really? They were doing this in Shal's bloody bedroom? He took a deep breath in and released it before trailing up after her like it was no skin.

Seeing Shal had spread her stuff out all over the rumpled bed, Cam claimed the chaise, leaning his guitar next to himself and pulling a sheaf of music out of his bag.

Two full metres between them should be ample.

Shal had made herself at home in the room. Colours and textures were sprawled across the floor, ending in a mountain of cast-off clothing by the walk-in wardrobe door, where a few unmatched shoes had come out to meet them.

Gone was the familiar smell of paint and new carpet, it'd been replaced with something girly and floral.

Recognising himself in a framed group photograph on the bedside table, Cam did a double take, surprised to see all six of the old crew together on the beach. Aroha was curled in Links' lap, his gangly legs spread out in front. Cam and Katie were slightly off to the side on a log, with Mason and Shal linked together in the foreground, his arm proprietary around her neck.

Cam dragged his gaze away from the image, uncomfortable with the memories that surfaced with it.

Once they started practicing, time disappeared. It was six-thirty when he pleaded starvation. Escaping downstairs to raid the fridge, he poked his head into the bathrooms to check on progress and workmanship on the way. By the time Shal joined him in the kitchen he was almost finished putting a ham and salad sandwich together.

"Can I make you one?"

"No, thanks. I had a really late lunch with Jac after going over the spring line with a fine-toothed comb. But I'll have a cuppa."

He flicked the switch on the kettle on his way past, and munching on his first sandwich, started stacking a second.

"Won't you spoil your appetite?"

"No." His mouthful muffled the word. "I'm *feeding* my appetite."

"You've got a dinner date, though?"

"Ah… No?" Cam took another bite, watching the emotions flit across Shal's face and trying to guess what she was thinking. "You mean the seven o'clock thing? That's just a sound check. I can be a smidgen late." He covered his mouth, because again, he was speaking with his mouth full. His ex would've rolled her eyes and told him he was being a pig, but Shal forged on without batting an eyelid.

"You've got a gig tonight?"

He hadn't meant to compare the two women, and was pissed off with himself when he realised he'd just done exactly that.

"Yeah. Jazz ensemble with Davis and a couple of others. I'd invite you along, but it's a private thing. Sixtieth birthday party or something."

"Oh." Shal's voice had lifted at the mention of a gig, but now fell a little flat. "Maybe next time."

Cam stopped chewing, remembered to swallow, then looked across the kitchen island at the most stunning woman he'd ever had the misfortune to fall for. She was perched on her bar stool, looking a little forlorn.

"You don't even like jazz."

"That's not entirely true," Shal replied a little huffily. "I find some of the modernist stuff inaccessible, but I like the older standards. If they have a vocalist I'm much more invested."

"Lyric snob."

"I'm *not*..." Shal started, before realising he was baiting her. "Well, I'd love to see you play, regardless."

"Come for the sound check if you like?"

———

Shal began to feel a little silly. She was grasping at something to do because she'd felt lonely today, but the last thing she wanted to do was come across like a teenage groupie.

"No, that's okay. I've got some work to do here."

Cam shrugged, sliding a perfect cup of tea across the bench without needing to ask how she took it.

Wearing classic dark jeans and a black V-necked T-shirt snug to the planes of his chest, Cam looked smart, fresh, and really very tasty. He certainly didn't look like a builder anymore. No sign of work boots, sawdust, or the five-o'clock shadow from yesterday.

Was he still seeing the ice maiden? Jodine? Jada?

Jody.

No. Katie had definitely said ex.

Maybe Pieta? The two women flaunted the same kind of fragile-blonde appeal...

For no concrete reason, Shal really hoped not. It was on the tip of her tongue to ask Cam if he was dating the songstress, but she found she didn't really want to know, after all.

When they headed back up to the master bedroom to go over the second song, Shal was quickly able to relax back into it. She loved building layers—hearing the harmonies come together. Bouncing ideas off each other and deciding on the right mix felt so right with Cam.

It was just before seven, and Cam was packing up to leave, when Rue called him on his cell. Shal's head snapped up at the ringtone; Sting's *Englishman in New York* was unmistakable.

She listened unashamedly to Cam's side of the conversation, figuring if it were private he would take it somewhere else. But Rue was merely passing on the name and number of a prospective client.

"Got a pen?" Cam asked Shal, wedging his phone between shoulder and ear.

She got up to pass him one.

Using his thigh as a table, Cam wrote the details on the corner of a lyrics sheet in his loose, long-tailed scrawl.

Shal was leaning over his shoulder to watch, smelling the soap on his skin. It was doing something very strange to her heart rate. The cords of Cam's neck were smooth and tempting under his fresh shave, and she became acutely aware how *weird* it was.

Cam was so familiar, yet so *different* from before.

Their faces were close, and when Cam finished the call and turned to look at her, his eyes caught the light from the bedside lamp. He had pretty golden shards radiating out from the pupil.

The two of them were close enough to kiss.

The thought came to Shal randomly, and her gaze shifted down to Cam's mouth.

She *could*…

Shal felt the flush rise and moved back slightly, blinking at Cam in embarrassment.

Cam cleared his throat. "One before I go?"

"Pardon?" Shal looked even more flustered.

"Shall we go over *Fallen* one more time?" he asked innocently enough, but his pulse was thumping.

He hadn't been planning on making a move. Not yet. He'd

figured they needed some time to reconnect before he broached the idea of something more.

What would her reaction be?

Interested? Insulted? Or just plain freaked out by a friend trying to move the boundaries on her?

The timing had always been wrong. It was *still* wrong, with too much left unsaid.

But Shal's eyes had been wide and dark for a moment there when she'd taken the time to stare at his mouth, and he'd almost believed she was about to lean in…

If Shal ever made the first move, he'd be toast.

Cam swallowed, hoping it wasn't audible to anyone but himself.

"The Brooke Fraser one." Shal climbed back onto her bed and hid her face behind the lyric sheet, effectively concealing what she was feeling, but in no way putting a stop to Cam's speculations.

When Cam left, Shal took out her reactions and examined them. She'd been confused to find her old flatmate so attractive this trip, on a different level than anything she'd ever noticed before. But now she was thinking about kissing him?

No doubt because she'd felt the bite of being alone today after Jac left. Empty, and looking for some sort of solace.

Wrong avenue to travel down. She'd definitely have to watch that.

Maybe the music had put her in a romantic frame of mind and loosened her inhibitions some? The songs had sounded good—better than she'd imagined. Cam was pretty damn amazing on guitar, and he'd been very accommodating with her sliding in on vocals and moving the arrangements wherever she liked.

More than that, it'd been fun just hanging out with him again.

She loved the camaraderie, and his gentle manner. And he *was* sexy—a real honey. It was only natural her body would notice that and wonder what it would be like to…

No. Best not.

Her reputation preceded her, and the last thing she wanted to do was use a friend—potentially hurt him.

The following day, Shal was booked to have lunch at Poppy's place, but there was a free morning to sink her teeth into first and a bunch things to fit in. The independent shoe store on George Street had caught her eye on arrival, so she ambushed that first. She introduced herself to the owner, handed over her business card, then moved the conversation towards both the 2-PEAS opening and Katie's wedding.

Two birds with one stone. Easy-peasy.

Her job was made even simpler due to the fact the place was a true shoe-Utopia, and she could exclaim over the well-chosen stock with pure and honest enthusiasm.

When she left, it was with a pair of frivolously strappy dress heels she couldn't wait to show Katie. Along with potential bridesmaid's sandals on hock, she'd just gained a very useful business advocate along with all the local retail gossip, leads on staff and modelling prospects, and the addresses of her next two stops.

Her morning was shaping up well.

By the time Shal arrived at Poppy's place she had a fresh manicure and her hair had been treated to a deep-conditioning mask. A huge bunch of lilies from the local grower had taken up residence in the back seat, too.

All new contacts in the network.

Shal heard the raucous laughter before reaching the steps to the deck, and was relieved to see it was just Katie's mum, Rosa, making Poppy guffaw. The sisters were both wearing ridiculously oversized sunnies when Shal rounded the shrubbery.

Cam's mum was fond of the outlandish and had a distinctive signature style, merging bohemian with a touch of kooky sass. Her shock of unruly hair was trimmed short, the same dark caramel as Cam's.

Both women exclaimed over Shal and made a fuss, gushing over her faux-suede jacket from last year's winter collection and the gem detailing on her fresh manicure. It took some time to get around to giving Poppy the flowers she'd been hiding behind her back, but the reaction was worth the wait.

Over lunch, the three of them got down to the serious business of finalising and securing the bookings for Katie's hen's party.

As Shal got up to leave, much later than she'd intended to, Poppy deposited a large, brightly wrapped present on her lap with aplomb.

"Oh, Poppy. You didn't have to get me a gift."

"Don't get too excited." Poppy laughed. "It's not your everyday present, but I saw these and thought of you."

Rosa, plainly impatient with Shal's snail-paced pick-at-it style of unwrapping, leant forward to tear a large hole in the corner so the contents of the package plopped out onto Shal's lap.

"Oh!" Shal began to laugh. "God, Poppy. They're just *awful*." She clutched the huge faux-fur slippers to her chest, tears smarting partly from the laughter and partly from another emotion entirely. In a roundabout way, Poppy had remembered her birthday. "I absolutely *love* them."

"I hoped you would." Poppy had a way of putting her head to the side and really considering a person. It was strangely disconcerting because Shal recognised the gesture as Cam's. "You're Pisces, right?"

"Yes, I am."

The slippers were ridiculous. A huge, sequinned pair of fish, complete with shining eyes, little side fins, and tails poking out the back. Shal slid her feet into the plush lining and mimicked a catwalk model across the deck, scissoring her legs overtly. More laughter ricocheted around in the afternoon sun.

Hearing a familiar song starting up somewhere nearby, Shal whipped around, trying to find the source. "Where's that music coming from?"

"Cam's phone. He dropped in for breakfast this morning and left it here. I'm a firm believer he'd forget his head if it wasn't screwed on," Poppy muttered, distracted. "Don't bother answering it," she advised as Shal discovered Cam's cell in the centre of the outdoor table behind some potted herbs. "It's just Cam calling on Jonno's phone. *Again*. I've already told him he needs to come back and get the damn thing himself. I'm not here to run around picking up after him like he's all of three years old."

"How do you know who's phone he's calling from?" Shal held

49

up one finger, concentrating on the ringtone. *'I'm a lover, I'm a sinner, I'm a fighter. Gonna set your soul on fire...'* "No. On second thoughts, don't tell me." Zed's Kiwi anthem was unmistakable. "Renegade Fighter could *only* be Jonno." The tune cut off, and Cam's phone was once again silent.

Poppy grinned. "You've met Cam's business partner, then?"

Shal laughed. "I have, yes." She thought back to yesterday and her practice with Cam. *Englishman in New York* had played when Rue called. "It's an app, right? You match a ringtone to each contact."

Poppy hesitated. "Right." Looking uncomfortable all of a sudden, eyes flitting to Rosa then back again, she began gathering the cups and teapot back onto the tray in a show of tidiness wholly unlike her.

Suspicion crept in.

"What's yours?" Shal wondered aloud.

"Ah, I'm not too sure." Poppy grimaced slightly as she looked up from her task. "It was *'Slice of Heaven'* a while back, but I think that was more to do with my banana loaf. Speaking of which, would you like to take some back to Dundas Street with you? I'll wrap a few slices." Her voice was a touch too chirpy as she motioned towards the leftover cake.

"Oh, good idea," Rosa bustled in with her two-cents-worth. "Lovely toasted up for breakfast, Shal."

Shal put her hands on her hips.

Poppy was making evasive manoeuvres and Rosa was fluffing— both of which were unprecedented behaviours. The women were usually as straight shooting as Katie. It ran in the family.

"What's *mine*?" Shal demanded.

"Umm..." The two older women glanced at each other, then away.

Hole in one.

Shal pinned first Poppy, then Rosa with a hard stare. Both appeared sheepish, and Poppy's shoulders rose in a slight shrug.

What the hell was going on?

Storming over to her handbag to get her phone *should* have conveyed some semblance of no-nonsense authority—if only Shal wasn't still wearing a pair of massive bug-eyed fish on her feet.

Rosa stifled a nervy giggle.

"We'll just see, shall we?" Shal huffed, placing a call to Cam.

Her ringtone was definitely a song, but it took her a moment to recognise the tune.

Creep, by Radiohead.

Creep?

Out of all the bloody songs on the planet, Cam had chosen *that* as her ringtone?

Rosa reached over, rejecting Shal's call as it softened into the verse.

"Let me get this straight." Shal's voice was reaching upper octaves. "He gives you *Slice of Heaven*, and I get *Creep*? Well, *that* sucks."

"It's nothing but an old joke. And of course it's referring to Cam, not…" Rosa earned herself a sharp glare from Poppy and clammed up mid-sentence.

6

Listening to…
Creep - Thom Yorke
From the album: Pablo Honey - Radiohead

Shal sat in her car, parked up below Poppy's house, and tried to pull up the Radiohead lyrics on her phone. But she'd forgotten to charge it and was shit out of luck on the battery front.

She was also obsessing.

Hoping it was still there, Shal drove to the music shop she remembered off George Street, recharging her phone along the way.

Replay Records was an old haunt, relatively unchanged by the passing of years, though Shal didn't remember it ever looking this unkempt. She wondered how it had survived alongside the download-music-world as she sought a staff-member's help.

"I'm looking for Radiohead's *Creep*. I just want to check out the lyrics."

"Sure. The Pablo Honey album?" Underneath the neon vinyl jacket, the long-limbed shop assistant had real potential to model. Androgynous enough to be truly beautiful, despite the heavy eyeliner.

"Ah, I don't know." Shal followed the eye-popping lime jacket around stock trestles.

"If we don't have it, I can Google them for you." The girl flipped through the Rs. "No. Here it is."

The sales assistant slid a long talon across the pricing sticker, splicing it open. "Still has the lyrics sheet. Classic crush song."

"Classic *what?*" Shal squeaked, blinking.

"Crush. Unrequited love. Lust. Whatever you want to call it."

No, it wasn't. Surely not. How could it possibly be?

She stared at the younger woman, feeling vaguely light-headed as her hand reached out for the lyrics on autopilot.

"Just bring it back to the counter when you're done, okay?" The shop assistant placed the small booklet in her hand. "I need to seal it back up again."

Lunch churning in her gut and fingers shaking, Shal hunted in vain for the corresponding lyrics. Why did they print everything so damn small?

"D'you want to hear it play?" The sales assistant twitched a studded eyebrow upward. "Says it's in good second-hand condition, but I wouldn't guarantee it. There's a headset stand." She nodded to the left.

"Okay." But Shal still hesitated before putting the headphones on.

The could-be-model loaded in the CD and disappeared.

Creep was second on the track list, settled amidst the buttery yellow stamens of the cover artwork.

Beautiful.

More than that, haunting.

Aching.

Shal groaned, pressing her fingertips to her eyelids. How could she have been so unbelievably stupid?

"Hiya." Katie finally answered her phone and Shal huffed out her relief, releasing her bottom lip from between her teeth.

"Katie? Thank God! Where are you?"

"Workshop. Filling orders. I've got beeswax in the double boiler for lip balm. Can I call you back in five?"

Shal could imagine the smell of the fragrant golden liquid—mint and honey, her favourite.

"No. Cam's ringtone. I didn't get it. Really didn't. I thought it meant *I* was a creep. I bought the CD."

"The CD?"

"Pablo Honey."

There was a telling pause. "Oh, shit."

"So, you *knew*? Rosa said it was an old joke."

"Ah…" Katie hesitated again. "Shal, he's my cousin. It was written all over him. Of course I knew."

"And you didn't *tell* me?"

"It wasn't mine to tell. It was all such a long time ago. You weren't interested, so…" Katie was stirring something furiously by the sounds of it—metal on metal—and an alarm began to bleat in the background. "Look, I've really gotta go, this stuff's gonna set on me."

"I'm coming over."

That might've sounded like a threat, but Shal didn't care.

"Okay, see you soon," Katie agreed, not bothering to disconnect.

Shal listened to the phone clatter down and Katie banging about in the workshop for a few moments more, the sound of industry settling her nerves a little.

Practical, fix-everything Katie would know what to do.

Katie was sitting on the front porch of Roseneath nursing a cup of tea when Shal arrived post-haste.

"That was fast," Katie called down the path. "You know there's a speed camera on the first causeway?"

"Crap! Really?"

"No, not really. But I wonder what it would have pinged you if there actually was one?"

Shal could read Katie's smirk more clearly as she drew closer.

"I just… I really missed you." She smiled back a little sheepishly, holding both palms up. At least her sense of humour was hanging in there.

Katie patted the step beside her. "Take a load off." Lifting her still warm cup of tea, she offered it to Shal as she sat down. "Camomile to calm the nerves. I needed this, and figure you might, too?"

"I feel like such an egghead." Shal sipped tentatively, and finding the tea a good temperature took a longer draft.

"You *are* an egghead." Then, as if to soften the sentiment, Katie added, "I find it's one of your most endearing features." Leaning against the porch post, she twisted to face Shal. "He's a mammoth egghead too if that makes you feel any better. I'm surrounded."

Shal groaned. "Please tell me I've misread this."

"Ground rules first. I don't want to break any confidences. I can tell you what I've seen—what a *blind* woman would've seen." Katie accentuated the little jibe with a poke at Shal's arm. "But not what's been given to me in private conversation."

"Fair enough." Shal thought for a moment. "We're talking about a mental connection, right?"

Katie pursed her lips together. "No, I wouldn't call it that. Not entirely, anyway."

"Some sort of crush?"

"More on the mark."

"Hence the creep song."

"Okay, so that was my fault. I planted that ringtone on Cam's phone. My way of harassing him whenever you called." Katie had the grace to look a little contrite.

"Cam told you he had a crush on me?"

Katie went to speak, then closed her mouth and mimed zipping it closed. She was walking a thin line. Friend on one end, cousin on the other.

Suddenly self-conscious, Shal tucked her hair behind her ears before approaching again from a slightly different angle. "What made you think Cam had feelings for me?"

Katie pressed the heels of her palms into her eye sockets, and groaned. "Where do I even *start* with that?"

"At the beginning?" Shal prodded hopefully.

Cam had been twenty when Shal had arrived on the scene (cue a massive crush) and twenty-one when she'd left (cue a solid year of hang-dog), according to Katie's recollection. And apparently, as his closest tuahine, she'd taken it as her due to hassle him mercilessly about his 'untouchable' flatmate.

They'd grown up more like siblings than cousins, and Katie knew Cam too well for him to hide his body language or emotive state. In Katie's words, it'd been written all over him like 'neon piss,' and was excellent fodder to annoy him with.

Shal stared at the shaggy macrocarpa along the boundary as Katie explained, trying to remember any vestiges of the conversations her friend was alluding to.

'Cam, I notice you changed the subject. Hands in your pockets, got something growing in there? Hey Cam, you've got that muscle thing happening in your jaw again—don't break a tooth!'

Why couldn't she remember any of that?

"I was always so crap at reading body language," Shal offered, toying with her ear lobe and lamenting her own youthful obtuseness.

"Oh, I absolutely agree," Katie razzed. "I was a real pain in Cam's butt, poor guy, rubbing his nose in it all the time. It's not like I was the only one to notice or take the mickey, but looking back, I could've been a lot less obnoxious about it."

"So why didn't I?" Shal wondered aloud. "Notice, I mean."

"Well, you did have a shitload of other things going on at the time." Katie conceded. "My guess is you were tied up in Mason. That, and the fact you're kind of used to the attention."

"Used to the...?" Shal floundered. "What's that supposed to mean?"

"Don't jump down my throat. When someone notices me, I *notice* them noticing, because it's not an hourly occurrence, or even a daily occurrence. I'm not knocking myself here," Katie added hastily as Shal tried to protest. "Just stating the facts as I see them. I get enough attention for my liking, thank you very much. The thing is, you're stunning, Shal. When you walk into a room the air changes, and *everyone* notices."

"Oh." Shal brought a hand up to her chest, flummoxed. "I think that's the most complimentary thing anyone's ever said to me."

"You're shitting me. Seriously? Those North Island guys need their heads read," Katie muttered. "I assumed at the time you noticed Cam noticing, but chose *not* to notice, if you get my drift?"

Shal was beginning to.

"Aroha, being a law unto herself, decided you'd blown Cam off," Katie continued. "Not good enough for you, not well-off enough for you, not pākeha enough for you—that kind of carry on. But I told her you hadn't even come close to picking up on it in the first place. Right?"

"Jesus! Aroha knows?" Shal wailed.

"Ah, *duuuh!*"

Placing her forehead carefully on her knees, Shal concentrated on the solid wood beneath her feet. Strong. Sturdy. Dependable.

"Links, too?" she queried weakly.

"I think you can pretty much assume the whole of Ōtepoti on this one," Katie assured her blithely. "Look, no offence, but it was pretty frickin' obvious Cam wanted to do more than just play house with you. But it was just as clear you didn't like him in that way. I half expected him to make a move, or at least say something to you after you and Mason broke up."

"He *didn't.*" Shal raised her head smartly.

"No. You were pretty raw." Katie looked across at her with a sigh.

It was so like Cam to stay on the back-foot and keep the pressure off. It had been a real effort to perform even the simplest functions after her breakup with Mason. She'd been slowly coming right, sliding out of the worst of it, when the accident had hit.

Hell-on-wheels for all of them. Links in intensive care, Mason in the morgue.

Shal swallowed before murmuring, "Yeah." Raw was one word for it.

"So, what did Cam have to say about it?"

"About *this*?"

"Wait. What? You haven't talked to Cam?" Katie's face was a picture of censure, eyebrows drawing together .

"I have no idea what to say to him."

"That's crap. You two are surf buddies from way back for God's sake. It's not like he…" Katie trailed off somewhat cryptically.

"It's not like he feels anything for me anymore?" Shal guessed, surprised to feel a decent dose of deflation in the knowledge.

Of course not. It was all such a long time ago.

Katie hesitated before answering, her fingers busily twisting her engagement ring. "You'll have to ask Cam about that part." She eased up to standing. "I guess it happens all the time; one friend develops deeper feelings than the other. Anyway, you were with Mason so the point was moot."

"Head-over-heels for him," Shal agreed, downcast.

"Yeah. Pity it turned out he was screwing everything with legs." Katie winced. "Sorry. Not nice of me to bring that up."

"No, don't apologise. I'm glad someone else is still angry about it."

"Not nearly as pissed off as I get about him not using protection. And don't even get me started about him driving drunk. What the hell was he even thinking?"

The women nodded solemnly at each other. Shal started to well up, and her voice was wobbly when she tried to speak again.

"He didn't give me the chance to tell him how furious I was. The *guilt*. He bowed out and left us all with the mess. I'm still mad about it. God. I was so naïve, I would've followed that guy to the end of the earth. He knew how much he meant to me. The whole thing was just so... so *Mason* of him."

Adversely, they both began to giggle at that. Shal got the hiccups, and suddenly they were out and out laughing till tears ran down their cheeks.

Shal happened to have the hanger bags for Katie in the back of her car, so she laid the samples over the back of the dining chairs at Roseneath while Katie put the kettle back on.

They weren't strictly 'samples,' but Katie didn't need to know that. Shal had Katie's size and shape memorised, and always pulled whatever she thought would suit her friend from the current range for her to pick and choose from.

She'd also brought the new option for bridesmaid's sandals with her—excited to see if Katie would go for them.

Katie closed the fridge and moved closer, at ease within the crisp white tiling and slate-blue cabinets.

"I love your kitchen."

"Yeah. Me too." Katie offered Shal another cup of camomile tea. "When the sun pours in here in the morning, I look out over the water and have to pinch myself it's ours."

They leant against the edge of the bench to drink in the ocean view with their tea.

All of Katie's pronouns had moved so easily to accommodate Rue. She now spoke seamlessly of *we*, *us*, and *ours*. It clearly suited the redhead's way of being to be one of a pair. Like turtle doves. Like geese.

"Geese?" Katie's bemused question jostled Shal out of her daydream, making her realise she'd spoken the word aloud.

"Mmm? Oh, geese. Yes. They mate for life. I was just thinking Rue's your gander."

"I don't know about a gander, but he's a goose alright," Katie muttered.

When Shal was little, her mother, Carol, had periodically taken her on trips back to Sweden. How old had she been…? Ten, or thereabouts, the trip her grandfather had been dying.

Her Morfar had seemed too young to be terminally ill, but cancer suffered no remorse about age and rode roughshod over his once robust body. His remaining height had seemed somewhat concave without the usual stuffing holding it up.

It was only later Shal realised Carol had made the trip to say goodbye to her father. Everyone must've known it would be the last time.

Everyone but Shal.

They'd spent a sunny morning walking around the heavily reeded lake near her mother's childhood home in Rönninge. Carol's brother and mother had been taking turns pushing Morfar in his wheelchair over the root-strewn path, winding through the tall trees around the lake edge.

Carol wasn't an emotive woman, so Shal had been surprised to spot tears in her mother's eyes. She'd laughed in her brittle way, squatting next to her father's wheelchair to reminisce about skating on the lake as a child. Her brother Henke's hand-me-down ice-hockey boots hadn't been at all pretty, but they were faster than any of the other girls' beautiful white figure-skates. Carol's voice had taken a bitter twist, and Morfar's withered hand had reached up to pat her blonde head as it came to rest near his shoulder.

Carol hadn't allowed the physical affection for long; had pulled away, as was her custom.

Growing tired of standing still, Shal had moved on ahead to see what was around the next corner, wandering away from the group. It was her full-blooded scream that had hastened her Uncle Henke to sprint around after her.

Already turned back on the path, she'd collided with him, burying her face in his shirt. He'd always smelt of the woods. It was incredibly reassuring—like squeezing a big, solid tree.

Taking her hand resolutely in his own, Henke had drawn her back to what she'd found on the hard packed earth at the water's edge.

She'd thought the large bird was sleeping at first, though one wing was spread out as if dreaming of flight. It wasn't until she'd gotten closer she'd seen the long metal shaft thrust into its breast, sticky dark ooze staining pale chest feathers.

Shal hadn't recognised the words had Henke used, but was pretty sure they were colourful ones. As he'd knelt to get a better look, a second wild goose had squawked and complained, batting its wings at Henke furiously. It appeared uninjured, but wouldn't quit the frenetic noise.

The rest of the family had emerged along the path, and Mormor had stepped down the bank to join them. Despite Henke's objections, his mother wrapped the dead goose in the sweater she'd had tied around her waist—folding the outstretched wing and cradling the bird as gently as if it were one of her own sleeping grandchildren.

Shal had noted, with some concern, that her grandmother's cheeks were wet with unchecked tears.

"Was it a special goose, Mormor?" she'd asked solemnly, artlessly.

"Very special, *älskling*." Mormor had sat down on the raised path edge and opened the sweater a little. "See how big he was? That means he's the gander—the boy." Mormor gestured towards the smaller, similarly feathered bird, still agitated and now alone on the bank. Her voice had tightened. "And this was his sweetheart. The little one's the girl."

"Why was he so very special?" Shal had tried so hard to understand the significance, because she could clearly see there was one. To her grandmother, this somewhat gory discovery had been nothing less than devastating.

"Oh, *lilla flicka*." Mormor had held one hand outstretched for Shal to hold. "Geese choose a partner and stay with them forever." Her voice broke on the last word, and she'd seemed suddenly fragile. "Like your Morfar and me. What ever will she do without him?"

Henke had come to sit beside his mother, swinging an arm around her shoulders and tucking her close to his large, warm frame.

"Your Mormor has a soft heart, just like you, *Fredslilja*. She's sad for the little goose, who'll miss her sweetheart terribly." Henke had reached out his free hand and ruffled Shal's hair, so much darker than his own. "And she'll be mourning the boy, too, because he'll never get to fly with his *älskling* again." The older woman beside him had let out a strangled sob. "Go on now and walk with your mama. Your Mormor and I are going to sit here a little longer."

———

Shal had been gazing out at the harbour, but she brought herself back to focus on the kitchen, on Katie.

Deciding the anecdote about a dead goose was a bit too morose for a girlfriend who was about to marry her gander, she turned the conversation back to the wedding instead, asking about the catering and flowers.

Her bridesmaid to-do list was burgeoning, and if she was going to do a decent job she needed to focus more on the task at hand and less on her own history.

7

Listening to...
Together Alone - Neil Finn, Mark Hart and Ngapo 'Bub' Wehi
From the album: Together Alone - Crowded House

Shal didn't sleep well. Her body should've been soothed by the delicious before-bed foot scrub she'd indulged in, complete with Katie's rosemary rejuvenation cream, but her mind kept churning around in circles. Dead geese, sequinned fish, Cameron Dante, and Mason Knox kept popping up in her stress dreams, tying themselves strangely into storylines.

She awoke after a particularly vivid one, where she'd knocked on the door of Dundas Street... Only it wasn't Cam, but Mason who'd come out to greet her—to kiss her.

Dread seeped all the way down to her toes, because even semi-conscious she knew *that* wasn't right.

Mason was long gone.

According to Shal's red-faced alarm clock, it was two-fourteen when she threw the bedclothes off, heart pounding with the queasy after-burn. Shitty what your mind pulled out of you while you were sleeping. Why couldn't she dream of flying like she used to when she was a child?

"Not your best look," Shal told herself in the ensuite mirror later that same morning, checking out her dark circles before stepping into the shower. She willed the steam and hot water to rinse off the disquiet plaguing her.

Finding her huge Pisces slippers peeping out from under the chaise lounge, she slid them on, grateful for their warmth and unmitigated cheerfulness. A cup of tea could fix all manner of ills, and she padded down to the kitchen to put the kettle on.

It was already midweek, and Shal's day was spread-sheeted into a tidy schedule. First up, supporting the bride-to-be at her dress fitting at nine. Katie would be swinging by to pick her up in… *fifteen minutes*!

Shal groaned, trying to swallow her too-hot tea while figuring out how to work the fancy toaster all at the same time.

Her phone bleated.

"*Shit!*" Jumping with a start, she slopped tea on the tiles, narrowly missing her fish-feet as she scrabbled to answer the call.

"Morning. You're up?"

Cam.

"Yes, I'm up." Sort of. "Going out in a tick though." If she could get her act together.

"Wondered if you'd be keen for a surf later this arvo? I can't make your two p.m. progress meeting with Jonno, but I'm heading down to St Clair after four."

St Clair, Shal's favourite surf beach in the whole, wide world.

She didn't answer right off the bat, weighing up the offer and the consequences. Did she really want to see Cameron Dante today?

Probably not a great idea.

Did she want to surf, though?

God, yes.

"I've got Katie's old winter wetsuit and a spare board," Cam started again, but still Shal remained silent, mulling it over. "I can easily chuck it in with my gear if you want to get out on the water? I've got booties and a vest that'll fit you," he added coaxingly, knowing her foibles far too well.

Shal sighed. "Thanks for that, can I let you know later? I've got a lot going on today."

"Sure. No worries."

Shal knelt on one knee with a paper towel, wiping up spilt tea and wondering if Katie had talked to her cousin, or whether the zipped lips went both ways?

"Cam?"

Did *he* know that *she* knew?

"Yeah?"

Shal had too much in her head—circling questions she wasn't sure she wanted to know the answers to. This trip would've been a damn sight easier if she'd remained buried up to her neck on this particular point, like an ostrich with its head in the sand.

"Thanks."

"Don't mention it, Surfer Girl."

Shal took the stairs at a jog, a mere handful of minutes remaining to get dressed and hunt through her suitcases for a swimming costume to shove into her handbag, just in case.

Three blocks away, Cam disconnected and slipped his phone into the back pocket of his jeans. He'd planned to keep out of Shal's way for a couple more days, but the sun had risen warm and cheerful this morning and the surf forecast was good.

The sound of her voice lifted him, but knowing he might see her today was even better. He hadn't caught up with her yesterday, and whether it was a smart move or not, he'd missed her.

Grabbing his tool belt in one hand and the belt-sander in the other, Cam headed back into the bare bones of the Park Street villa, getting back to work with a lift in his step and a whistle on his lips.

A large, pithy hill residence, the dressmaker's turreted mansion high on the hill smacked of history and long faded wealth, the two front bay rooms now a showroom, fitting area, and sewing room. Specialising in bridal and evening gowns, the owner's work was meticulous—unfaultable.

The woman had been a godsend, only too happy to work in with Shal's designs, patterns, and fabric choices for Katie's wedding. Not every seamstress would have been so accomodating.

When Katie was last in Te Whanganui-a-Tara, Shal had dragged her through multiple bridal boutiques, getting a feeling for what she liked, and more to the point *didn't* like. Katie was cajoled into trying on more dresses than she'd probably worn in her lifetime that weekend. The resulting bridal design they'd come up with would perfectly complement the redhead's curves.

The sweetheart neckline and capped sleeves in antique lace were a traditional nod to Katie's Scots heritage, framing her in off-white, while the high hexagonal cut-out at the back was a lot more modern.

Knowing every detail of Katie's dress didn't come close to preparing Shal for the effect of seeing her friend walking into the room wearing it, though.

Rosa promptly burst into tears, holding a hand up to her mouth while Katie's aunties stared for a stunned moment.

The bride glowed. Radiating happiness and excitement, she did a little twirl before skipping over to her mum and giving her a tight squeeze.

"Don't blub, or you'll make *me* blub. I take it you like it?"

"Like it? I *love* it." Rosa's voice was a little strangled. "Oh, Katie, I wish your Nana Nona could see you in that dress. How did you get to be so beautiful?"

"I come from good stock," Katie offered with a dewy smile.

Everyone spoke at once, exclaiming over details. Fingering the heaviness of the fabric, they were all enchanted by the pearl detailing stitched into scallops of lace. Katie caught Shal's eye over the throng of older women, her face shining with the joy of the moment. '*Thank you*', she mouthed, touching her fingertips to her lips and blowing her head bridesmaid a kiss.

Following the fitting, the women all laughed, talked, and drank their way through lunch and well beyond. The food was beautifully presented in the little French bistro, upstairs off George Street, with zero eyebrows raised at the sheer volume of midday wine consumed.

Rosa, Poppy, and a third sister, Lily, bounced ideas off each other and finished each other's sentences. As well as the hot topic of the wedding, they talked of family, work, travel, fashion, food, and the men (or in Lily's case, woman) in their lives.

Shal could see why Katie had insisted on driving them all. The sisters would be in no state to get behind the wheel after their liquid lunch. Their raucous behaviour extended right through to Shal's two-p.m. appointment with Jonno, which she almost forgot about in the medley.

Realising how late it was getting, she hurriedly made her goodbyes, and was followed down the narrow stairs by wolf-whistles, catcalls, and much laughter.

The boutique was only three blocks up, but Shal was already late. She texted Jonno with her ETA as she walked, thankful she'd worn flats and for the fresh air clearing her head.

It wasn't just the wine at lunch she wasn't used to, it was being absorbed wholeheartedly into a noisy family group full of extroverts and energy.

Exhilarating, but incredibly draining.

Jonno's furtive glance behind her as she entered the boutique wasn't lost on Shal, though she couldn't tell if it was relief or disappointment that flashed across his face.

Her business partner obviously hadn't informed the burly builder she'd be flying out.

"No fire-breathing sidekick today?" Jonno quipped.

Shal muffled a snort of laughter in surprise. The man actually had a sense of humour.

"No. I'm flying solo."

"Phew. Disaster averted." Jonno's lips twitched, and Shal was amazed to see a small dimple flicker on one cheek. The grim tradesman appeared to be holding back a genuine smile.

Jonno was an entirely different person without Jac on the scene. He held a calm and intelligent conversation, treated Shal respectfully, and didn't swear once. He also had his eye on the ball. With plans laid out on what would soon become the boutique counter, they went over the details and timeline for finishing up. How much of the budget was left, (none), and how much more Jonno estimated he'd need before laying down tools.

Shal carefully avoided all mention of Cam. Her head was busy enough, swimming with numbers, dates, and what she had to get done. The addition of alcohol in her system was in no way helping matters.

"Okay, so I'm going to go ahead with all the advertising and invitations for the opening event on the evening of March twenty-seventh." She re-checked the date, inputting a note on her calendar app and sharing it with Jac. "Which means our first day open is Saturday, March twenty-eighth." Lowering her device, Shal looked Jonno over.

His long denim shorts appeared relatively unscathed, but the T-shirt he was wearing was streaked with paint and wood varnish.

"It'd be great if you could come to the Friday night do." She watched with some humour as the builder took a small step backwards—physically removing himself from both the concept, and her—and was able to mockingly congratulate herself on being able to read this most basic of body languages. "I'm sure you scrub up just fine, Jonno, and there'll be food," she wheedled. "You can keep Cam company."

"Not really my scene."

"And beer."

"Ahh." Jonno's hand came up, and he rubbed at the scar tracking down his temple.

"Wine?"

"I don't drink, actually. The thing is, Shal—"

"Jac."

"What?"

"The thing is Jac, isn't it?" Shal leant her hip on the counter and folded her arms. "Look, I'll do my best to keep her in check, though that's not promising much when she's clearly on the warpath." She narrowed her eyes at him. "I don't know what you did to piss her off so soundly, but her bark is worse than her bite. Mostly."

"I can handle Jac." But Jonno looked down to the toe of his boot as he spoke, scuffing at the floor as if he'd found a raised nail.

"Then I'd be really grateful if you'd come to the opening. You've had so much input on the refit."

Jonno looked across at her, silent.

"Bring a date, if you like." Shal fished around for a bit more information.

"I might just do that," Jonno answered with a slow, thoughtful nod.

———

Shal walked up to the Octagon, buying a bottle of water on the way. She found a prime people-watching position on the Cathedral steps and hugged one knee, sipping water and procrastinating.

She had to call The Bank of David for another draw-down of funds, and she wasn't looking forward to it.

Not exactly *guilty*. Guilt was an emotion Shal was trying to eradicate from her vocabulary. She'd rather be standing on her own two feet at twenty-eight, though—not calling her father for cash. Not that the money was *his*, exactly. It was New York Nana who'd set up the Hoffner trust for David's offspring.

A trio of them, so far.

David was just one of three trustees. Shal's great uncle Samuel and New York Nana were the ones she'd rather be contacting, but it was the wee small hours of the morning in the northern hemisphere right now, so if she wanted to get the ball rolling it had to be through David.

Shal's father had settled in New Zealand in his thirties. Hailing from old family wealth, he'd travelled a lot for his trading advisory firm between Tāmaki-makau-rau, Aotearoa's largest city, and Te Whanganui-a-Tara, its capital. But he'd had no trouble making himself at home—figuratively and literally—in both cities.

Stock trading was the perfect playground for David, though some of his tactics may've been questionable. Holding the truth close to one's chest was imperative in the high stakes game, and he was certainly a master of that. With an ego to match his good looks and soft American accent, even Shal could see he carried a certain mystique.

He also knew damn well how to play on it.

Shal was eighteen before she'd found out about her father's other families; his other children. Back then, sweet, pigtailed Bianca had lived with her mother in the capital, and little Eliza was still in utero in Tāmaki-makau-rau. It was like something out of a movie; a black comedy of epic proportions. None of the key players were laughing, though. David's collective partners and children had all been blindsided, sucker punched, and left gasping for air.

Shal had never had an inkling of David's duplicity, not a single one. Her daddy had been her entire world, and she'd innocently believed she was his. With 'my princess' this, and 'my pearl' that, who wouldn't?

She'd never really managed to gel well with her mother. Since early childhood it had become clear Shal wasn't much more than a splinter in Carol's perfectly manicured schedule.

In a choice made simple, Shal had loved David instead; entrusted her whole heart to his generous nature and sense of fun. It was no hardship, the man was magnetic.

Unfortunately, the word liar didn't even come close to describing how her daddy had conducted himself.

During her parents' divorce, teenage Shal became piggy in the middle—the meat in the sandwich—as insults and bombshells flew. When asked to describe her family to her therapist in later years, she'd given the analogy of a sloppy club-sandwich; with multiple slices of bread and multiple fillings…

She hadn't touched a club-sandwich since.

Shal took a deep breath and talked herself around, searching through the Bs in her contacts. She'd purposefully set her father apart from other family members by listing him under 'Bank of David.' It was supposed to be a dig at him, but each time she saw the onscreen pseudonym she was confronted by the money-hungry nature it portrayed in her.

He owed her, the least he could do was sign the paperwork and get it underway. What else was the money doing but sitting there, earning interest? It was her inheritance after all. New York Nana's money.

All the reasoning in the world couldn't persuade Shal to feel good about it. There was another scheduled payment due in two years' time, on her thirtieth birthday, but in order to finalise the boutique she needed that date brought forward.

Shal still remembered how to play Daddy's Little Princess reasonably well, and was able to keep her tone light and bubbly; friendly and non-judgemental. She even remembered to ask after her latest soon-to-be stepmother, who was ridiculously young for David at thirty-two.

The same age as Jac, for heaven's sake.

Shal wondered, but didn't ask, if he had a mistress on the go this time too. And if so, did the poor woman have any inkling there was a fiancée and a veritable string of pearls and princesses trailing in his wake?

It didn't bear thinking about.

She allowed David to call her Shalom (even though it rankled) and his pearl (even though it scalded with an intense burn). She knew for a fact David called Bianca his pearl too, and that should be fine. Only it wasn't. Because for years, he'd led each of them to believe they were his *only* one, and Shal had a sneaking suspicion he called everyone by the same generic pet-names just so that he didn't slip up.

Shal didn't mention the boutique until her father did, and even then, was careful to make sure the second early disbursement of funds was *his* idea, not hers. From there, she could play out the surprised-at-his-generous-idea scene.

Maybe her father was as good at playing this duplicitous game as she was. She wouldn't put it past him. They were both so habitually dishonest with each other now, she found it hard to know who was the better actor, David or herself.

Immensely relieved when the call was finally over, Shal turned her face up to the sunlight valiantly struggling to break through the clouds. As always, conversing with her father left a tarnish on her day due to the lies told, and the truths unspoken.

8

Listening to…
Sway - Bic Runga
From the album: Drive

As soon as Shal climbed into Cam's ute, she let him know she wasn't going to be great company. In fact, she'd begun to wish she'd flagged the whole surfing idea and gone lane swimming instead. She really needed to be alone.

Instead she was in the cab with the guy who'd had a crush on her back in university, *#feelingawkward.*

She'd always been relaxed around Cam, but the knowledge of what he'd felt for her in the past was sitting oddly. They hadn't talked about it, and until the air was cleared she'd continue to feel weird.

Cam was nothing if not thoughtful, though, getting gear together and taking her out on the water. He'd also put one of her favourite old songs on, and knew how to back off when someone was in a sketchy mood.

Shal stole a quick glance his way.

He *seemed* calm, much more relaxed than she felt. The spring inside her got wound tight sometimes, and talking with her father today had added to the general stress. Their sporadic father-daughter lip-service made Shal feel like an imposter in her own life.

Seeing Katie in her dress this morning should've been the highlight of her day, but Shal had been shocked at the same time. She hadn't been expecting to feel any negative emotion, and could still taste the tang of her own disloyalty. Because when Katie had glowed prettily in her gown, Shal's gut reaction hadn't just been happiness for a friend. Not entirely.

The elation had been contaminated by a slow, sliding envy.

What kind of person felt that in the face of such joy? What the hell was wrong with her?

The thing was, Katie knew how to play this game. It was as natural to her as breathing. She knew how to love and be loved, how to trust and be trusted...

And Shal didn't.

It was confronting to acknowledge that somewhere deep within herself was a child wistfully longing for her very own fairy-tale ending.

Shal made it clear she wanted to be alone on the water, but Cam couldn't help it if his eyes were drawn to her time and again, with the Bic Runga song from the ute still playing in his head. She was off her game, daydreaming, faffing around and getting bowled more than once by the surf in payback.

Cam was just thinking the break was getting crowded when Shal had a near miss with a longboarder. She wasn't one to give up or throw in the towel, so he knew something was up when she paddled in on the next wave.

He followed suit.

Strolling up the sand with his board under his arm, flicking his head to shake the dripping salt out of his eyes, it took Cam a moment to realise he wasn't the first to reach her.

The longboarder had beat him to the sand.

From her stance, Shal was fuming, and it didn't look like she'd be calming down anytime soon. The longboarder had some balls to even continue on approach.

"What do you want?" Shal spat angrily at the other surfer as he neared.

The longboarder stopped in his tracks, putting one hand up in defence. "Just checking you're okay. I wasn't sure if I clipped you."

"Yeah, you did." Shal indicated to her right thigh.

Heart in his throat, Cam dumped his board and lunged forward. Zeroing in on Shal's leg he checked for signs the wetsuit—or the body underneath—had been damaged.

She shoved his hands away in irritation.

"What the hell *was* that? Trying to slice me open as shark bait?" Shal all but snarled at the other man.

The longboarder got angry right back. "That was on you, lady. You nearly ruined my wave. Pay attention and get out of the bloody way next time."

Cam recognised the surfer as one of the regular set. He was built like a brick shit-house, reminding Cam of his own brother at the height of his rugby career, with broad shoulders, muscular thighs, and an immovable stance. He was clearly pissed off, but didn't look like he was going to get physical about it.

Shal, on the other hand, was just getting warmed up. She'd already chucked her board down on the sand between them, and her fists were fused to her hips.

"*I* nearly ruined *your* wave? You arrogant son-of-a—" she began.

"Peace, e hoa," Cam tried to intervene before it got too ugly, but found himself copying the longboarder and raising a hand in defence when Shal spun, turning fiery eyes on him.

"*Peace*? Oh, that's priceless, Cam." Turning, she pointed fiercely. "He nearly took me out!"

"He was on the wave, Shal. He was up and riding and you were daydreaming," Cam reasoned, getting up to stand and taking a surreptitious step backward. "Honestly? I think he did well to get around you, all things considered. Buggered if I could on that board." He indicated the sheer size of the thing.

The big dude seemed to take that as a compliment, and relaxed a little, nodding.

"Get *around* me? He clipped me! You're taking *his* side on this?"

Shal hiccuped loudly, and her ears burned pink—with fury or embarrassment? Cam couldn't be sure.

"I'm heading back out. Don't either of you even *think* of coming anywhere near me!" Snatching up the borrowed board, she stormed back down to the shoreline, stopping only to re-attach her leg rope and hiccup once more before paddling out with deep, determined strokes.

No sign of a limp, so not too badly injured.

After a bemused silence, the longboarder finally turned to Cam. "What the hell is her problem?"

"Aucklander," Cam offered lightly. The mere mention of the northernmost city was usually all the explanation needed this far south.

He watched Shal pull still further out—just a silhouette of black now.

"Ah, figures." Spitting salt out onto the sand, the other surfer watched too. And who could blame him? "Rides goofy?"

"Yep."

"Bit of a spitfire."

"You could say that, yeah."

"Yours?" The longboarder flicked his chin towards the now small figure in the surf.

"No, 'fraid not," Cam admitted with a touch of bona fide regret.

The longboarder grunted, taking a long steady look at him before nodding again. He headed back out, this time to the right point, giving Shal a wide berth.

Cam turned to walk his board up above the high tide line.

He'd sit and wait. Better to give Shal some space and let her cool down in her own sweet time.

Spitfire? Yes, she was.

It wasn't the first time Shal had been pissed off at him down on the beach, and it probably wouldn't be the last.

They'd all been mucking around on the peninsula once, years ago, and at Links' instigation the girls had raced each other on the sand. Aroha, unhappy with her initial loss, had insisted on best-of-three. In every race Shal had led with her right leg. Not problematic, just interesting. Back then, Shal had surfed regular—left leg leading.

Her weaker side, as it turned out.

Shal was naturally goofy, though she hadn't thanked Cam for his surprised observation at the time.

Shal took another half hour to catch a couple more waves. Not her best day on the water, but the concentration needed expedited her calm-down process.

Shal's father getting married again didn't have to pose a problem, she wouldn't be expected to have much to do with the mismatched couple. And down to earth Katie *deserved* the fairy-tale romance; the happy-ever-after. No one was more worthy, or more capable of making it work.

Cam had taken the other surfer's side? She could chalk that down to a male-ego hang-together moment. And the fact he'd held a candle for her, years back, was a compliment if she could only see it as such.

Shal hated being left out of the loop, though. It smacked of secrets and betrayal. More than anything else, she hated not knowing. Everyone around her had been aware the-boy-down-the-hall had the hots for her. They'd talked about it, and from the sounds of it openly joked about it, but she'd never had an inkling. That made her an unobservant noodle, didn't it? Just plain goofy.

Would things have played out differently if she'd chosen someone else over Mason, rather than it being the other way around? Maybe Mason would still be alive? Maybe Links would still be running?

But the Shal who'd been in love with Mason never would've chosen to make that break. Not without a decent shove. She'd believed in monogamy and happy-ever-afters.

Cam had been a good friend, and she'd loved him as that— missed him as that. They'd been close, and she'd absolutely taken that closeness for granted. He'd never looked at her with that sex-on-the-brain slant guys got. Not that she'd noticed anyway.

The kicker was, she'd always felt safe with him.

They'd texted and emailed a bit after she left. Kept in touch but remained distant at the same time. She could count on one hand the times she'd actually seen Cam face-to-face since she'd left Ōtepoti.

He'd been there at Mason's funeral, of course, though that was all a bit of a blur. The whole fortnight leading up to that event was a hazy cluster of images and emotions, like the disjointed angles in a broken mirror.

How had she managed to stand up and breathe in and out?

Though there'd been plenty of opportunity, Cam had never made a pass at her. Hugs when she'd asked for one, the odd light punch on the arm in passing, or teasing when she was dressed up. He had always been supportive.

Stuff your brother would do? She didn't know; didn't have one. Stuff a friend would do. Stuff Katie would do.

Though it'd often been just the two of them alone together, Shal had never considered Cam in any other light. But the attraction she'd been feeling for him this trip was only gaining traction— elevated heart rate and flushes of shyness. How was she supposed to equate *that* with friendship?

Good-looking guy. Acutely so, as it turned out. And sweet.

Carry on as before? That was infinitely better than confronting Cam and embarrassing him about something he'd felt years ago— exposing her own obtuseness. With less than two weeks left until Katie's wedding, and the boutique racing on ahead of schedule, Shal would soon be back in Te Whanganui-a-Tara anyway. Well out of the way.

It was ancient history, after all.

"Just an old crush," Shal muttered to herself, coming to a clear decision.

Her thigh was aching where the longboard had clipped her, and she decided her next wave in would be the last.

When she emerged out of the surf, Cam was waiting for her on the sand. He looked relaxed, part of the stunning scenery, leaning back on his elbows and watching the other surfers. His hair was a little long, curlier than usual from the salt, and lighter on the tips than the rest. The wetsuit showed off his lean, athletic frame, and broad shoulders.

A bloody good-looking male—her body gave a hearty pulse of approval.

A bloody good friend, she reminded herself.

"Not a bad ride, that last one," Cam observed calmly.

"Felt good," Shal returned, easing herself down near him, but not too close. Waiting to get her words right in her head, she scanned the surf. "I need to apologise. I totally lost my cool." Squinting out to the horizon, she was embarrassed to remember how she'd barked at him.

Not what a good friend would do. Not even close.

"No worries. How's the leg?"

"Sore," she conceded. "But I think I'll live."

Cam nodded and left it at that. They remained silent for a while, watching the other surfers ride.

How different they were. Cam let insults and bad temper slide right off him like water off a well-waxed board.

The sun was creeping lower, the tops of the coastal hills swathed in rose-gold light.

"It's just…" Shal shivered. "I had some stuff on my mind, and took it out on you."

Like a sore tooth, she was worrying at what sat uncomfortably within her.

"Yeah, I could see that." Cam turned to look at her, his eyes honey-brown and questioning. "You're alright, though?"

"No. I mean, yeah." Shal faltered. "Actually, not great. A few things going on." She mimed 'loopy' with a finger circling off her right temple. "My father's getting married again."

"Right." Cam raised his eyebrow a notch. "Ah, congratulations?"

"Ha. Well at least she's older than me. Just." She fiddled with a piece of loose stitching near her ankle. "I also blew my budget on some copper detailing in the boutique. It's going to look amazing, but you know…" She raised one shoulder, then let it drop as she turned slowly to face him, still wondering if he'd been given a heads up and needing to gauge his reaction. "I went out and saw Katie yesterday, too. After I'd had a rather illuminating lunch with your mum."

That got his attention. Cam's eyes narrowed and he became perfectly still. The hand that had been picking up dry sand and filtering it out like an hourglass froze, then clenched slowly into a tight fist.

"Mmm?" He hummed noncommittally, but he was watching her with an intensity that began to make her feel uncomfortable.

"And I found the old music shop in town we used to go to."

"Right." Cam's brows were clamped together, but he still held back from asking any questions. Silent. Listening. Letting her get whatever it was off her chest.

Shal took a deep breath before admitting, "I heard my ringtone, I mean on *your* phone. I was in a shitty mood about that. Confused, I guess. I thought you were calling *me* a creep."

A wave surged further up the beach than the last set, sending the gulls scattering. It was followed by an even longer reaching second, then third. The tide was coming in, and still Cam said nothing.

"So, is everyone nuts, or did you actually feel something for me back in university?" The question came out rushed, the words too compressed together, and hung in the air for them both to contemplate like laundry on the line.

Cam didn't move. He blinked once, and Shal noticed the muscle flickering on his jawline again. The pause was telling, but when he eventually spoke, he made light of it.

"Oh, I'm sure I wasn't the only one. We were all a little bit in love with you, I think." His smile didn't reach his eyes.

"In *love* with me?" Shal yelped.

9

———————

Listening to…
Monarch - Shapeshifter
From the album: Delta

In love—an inflammatory pair of words to use, even if Cam had meant them in jest.

Which he hadn't.

Going by the dumbstruck look on Shal's face, he should've kept his mouth shut.

"Hell, anyone with a pair of eyes and half a brain would've fallen for you, Shal. Half of the English department for all I know. It must've been pretty damn clear I was part of the ranks." He brushed the sand off his hands, irritated with both himself and the situation. "You were smart, beautiful, fun… Sounded good behind a mic and even found some of my lame jokes mildly funny." Their shared sense of humour had gotten them both through some tough times. "Plus, I could talk to you. I mean really talk to you. About Dad. About anything. It wasn't a conscious thing—I didn't choose it —but I guess I let you get under my skin." He aimed for casual and used past tense, but to his own ears it all sounded a bit strangled.

"I thought we were friends. We hung out a lot, but you never said anything to me about this. Not one thing. Now I look like an egghead for not realising."

Ah, she was miffed about missing the clear cues and markers? Cam cocked his head and considered her.

"Of course we were friends. *Are* friends. I've never been dishonest about it, and it was never my intention to fleece you. You were with someone else. What was I supposed to say? 'Oh, by the way, I've fallen for you—dump the dickhead?' "

"A heads-up would've been preferable," Shal muttered, clearly still sulky.

"We weren't much more than kids," he countered.

"I was *twenty*," she spluttered.

"Nineteen, then twenty. But pretty green, you'd have to admit."

"Green!"

"That wasn't an insult." Though Shal had clearly taken it as one. "We were *all* green. You were crazy about Mason. That smacks of green, wouldn't you say?" He turned to look out across the bay again, away from her confusion and affront. "He was a mate, and you didn't feel the same towards me. End of story. There was no point mentioning it to you," he added, feeling her eyes on his profile but not turning to meet them.

Mason, for all his faults, had been a friend. They'd all been young, and admittedly reckless at times. Bulletproof. It could've been any one of them who hadn't made it past twenty-one. Just the luck of the draw and a particularly boneheaded choice that had spun the bony finger of fate to point at Mason.

"I don't think it's fair to say there was no point *mentioning*—"

"You were with someone else, Shal," Cam cut her off, exasperated to be talking circles around a situation he'd had no control over then, and even less control over now. "Then, after the accident..." He held both hands up in a helpless gesture.

After the accident, Shal was gone.

"I've always assumed you knew. You had to've known on some level." Cam had been told it was painfully obvious. Though he'd tried to push the whole thing aside, keep it on a platonic plane, there was only a flimsy partition between friendship and what he'd really hankered for.

Cam turned back to Shal, studying her face for duplicity and coming up empty. Hollow eyed and a little sad, she stared back at him.

He shrugged, trying to shift the weight of secrecy that had been settled on his shoulders for years. "It's not important."

"I was so tied up in..." Shal's eyes widened. "Did Mason know?"

Cam raised both palms in an are-you-effing-kidding-me gesture.

Of course Mason picked up on his flatmate's highly inconvenient crush, and had been a total asshole about it.

"I probably should've moved out of the flat, looking back. But at the time I figured I was there first." He looked down at Shal's bootied feet, furrowing deeper into the sand. "What did I know? I wasn't what you'd call experienced."

"When did you start to think of me that way?"

Cam took a long time to answer her, not sure if it was particularly wise to get into the details.

"At the beginning."

"*What* beginning?" she insisted.

"Probably the first day," he reiterated softly after another long pause.

Shal's face was sun-kissed, washed clean by the ocean, and Cam got lost in studying it for a moment.

He remembered her as she had been, standing on the front stoop with her stunning eyes, catlike in their intensity. Noting the small changes maturity and confidence had given her, he thought of everything she'd achieved for herself since that time. Dragging herself up from rock bottom after Mason's death, believing in herself and forging forward, Shal had built her own little empire.

Green? No, he couldn't call either of them that anymore.

She was more beautiful now than she'd ever been, and more desirable to him than she'd ever believe.

"But you didn't even know me then," Shal discounted almost wistfully.

Cam gave her the ghost of a smile in return.

How did he begin to explain how it had felt to have a freight train slam into his chest when the girl he'd just met had smiled shyly at him? Such a sad, hopeful smile, offering zero chance of survival.

A Cam-cataclysm just itching to happen.

Love and longing, grief and abstinence, all contorted into silence by one flatmate desperately trying to respect the boundaries laid out by another.

"When did it end for you, then?" Shal continued matter-of-factly, as if there'd been a moment in time when he'd conveniently fallen out of love with her.

How the hell was he supposed to answer that?

Cam hesitated. "I guess I got over it when you left." The only vague untruth he'd told her. He couldn't look at her when he said it, turning to pick up his board instead.

"Ah. So just puppy love, then?" Shal surmised with a touch less gravity.

Let her believe that, if it was easier.

From the corner of his eye, he saw her pull her knees close into her chest.

"Well, I'm flattered you saw something in me."

Flattered? A step up from insulted, at least.

Cam was sorry Shal knew, especially as it had clearly changed things between them, but at least he was finally clear on where they stood. When they came off the beach and his hand brushed Shal's accidentally, she sucked in her breath and pulled back as if he'd pinched her, eyes snapping to meet his.

He was fighting for some sort of normal here, not wanting to slip into awkwardness. But any form of touching was now off limits, obviously.

"It's alright. I won't jump your bones," Cam joked lightly, but Shal's reaction had stung.

He'd never tried to take it past flatmates with anything physical. They'd always been clearly in the friend-zone, with Shal never giving any indication she'd be interested in anything else.

More than ever, Cam wished he could cut the desire; neutralise it somehow.

If he could just ignore the underlying sweetness that grabbed him by the guts, the vulnerability hidden under the pristine facade she showed the world. He couldn't begin to explain how much it meant to him, the way she opened up when they were alone together. If he could sure-up his heart and forget all about his protective mode, always and forever ready to kick into action wherever she was concerned... But it was no use. Shal was everything he'd ever wanted; right-brain-creative about everything she did, intriguing him with her business acumen, and making him laugh with her dogged determination to do everything her own way.

Making him *want*, much more than had ever been on offer as a friend.

He'd believed he was well over it, and expected this latest bout to ease like a bellyache, not build like a bloody stomach ulcer. What the hell was he supposed to do about it now? No chance of getting it back to what it had been, and not a shit-show-in-hell of moving it forward.

Avoidance. That's all he had.

Cam sighed, strapping the boards down before pulling two towels from the cab. Chucking one towards Shal, he turned his back to give her some privacy. Rubbing salt crystals out of his hair, he unzipped the torso of his wetsuit and peeled it down to his waist.

"Um, Cameron?" A small voice interrupted.

He turned to see Shal out of the vest but still suited up.

Katie's wetsuit fitted her surprisingly well, considering their differences. Where Katie was shorter and curvier, Shal was lithe and slim hipped, arresting in the skin-hugging rubber.

———

Shal noted Cam's wetsuit, or lack of it, and found herself admiring a very muscular, tanned expanse of male skin. He looked good. *Really* damn good. And she was ogling him like candy in a window display.

It's just Cam, she reminded herself.

But the guy-down-the-hall had grown up, and she was having trouble looking at him in quite the same way. Worse still, she was fighting another rush of warmth to her cheeks.

Who was acting like they had a crush now?

"C-can you help with this?" she stammered, trying to convince herself her inability to talk was expressly due to the cold. Turning, she presented Cam with her back. "My hair's caught."

Loops of hair, still wet from the ocean, had worked themselves loose from the quick bun she'd thrown it into and were now hooked into the Velcro at the top of the chunky zip.

"Oh, right. Stay still." Cam stepped forward and carefully worked her hair free, apologising when it tugged once. Twice. "Done." He stepped back and turned away from her again, wrapping a towel around his waist and working the legs of his wetsuit off.

Struggling out of Katie's suit, Shal continued to send surreptitious glances his way.

It wasn't rude to check out someone who was getting changed in public, right? Anyone happening to walk past would be remiss not to take a second peep at all that muscle tone, or the tattoo on Cam's shoulder blade.

Or both.

Perhaps a third look, if they were into contemporary Māori designs, or contemporary Kiwi guys.

Cameron Dante really was an attractive package. He obviously stayed fit with the manual labour of his job, and surfing no doubt helped. Shal flipped her borrowed towel over one shoulder and stroked her hands down her own stomach. Her own abs and arms had gone through a decent workout today.

She bent sideways to try and check out her sore thigh. It must've been the side of the board that grazed her, rather than the tip. She'd have a hell of a bruise there tomorrow but it didn't look too bad, and wasn't affecting her movement.

"Ready?" Cam was now standing in jeans with bare feet, pulling a soft grey sweater over his head with no shirt underneath.

Shal could still see an appetising chunk of his chest in the low V of the open-neck zipper, along with his familiar jade pendant.

He'd caught her daydreaming.

"My body's going to tell me all about this tomorrow," she surmised, hopping from foot to foot in a vain attempt to escape the frigid concrete and handing Katie's inside-out wetsuit and vest to Cam.

Her swimsuit afforded zero warmth, and she was sporting goosebumps on her goosebumps.

The muscle on Cam's jawline clenched as he clocked her state of undress. Standing with one hand scuffing up the back of his hair, he grabbed a random sweatshirt from the cab, a frown clamping his eyebrows together.

Shal's interest piqued. Did he still feel something for her? She took a tentative step towards him.

Cam thrust the sweatshirt at her midriff. "You look half frozen. Put that on." He spoke roughly, pointedly looking anywhere but at her as he turned on his heel to walk around to the driver's side of the cab.

Shal pulled the fleeced cotton over her head and jumped into the passenger side.

"You're gonna have a shiner there," Cam muttered, but was once again staring straight ahead when Shal turned to study him. Sitting in the driver's seat, he may as well have been on Mars for all he was connecting with her.

"Where?" she questioned nonchalantly.

"On your..." Cam glanced down at her thigh, then caught her eye, cottoning on to the fact she was razzing him. "You bloody know where," he growled.

Shal mulled it over in the ute all the way back to Dundas Street, heater blasting. Wearing the sweatshirt that smelled decidedly masculine and intriguingly of Cam, she sneaked peeks at him when he wasn't looking.

———

It was a bit of an ask for Cam's body not to react to Shal. Especially when she'd been standing in front of him in a sporty black swimsuit, for pity's sake.

Anyone would have had trouble with that, right?

The drive home was uncomfortable. Cam ignored the conversational elephant settled between them and asked Shal about the shop, then made small talk about the wedding. But she was a closed book and he couldn't fathom her mood—quietly huddled in the passenger seat.

Eventually he just gave up, letting the silence settle.

Shal brought her knees to her chin, tucking her legs up inside the old sweatshirt he'd loaned her. She looked like a sand-tumbled Humpty Dumpty with just her toes peeking out the bottom.

Humpty Dumpty with fuchsia-pink nail polish and chattering teeth.

Cam risked another glance her way to check how blue her lips were. The heater was already up to full blast and he squashed the urge to pull over and wrap her in a warm bear hug. Kiss those lips back to pink.

His fingers tapped a drumbeat on the steering wheel instead.

You can do this—he coached himself. *She's just a mate. Pretend she's a bloke.* A laughable concept, considering Shal's figure in a swimsuit.

Cam insisted on walking Shal to her front door. It was starting to get dark and he'd sleep better knowing she was safe. She'd wrapped a beach towel round her legs and still wore his sweatshirt.

"Do you need this back?" Shal lifted the hem with both hands as if she was going to pull the cotton up over her head, right there and then.

"No!" Remembering all that smooth, bare skin, Cam put a hand out to stop her movement, then rubbed at his eyebrow with it instead. Trying to mask his overreaction, he toned down his voice to reiterate, "Ah, no, that's sweet. No rush."

Shal stared at him, narrow-eyed and watchful—figuring him out.

"I've made you feel awkward." The air around them was thick with it. "I'm sorry you had to find out how I felt from someone else." Cam shifted slightly, making sure he wasn't standing too close. "Maybe I should've told you at the time, but I assumed you could tell. And it seemed uncouth to lay anything else on you after Mason..." Not knowing what to do with his hands, he slid his thumbs into his front pockets and scuffed one bare foot backwards and forwards across the concrete. "You needed support then, not someone wanting something more from you." Standing one step above him, Shal was still and quiet in the deepening shadows, making him nervous. "Don't feel weird about it, eh? It was a long time ago—no big deal."

"It *does* feel weird, though. You changed our history on me."

"I'm sorry. It was out of my hands." He held the palms in question out and considered their rough texture. The lines and creases were still embedded with deck stain, even after being out on the ocean.

Cam was surprised into silence when Shal reached out and placed both her palms in his. He felt even less steady when she squeezed his fingers and searched his face, eye-level with him.

"You said that already," she whispered.

"Yeah. Look, I guess you get a lot of this. I'm not looking to complicate things for you. If we could just play it like it was, that'd be sweet." Touching her was making Cam twitchy, and he pulled his hands out from under hers, rubbing them on the back pockets of his jeans.

He took a half step backwards on the path, aiming to go.

"Wait. What do you mean by that?" Shal spoke quietly, but her words stopped Cam from scarpering.

She'd been following his actions carefully, trying to weigh them up against what she now knew. It was incredibly hard to follow his body-language and their conversation at the same time.

"What? Play it like it was?"

"No, that I must get a lot of this. What exactly do you mean by that?"

"You know, guys hitting on you."

So, Cam had come to the same conclusion as Katie.

"It happens on occasion. But the point is, you've *never* hit on me." She sighed. "You treat me like a person rather than a walking pair of boobs with an ass attached, which is frankly what I usually get."

Cam stared.

"I assumed it was because you could see I had a brain," she continued mildly.

"Of course I see your brain, *and* your person, but a guy would be blind not to notice the packaging it comes in. You're beautiful, Shal."

She lifted one shoulder in a faint shrug. "Thanks." It was tricky to know what to do that. Men used lines like that all the time, but it was a little weird to hear Cam saying it. Compliments from the opposite sex were nice, but rarely meant more than someone was aiming to get you in bed—and Cam seemed to be angling in the other direction.

"This is just my skin, you know. My scales. My shell. It doesn't define me."

"No, I know that." Cam smiled, maybe a little self-consciously. "Just so you know, though. I wasn't after the wrapping, but everything that went with it."

Rather than softening her, the sentiment made her more scratchy.

"You weren't actually 'after' anything at all." Her fingers drew the quotation marks in the air between them. "You never made any kind of play. I can't read minds." And that was the crux of it. She was beginning to wonder if she knew Cam at all. "I'm the opposite of psychic," she added in a mutter.

"Trust me on this one, Shal. I was interested in everything about you." Cam rubbed a rough hand over his eyes. "I just didn't have the guts to put it out there."

"Maybe if you'd told me, things could've ended differently." Shal could hear the censure edging into her own voice—not necessarily rebuking Cam's past choices, but all the poor ones she'd made herself.

Cam held up a hand in resignation. "I get it. You mean with Mason? They wouldn't've, Shal. Only more awkwardly."

"You don't *know*—"

"Hold it!" Cam lost his cool; cutting her off and raising his voice with one finger pointed in her direction. "Can you honestly say you were interested in me in *any other way* than as a friend?" When she opened her mouth to speak, Cam lowered his tone in warning, repeating each syllable in exaggeration. "Hon-est-ly."

"No," she admitted.

Cam sighed and looked away, eyes squinted towards the top of the towering ngaio on the neighbouring property. "So, if I'd brought it up I would've made life uncomfortable for everyone. It was just a crush, Shal. Like I said before. No biggie."

"I guess you're right." But it did warrant the question, could their friendship have built into something more, given half a chance?

"Want to go surfing again tomorrow?" Cam suddenly switched

tack on her, cocking his head to one side as his gaze slid back to hers.

Shal blinked at him, frowning again.

"Is that like… Are you asking me out?" She tried to get a handle on their ambiguous grounding.

Cam hesitated, but only for a second. "No. I'm like, asking if you want to come surfing tomorrow." His dimples were twitching, a sure sign he was holding back a smirk.

Shal huffed, stomped up the final step and managed to get her key in the lock before turning back to him testily.

She'd never been great at reading people, and although some of that was on her, it seemed very much like Cam was purposefully sending mixed messages.

"Yes!" she snapped.

Cam's smile finally broke through, sunny and relaxed. "Sweet. Pick you up just after four." Then he was off down the path— whistling like he didn't have a care in the world.

Back at Park Street, Cam leant the boards on the garage door and hosed them down.

Salt and sand ran in rivulets down the foot treads and trickled down the warm concrete under his bare feet.

It smelt like summer, though autumn had already begun to take hold.

Chucking both wetsuits and the vest over the washing line, he gave them a good soaking too before leaving them to drip dry, all the while mulling on his conversation with Shal.

Surely she could see the effect she still had on him? She had a quiet confidence, a tangible self-respect, but occasionally seemed unable to rate her own calibre.

Way out of his league, and always had been.

Out of Mason's league too, but that hadn't stopped the canny bastard.

Was it feasible Shal hadn't noticed Cam falling all over himself wherever she was concerned?

No. Not bloody likely.

It was more probable Shal was pulling his chain to see if it still had bells on it. She'd get more than she bargained for if that was the case. 'Puppy love' this wasn't.

Surf gear done, Cam moved to clear out the cab of the ute, finding a tidy little stack of Shal's clothes under a discarded towel. Undies tucked neatly into a bra, both in dainty blue lace.

Try not to imagine her in that, he challenged himself, shoving the pile into a paper supermarket bag and failing epically.

A memory of the midwinter plunge at St Clair came back to him like an old movie, cut and spliced into individual slo-mo segments. Links wet and laughing, seawater sitting in droplets on his wiry chest. Mason with his boxers plastered to his skin, dragging a squealing Shal into the waves in her underwear.

Already in the surf, Cam had turned his back on the scene and gone under—low and deep. He'd let the undertow draw him down until the aching cold closed over his head like a frigid clamp.

Freeze out the feeling.

Wash away the want.

Shut it down.

They'd all stripped down to their undies and gone in, along with a hundred or so other crazy Ōtepoti-ans. The winter solstice event was popular, though you could easily turn into a Popsicle in the icy southern water.

Someone from St. John was handing out silver anti-hypothermia sheets, gossamer-fine but effective, and the beach had been peppered with euphoric shivering bodies wrapped in foil, like the survivors of some futuristic cleansing ritual.

10

Listening to...
How Bizarre - Alan Jansson, Pauly Fuemana
From the album: How Bizarre - OMC

Shal was curled on the sofa at Dundas Street watching Shortland Street, mentally picking apart the wardrobe department rather than following the drama, when her cell rang.

She'd just christened the communal upstairs bath with an apple scented bath bomb from Katie's gift pack, having been given strict instructions by the tilers not to use it until today. Replete with PJs, fish slippers, and a bowl of cereal, she deliberated whether she could actually be bothered getting up to answer her phone.

When she saw it was Katie calling, Shal's recourse tangled even further. She'd been semi-ignoring her friend's texts, knowing there'd be a multitude of questions and unsure if she was ready to address a single one.

It might've been more practical to drive down the road and meet the barrage head-on, but the two were used to phone conversations. Like spilling your guts in a confessional, it was easier when no one could see you.

Not for the first time, Shal surmised she should've been born Catholic, and sighing, answered the call.

The second time the phone rang, it was Aroha, and Shal turned off the distracting TV program altogether. Aroha could be considered a friend, but a testy one, and Shal was still feeling a bit singed around the edges after Katie's grilling.

The call wasn't nearly as bad as Shal had braced herself for. Aroha was merely passing on the details of her and Links' flight down the following week.

Both women were Katie's bridesmaids, along with Adele, Katie's sister, so they had the wedding in common and plenty to discuss. They even managed to laugh together about Katie's interminable aunties, who'd been arriving in Ōtepoti sporadically and were now terrorising the small city en masse.

There wasn't any sort of awkwardness until the end of the conversation, and even then it was mild, in Aroha terms.

"Links spoke to Cam today," Aroha offered, the words sounding more hesitant than her usual style.

Shal closed her eyes tight, loathe to open that particular can of worms again. "Did he?" she murmured.

"You told him you didn't know he had feelings for you."

"Well, I—"

"I find that hard to believe." Aroha had a habit of interrupting both Shal's words and her thought processes.

"I knew he cared for me as a friend." Always on the witness stand with Aroha, trying to prove herself, Shal refused to concede a point this time. "That's *all* I saw."

Aroha harrumphed, then let it go.

When they finally disconnected the call, Shal sat staring at the phone in her hand for some time. Any form of sparring with Aroha left her a little winded, as if she'd run into a surprise brick wall.

Shal shook it off, but not before drawing some similarities between her relationship with Aroha and her long-standing discord with her own mother.

Carol always seemed to be dissatisfied with her as well.

Some women had stingers in their tails, and Shal had mentally placed the two females into the same sub-species long ago.

When she'd first heard the rumours about her father's infidelity, Shal had gone to Carol, hoping her mother would somehow prove the story false—maybe even laugh it off as ridiculous. Instead, Shal had poked her stick into an already buzzing wasp's nest.

It hadn't been hard to hunt out the address of her father's ex-PA, ex-lover, ex-girlfriend—or whatever Shal was supposed to call Danielle. There wasn't a lock on the filing cabinet in her father's Tāmaki-makau-rau office.

Only six years Shal's senior, Danielle had stood tall and willowy in her apartment doorway—save for the basketball shoved up her jumper. Though civil, her reception could in no way be interpreted as friendly.

Shal had thought she was being savvy, gathering what intel she could after her parents' split. At eighteen, she'd been immature enough to completely underestimate the minefield she was walking into.

Perhaps Cam wasn't so far off with his 'green' comment.

Turning up unannounced on her father's pregnant ex-girlfriend's doorstep, introducing herself and pushing to gain some sort of sibling connection had been a fairly insensitive move. Danielle had certainly thought so. She hadn't invited Shal into her apartment, or into her child's life, but she *had* taken the time to drop a second bombshell.

David had another family in Te Whanganui-a-Tara. Another house, another wife, and another child.

The lead up to Shal's Te Whanganui-a-Tara confrontation had been that much worse, because she already knew how badly it could go. Standing outside the picket gate, unable to take the steps that would lead her to the door, she'd waited for her nausea to ease. She'd also waited in vain for her eyes to tell her that this family had meant somehow *less*.

Less than her own.

But it wasn't some dingy flat, as she'd imagined from the central city address, it was a beautifully maintained villa. Potted lavender on the veranda, a trampoline on the side lawn, and fresh white sheets billowing on the line.

It was a home, just as hers had been.

And it was too much, too soon.

In the end, it was the princess shoes that had swayed her. Hastily removed, or likely kicked off, one hung precariously close to the edge of the step while the other lay on the concrete path below.

Blue plastic Cinderella pumps, with glitter heels.

Shal had spent her life as an only child, and regardless of the circumstances, the little girl who wore those shoes was her sister. A half-sister she had a chance to meet, maybe even *know*, if she could just hold down her lunch long enough to knock on the door.

The Te Whanganui-a-Tara trip had been a pit-stop on the way down to Ōtepoti, over eight years ago now, and Bianca, the little six-year-old with two front-teeth missing and a cute lisp, was now almost fifteen.

Perhaps the age gap between Shal and Bianca had made it easier. Bee had been a verbose little girl, with only a vague comprehension of what it meant to have a full-grown sister turn up out of the blue. Chattering away like a little pīwakawaka, Bianca had proudly shown Shal her toys, her room, and how well she could cartwheel.

They'd become a bizarre sort of quasi-family group—Shal, Bee, and her mother, Carmel. Against all the odds the three of them had managed to build something warm out of the rubble David had left behind.

Shal spent the next morning alone, leaving the house only to walk down to a local café for a muffin and a cup of tea. She had a full office day scheduled; replying to emails, adding to the Pinterest page she was sharing with Jac, tweaking her finances, and sketching some ideas for the new line.

The upbeat music in the café made her realise how quiet it had been working alone at the house. Standing in the cashier queue, the usual calm of being on her own was pierced by a shard of loneliness so acute it brought tears to her eyes.

There were couples and groups, chatting and sharing their day, coming in together or meeting there. The mood inside the eatery was relaxed and almost festive in the early autumn sunshine.

Shal blinked rapidly, her gut reaction being to order take-out and remove herself. Escape.

Chicken.

"Actually, can I change that to eat-in?" She attempted an apologetic smile. "And make that a pot of tea, instead of a cup?"

"No problem." The young guy at the counter returned the smile, cancelling her order and re-entering it. "You *deserve* a pot," he joked.

"I absolutely do," she agreed.

Shal paid, took her order-number, and claimed a stool in the front window, forcing herself to examine her raw emotional state.

She never felt this way in Te Whanganui-a-Tara. Why did Ōtepoti have this effect? She'd come across it twice in the space of a few days.

Because Jac had gone, and Dundas Street felt big and empty without all the tradies?

No. Not entirely.

More likely due to the memories Otago stirred up—how it had felt to be half of a whole when she'd lived here with Mason. The trust had come so naturally, so implicitly, because she'd honestly believed he would never intentionally hurt her.

Shal poured her newly arrived tea, remembering how she'd left the guys' flat after the break-up and moved in with Katie. Links had rustled up a single mattress for her on the floor next to Katie's bed, because everything within Shal had gone numb, and sleeping alone was near impossible.

Katie had come to hold her hand at the women's health clinic, too, and Shal was grateful for that. She'd finally broken down in the consultation room, realising she didn't have any answers to their questions.

How many partners had Mason had? Male? Female? Had he used protection? Been AIDS tested?

Shal hadn't been able to continue lying to herself about her ex-boyfriend's actions and intentions after that. He was a selfish con artist. A cheat.

The humiliation of it had almost outweighed the hurt.

Shal sighed, putting her chin in her hands to contemplate the trickle of humanity filtering past on the footpath in front of the café. It was better to extricate yourself before relationships got serious, *much* better to establish ground rules before you even began.

Lesson learned.

The tea tempered her emotions. The muffin helped too, making her realise she'd unconsciously skipped breakfast and was probably feeling low due to that. Alone wasn't necessarily *lonely*, it was safe, and familiar.

Shal's vibe was much more positive by the time she returned to the house.

Finishing her emails for the afternoon, Shal locked Dundas Street and went to wait on the front doorstep, catching up on her texts. There was another one from Katie, checking she was okay.

Was she?

Shal texted back a thumbs-up emoji, not knowing how else to answer that one.

It was just after four when Cam pulled up, and he wasn't alone. Katie jumped out of the twin-cab ute, and Shal's surprise turned to excitement on realising there were three boards strapped on the back.

Even with her muscles complaining about the overindulgence, it was great to be back out on the water. Cam eased off by himself, so Shal stuck to Katie. It was the first time the two women had been surfing together in years but it almost felt like old times, relaxed and free of any responsibilities.

Shal was laughing with Katie over a ridiculous YouTube clip, shared earlier in the week, when she turned to scope out the other surfers on the break. Mirth dried in her throat and she made a strangled sound, not believing what she was seeing.

Mason.

"Oh, God," she groaned.

"What?" Katie turned to her swiftly, then followed her gaze.

For a second it had looked like Mason, silhouetted against the horizon but too far away to make out clearly.

No.

Cam, not Mason, who was waiting out the low set. Cameron Dante, without the signature dreadlocks he'd had in the past.

The hair had thrown her.

"I thought I saw something, but it's nothing." Shal raised her voice over the surf so Katie could hear, forcing a smile.

"Seeing sharks that aren't there?" Katie called back.

"Yeah. Exactly that."

The image was hard to shake, taking some shine off her afternoon. Even when all three of them headed back along the sand toward the car park, Shal's laughter felt a bit hollow.

They moved differently, she decided. Where Mason had walked with a tightly wound tension, Cam was more fluid, more relaxed.

The two men had been a similar height, though Cam was broader now than he had been back then. Perhaps Mason would've been more muscular too, at twenty-nine?

Or, would he be thirty now?

Shal realised with a jolt she'd forgotten the milestone of Mason's birthday for once—flown straight through February without it even crossing her mind.

That meant Cam would be turning thirty this year too, in November. But apart from age, height, and a deep-seated love of the ocean, the old flatmates weren't at all alike.

Tawny-caramel hair, not blond. Golden eyes, not blue. Friend, not foible.

Shal tried to dismiss what she'd seen on the water, because it didn't sit easy. It must've been this particular beach that'd brought it on, or perhaps the high surf?

Mason had liked the waves big, stormy and fierce, while Shal found the ocean frightening when moody.

The day was cooling by the time the three reached Cam's ute to towel off, but many were just turning up to the beach after knocking off work. Shal thought she caught sight of the longboarder she'd had a run in with the day before. Several cars down, he was unstrapping his board from the roof of a pristine 1970's Holden.

She turned to Cam. "Isn't that the guy from yesterday?"

"Ah, yep." Cam turned to double-check, towel slung around his neck. "That's him."

"Do you know him?"

"Just the face and the car. He's often down here, or on the peninsula."

Shal offloaded her vest, booties, and towel in the back of the ute before strolling barefoot down the esplanade towards the Holden.

She owed the man an apology.

"Shit." Cam stared after Shal.

Buggered if Katie's old wetsuit didn't look like it was made expressly to hug the designer's pert behind.

"Problem?" Katie joined him on the curb, watching as Shal retreated back along the esplanade footpath.

"Could be. She had a bit of a bitch at the guy yesterday."

Katie placed her hands on her hips and raised her eyebrows until he elaborated.

"She blocked his ride and he clipped her," Cam explained. "Got a bit of a knock to her leg, and her ego."

"Right." Katie waited a split second. "Was that before or after she had a bit of a bitch at *you*?"

"Before. She told you about that? It wasn't so much of a bitch in that instance, more like an interrogation." He injected a shot of blame into the look he aimed at his cousin, which she chose to completely ignore.

"Mm…" Katie brushed her hands together as if dusting off sand. "Well, I might just go and play gooseberry then." She threw her towel over one shoulder and followed Shal.

Cam could see by the time Katie was halfway there she needn't have bothered. The two beside the Holden were all smiles. Shal was stroking the chrome on the restored car and chatting animatedly, while the big guy leant back on the paintwork, grinning stupidly.

Cam had seen that look before. It seemed to follow Shal wherever she went.

"Nice wheels," Katie announced her arrival, and Shal turned, surprised to have been followed on her errand.

"Katie, this is Steven," she introduced the two. "I just came down to apologise. We met yesterday, but I was completely out of line. So sorry." She turned again to smile at the longboarder, who didn't seem to be in any particular hurry to get out on the water. "I was having a bad day and took it out on everyone around me."

"Like I said. No skin. Just glad you're okay." Steven turned to Katie and held out a large hand. "Steve."

"Katie." Katie put her hand in his to shake.

Steven was a big man, but his demeanour was friendly and open. Today, anyway.

"You two finished for the day?" he wondered aloud, grey eyes the colour of the sea after rain.

"Yep, just heading off," Katie confirmed.

"Might see you around another time, then?" Though he was responding to Katie, Steve's eyes never left Shal.

"Yeah, might," Katie returned, touching Shal's arm lightly and lowering her voice. "Let's go."

"It was nice to talk to you, Steve." Shal smiled again before moving off, turning back to add, "I love your car." It was perfectly suited to its driver—squarely solid. Trailing her fingers down the nose of the bonnet, she stepped back onto the footpath with Katie.

"Jeez, Shal, just bring a shotgun next time and nail him between the eyes," Katie advised sarcastically when they were out of earshot. "Put the poor guy out of his misery."

"I don't know what you're talking about. I was just being polite."

"Oh, *Steve*, It was *so* nice to talk to you. I just *love* your car." Katie hammed up the rendition, laying it on thick.

Shal laughed at the caricature of herself. "I don't sound like that."

"His jaw was hanging open and I'm pretty sure he was salivating."

"Don't be ridiculous." She was still smiling. "If he was interested he would've done something about it."

"You don't think he was interested?" Katie stopped abruptly, putting a hand on Shal's arm to turn her about-face.

"Not particularly." Shal lifted a shoulder. "He didn't say or do anything about it if he was."

"He said he might see you around."

"So?"

"So, he'd *like* to see you around."

"Then he should've *said* so."

Katie appeared to think on that for a minute. "Just out of interest, did you like the look of him? Would you've given him your number if he'd asked?"

Shal put one finger to her top lip, considering. "Maybe? He seemed quite nice. Pretty eyes. Not my usual type, though."

Really big guys sometimes made her feel insubstantial. Inconsequential. Indistinct. But she was unsure if that was due to their size, or an attitude of superiority she'd come across a few times.

Perhaps both?

"God." Katie glanced behind them somewhat uneasily. "If that's you with a 'maybe,' we should definitely bring a body bag for anyone you really like the look of. Why didn't you ask for his?"

"His number? Oh..." Shal readjusted her shoulders, uncomfortable with the idea. "That wasn't the reason I went over. I really *did* owe him an apology." She turned towards the railing, the only thing between them and the churning ocean, metres below. "Anyway, I don't make the first move, as a rule."

"No, you don't. Why *is* that?"

Shal chewed on her lip, seeking to end the conversation. "Not a great track record," she finally offered before trying to move off.

Katie tightened the grip on her arm, and Shal looked down at it with some trepidation. They both knew if Katie wanted more information, she just had to look at Shal a certain way.

"Shouldn't we get back?" Shal wheedled.

"He'll wait."

Flicking a look at Cam, still a couple of cars away, Shal could see waiting was exactly what he was doing. Waiting and watching.

"I asked Mason out in high school." The words came out in a rush. "He didn't know me from a bar of soap. He was a year above me, he surfed, and he was gorgeous. I picked up a superstition about it after that, you know? I mean, look how well *that* turned out." She offered Katie a half-assed smile. "Anyway, it figures if they start it, they don't get so offended when it ends. It's better than me switching on, then off again, right?" Moving forward, she broke contact.

"Try again."

"What?" Shal turned to stare at Katie.

Katie cleared her throat. "Don't Let Mason dictate how you run your life. Try again. You deserve another chance."

"With Steve?" She aimed a thumb surreptitiously toward the Holden.

"No. Not necessarily." Katie glanced toward her cousin, who'd stowed all of their gear and was leaning on the front bull bars drinking deeply from his bottle of water. "You choose. If it feels right, trust yourself. You're not sixteen anymore."

Shal didn't have a reply to that, because it was true. She *wasn't* sixteen anymore.

"Mum called. She's invited all of us up for a barbecue tonight." Cam passed on the invitation as they neared, handing out two more bottles of fresh water and looking from one woman to the other, no doubt picking up on the strange tension between them. "Rue's already up at the house if you guys are up for it?"

11

Listening to...
Isabelle - Greg Johnson
From the album: Everyday Distortions - The Greg Johnson Set

The view from Poppy's deck was second to none, and Shal sunk into the hanging chair with a contented sigh, tucking her bare feet under herself. It was like a cane hideout, the large squabs moulding the interior and blocking out the sounds of conversation.

She'd been stuffed to the gills and banned from doing dishes. Poppy had made the most delectable Mediterranean lamb-patties, with a tzatziki dipping sauce.

"How's my northlander doing?" Poppy poked her head around. "Room for dessert?"

Shal groaned. "Poppy, I couldn't squeeze in another mouthful."

"Cup of tea, then?"

That was a different story.

"I'd love a cup of tea." Shal made to get up. "I'll get it, though."

"No. You stay right there." Poppy patted Shal's knee, already on a beeline to the kitchen.

When Cam's mother returned with a pot of tea on a tray, she handed Shal a soft blanket.

Shrugging the blanket around her shoulders, Shal smiled.

"Thank you. As always, the Dante service is above and beyond." Poppy was still in short-sleeves, a testament to her southern blood, but evidently hadn't forgotten how Shal felt the cold. "You always manage to look relaxed and in charge, no matter how many people turn up at your table."

"Being surrounded by the people I care about is one of life's greatest pleasures." Poppy returned the smile, opening the lid of the teapot to check the brew before pouring into two waiting cups. "Feeding them's an added bonus."

"You and Katie have more in common than lineage, then."

"Yes." Poppy turned to her with her eyebrows raised. "Katie shows love through food too. It was something my mother—Katie's Nana Nona—instilled in all of us. I swear there was an added sweetness to her food from her pure love of making it."

"You miss her."

"Mum? Every day." Poppy handed Shal her tea.

She studied the beautiful glaze, transitioning from deep blue to the iciest cyan. "I'm not so close to my mother."

"No. Why's that?"

"Why?" Surprised by the question, Shal mulled on it. "She's distant. I get the feeling my turning up was a bit of an inconvenience."

"By 'turning up,' I'm assuming you mean your birth?" Poppy sounded a trifle growly. "Was she unaware how conception worked?"

Shal snorted, bringing her eyes up to meet Poppy's light sarcasm. "Um, no. I wasn't her first child, actually. My mum, Carol, was just a teenager when she had my brother. He died."

She'd never told anyone but Cam that before.

"Oh! I'm so sorry to hear that." Poppy's big hazel eyes were quick to glass up, and she didn't bother masking the fact.

Shal shrugged. "She can't talk about it. I think the softest parts of her stopped living when he did."

"What was his name?"

"Sebastian. Seb. Mum left Sweden after that, and can't seem to settle anywhere else. New Zealand isn't home to her. *I'm* not home to her."

"Does she feel like home to you?" Poppy wondered aloud.

"You know you sound like a shrink, don't you?" Shal twisted her lips in a wry attempt at a smile, then turned back to the sea view. "No. She doesn't. To be honest, we don't know each other that well." Down past the southern pohutukawa, the horizon was deepening into indigo. "She's the black sheep, though. Her family are pretty open with their affections, as a rule."

"*Your* family."

"Pardon?"

"You said 'her family,' but they belong to you, too. Your mother doesn't have full custody."

"True." Shal sighed. "And there were times when I *did* have them all to myself. Uncle Henke and his partner Ulrika were in Stockholm, and I'd get jumbled in with my cousins while Mum jet-setted around. They have four kids, all older than me." In the soft evening light, she visualised the archipelago she'd loved so much in her childhood—swimming, making daisy chains, playing Vikings…

Big family. More love. Less pressure.

"Are they still together?"

"Who?" Shal blinked.

"Henke and Ulrika."

"Oh! Yes. I don't see them often enough. We video call, but…" She lifted one shoulder. "It's not the same."

"They're still in Stockholm?"

"No. Hong Kong, actually. Henke's a travel writer and they move around a bit. I'll be heading over soon for a buying trip, so we'll catch up."

"Do you consider Sweden home, then? Or is Te Whanganui-a-Tara…?"

Shal shook her head, suddenly not trusting her voice.

"Tāmaki-makau-rau?" Poppy tried again.

How had Shal gotten into this touchy topic with Poppy? She'd said too much and was now caught up in the nostalgia of it, missing her family and feeling vulnerable.

Although she had an apartment and a life in Te Whanganui-a-Tara, it wasn't exactly home, and neither was her birthplace, Tāmaki-makau-rau. Sweden was a world away; a million miles from who she'd chosen to be, while in the States she was little more than a novelty. The quirky cousin with the 'cute Kiwi accent,' and the 'dressmaking hobby.'

"None of the above," she murmured.

Obviously realising her question had hit a raw nerve, Poppy moved to cover Shal's hands, enclosing them around her still warm teacup.

"You know you have a home here, if you ever want it, Shal. I've plenty of space, and I'm only around half the time. I would've invited you long before, but I thought you were happy off in your own world. I consider you part of the family." Poppy was leaning forward, her eyes penetrating, and Shal could pinpoint precisely when she'd seen that look before.

It reminded her of the two week block between Mason's accident and the funeral, when Cam had transferred her from Katie's home to Poppy's.

Shal had been floating in hollow space; a yawning black hole—beyond caring what happened to her and incapable of attending to anything beyond basic functions. Katie and her family had been stretched thin, supporting Aroha at the hospital as Links went through operation after operation to try and save what was left of his lower legs.

Under Poppy's iron rule, Shal began to eat properly, but sleeping had still been a real issue. She'd needed company to help ward off the nightmares.

"*Don't*, Poppy," she whispered hoarsely, pulling her hands away as tears threatened. She'd been hoping to show at least some semblance of having it together this trip. "You're incredibly kind, but I'm fine. I'll be just fine."

Key people had been there to help scrape her together, and yes, they were like family. But they'd *all* been in a world of shock and disbelief, not just her. Deep in her own pit, Shal hadn't been capable of acknowledging that at the time, and she'd vowed never to load that kind of pressure on friends and found-family again.

She raised a finger to check no tears had escaped, before painting on a shaky smile for Poppy.

"Right, then. I'll pour us another tea, shall I?" Poppy decided overly brightly.

"Me and Rue have talked Cam into a walk-through of the latest refit." Katie jostled up next to Cam and elbowed him surreptitiously in the ribs.

Meaning he had to go along with the idea?

Probably.

The four impromptu dinner guests were already gathering their gear to leave Poppy's, and Cam raised one hand in a suit yourself gesture. It was the first he'd heard of the plan, but didn't care either way.

"Rue and I," Rue corrected automatically, before blushing crimson.

Cam grinned at the resulting expression on his cousin's face. Katie did *not* like being put in her place in any way, shape, or form.

As if to prove Cam's point, Katie poked a finger into her husband-to-be's chest.

"Yes, *professor*."

"Ohhh! I'm coming, too," Poppy jumped in, all eager and excited.

"You were just there yesterday, Mum," Cam intoned.

"But I want to see what Shal and Katie think of it," Poppy returned impatiently, as if that much should've been obvious.

"So, you've been dragged into this as well?" Cam turned to Shal, surprised to find her eyes red-rimmed. Lowering his tone for her ears alone, he sent an accusatory glare across at his mother. What the hell had she been saying to Shal during their little tea-party-for-two? "Are you okay?"

"Yes." Shal's chin went up. "Fine. And I've been wanting to see Park Street too."

Cam sighed, thinking of the state of the floors and general lack of interior wall cladding. "You know it's a bomb site, right?"

But there was no stopping Katie on a mission, Poppy within cooee of a social event, or Shal trying to prove a point.

Shal found herself alone with Cam in his work ute on the short drive to Park Street. Poppy had suddenly, inexplicably, needed to keep Katie and Rue company.

There was a vaguely strained silence for the first few blocks.

"Can I put some music on?" She tried to figure out how to switch on the car stereo.

"Sure, here." Cam leaned across and opened the glove box, handing her a well-used iPod in a battered casing and leaving her with a faint whiff of pine and ocean.

She flicked through Cam's playlists, looking for something to catch her eye.

Something did. *'Shal's Playlist.'* What the hell?

"How old's your iPod?" she wondered aloud, surprised he still had her favourites on file.

"Ancient. I don't know. Still plays." He handed her the plugin to connect it to the stereo, and she chose a New Zealand classic off her old list.

How Bizarre.

The lead singer had died very young, she remembered.

Shal didn't hear Cam speak, so nearly jumped out of her skin when his knuckles nudged her knee to gain her attention.

"Sorry. Didn't mean to spook you. I said, did Mum upset you tonight?"

God. Was nothing private around here?

"No." Shal went back to looking out the window.

"If there's anything I can do…?"

Shal sighed, turning in her seat till she was facing Cam. He glanced across at her then back to the road, concern obvious.

"I'm good. Honestly. I know you're a master at repairing things, Cam, but despite what you might've heard, I don't need a patch-up job." Whatever was broken within her seemed irreparable.

Leaning her head sideways on the headrest, Shal studied his familiar profile.

"I'm really fond of Poppy, and she was only trying to help. She *did* help," she amended quickly when Cam's brows lowered.

"She interferes."

"No. I disagree. She cares." Shal settled herself forward-facing again and pulled her knees up to her chin, considering the vast differences between Poppy and her own mother. "Don't be grumpy at her for giving a damn. The alternative is a thousand times worse, believe me. Poppy just hoped I'd be happy down here, so invited me. Formally. As part of the family. She wants to see me settled —content."

The sudden tension in Cam caught Shal's attention. The hand on the column shift, changing down for the steep hill climb, was taut. And the muscle spasming in his jaw added a strain that was unfamiliar around his mouth.

Cam groaned inwardly, imagining Shal and Poppy's conversation. It looked very much like his mother, knowing his feelings all too well, had wasted no time in trying to shunt him into Shal's future. Whether she wanted him there or not.

"With me," he muttered, fuming.

How goddamn embarrassing for Shal. How confronting—and clearly upsetting—to have to turn him down through his bloody *mother*. No matter how well meaning, it wasn't Poppy's right to act as self-appointed matchmaker.

"What? No. With her."

Caught between a rock and a hard place, Cam was silent for a full minute.

"What?" He finally fished for a bit more clarity.

Shal blew out a puff of air. "Poppy said I always had a place here, with her. She said if I ever needed a home…" She shrugged. "You know." She turned to look at him again. "What were you meaning?"

"Ahh." He drew a blank, then grasped at the obvious explanation. "You have a lot of close friends here."

"Yes. I do," Shal said evenly, and still he could feel her eyes on him. "People I care for a great deal."

People, not one person.

"Yes," he agreed grimly, refusing to look at her even when he'd pulled in and parked the ute in the short driveway, cutting the music off mid-chorus.

"Cam?"

He finally turned, one hand clenched on the handbrake, the other tapping the steering wheel in a nervy tattoo.

"Yeah?"

"What am I to you?" Shal whispered, her eyes wide in the low light of the dash as her fingers came to rest lightly on his hand, still wrapped around the brake.

Everything.

She could be everything.

Looking down at Shal's fingers, which had begun to stroke his knuckles, he was struck by how bare they were without her usual rings and bracelets—how naked and vulnerable. Her face was washed clean of makeup by the sea, features soaked in freshness, and there was a granular dusting of salt in her hairline.

Shal was stunning like this. Familiar, honest, and almost within reach. He turned his hand until it was palm up, and Shal wove her fingers into his as if it was the most natural thing in the world.

Cam had heard of Shal long before they'd met; had known she was arriving to share the flat. Links and himself had been wary of a girl in their all-blokes domain, but the drop in rent had been more than welcome.

He'd opened the door on a sweet February afternoon to a sweet February smile, dark gypsy hair, and ocean eyes.

God—those eyes. The most expressive he'd ever seen.

Helping Shal lug her suitcase and surfboard up to Mason's double room had been easy. Falling so hard and so fast for his flatmate's girlfriend? Much trickier.

Cam released the steering wheel, and trancelike, traced a feather-light finger along the angle of Shal's jawline. She was caught in silhouette with the streetlight behind, skin silky-smooth and warm to the touch.

He cleared the sandpaper lodged in his throat. "Actually, Shal—"

"*Shit*!" Shal jumped for a second time in fright, as Rue tapped on the passenger window directly behind her head.

"Getting frostbite out here," he complained, hopping from one foot to the other. "Any chance one of you could hand over the keys?"

12

Listening to...
Modern Fables - Julia Deans
From the album: Modern Fables

The Park Street property was a wooden two bay villa boasting over a century on the hill. Her bones were solid enough, but given years of abuse and neglect it was hardly surprising her skin and fleshing-out were a little less desirable.

Cam let Poppy take the reins and show the others through the house as he stepped ahead, moving debris and drop-sheets aside to clear an easier path.

Poppy, sounding very much like a tour guide, regurgitated all the information Cam had given her on her last walk-through.

He could hear snippets of her spiel from the next room.

"Removed this wall and opened through... converted the attic... rebuilding the window box... recycled panelling."

Cam escaped to put on the kettle, unnerved by the unfiltered pride in his mother's voice. It reminded him of how she talked about Daniel when his brother wasn't around to hear it.

Managing to scrounge up five coffee mugs in various states of repair, Cam offered everyone tea and instant coffee in the lounge, the only room other than the master with any form of furniture.

A solid leather sofa stood against one wall, and an old piece of carpet overlayed the uneven tongue-in-groove flooring. The gib board was on though, and even some of the skirting, so the drafts were minimal in contrast to the rest of the house.

Shal half-heartedly considered cornering Cam alone and demanding a replay of what had happened in the ute, or at least ask for a better grasp of where they stood.

She could still feel his touch on her skin and it was so, *so* different from before.

Somewhere during that moment in the cab, friendship had shifted and slid silkily into something unknown. Shal knew this was neither the time nor place to discuss it, but that didn't stop her wondering.

Over hot drinks, the conversation turned to a piece of land Cam was banking for himself on the hills above the green belt. At Poppy's insistence he laid the approved blueprints out on the floor.

A large, modern home, it would be an entertainer's paradise when complete, with acres of glass facing the view of the inland hills.

"It's going to be stunning," Shal decided, straightening up on her knees and turning to study Cam.

It wasn't the sort of house she'd ever imagined him in.

"Quite a long way from the beach, though," Poppy slid in knowingly. "Jody's idea, wasn't it?"

Cam turned to his mother and met her raised eyebrows with a cool stare, but she merely laughed off his distemper.

Shal got up to leave after finishing her tea, insisting she didn't want a ride home. She was keen to walk off Poppy's meatballs with some fresh air, and to gain some alone-time to think through the Cam equation.

"I might join you," Katie invited herself, standing too. "Could you swing by Dundas and pick me up in half an hour or so?" She leant in to buzz a kiss over her fiancé's cheek.

"Your wish is my command." Rue nodded. "I'll drop Poppy home first, then come back for you."

"In that case, I could join—" Cam made to get up off the sofa.

"Don't even think about it." Katie turned to stare her cousin down, zero camouflage on the fact she was aiming to get Shal alone.

Silently easing his frame back onto the firm cushioning, Cam shut his mouth in a resigned line.

Shal laughed along with Poppy at the not-so-subtle snub, but in addition to humour she felt a pinch of trepidation. Katie clearly wanted to talk and was not taking no for an answer.

The evening was cooling off as the southerly change began to creep in. The heaviness in the atmosphere grumbled of rain, and leaves flurried in circles around their feet as they began their downhill trek.

Shal gathered her jacket tightly around herself, grateful the exercise was reawakening warmth in her extremities.

Park Street was a beautiful old building, but with so much work to do it was hardly liveable. Why wasn't Cam in one of the finished rooms in Dundas Street, sharing the house with her? Had her arrival pushed him out? He should be living in the lovely master bedroom, relaxing after a hard day's work, not shivering in the draughty shell of a half-finished house.

Cam seemed content enough with the situation, though, displaying simple needs that appealed. Guitars on the wall, and a fire for company…

Her own lifestyle was so far removed from that. Tied up in the rat-race of the fashion world, the constant materialism and throwaway nature of last season's fabrics and accessories didn't always sit well with her views on sustainability. She struggled with that contradiction on a daily basis, trying to incorporate carefully sourced and recycled materials with local workmanship while maintaining 2-PEAS' high-end status.

"You and Cam seem to be getting on well." On the steep downward slope, Katie approached her topic without any mucking around, as was her style.

"Yes."

"What did Rue interrupt in the car?"

"Nothing," Shal answered on reflex before reconsidering, and reiterating with, "Nothing much," a little more thoughtfully.

"Bloody obtuse Englishman," Katie huffed. "Barging on over. Totally oblivious there was a private moment going on."

"No, it was fine. Just a bit strained, that's all."

"Strained?"

"Little things." Shal chewed on her bottom lip, deliberating about how much of herself to expose. "Almost everything, to be honest. I've been studying up on body language, Cam's in particular."

"Heaven help him." Katie hooted a laugh.

Shal conceded a smile at her own expense. "I'm the first to admit I'm a nube, but I'm getting better." She kicked a stone out of her path. "I'm pretty sure Cam wants to touch me, in a no-longer-friends sort of way."

"Right." Katie ended the word on an upward note, questioning.

"But he won't."

"Of course not! He's not a *complete* numpty."

"Mmm." Shal stopped to snap off a sprig of rosemary from the profuse climber on the retaining wall, bringing it up to her nose to breathe in the astringent tang. "The thing is, I'm beginning to realise I want him to."

"You *want* him to? Cam." Katie studied Shal with a flickering frown of uncertainty. "You want *Cam* to?"

"Yes." Under different circumstances it might've been amusing to watch the range of emotions play over her friend's face, but this thing with Cameron Dante was in no way laughable. "He's sexy."

Katie wrinkled up her nose. "You can't say 'sexy' when you're talking about Cam. It's just too weird. He's like my brother."

"I know." Shal put a hand on Katie's arm, steadying them both. "But he's not *my* brother, and there's something physical building between us."

Katie's eyes, as blue as the channel they'd surfed today, showed a surge of panic. "Don't hurt him," she blurted.

"Of course not!" Shal was taken aback by the insinuation, enough to remove her fingers from Katie's tense forearm. "I'm just saying it might morph into a sexual thing. That's what it feels like at the moment." Her gaze flicked towards Katie, then away again, before settling on the less confrontational church tower below.

Katie groaned. "Shal. This isn't what I meant about trying again.

I meant *love*. You could walk down the street and choose a 'sexual thing' with any number of candidates. The big surfer, what was his name?"

"Steven?"

"Yeah. Steve. He looked good. Choose him as your next plaything." Katie's chin had winched up in battle-mode.

"But why? If Cam—" Her own hackles were rising.

"Because Cam's not *for* you if you're just looking for a fling."

"You get a say in who I sleep with, now?" she snapped.

"Not my territory," Katie admitted with a little less heat. "But Cam cares too much. He'll get hurt." Reaching out, she gripped Shal's hand and squeezed, inadvertently crushing the rosemary stalk into her palm. "You *know* this. He's in the market for something permanent. I'm not trying to choose who you hook up with, Shal, but please don't go down this path. Not unless you're considering something serious; a potential long term thing." The underlying sadness in her eyes added entreaty.

"Long term?" Shal knew she wasn't capable of offering that. Not since Mason. Perhaps there was too much of her father in her, after all? "Cam knows me. He knows my background. He'd never expect that from me."

"You know I love you, Shal, but—"

"But your cousin's too good for me?"

"No! That's not what I'm saying. But he deserves more than a quick roll in the hay!"

Mild irritation boiled over and anger rose in its place. "Maybe all Cam *wants* is a quick roll in the hay. Maybe I'm just the woman for the job!"

"I don't want to fight with you about this."

"Too late, by my estimation."

Katie sighed, slipping her fists deep into the front pockets of her jeans. She always wore them baggy, cinched in at the waist with an oversized belt.

"I'm not judging your lifestyle choices, Shal. I just want you to be clear on this. Cam won't be as relaxed about it as he makes out. His feelings run deep, and he's been hurt before."

"He's a grown-assed man," Shal replied mulishly.

"I know. And he'll choose whichever way he wants to go. But

with regards to you it's all tangled up in everything else that's gone on in the past. When you put an end to it, it could wipe any friendship you two have left."

"No. It won't. And who says I'll be the one to finish it? Cam could—"

"Like hell," Katie muttered, and the resignation in her tone made Shal falter a step.

———

Katie was completely right, of course, which was infuriating in itself. Friends *should* be off limits.

The fact Katie had so adamantly placed her cousin on an unattainable island was still niggling at Shal two days later, even though she'd come to the same conclusion herself.

She was down in Ōtepoti by special invitation and it was beyond time she started acting like her position as Katie's bridesmaid meant more to her than the new boutique, or a quick fling with an old mate.

It was the third time Shal had been given the honour, but the other two brides she'd attended had been her cousins, and both times she'd been in her teens.

As Katie's only bridesmaid present in Ōtepoti, Shal found herself in charge of the hen's do, with background support from Poppy and Rosa. The responsibility of it all going well was sitting heavily on her shoulders, and she was consequently bird-brained on Saturday morning in the lead up to the bookings; anxious, flappy, and feeling vaguely nauseous.

Hot rock massages, aromatherapy, facials, deep conditioning hair treatments, manicures, and pedicures for the hens. With all credit going to the beauty therapists who took care of the large, eclectic group of women, it went rather swimmingly.

The feedback from the pampered women was all positive, but for some reason, Shal still wasn't able to fully relax and enjoy herself.

It should've been blissful, and yet her mind kept flitting elsewhere.

She knew Katie's dad, Amos, had arranged to take Rue and Cam up the Clutha River this weekend, fishing for trout. They would've left on Friday evening after work.

And now? Where would they be now?

Up at the boutique apartment, Shal squinted at a flat pack instruction sheet with growing frustration. She hadn't intended to spend her entire Monday morning on this shelving unit, but the assembly was nowhere near as simple as the sales pitch had made out.

A text from Poppy, inviting her over to Katie's for a wedding-preparation stitch-n-bitch gave Shal an excellent excuse to leave. She piled the confusing stack of boards, bolts, and Allan keys on the carpet and left without a backward glance.

Surely it didn't take four women to attach pearls onto a veil? Katie and Rosa had gone out to deliver a carload of Katie's products downtown, and in their absence a full contingency of aunties had been left with the hand-sewing.

Three of them sat at the dining table at Roseneath with reading glasses and needles, tiny scissors, threaded pearls, a sea of scalloped lace surging between. Apparently Katie's younger sister, Adele, was the last to have donned the veil, sans pearls.

"I don't like the smell of what's going on between Adele and James," Poppy sighed, referring to her niece and what she considered 'the loaded, pretty-boy' husband. She squinted first through, then over her reading glasses. "He's coming across for the wedding, then he's not. I wish he'd make up his damn mind."

"Don't you worry, Katie will figure out what's going on," Lily assured, stitching a tiny pearl droplet onto the edging. "It's hard to keep anything from a sister, and weddings always bring people together."

"Gray and I eloped to England, then honeymooned in Italy," Poppy murmured to Shal as an aside, referring to Cam's father. "Easier without all the fuss. My father was totally against us marrying, racist old bugger, and I thought it a romantic notion to run away."

Giving up on threading the needle and turning her nose up at the magnifying glass Lily offered, Poppy instead handed the cotton and needle to Shal with a hopeful smile.

Shal deftly threaded it and handed it back.

"Although you do miss out on the big party, and I'm glad we had some sneaky engagement photos taken beforehand. He was so damn handsome. A month in Italy." Poppy sighed dramatically. "God, it was beautiful. We'd planned to wait a bit to have children, but by the time we made it back I was well and truly up-the-duff with Daniel. I never could resist Gray, bless him. Those amber eyes." She chuckled. "Fiery too, but that's what you get for taking on a Leo when you're a fire sign yourself."

Poppy's birthday was coming up in April. Did that make her a Libra? Shal had minimal knowledge of zodiac signs, but Poppy liked to talk-the-talk.

"Graham was a looker, alright. Cameron takes after him, only without the breadth." Lily spread her arms wide to illustrate her point.

"Watch it!" Daisy, the quietest of the sisters, and the one Shal knew the least, eyed the needle hovering too close to her face. "I disagree. Daniel has the look of his father, and Cam's a masculine version of you." She directed this observation towards Poppy, while handing Shal another two needles to thread.

Shal began to get an inkling why the three older women had been so eager to have her along.

"I think Cam looks like you," she whispered to Poppy, threading the needles and reaching for a couple more. "But then, I never met his dad." Cam had told her a lot about his father, who'd died when he was a teenager.

"Sometimes it's the mannerisms you recognise, more than the colouring. Cam's very like his father in personality. Loyal and dogged. Just chugs away at it until it's done. Especially if he's got something on his mind. He's a lot calmer than Gray, though. More measured. Water sign." Poppy leaned back in her chair and sighed, laying down the anchor comb she'd been hand stitching new lace onto. "When he's being stubborn, he's *very* like Gray. I'm not sure what's eating him at the moment, but he's working like a dog all the God-given hours on earth. Hasn't even got time to drop round for a meal. Apparently he's given himself one night off this week. Tonight. Which just happens to be my book-club night."

"He's avoiding you," Lily stated matter-of-factly.

"Well of *course* he's avoiding me," Poppy scoffed. "What I want to know is, why?"

Inexplicably, all four pairs of eyes turned to study Shal.

Maybe she hadn't been invited just to thread needles, after all?

"Don't ask me." She put both hands up in surrender, one still in possession of a needle. "He's avoiding me, too."

"Is he?" Poppy exclaimed, as if she'd just experienced an ah-ha moment. "Well, now. *That's* interesting."

13

Listening to…
Down in Splendour - Straitjacket Fits
From the album: Melt

Shal was now positive that Cam was actively steering clear.

Though the guys' fishing trip was done and dusted, Cam hadn't turned up to any of Katie's family get-togethers—not to Dundas Street or the boutique—nor could he 'find the time' when Shal badgered him for another music meet-up.

Yes, he was a busy guy, but Shal wasn't used to getting no for an answer.

Cam was free tonight. Poppy had managed to weave that thread of information into the conversation—along with worrying aloud about the state of Adele's marriage.

Rather than call first, Shal took a punt and picked up two kebabs on her way up to Park Street, getting there right at four when she knew Cam usually knocked off. She hadn't been expecting the full crew to be crawling all over the villa like ants, but the progress achieved from having all-hands-on-deck was pretty impressive.

Cam blinked at her in surprise from the top of his ladder when she arrived unannounced, but his eyes lit up when he noted the familiar food packaging, and his pita pocket disappeared in record time.

An unnatural strain hung between them as they ate; a shield of silence Cam was hiding behind. So when Jonno entered, stomping all over their awkwardness with jovial friendliness, Shal welcomed him with a relieved smile and the second half of her pita-pocket.

"I wondered who'd arrived when my apprentice lost the ability to string a coherent sentence together." Jonno grinned at her before tucking into the kebab. "I'm not sure if it was the Alfa Romeo, the heels, or the fact you were carrying take-away food, but he's gone home in a state."

Shal crossed one leg over the other, precariously perched on a sawhorse amidst the organised chaos, and laughed.

"Three sure ways to a young man's heart." Twirling her foot, she studied her newly purchased peep-toe pumps from several angles.

She needed a new pair of shoes like she needed a new hole in the head, but she'd fallen in love with this pair's cheeky red shine and found she couldn't actually leave the new-arrivals in the store when it'd come to the crunch.

"Yeah. Might just be onto something there. The shoes definitely do it for me," Jonno conceded drily, wiping his mouth on the shoulder of his already well-used T-shirt and not-so-covertly checking out her legs.

Cam was still sitting on the floor where he'd just eaten, his back against the gib board, legs bent, and elbows on his knees. There was a mask hanging around his neck and a clearly delineated line where it'd bridged his nose while he'd worked. The rest of him was covered in dust. Shal saw him catch his business partner's eye, and the look he shot across the room at Jonno was anything but warm.

Ignoring the undercurrent, she continued on with her agenda. "Are you free for a practice tonight, Cam?"

"Now, what would you be *rusty* on, Cam?" Jonno prodded, clearly happy to be given the opportunity to niggle.

Still scowling, Cam turned to look at her. But the black look on his face softened a little, and she was suddenly glad she'd come.

Shal was looking fresh, and way too pretty for the work site, her hair swinging in a curtain of ebony as she leant forward to catch his answer. Jonno was right, and Cam silently cursed the builder for it. Shal's legs were something else in those heels, all smooth and tanned, and eye level to his current position.

"Ahh…" He stalled, wishing Jonno to hell or somewhere equally distant, wanting some semblance of privacy while he scrabbled for an excuse.

He'd taken a step sideways from Shal this week, and could tell by her determined look she wasn't going to take it lying down.

He also knew Jonno was just hanging around to piss him off and pay him back.

Cam hadn't been the best version of himself today, and had no doubt been a shit to work with. Gritty, short tempered, and distracted. More than once he'd taken it out on the other builder.

Jonno knew how Cam felt about this woman, the least he could do was bugger off and leave them to their awkward silences.

After Shal left, taking her tantalising scent with her, Jonno stayed on for another half hour to help with the clean up. The other builder clearly saw it as an open invitation to wring Cam for more information, and started in on him straight away.

"What are you two practicing then?"

"Music for the wedding."

"You're getting married, now?" Jonno hassled. "And here was me thinking you'd been avoiding the pretty wee thing."

That's exactly what Cam had been trying to do, as Jonno knew damn well.

"*Katie's* wedding."

"Mm-Hmm…" Jonno poked his head into the main bedroom, which was further along than the rest of the house now, but still unpainted. "Better change the sheets, then."

"Get fucked."

Jonno laughed, "That's the spirit Cam. 'Get fucked.' Roll with that."

"She's not into me that way, so leave off with the sex chat." Cam ran a forearm over his weary eyes, coming away gritty.

"Is *that* what's got your goat these last couple of days?"

"No."

Possibly?

Probably.

"You've just been a grumpy shite for the hell of it?"

"Jesus, Jonno. Are you going to help clean up some of this crap, or just mouth off? You've told the apprentices to piss off, so the least you could do is pick up where they left off."

"I'm helping, I'm helping." Jonno picked up the well-used broom to prove it, getting to work in the front room.

Clearing broken gib board, Cam dumped a couple of wheelbarrow-loads in the skip before checking the site for missed tools and materials to lock up. More and more, working sites were being broken into. It was a pain in the ass, and it was getting bloody expensive.

"You look like hell," he observed when they got outside. Jonno stood in the open roller-door of the garage, holding the stacked sawhorses and a hand drill. Sawdust and plaster dust ran through his hair, and smudges of grey were smeared across his face where his mask hadn't reached. His coveralls had once been white, but now sported an array of colours and a sheen of fine grey dust.

"Ditto," Jonno grinned back at him.

Most likely in a similar state, Cam peeled his coveralls off his shoulders. "I'm heading for a shower. Can you lock this up?"

"Yep."

Cam moved off, leaning forward to brush the worst of the crap out of his hair and climbing out of the oversized suit, shaking it out as he walked.

"Shower's a good start. Still think you should reconsider changing those sheets, though!" Jonno called after Cam, making him loosen up enough to laugh as he swung through the kitchen door.

The last time he'd seen Shal, he'd been on the verge of telling her he was still crazy about her—wanted to be with her. If Rue hadn't tapped on the ute window...

As long as he kept his thoughts and hands to himself, he'd be fine.

"Sure," he'd found himself saying to Shal when she'd asked for a practice. Though he wasn't clear exactly why he'd agreed to her suggestion of doing it up here at the worksite.

Cam scoped the shambles left by the plasterers and carpenters, and sighed.

Shal handed Cam a hot caramel sundae—slightly melted—the moment he answered the door.

"Still your favourite?" She asked with a tentative smile.

"Yeah." Cam grinned back, allowing Shal to relax a little; relieved he seemed to be in a more approachable mood.

"Strawberry's still yours, I see." Cam tapped his plastic cup against her syrup topped one. "Cheers."

"Can't beat it." Looking him up and down, she admired the fit of his jeans. "You're a lot cleaner than the last time I saw you."

"Yeah, plaster sanding's a dog. Did you walk?"

"Yes, I did. And it's a testament to the outdoor refrigeration system you Ōtepotians insist on running down here—the ice cream's hardly melted."

Shal followed a laughing Cam down the hall, through a plastic hanging sheet keeping the majority of the dust out of one end of the house, and breathed in the smell of paper and wood burning. The fire was reaching up to take in the kindling, and the flicker of real flames instantly filled her head with memories of their shared flat.

"I haven't seen an open fire for so long." Shal chose to sit close by on the floor rug, pulling off her jacket and boots before stretching her socked feet towards the crackle of the fire.

"Much cleaner burn with gas, I guess." Cam lent one arm on the solid rimu mantle, forehead to forearm, to watch the burn settle. "But you can't beat the real thing." He chose another log from the basket next to the fireplace and crouched down on the tiled hearth to settle it in place.

Shal finished off the last of her sundae in silence, watching the fire discover and claim the wood, licking hungry tongues of heat up towards the chimney.

"Remember when we came home drunk that night," Cam mused, his eyes taking on a faraway look as he gazed at the fire. "We stole some pickets off the fence of that abandoned house on George Street?"

"I was *just* thinking about that night! Losing Battle of the Bands," she added, with a bit more sobriety.

"Coming a respectable third," Cam paraphrased.

"That sounds better, but it's not how it felt at the time." As she spoke, a shiver—from the ice cream, or the memory—crept up her spine.

She shouldn't have taken her jacket off.

"No, agreed. It felt like shite." Cam took a stride to the sofa, pulled the soft grey blanket off the arm, and handed it to her.

Shal snuggled it around herself, smiling her thanks.

"Mason and Links didn't seem to think so. They stayed out celebrating way longer than us. Did they even come home that night?" she wondered aloud, wrinkling her nose as she tried to remember.

Had Mason been hooking up with someone else, even that far back? A sobering thought. Shal opened her mouth to ask Cam if he could confirm her suspicion, then changed her mind. She didn't want to know that detail after all.

It'd taken weeks of jamming, debates on song choices, key changes, and practice, before they'd entered Battle of the Bands. Or B-of-B, as everyone called it.

It was a long-running gig by one of the popular bars near the university campus, with the obligatory sticky carpet and overused toilets. The flat had pulled together as a group and agreed on the name Stagger—the way Links used to walk when he'd had a couple.

A bit of a sick joke now he couldn't walk without the aid of prosthetics.

They'd made it to the final round, which was no easy feat. Mason was solid on drums, and Cam and Links wielded the advantage of having played guitar and bass together for years.

Stagger managed to snag a couple of tiny cover spots before B-of-B, but nothing compared to the event itself. Wearing a strappy vintage cocktail dress and Adele's artfully applied makeup, Shal's sheer exhilaration of performing had overridden her nerves.

Right up until she'd forgotten the lyrics.

"I'm sorry. I often think about that night. If I hadn't screwed up—"

"Shut up," Cam countered without any heat. "I told you before, there were four of us up on that stage. The other bands were just better on the night, that's all."

B-of-B had been a roller coaster of emotions, and after Shal's initial nerves—including a quick visit to the alley for a dry retch—she'd been incredible.

Husky and soulful. Mesmerising.

Cam's usually quiet flatmate had spun magic out of thin air that night, and held the crowd in the palm of her hand. If Cam hadn't already fallen, hook, line, and sinker, he would've been a gonner before she's finished singing her first line.

"So, we lost." Cam shrugged. "Then you talked an innocent flatmate into stealing a picket fence."

"I was cold!" Shal laughed. "God it was freezing that winter, the coldest nights ever."

"Yeah, one for the record books." Though Cam had hardly noticed, he'd been so caught up in her.

It'd been Shal's idea, but he'd been happy to rip off a few pickets to take home for the fire. There was no cash left in the kitty that week, and the cord of wood delivered at the beginning of the season had been well gone by then.

Judging by the state of the fence, they hadn't been the first to think of it, either. The pickets were tinder dry, the paint long ago stripped by the weather, and were nothing more than ash all too quickly.

They'd shared the old checked blanket across their backs, and Shal had asked him about his father.

For the first time, Cam had felt comfortable talking about his dad with someone other than family. What it had meant to have him, and what it had meant to lose him to the sea.

In a strange way, Shal had been through a similar emotional severance with her father, though the man was still alive.

Shal knew the final song of their set, *Gray Flow*, was written about Cam's dad, and that was probably why she'd been so upset about forgetting the lyrics on stage. No one who hadn't already heard the song would have even picked up on the slip-up. The band simply covered her with a second bridge, and Shal had picked up the vocal lead the next time around.

Cam had assured her it didn't matter as they'd watched the pickets disintegrate, and he'd meant it. His flank burning with heat where Shal's body innocently grazed against his, he'd been in heaven, and he'd been in hell. It had always been that way for Cam where Shal was concerned.

They were close, and they were as far apart as Rā and Marama.

Cam pushed away the dregs of his ice cream, then lifted one of the guitars down off its wall hanger and absently began to tune it. Although the place was blatantly unfinished—no architraves, pieces of skirting missing, floors scarred and unvarnished—the man's favourite musical instruments were on display mounts within ready access.

He brought his ear low to the curved honey-wood, gently turning the toggles as he played each string. The sound was deep and resonating, and Shal felt it bone-deep.

The low notes of the guitar blended with Cam's baritone in a masculine harmony that started a warning buzz of awareness in her.

Obviously satisfied with the tuning, Cam strummed once and lifted his head to smile at her. His dark eyes took on golden tones in the firelight, crinkling and warming as they met hers.

Shal felt the shock of it as if she'd just taken an unexpected wave to the chest. Her heart stumbled with the shift in footing, before thundering into a hip-hop rhythm as she went under.

Pheromone overload.

And exactly like those few moments of disorientation as she fought to find which way was up—the proximity of Cam, his voice, those eyes, and his hand resting on the curved waist of the guitar—all systems freaked before re-booting.

Shal had lived under the same roof with Cam for a year, but had never once considered him on a sexual level. What the hell had been wrong with her? So wrapped up in her doomed-to-fail relationship with Mason, she hadn't seen what was staring her right in the face?

Shal took a deep breath in, releasing it out in even measure.

Cam's head cocked to one side, and though his eyes were still smiling, they were quizzical as well. "You okay?"

"Um, yes?" She'd made that sound like a question. "Yes," Shal repeated, with much more conviction. The silence stretched. "Ah, do you still write?"

"Sure, every now and again when the mood strikes. Don't you?" Cam's hands stilled and he studied her face more fully.

"Not really. Poetry sometimes. But songs? No."

"Same difference." Cam shrugged.

"Mm." Shal tucked an errant piece of hair behind her ear. "I created a fabric line with script overlaid last season. That was fun."

"You used your own lyrics on it?" He appeared genuinely interested.

"Yes. My poetry, my script, and my photographs backing it. The poem was called *Ebb and Flow*, so we named the summer line that, too. Tried something new and printed onto bamboo fibre—lots of leafy greens and soft greys."

"Ebb and Flow. Tidal. That's you."

"Yes." She grinned. Cam knew her well. "Play me something new, then."

Within the shift back to comfortable and relaxed, where was she supposed to slot this odd new sensation of *wanting* him? It was a question she had no answer to.

"Tell you what, I'll play you a song if you recite your poem. Tit for tat," Cam decided aloud.

"You'll show me yours if I show you mine?" she teased, laughing.

He actually blushed.

Shal stared at the rising colour on Cam's neck in disbelief.

"Okay, so, something new," Cam coughed, hiding his face from view by looking down at the instrument.

Covering up?

Definitely covering up.

He chose a playful, upbeat song about the sun—longing for summer with sand in his jandals. His voice was familiar, cruisy, like an afternoon on the beach. And by both playing the chords and using the body of the guitar as percussion, flicking and tapping beats to give the illusion of multiple instruments, he made it fun.

The timbre of the acoustic was low. A bass, Shal realised belatedly, though Cam was playing modified chords as if it was a regular six-string. And just like that, Cam seemed to be himself again, self-possessed and confident without any hint of fluster.

Shal drank in his easy smile and those long creased dimples that ran down each cheek to his jawline. His clean shave showed off nicely carved cheekbones, and the corded lines of his neck.

Fire was glinting in his eyes as he finished the song, and Shal wondered if the warmth she'd picked up earlier was nothing more than a reflection of the flames.

"I like that one," she complimented him simply.

She liked all his songs.

"I have an idea," Cam said, and she could tell by the twitch of his lips he was about to tease her. "You could take the lyrics and base a whole line of clothing on it."

"Idiot." She laughed, fisting one hand and leaning forward to hammer it in mock anger on his socked foot.

"Okay, I'm an idiot," Cam conceded, grinning as he raised his feet up sideways on the sofa so she couldn't reach them. "But in all seriousness, I think it's cool you find creative outlets in your work. Clothing designer, poet, photographer, sustainable resource manager… It must add a few dimensions to your workday. Definitely right-side-brainiac. I mean, even the way you surf is 'creative.' " Cam wiggled speech marks with his forefingers.

Shal snorted. "Yeah? Well I had some 'creative' surfing advice early in my career." She copied his gesture. "Put me all goofy."

A shared grin in the firelight felt good, even when it was suffused with growing want, curled low in her belly.

"So this one's a bass?" she queried.

Trying to be cool and act normal had never been this problematic before.

"Mm-hm." Cam nodded, and Shal's nerve endings hummed along with his soft tone—with the fact he didn't take his eyes off hers when he answered. "Acoustic bass. She's got a lovely round sound. Beautiful to play." He'd been stroking the drum of the bass guitar, and Shal was drawn to his long, able fingers. "She was my first, and I always seem to be drawn back to her."

Cam's hand was gentle on the wood and Shal remembered his light touch on her skin when they were parked up in his ute, stroking down her jawline.

She chewed on her lower lip, eyes flicking to his. Was Cam stringing her out on purpose? She couldn't be sure. There was intensity in his direct gaze, but nothing crude or overt about what he was saying or how he was acting.

No matter Cam's intentions, every feminine cell in her body was standing to attention with the sheer temptation of him.

Shal cleared her throat, and tried to clear her thoughts as well before querying, "She?"

"Well, I couldn't exactly call her a bloke now, could I? Not with a body like that," Cam scoffed, holding the bass aloft by her long neck to show off her womanly contours.

Turning back to Shal, his grin faltered, and if she wasn't mistaken the flush was edging back.

14

Listening to…
The Sum of Us - Ruth Carr
From the EP: The Sum of Us - Minuit

Cam's gaze unwittingly dropped down to take in Shal's curves, beautifully lit by the soft firelight as she leaned back on her arms. She was listening intently from her position on the lounge floor, and his physical awareness ratcheted into overdrive.

It was kind of crazy how much she still affected him. Out of practice navigating these waters, it was becoming increasingly difficult to keep his waka on an even keel.

The blanket around Shal had slipped, showing off one fluted collarbone and giving her an air of fragility. A few long ribbons of raven hair had escaped her hair-tie and lay over the silhouette of her breast.

Shit. He'd lost his train of thought.

The woman—her shape. Similar to that of his guitar.

Right.

"I can't think of a guitar as anything other than female. Calling her male would be like…" Cam failed to finish his sentence. Shal's fitted jeans showed off the length of her legs, ending with the high arches of her narrow feet, encased in fine black wool.

Hell, even her socked feet were sexy.

"It'd be like…?" she prompted.

It'd be like calling Shal a bloke, when clearly she wasn't. Every bone in his body proclaimed her the most feminine creature to walk the earth.

Too late, his eyes snapped back to hers.

"Ah, coffee, tea?" Standing hurriedly, he struggled to prop the bass against the sofa. Caught out, every one of his digits were suddenly clumsy.

Get a grip, Cam counselled himself, moving towards the kitchen. Hot drinks—the perfect way to winch his overextending imagination back into friendship mode.

"Do you have any herbal tea?"

"I know there's some here somewhere," he called back, flicking the kettle on before routing around in the single cardboard box he kept as a pantry. Now he was out of Shal's immediate vicinity he felt much calmer and more in control.

"Peppermint, or Ginger and Lemon," he finally called, placing two cups on the temporary bench-top; fashioned from a scaffolding plank laid across the battered old cupboard framing.

"Peppermint, please." Shal spoke from directly behind him, and Cam turned with a start, wondering how long she'd been leaning on the doorframe watching him.

"Sweet. Okay," he readjusted his volume to suit the confines of the space, tearing the paper wrapper off her teabag.

Shal laughed. "You and the other guys always used to say that. '*Sweeeeet,*' " she mimicked.

"Old habit, I guess." He grimaced, heaping a teaspoon of instant coffee into his own cup before adding boiling water to both.

"Do you have any other old habits you hang onto?" Shal's mouth formed the words before her brain had decided just how smart it was to take this any further.

She swallowed, stepping forward to better read Cam's profile as he concentrated on brewing her tea. But the move positioned her too close for comfort when he turned, and looked directly into her eyes.

In her three-inch heels they'd probably be about the same height. But in socks, she had to look up to him.

With Cam's full focus suddenly on her, Shal didn't feel nearly as calm as she was trying to make out.

She'd noted the grazing glance across her body when they were in the lounge, the warmth on Cam's face, and the swift change of topic. Had he always reacted to her like this? She didn't think so, but then, maybe she just hadn't been ready to see it?

Relieved she didn't appear to be the only one feeling the heat, Shal was also ridiculously nervous to realise Cam wouldn't be making the first move.

She *never* made the first move, but the ball was clearly in her court this time. She just had to figure out how best to hit it.

"Are you *sassing* me, Surfer Girl?" Cam spoke softly, the old nickname mellow off his tongue. His eyes were dark, but humour tugged at the side of his generous mouth.

Mmm… That mouth. Full bottom lip bracketed by deeply creased laughter lines.

How would it feel to taste that mouth?

Shal realised she'd been gazing at Cam's lips for a fraction too long, and maybe a fraction too longingly. His grin began to fade, and when her eyes shot back to meet his there was a different glint there.

An awakening. A recognition.

"You *are* sassing me, right?" Cam spoke even more quietly now, as soft as a caress.

Shal knew she only had to take a step forward and Cameron Dante would kiss her. She'd brush those lips with her own and test the chemistry she could sense zipping along her nerve endings.

Easing out the breath she'd been holding, she let her body decide.

Shal was just fooling around with him. She had to be.

Relax, for God's sake.

But relaxing was beyond Cam's capacity. The air in the kitchen turned electric as Shal took a small step towards him, closing the gap between.

Her eyes never left his.

"Do you have any other old habits?" Shal repeated, glancing at his mouth before sweeping her gaze up through long lashes to look him in the eye. When she reached forward to touch the fingertips of one hand tentatively to his chest, the contact sent a shiver through him. "Like, wanting to kiss me?"

Cam narrowed his eyes, trying to figure her out. Shal was leading him on, but why? This was a high-risk game to play between friends.

Watching for her reaction, his hand went lightly to her chin and lifted.

"Kiss you?" He held her gently, all too aware his hands were work-rough. But Shal didn't pull back and his heart kicked into a jerky rhythm in response, because he'd half expected her to.

Giving her ample time to move away, he lowered his head. Shal's lashes fluttered down as he brushed the softest butterfly kiss on her left cheekbone, then retreated, allowing the coolness of space between them.

Opening her eyes, Shal began to doubt.

"Don't you want to kiss me?" She pulled back slightly, the drop of unexpected rejection crystallising to cool her confidence.

Maybe she'd read him wrong. Maybe she was too late.

Years too late.

But Cam's gaze didn't deviate from hers and there was a quiet steadiness there, quelling her uncertainty. Cocoa and honey eyes— reassuringly familiar. So why did she feel like she was looking into them for the first time?

"Shal, I've wanted to kiss you since the first time I saw you." Cam's voice was husky as he lowered his head again, this time brushing her other cheek with the gentlest of kisses.

The faint rasp from his clean-shaven jaw sent tingles skittering across her skin as he murmured against her ear.

"And every living, breathing moment since then."

"Oh…" Shal melted into the sweetness of his words.

Cam's hand was still cradling her jaw as he drew back, watching her, and she knew he was once more giving her time to change her mind.

Not bloody likely. She wasn't backing out, she was climbing in—right here and right now.

The tension between them was building like a static storm, and Shal's senses honed in on the familiar smell of him. Fresh soap, pine and ocean—a magnetic mix of comfort and aphrodisiac.

"Then, what are you waiting for?" she whispered a little unevenly.

But Cam would not be hurried and took his own sweet time. Warm eyes anchored her as his lips gently descended, brushing hers with a whisper of a kiss.

Shal surrendered her mouth to the sensation, closing her eyes to let everything in her mind fly free. Reaching from Cam's chest to his neck, her hands found their way up into the back of his hair, curling the softness through and around her fingers.

Pulling Cam closer as she stood on tiptoe to curve into him, Shal invited him deeper into the liquid heat wave. She was drowning now, revelling in the taste of him, the feel of him. Cam's arms were around her and his mouth was insistent, scorching.

A helpless groan from him sent another surge of pleasure down her spine.

The chemistry between them was unbelievable. Undeniable.

The nerve endings on Shal's skin sparked and lit wherever they touched, and when Cam's tongue traced the line of her upper lip, a hot bolt of need struck low in her core and began to pulse there.

A single whimper escaped her, unbidden.

Holy hell.

This was a much more intense burn than she'd expected.

"Cam," Shal groaned, unable to get enough of him. Back to stroking his chest, she worried at the light cotton of his shirt, wishing it wasn't between them.

In answer, Cam's hand roved around to cup her butt, fusing their pelvises together. His other hand was sliding down her side—rib cage, waist, hip, thigh—then tracing its way back up again, discovering her curves.

So hot.

The hard thrust of Cam's sex nudged against her own ache. He clearly wanted her, there was no room for question. And the intense need in her was building, too—tipping her over the edge into lust, where nothing but their combined bodies mattered anymore.

So, *so* hot.

Shal nibbled on Cam's sensuous lower lip, wanting him naked, longing to explore flesh on flesh. Breath coming in short pants, she slid both hands into Cam's open-necked shirt, relentlessly twisting buttons and tugging fabric free from his jeans, urgently yanking cotton off his muscular shoulders.

There. Much, *much* better.

Cam moaned low and deep as Shal's hands grasped and slid over his near-naked torso, and she sunk herself back into his kiss.

Burning hot.

Then suddenly, not.

The mouth and pelvis that had been fused with hers were gone, leaving her bereft. Strong hands now gripped her upper arms as Cam placed her bodily away from the heat and contours of his chest.

Shal made a sound of protest, blinking up at him, her brain foggy and questioning.

Cam appeared to be struggling for control, too, his breathing ragged and eyes lust-filled. His skin was taut as he held her away, shirt still hanging off one arm and tucked into the back of his jeans.

Endeared by Cam's ruffled hair, and drawn to his muscular frame, Shal tried to lean back into him. Incredibly turned on by the searing heat, she was keen for more and cold without him.

"No, Shal. Stop." She almost didn't recognise Cam's voice, so gravelly and uneven. "We should stop this now before we…" He shook his head as if trying to clear it.

"Stop?" Her mind refused the suggestion point blank. "What?"

And even more crucially, *why*?

It was easier to think with Shal at arm's length; clearer to see where he should be headed. "Look, no offence, but I know how this ends."

Cam attached his hands firmly to Shal's elbows and tried to rip his mind away from her lips and body.

"You mean, in bed?"

He looked up at the ceiling and counted to five—counted to ten for good measure.

"Are you counting?" Shal asked, eyes narrowing.

"Are you going to stay on your side of the kitchen?" He skirted the question with another, releasing her arms to move back a metre, hands still raised in a defensive position.

"Fine," Shal huffed, folding her arms across her chest.

He wasn't the only one on the defensive, now. "Okay, so..." Taking a deep breath in, he released it out again just as slowly.

Back on even ground. Altitude returning to normal. Those little noises Shal made when they kissed could smack a guy clear out of the bloody atmosphere.

"Correct me if I'm wrong, but you're aiming to...?" Once again Cam got lost for words.

"Bonk." Shal ended the sentence helpfully, and he winced at the term. "Screw?" She supplied a second option with a pinch of artificial sweetener.

He looked up at the ceiling again. She wasn't making this easy.

"Make *pretzels*?" she ground out.

Noticing she'd inched forward, he stepped backward again, shrugging his shirt back onto his shoulders and beginning on buttons.

"Make pretzels, okay. So we make some pretzels. They're amazing pretzels. Incredible pretzels, if that taster was anything to go by. But we're mates, and we have a lot of mates in common so it gets awkward. Our timing isn't great. There's a wedding in less than a week. I'm one of the best men and you're one of the, um... the best women."

"Bridesmaids," Shal corrected him.

"Bridesmaids! See? I knew that." Cam tapped at his temple, more to wake up his brain than to indicate there was anything coherent going on in there. "So, that's no good for the bride and groom, stuck in the middle of our, ah, our pretzel dough."

He'd reached the other side of the kitchen and gripped the low windowsill behind him like his life depended on it. His shirt was back on, but hurriedly so, and when he ran a hand down the front he could feel he'd buttoned it unevenly.

"Why does it have to get awkward?" Shal shook her head and raised her hands in a *mamma mia* gesture. "We're grown ups. I get the feeling after that kiss you still have the hots for me. I *definitely* have the hots for you." Shal openly considered him from head to toe. "Any hotter and you'd be molten lava."

He blinked across the room at her, completely floored by that flippant compliment.

"We don't see each other enough for it to be a problem," Shal continued, moving a smidgen towards him again. "Friends with benefits, if you like." One shoulder shrugged up and down nonchalantly.

She made it sound so easy. Fall into bed—fall out again.

"You don't have to announce it to anyone, Cam. It can be just us, fooling around. No strings attached."

And that was the crux.

Friends with benefits. Fooling around. Shal couldn't have presented the proposition in a less appetising way. Either offer could be taken as a cold, hard slap in the face.

Good enough for sex, but not good enough to keep. More insulting than Cam would like to admit, even to himself—but what had he expected from this particular woman? Happily-ever-after?

Idiot.

It was easier than he'd thought to step aside, after all.

"Actually. I'll pass, thanks." His voice was cool, but he'd felt pure, hot anger flash through him for a second there. He was furious with himself, and furious with Shal. "Friends with benefits might cut it with all the guys up north, but you can count me out."

Far too much at stake. Shal knew damn well he'd willingly give her everything he was, everything he had. And she'd happily take it.

"You'll *pass*? Like I'm offering you a beer? Jesus, Cam, what do you want from me?" Shal was instantly spitting tacks. "You felt it too!"

"Yeah, I *felt* it, I'm not a fuckin' iceberg! I want everything, Shal. The whole bloody shebang!" Realising he was shouting, Cam took a steadying breath. It was such a hopeless request. "I'm worth that."

He tried to shrug off the resentment and let some of the fire ebb out. "I'm sorry. You don't know *how* sorry. I want you more than I can say, but I'm over sleeping around for the hell of it. I'm looking for more." He attempted to re-button his shirt more evenly. "I want what my parents had." A wash of pure hopelessness threatened to close his throat, but he forced the words to keep coming out of his mouth. "I actually *want* the strings. I know you can't give me that. I know you wouldn't give that to anyone. So let's just say, for my own self-preservation and with no offence—thanks for the compliment, but I'll pass on the offer. Stick to friends. We're good at that."

He attempted to smile and smooth it over but there was no social nicety left in him, just stone and fire. His body strongly opposed the decision his brain had just made, and he was still fighting the intense urge to find out exactly what making pretzels with Shal would be like.

God knew, he'd dreamed about it often enough.

Shal was in shock. Needing to busy her hands, she grabbed her herbal tea off the make-do countertop, fingers not completely steady.

"You're telling me… You think… You think I'm incapable of loving someone?" She tried to sound angry, but she was hurt. 'No offence' was almost laughable.

"No, That's not what I said," Cam replied woodenly. "I said you *wouldn't*. It's entirely your prerogative. No one can force you. You either feel something or you don't." Cam hesitated, his eyes not quite meeting hers. "But I think maybe you prefer it…"

"Prefer it, *what*?" Shal eyed Cam suspiciously when he stopped talking altogether and started concentrating on his feet.

"Alone," he finally finished.

"I'm not alone! I see people. I have relationships. I love my friends. And. They. Love. Me. Back!" She punctuated each word with an index finger stabbed in Cam's direction. "I love my… my family." She stopped mid-rant, her cup beginning to shake in earnest.

Damn her stuttering mouth. Her mind had raced immediately to the two people who should love her unconditionally; the only two people she couldn't rely on.

Her mother and father.

And they love me back? No. It wasn't anywhere near so clear cut, and that shit hurt.

Alone was exactly how Shal had felt this week, after Jac left.

"Of course you *love*. But I'm talking about partnership love. Fidelity. Trust. Commitment. Katie and Rue love, Aroha and Links love. That's what *I* want. That's what *I'm* looking for." Cam ran his hand up the back of his neck. "I don't know if you sabotage it, or just run away, but you make light of it. Poke fun at it, like you don't want to believe in it anymore."

"I don't need your psychoanalysis, Cam."

Shal was a master at willing tears to piss off, but it was getting harder. The emotion wanted to overflow because Cam had just hit the nail on the head. She didn't believe she was capable anymore. Something in her had disengaged when Mason had shattered her trust into a thousand little pieces, something necessary to carry on a regular relationship and love someone back.

When in doubt, attack. It was the motto her mother had survived with every damned day of her life.

"You want to pick holes? Where is the love of *your* life? Been married lately? Engaged to your high school sweetheart?" she snapped.

Cam's demeanour shifted, and if anything he became more guarded, more watchful.

"Engaged. Yeah. But that's been off for a while now," he murmured.

Shal's head snapped back. "Engaged?" She felt a little winded. "To who?"

Ignoring her spluttering, Cam went on as if she hadn't spoken. "I know you got thrown in the past, but it's like you won't allow yourself to get back up on that horse or let anyone prove themselves to you. First your father, then Mason—"

"Don't you *dare* bring them into this." Her father? Shal was mortified Cam had brought David up, and what had happened between Mason and herself was goddamn private. "They have nothing to bloody *do* with this!" she denied with a vehemence she couldn't actually back up. "This is between you." She gestured wildly. "And me." Peppermint tea slopped around indiscriminately, and she didn't care.

"But they do, Shal. Experiences mould us."

"Oh *screw* that. I refuse to be the sum of all the shit that's happened to me, and I will not stand here bearing witness to all the things you think are *wrong* with me. Screw that too. You want commitment? You're barking mad. It doesn't *exist*. Marriage is nothing more than a signed shopping list. An empty promise, not even worth the paper it's written on."

Shal slammed her tea back on the scaffold plank, spilling more in the process. The cup was half empty and she hadn't managed to drink any of it, which pissed her off even further. She fisted her hands at her sides as a tangible spike of hysteria rose and fell, leaving her hollow.

Of course Cam hadn't brought up marriage, Shal had. She'd lumped it all together with shopping lists, madness, and empty promises.

Cam rubbed the heels of his hands into his eyes.

"I'm not trying to tell you what's wrong with you. I don't want to trap you, hurt you, or change you in any way." Dropping his arms to his sides, he stared at Shal across the room, willing her to understand. "I'm trying to tell you why we shouldn't start this. Why I can't do this—not with you. I can't remain detached. Don't you get it? Catch and release. No strings. I think it'd kill me. I want all of you, Shal. I always have. And I want you to want all of me."

Cam was sliding dangerously close to the edge, where what he wanted was not as relevant as what his body wanted, and that was to take Shal's shaking hands in his and hold her close. With every atom of his physical body, he wanted to make love to Shal and *make* her love him back.

"It feels like I've been in love with you forever, Shal. I don't know how to not be in love with you."

"You're in *love*?" If anything, Shal seemed more incensed by the words. "You're in love with a figment of your own imagination, then. Someone you thought you knew way back when. She doesn't exist anymore. Maybe you even made parts of me up. I can't... I'm *not* that naïve young girl anymore." Her voice wavered dangerously, then thinned to a whisper, "I can't ever be her again, Cam. She *broke*."

Cam's heart went out to her. She was tearing herself up, and he'd pushed her to it.

Tears began to smart, and desperate to salvage what remained of her pride Shal spun on her heel, urgent to escape.

"You've got some fairy-tale going on about what kind of person I am. You *can't* be in love with me, because I *can't* love you back." She was ranting, knowing it made her sound crazy but powerless against the need to get it all out.

Striding into the lounge, she began searching for her stuff.

"It wouldn't work. It really wouldn't." Compiling a list of suitable safeguards, she reeled them off like a soothing mantra. "No promises, no commitment, no strings, and no exclusive rights." She hiccupped loudly, startling even herself. "That's really the only way. No one gets lied to, and no one gets hurt."

Grabbing her coat off the chair on the way past, she stomped over to collect her boots from beside the sofa, hiccupping again.

Bloody body! Couldn't it just behave for once and let her exit with some semblance of dignity?

Cam called after her as she stormed back towards the hall.

"Wait, Shal. I'll drive you."

"I don't want you to (*hiccup*) drive me!"

"Then I'll call you a cab."

"I don't *want* you to call me a cab. I don't want anything from you, Cameron (*hiccup*) Rimutaka Dante. Just leave me—the hell —alone!"

(*Hiccup*).

15

Listening to...
Wandering Eye - Fat Freddy's Drop
From the album: Based on a True Story

Cam let Shal go, his heart down low in his woollen socks.

"Shit. You could've handled that better." He scrubbed both palms across his jawline as he berated himself, wondering if he could've handled it any worse.

He listened to Shal thrusting on her boots and clothing down the hall, fully expecting, but still wincing at the force of the slammed front door.

Damned if he wouldn't see that she got home safely, though. He grabbed his jacket, phone, and keys, and put up the fireguard before locking the villa.

If Shal knew his ute was tailing her home, she didn't give any indication. Cam stayed well back and gave her plenty of space, waiting until she'd turned the corners before creeping round to park again.

Shal wouldn't have noticed if an eighteen-wheeler was cruising along beside her—she was in the midst of an emotional free fall. Tears, anger, the odd hiccup, then tears again.

Of course she could love. It was being *in* love that seemed to be the problem. But she was only twenty-frickin'-eight for heaven's sake… Plenty of time to figure it all out.

She knew every man wasn't her father, or Mason for that matter. She had complete control over her own life, and no men—past or present—held any sway.

Cam had been out of line, making out like she was sleeping with 'all the guys up north.'

She dated, sure. Enjoyed her freedom, absolutely.

And if she chose to keep it strictly casual? That was her own prerogative and no one else's business. She was damn picky about who she said yes to, and completely upfront with every guy she went out with. Plenty of women were opting not to get serious or hitched nowadays. She was in bloody good company. There was no point tying yourself to someone you couldn't promise to love forever, right? Much better to keep your options open.

Or was Cam right?

Sabotage it… Run away from it… Make light of it…

Was that how she was choosing to live?

The further Shal walked, the more perplexing the whole Cam situation became. They were supposed to be friends, not attacking each other and trading insults. Sure as hell not meant to be kissing each other senseless—though that part had been totally her fault.

If fault was even the right word.

Cam had been hot for her as well. She may be obtuse, but she'd felt it. She *knew* it, right down to her bone marrow. She'd put herself out there, offered pretzels, for God's sake, but that hadn't been enough.

He'd turned her down.

'Thanks for the compliment, but I'll pass…'

How mortifying!

And he'd been engaged. Why hadn't she heard about that?

To Jody, the Ice Queen?

Another pertinent point kept niggling in the back of Shal's mind, jostling to be reviewed.

Cam had said he was in love.

Of course that couldn't be true—but if it *was*, then the damage was already being done. Because she wasn't 'in love' with Cam back, was she? She loved him though, and for that reason alone she should've walked away from this well before it had gotten any more involved.

When Katie had implored her not to hurt Cam, Shal had almost allowed herself to believe she wouldn't; that she *couldn't*.

It was a short walk between houses, but the exercise and frigid air did her good. By the time she'd reached the front door of Dundas Street Shal was much calmer.

Cam waited until Shal was inside the house with the interior lights switched on. He could see her silhouetted against the stained glass, bolting the front door.

Leaning to turn his ignition key, his phone buzzed in his jacket pocket with an incoming text, and he flicked it a quick look.

Shal.

Home safe.

Cam put both hands at twelve o'clock on the steering wheel and laid his forehead on them, groaning.

God, but he loved her.

She was angry, he was angry, and they'd both said stuff that'd hurt the other. But underneath it all, Shal knew he'd worry about her walking home alone in the dark.

Another text came through, and it made him chuckle aloud, appreciating Shal trying to end their argument on a laugh.

hiccup

He sat for a while longer with a thousand things to say to her, then simply texted back, *Thank you.*

The events from the night before were insidiously eating away at Shal's gut. To say she was upset would be a huge understatement. Embarrassed didn't cut it either.

Horrified just about summed it up.

She couldn't stomach the idea of breakfast so jumped in the car instead, heading to the large indoor pool on the hill to swim off her angst. Tuesday was clearly aqua-aerobics day, and her already busy brain didn't appreciate the perky dance beat.

Twenty lanes later, Shal had a mild chlorine head-spin, and by the time she'd hit the showers it was a full-blown, thumping headache.

She popped a couple of painkillers in the car as she left the complex, the meds beginning to soothe by the time she pulled up outside Dundas Street. Though last night had been a weeknight, she still had to avoid the obligatory shattered bottle in the gutter from yesterday's student partying. Life continuing on around her, as usual.

Perhaps nothing had changed in Ōtepoti, after all.

The car was blissfully quiet when Shal turned off the engine and laid her head back on the headrest, unwilling to move just yet. A white van parallel parked behind her, crunching over glassy green shards and pulling her out of her daze. She adjusted the rear view mirror to watch as a courier jumped out and headed to the front door. When he didn't get an immediate answer, he left the delivery on the porch and drove away.

Five minutes later, the throb in her head easing down to a quiet hum, curiosity got the better of Shal. She dragged herself and her swim bag out of the car and went to investigate.

The bouquet was beautiful.

A large arrangement of old-fashioned tea roses in muted dusky tones was surrounded by jasmine and tightly budded sprays of soft pink rosebuds. The heady scent reminded her of New York Nana, and the fact it'd been a full year since she'd last seen her paternal grandmother.

Far too long.

Shal could visualise her Nana's face, shadowy under the wide brim of her gardening hat, the skin of her hands crepe-like as she carefully chose stems to cut for her indoor vases. Diamond and platinum love trinkets would be nestled near her grandmother's wizened knuckles, catching the light.

Engagement, wedding, eternity, silver and golden wedding anniversary gifts…

The message was stapled shut.

Shal sat on the top step and tried to manoeuvre the sharp prongs open with her fingernail, not wanting to rip the card—yelping when she inadvertently stabbed the soft pad of her forefinger in the process.

It was a brief note, written in Cam's own loopy scrawl, so he must've gone in and chosen the flowers himself. He hadn't hand delivered them, though.

Understandable, considering she'd told him to leave her the hell alone.

Shal mulled on that for a while.

Cam was giving her some space. Or maybe he didn't want to see her, either? She could only guess. Stroking her fingers lightly over Cam's handwriting, a smear of her own blood smudged across her name.

I'm sorry for hurting you.
Peace please, Shal.
C. x

Shal tucked the note into her pocket, then brought the heavy bouquet onto her lap to drown herself in the scent as she sucked on her injured finger. The faint taste of iron was soothing in its familiarity.

"Lost your key?" A deep, male voice pulled her out of her sombre reverie.

"What? No… Hi." She squinted into the sun but was unable to make out any clear features of the man in the white light. "Just letting the painkillers work their magic."

"Are you okay?" The man folded his considerable height until he was squatting on the path in front of her—eye level—his face wreathed in concern.

"I am now." She smiled across at him. "Just a headache, but it's easing off."

Now the sun wasn't directly behind his head she could see who he was. His dark hair was a little longer than she'd seen it in photos, curling over his collar. He had hazel-green eyes that seemed to see too much, just like his mother, and a full, sensual bottom lip, just like his brother.

He was parts of Poppy and parts of Cam, but on a bigger, broader, and darker scale.

This was Dante D.

Shal offered her left hand out between them. The one she hadn't just been sucking on.

"I'm Shal, and you must be Cam's brother, Daniel." She shook his hand formally, despite being wrong-sided. "I believe I used to flat in your old room, years ago. It's nice to finally meet you."

"Tēnā koe, Shal. I've heard a lot about you."

"Ha! Likewise." She wrinkled up her nose and they both laughed. The man was a bloody rugby legend.

Shal rose with her keys as Daniel picked up his bag and suit sleeve, and followed her into the house.

———

They had brunch on the kitchen stools.

Daniel had taken one look at what was available in the pantry and fridge and muttered, "Eggs Benedict."

"You know how to make Eggs Benedict?" Shal had been quietly astounded at the big man's grace in the kitchen. Obviously in his element in the heart of the house, he'd just sauntered in and taken over.

He was welcome to it.

"You don't?"

"I know how to *order* it."

Daniel laughed. "Do you cook at all?"

"I like salads, so I tend to make salads." She smiled at his raised eyebrows. "I'm talking *exceptional* salads. I can also follow a recipe to make anything basic, if necessary." She shrugged. "But it's not my forte. Katie on the other hand—"

"Creates Michelin star worthy works of art," Daniel finished for her.

"Yes," she breathed the word out reverently.

"Well, mine's somewhere in the middle. I learned how to cook after Dad died. We all did. He used to be head chef at our place. I don't need a recipe, except with baking, and it's usually edible, though not always pretty."

Shal caught the key word and hung onto it. "You *bake*?"

Daniel was a breeze to get on with, so they just got on. It was easy to forget any preconceived ideas she'd had about the big rugby man. He seemed to be a regular Kiwi bloke, aside from the baking, perhaps.

And despite his size, he didn't make her feel small. Not in the least.

They talked and laughed over food, then went their separate ways. Before she slipped off to the boutique for another meeting with Jonno, Shal went upstairs to make sure Daniel had his own key. She was halfway down again before she thought about dinner.

"Daniel!" she called back up the stairs.

"Yep?" He poked his head out of his bedroom door, the smaller of the two spare upstairs.

"What are you doing for dinner?"

"Why? Are you paying?"

"What? No I—"

"You want me to shout? Well, that's a little forward, Shal, but I'm not opposed to it."

"No, I meant—"

"Oh, you mean forgo dinner and just…" He waggled his eyebrows.

Shal cracked up laughing, as Daniel had clearly meant her to, and he grinned back.

"Thanks for your thoughtful invitation." Daniel was taking a dig at her shouting at him up the stairs if the sparkle in his eye was anything to go by. "But I have a date tonight with my favourite woman."

Shal thought for a minute. "Poppy?" she guessed, and Daniel grunted a laugh.

"Hole in one."

Jonno left the boutique after another successful meeting, and Shal moved upstairs to measure for the final window treatments in the attached apartment.

Some of the furniture was now installed, and it was looking almost finished with just the kitchen and bathroom tiling to go. Walking towards the window with her tape measure ready she stopped mid-stride, staring at the wooden shelving unit up against the living room wall.

It fitted the spot perfectly now it was complete. Last time she'd seen it, the confusing components had all been lying in a pile on the carpet.

Bonus! Who'd done that for her? Jonno?

She must remember to thank him.

Orders for stock were set, interviews and appointments with key staff were complete, and the boutique keys were due to be handed over on Friday.

With only four days left until the wedding, Shal had no more reasonable excuses to avoid Katie (other than these unimportant blind measurements).

She hadn't made any attempt to tell the soon-to-be bride what had happened in Cam's kitchen last night, and the omission loomed. Katie had a habit of sensing subterfuge and asking very pertinent questions, and there was sure to be a large dose of I-told-you-so coming Shal's way.

She wasn't up for that yet. Better to wait until her confusing emotions had simmered down first.

Cam was right, pretzel dough was not something Katie should have thrust on her plate right now.

The feelings Shal had for Cam were confounding the issue. Love, of the friendship kind, meant she didn't want to hurt him, and she almost wished she'd remained unaware of his old crush.

Though that would've meant missing out on that scorching kiss…

"How old is Saffron?" Shal asked, tucking fresh sheets onto the borrowed single bed Rosa and herself had just wrangled up the stairs of Dundas St.

Daniel and his brawn were unfortunately out.

"She's just about to turn five, and a chatterbox. I'm afraid it won't be anywhere near as peaceful with Saffy in the house," Rosa described her grandchild succinctly, wiping one arm across her forehead before stepping back to admire their handiwork.

In tones of pink, the single duvet went well with the pastel patchwork on the main bed.

"I have a wee desk for this area, too." Rosa turned and motioned to a space along the wall. "Saffy's into anything artsy. The messier the better."

Shal looked around what was soon to be Adele and her daughter Saffy's room. It was clean and serviceable, if a little lacking in personality. The desk would be a nice touch.

Some art supplies? What about toys?

She began to make a mental list.

Dropping Rosa home, Shal ended up tangling with the floral sisters again. Maybe she was a sucker for punishment, or maybe she was getting used to it, but their brand of noise and laughter didn't seem so full-on, today. It kind of suited the big old house Katie had grown up in.

Poppy, Lily, and Daisy were entrenched in the living room, working on pew decorations for the church in off-white raw silk.

"Do you need any help?" Shal found herself asking.

"That depends how much experience you have with top-of-the-range fabrics," Daisy quipped.

A surprising amount, actually.

"And bows," Lilly added.

Nope. None at all.

"It's not *real* silk," Rosa told her conspiratorially, "Just a decent looking knock-off."

Poppy was cutting out, with Lily on the sewing machine hemming the wide strips.

Shal and Daisy got to know each other better whilst folding bows and hand tacking them so they held their shape, Shal increasingly enveloped into the warmth of the siblings conversation and laughter. Like the cottage garden their mother had named them after, the atmosphere was light and fragrant, crowded and familiar. One bloom eased cheerfully into another's space without seeking or seeming to need permission, and Shal suddenly missed her half-sister Bianca getting all up in her face.

When Katie arrived with Lily's wife, Maureen, there were hugs all around. Maureen had brought a pile of scrubbed horseshoes with her from the stables she ran just outside of Vancouver, and the women got down to the serious business of squabbling about how best to to pretty them up.

Shal moved off with Katie and neatly avoided the topic of a certain male, unwilling to start up another disagreement so close to the wedding. The friends concentrated instead on the timeline of the bridal party's arrival.

Adele and Saffy were flying in tomorrow, then Aroha and Links the day after.

Before Shal left, Rosa gave her the little desk to take home for Saffy's room. It was chambray blue with a liftable lid, but could've done with another lick of paint or some decoration.

Along with the desk came a basket of plastic animals and an old wooden dolls house with furniture. A small chair, a pile of art supplies, and a child-sized plastic apron completed the collection.

Shal's car interior was beginning to look like the tail end of a jumble sale.

"I'm not sure if I've got anything big enough to put down under the desk to protect the carpet," Rosa worried aloud.

"Don't worry. I'll get onto that," Shal promised, wanting to relieve some of the stress around Rosa's eyes.

"Super." The mother of the bride patted her on the arm distractedly. "I'll leave that to you then. Anything to settle Saffy in will be a godsend for Adele. Heaven knows she's got enough on her plate..." Rosa trailed off.

After leaving Katie's parent's place, Shal picked up what she needed at the shops, then bit the bullet and called Cam.

No answer. Again.

Not bothering to leave another message for him to ignore, she called Jonno instead.

"Hi, Jonno, it's Shal. You don't happen to have any big-ish pieces of lino off-cut, do you? I need some for an art corner."

When Shal knocked on the door at Park Street it was Jonno who answered, and he had the small roll of lino ready by the door.

"Oh, it's perfect!" she cooed, fingering the tan floor covering. "How much do I owe you for that?"

"I'll add it to your bill," Jonno answered, and Shal took his smile to be sardonic.

"Thank you." She gave him a hesitant smile back. "Is Cam around? I've been trying to get hold of him…" she trailed off as the builder shook his head, lifting the roll onto his shoulder.

"No. You just missed him. He's out on a pick-up."

"Right." Disappointment settled somewhere in the region of her midriff. "Can you ask him to give me a call when he gets back?"

"Sure. I can do that."

But something in the builder's manner told Shal she shouldn't hold her breath.

"He's not going to contact me, is he?"

Jonno grinned. "Odds aren't high."

"God, what a mess." Shal brought her thumb and forefinger up to squeeze the bridge of her nose. "I screwed up."

"Nah," Jonno replied evenly. "Cam and I butt heads all the time. I'd call him a stubborn son-of-a-bitch, but I know his mother, so…" He lifted his free shoulder in a half shrug.

Shal considered the builder, who seemed to be placing himself as an ally.

"We had a difference of opinion." Opening the passenger door, she stood aside for Jonno to slide the roll of flooring in. "And I really need to see him to patch things up. It's terrible timing." Realising the truth of that statement, she chewed on her lower lip.

Shit. She really *did* need to see him. Katie's wedding was mere days away.

"Well…" Jonno seemed amused. "If anyone can, you can, Legs."

Shal wrinkled up her nose at the sideways compliment. "Here's hoping. Though it's tricky when he's so damn set on avoiding me."

"Don't tell him you're coming next time."

"I *didn't*." She eyeballed the burly builder pointedly.

"Oops."

"*Oops,*" she mimicked, sending Jonno a wry smile. "*Not* helpful. Though, I do have to thank you for finishing the shelving unit. It was doing my head in."

"What unit?"

"In the boutique apartment."

Jonno shook his head again.

"You know, the flat pack?" She tried again.

"Nope. Not me."

"Who else has been up there?"

But Shal knew the answer before Jonno offered it. Cam had been steering clear of the boutique, but she hadn't realised it was only when she was scheduled to be there.

Shal had just enough time to drag the desk, the roll of lino, and the art supplies into the hall of Dundas Street before racing back to the boutique apartment to sign for the delivery of the queen bed, sofa, and dining set.

The beefy truck driver and his skinny sidekick hauled the bulky items all upstairs with minimum fuss, and remembering how long it had taken herself and Rosa to move Saffron's single bed up a much wider set of stairs, Shal was vaguely embarrassed by the comparison.

When the movers had gone she ran a hand over the completed shelving unit, deep in thought.

So, Cam had a penchant for putting together flat packs?

Taking the simple table and chairs out of their boxes, she left all the components in a pile with the instructions and Allen keys on top. Then, retaining a large piece of the cardboard wrapping, she wrote a note with the biro she found at the bottom of her handbag.

Cam.
Thank you for the flowers, they're beautiful.
I owe you an apology, so I've left you this flat pack as a peace offering.
I really appreciate you making up the shelving unit. It was driving me crazy.
This is silly. Please stop avoiding me. I feel like a leper. A mutual friend

warned me this would happen if I let my libido lead, and that's exactly
what I did. Sorry for coming onto you. That was uncool.
(Though if you change your mind, I still think you're hot).
Friends, e hoa?
Shal.

The embarrassment due to her behaviour the other night had dulled down, but trying to fathom her own complex emotive state was beyond her. She couldn't stop thinking about Cam, and knew enough to recognise kissing him had flicked a major switch. She wanted more, and the arm's length Cam was keeping her at was driving her nuts.

He was a damn pheromone grenade, and the pin had been pulled.

Folding her big cardboard note in half, she wrote Cam's name on it and tucked it under the first large table-section on the pile, so he wouldn't see it before he started, and no one else would see it by mistake.

Checking the time, she sent a text to Jonno.

If her radar was working right, he might just be willing to help her on the Cam front.

Another flat pack upstairs at the boutique doing my head in. Hopefully the Allen key fairy comes again this evening while I'm out. S.

16

Listening to…
Undone - Boh Runga
From the album: Mix - Stellar

Shal was trying to concentrate on prettifying the desk and chair set for Saffy in the dining room. She'd pushed all the other furniture aside and spread newspaper down on the tiles, but every half hour her nerves bumped up as her set alarm went off.

The first time her cellphone interrupted with its distinctive 'yoo-hoo!' she all but sprinted out the door, car keys jangling.

Arriving back fifteen minutes later, she felt a bit sheepish when Daniel looked up from his laptop at the breakfast bar, eyeing her suspiciously.

The second time the alarm yoo-hooed, she took the time to wash out the brush she was using and change out of her paint-flecked shirt before leaving.

Arriving back ten minutes later after yet another dummy run, Shal tapped the side of her nose in a mild mind-your-own-business gesture when Daniel gave her a second sideways look.

The desk and chair set were looking pretty cute by the time the next alarm went off. Clusters of pink rosebuds and white daisies stood out against the blue backdrop, and the chair had a matching bouquet on the backrest.

"Back in ten minutes?" Daniel joked.

"God. I hope not," Shal muttered, washing up the paints in the kitchen sink and drying her hands off on her jeans. "Wish me luck."

"Luck," Daniel offered the single word with a suspiciously bland expression. "Bring some chocolate back with you next time."

"Aren't you supposed to be going to some fancy rugby club dinner tonight?" Using the glass doors as a mirror, Shal pulled her hair out of her ponytail and fussed with it, staring for a moment at the dual image of herself presented by the double-glazing.

A girl with two faces. A woman with a tangible shadow.

She shook her head at her reflection, wanting to flick away the thoughts.

"That's an oxymoron. No such thing as a fancy-rugby-club anything. And chocolate doesn't count," Daniel stated baldly, as if it was a nutritional fact.

This time when Shal drove into town, Cam's work ute was parked directly outside the boutique. Her relief was short-lived, however. The disappointment she'd felt on the first two trips was now replaced by gut clenching nervousness, presenting itself as nausea.

Ridiculous.

It was just Cam.

Just Cam who'd been tying her up in knots. Just Cam she'd been obsessing about. Imagining. Missing.

Shal hesitated in the alley with her hand on the back door, though she had no intention of chickening out.

Letting herself into the rear corridor of the boutique, she made her way up the stairs in stealth-mode. There was no need to switch on the light on the landing, as plenty spilled onto the carpet from the open door to the living room.

At first, she thought Cam had a radio on.

The voices were indistinct, like talk-back in the background. It wasn't until Shal had almost reached the landing she recognised Cam's baritone. The returning laughter was definitely female.

She froze.

What was she doing? Sneaking around spying on Cam's romantic tête-à-tête?

Hell, no.

Cursing her lack of insight, Shal backtracked as quickly and quietly as she could, holding her breath as she re-locked the exterior door and trotted back to her car.

Her hands were shaking by the time she slid behind the wheel. Due to the shock, or due to the idiotic jealousy biting and twisting in her gut? It shouldn't matter, but suddenly the whole situation was just awful. Cam was up there with someone else.

"Calm down."

The command was easier said than done, but vocalising it gave Shal something to concentrate on. It wasn't until she had her keys in the ignition that she remembered her note, scribbled on cardboard and stuck in the flat pack pile.

"*Nooo*," she moaned, bumping the heel of her hand against her forehead. But short of storming the place, there was nothing she could do about it now.

When Shal returned to Dundas Street half an hour later, she brought a two-litre carton of choc-fudge ice cream and a box of Cadbury Favourites with her.

Daniel took one look at her face and had the smarts to accept the sweet offering without comment, and they ate bowls of decadent ice cream in relative silence.

He waited until Shal was clearing the plates to say, "Adele and Saffy fly in tomorrow afternoon, so I'm putting on a family dinner for them here. Does that work for you?"

She looked up from the dishwasher. "Sure. I can make myself scarce." Maybe head to the boutique apartment and start hanging the delivered curtains.

"No. I didn't mean that." Daniel's mouth twitched. "I mean, are you free? Would you help?"

"Oh, right. Yes, of course. I could, um…" Shal hesitated, a bit vague on what he meant by 'help.'

"Make a salad?" Daniel's mouth twitched a little more, into an almost-smile.

"An *exceptional* salad, or two. How many people?"

Daniel counted on his fingers as he reeled off names. "Fifteen... or, sixteen?"

"Six*teen*?" Flabbergasted, Shal blinked at him, unsure if he was joking.

Daniel finally laughed at her outright. "Maybe more, with the odd tag-along I've forgotten to factor in. That's just how it is on Mum's side of the family. You'll get used to it." Shal must've looked panicked because he added soothingly, "They'll all bring food and drinks. It'll be fine."

Adele and Saffron arrived to dismal rain and a southerly cold snap, so Shal went out of her way to make their room a little bit more welcoming. Taking one of her own bedside lamps and tables, she set it up next to the queen and fussed with some roses from Cam's bouquet, arranging them in a water glass.

Saffy entered the house stroppy, dragged in by her nana Rosa. The four-year-old dug her heels in like a little mule, complaining plaintively about her wet shoes and empty stomach, and repeatedly asking for her dad.

A frazzled looking Adele met Shal at the doorstep and snatched a quick hug, Daniel and Katie following her with two large suitcases.

Shal's tension increased a notch when she caught Cam's unmistakable laughter coming from the street. Still standing in the shadow of the porch, she watched as Katie's father, Amos, limped up the footpath with his nephew and turned into the front entrance.

Seemingly unaware of her presence, Amos leant heavily on his walking stick and carried on with his tirade about the perils and expense of having daughters, one of which was footing the bill for wedding buffets. Seeing her at the last minute, his face split into a wide grin.

"Shal! *Sheesh*, you hiding like a wee wood nymph in the shadows?" Amos handed Cam a walking stick to go with the umbrella he was already holding, and enveloped Shal in a huge bear hug.

The colour of Amos' signature beard was changing to embrace his advancing years, and white sideburns now merged into the russet chin that was tickling her face.

"Nice to finally see you." She squeezed him back, not caring that the dampness of the evening transferred onto her shirt. "I've been frequenting your place, but you're always out."

Amos grunted and muttered something about the house being full of in-laws.

"You look a bit more like Father Christmas every time we meet," she reached up to touch Amos' woolly facial hair as he let her go.

"*Ho, ho, ho.*" Amos played along. "I'm afraid the only gift I bought you this year was this suspect I picked up on the street." He gestured towards Cam, who hung back on the path looking uncomfortable, one hand pressed deep into his front pocket and the other gripping both the walking stick and umbrella.

"Hmm…" Shal looked Cam up and down, taking in the jeans and work boots, broad shoulders and slim hips. Slap on a Stetson and he'd just about pass as a cowboy. "Well done, Santa. He's just what I asked for." But she didn't move forward, because when Cam gave her that sad, lopsided little smile, she found her feet had become rooted to the porch.

The more people arrived, heavy-laden with food as Dan had predicted, the nervier Shal became. Acutely aware of Cam, she was unable to relax. Actively trying *not* to watch him, she kept catching herself doing just that.

Who had Cam been at the boutique with? Had he read her note? Where did they stand, now?

With the majority of adults populating the lounge, Shal retreated to the open plan kitchen-dining to make her favourite lemon zest and mustard dressing. It took her a while to realise Saffy was hiding under the large wooden dining table, pushed up against the wall to form a buffet for later.

Shal was somewhat envious of the bolt-hole the little girl had commandeered, right under everyone's noses. Deep down she wished *she* was able to retreat, too.

Perhaps no one would miss her…

Neatly sidestepping the floral sisters and Maureen, with their raucous laughter in the hall, Shal scooted up to her bedroom to retrieve a large gift bag from her wardrobe. Returning downstairs, she swiped the kitchen shears and knocked lightly on the dining table top, before poking her head under and whispering, "Can I come in?"

She was met by a solemn stare and a slight shake of the head. The beads on the ends of Saffy's cornrows chinked together twice, then lay silent.

"No? Oh, that's a shame." Kneeling at eye level, Shal looked pointedly at the gift bag, then back at the stubborn little face. "I was hoping to share my present with you."

That was all it took for the welcome mat to roll out, and Saffy and Shal became joint occupants of the secret cavern. Quiet as church mice, they opened the boxes to form a family of dolls, and for twenty blissful minutes all was well with the world.

People came and went from the kitchen, topping up wine, getting more ice, and popping caps off beer. If anyone noticed the disappearance of the two dark-haired girls, they didn't mention it. It wasn't until Saffy dropped one of the dolls on the tiles with a clatter that anyone ventured over to check under the table.

As woolly farm socks and jean clad legs wandered closer, Saffy clamped her hand over her mouth to muffle nervous giggles.

Shal had pulled her knees up to hide behind, so when Cam squatted down he was faced with two pairs of wide eyes. One the deepest, richest brown, the other oceanic.

"Hiding?" he whispered, looking from Saffy to Shal.

Both dark heads nodded in unison.

He took in the dolls, the scissors, the discarded packaging, and the cramped conditions.

Shal had bought a bi-racial family for Saffy. She definitely hadn't done that by accident and the knowledge softened his heart a smidgen.

"Room for one more?"

Both heads shook vigorously.

"Aw, pity. Because I have chips." Cam held up the big bag of ready-salted he'd been hiding behind his back, and Shal's eyes widened as her lips parted, letting him know she wanted some. So, apparently, did his little cousin-once-removed, Saffron, because she quickly scooted sideways and made room.

"You have to be quiet, though," Saffy warned in a stage whisper as he folded himself into the tight space, his lower spine crimped against the wall. "It's our secret hideout." She waited patiently as he opened the chips, then daintily removed a few from the offered handful. "You're very hot, and a bit *big*." The four year-old pruned up her mouth and pointed to his feet.

"Sorry about that." Cam held back a smirk, trying to wiggle his toes further out of sight from anyone in the kitchen.

Saffy sighed theatrically. "I guess you can't help it."

Turning to offer Shal the chips too, he conked his head on the table's crossbeam.

Her face was extremely close, and the situation ridiculous.

"Hi." He smiled tentatively.

Although she still looked a touch nervy, Shal smiled back.

"Hi."

"Chips?"

"If you insist." Shal cupped her hands, and he dumped the handful in before getting another small mountain for himself and Saffy to share.

Aside from the odd "Shhh!" from Saffy when she heard footsteps approaching, they all munched in a companionable, salty heaven until they reached the bottom of the bag.

Assuming director's rights, Saffron then handed Cam the dark-skinned male doll. Shal was just as solemnly given the one with long blonde hair, and Saffy held both the teen doll and the little sister with braids sticking out at absurd right angles.

Saffy's two immediately began to argue in whispered American accents about who was going to hold the plastic dog's leash.

Cam turned back to Shal, amusement obvious. The boyish grin made her stomach flip-flop as his doll moved to stand next to hers.

"You look beautiful tonight, sweetheart." Cam spoke softly, putting on a southern American drawl and somehow consolidating the cowboy image. "New dress?"

"Vaaaat, zis old sing?" Shal aimed for Hollywood Transylvanian. "Vy, it's ancient daaaarling!"

Cam's chuckle earned him a furious "Shhh!" from Saffy.

Looking deeply into Cam's eyes, Shal watched his mirth slowly drain and seriousness creep back in. "I wanted to apologise. I never meant to hurt you." Stepping out of character, he used his own accent—which gained him Saffy's attention again.

"What did you do?" The four year old managed to make the query an admonishment by using the age-old tone of *here-we-go-again*.

Cam blinked. Looked down at the doll, then back to Shal. "I hurt her feelings," he returned quietly.

"You need to buy her *flowers*," Saffy counselled, matter-of-factly.

The side of Cam's mouth tugged slowly back up into a sideways grin. "I did that already."

"Oh, then you need to kissandmakeup." Saffy shoved all four words together as if they were one.

Maybe they *should* be one.

Shal's gaze automatically moved to Cam's lips, and when she glanced up he'd followed suit, staring at her mouth. The mutual focus made her acutely aware of the last time they'd been this close, and she chewed on her bottom lip.

It was snug under the table and suddenly her cheeks were burning hot.

Feeling pressure against the doll in her hand, she looked down and laughed. Cam's doll was kissing hers, along with resounding sound effects.

When she looked up again, Cam was closer.

Much closer.

Her breath hitched, but she found she didn't want to pull away as slowly and ever so gently Cam angled his head under the crossbeam to kiss her lips.

Cameron Dante's mouth was designed for this very purpose. His generous lower lip softly caressed, and there was an underlying tenderness in the simple action.

It wasn't a sexual kiss, but neither was it one of mere friendship. There was something else moving into Shal's chest to settle there for those brief seconds when Cam's lips were on hers. The whisper of an unspoken promise. A question. A coaxing pull.

"There! *All* better," Saffy decreed before deferring focus back to her doll's squabble.

Shal opened her eyes to Cam's soft golden regard, and he smiled at her. The warm glow flushing her cheeks relocated smoothly to settle in her belly, like a sip of hot tea on a chilly morning.

"Thank you for the flowers, they're really beautiful," she whispered.

Saffy's four-year-old logic was near perfect in its simplicity, because after kissandmakeup, it *did* seem to be heading towards 'all better.'

The returning calm was welcome, and the unspoken truce held. Even when they crawled out from under the table to find Adele and Poppy regarding them with raised eyebrows from the kitchen, they held a united front.

It felt almost normal between them, right up until the casual, stand around dinner, when everyone piled into the dining area to load their plates with food.

Daniel, his paper plate topped up for the second time, stood next to Shal and made a big deal of complimenting her on her 'exceptional salads.' She didn't think anything of his gentle ribbing at the time, or of reaching up to pat the big rugby guy's arm and smiling at the private joke.

She happened to glance across the breakfast bar at Cam, and was surprised to be met again with a cool, narrow-eyed stare.

What?

A couple of kisses and she wasn't supposed to *talk* to other males now?

Cam left early. He couldn't stand being there a minute longer.

Bloody Daniel.

Bloody fuckin' Dante D.

Rather than head home, he drove to the lookout to sit for an hour and watch the sea shift and dance under the moon. Moana and Marama had nothing to say about his undefinable relationship with Shalom Hoffner, but the even whoosh and crash of the waves hitting the shore reminded him how to breathe in, and breathe out.

Shal bummed breakfast off Daniel the following morning. She came down to grab a cup of tea and he happened to be banging around in the kitchen making up a batch of French toast.

Her stomach growled loudly at the heavenly scent of hot butter in the pan, and Daniel laughed, adding a couple more eggs to the soaking mix.

A few minutes later Shal was presented with a mouth-watering plate of cinnamon-sugared bliss. The maple syrup and fried bananas on the side were an added bonus.

"I could get used to this."

"You'll have to put a ring on it then," Daniel joked. "I *am* available, in case you're wondering."

She wrinkled up her nose at him. "Really? You bloody Dantes are suckers for commitment. Offer you a ball and you'd gladly slap on a chain and shackle it around your ankle. Cam's just the same," she complained.

Daniel shrugged. "It's in the blood."

"Yeah. I know." Shal sighed. "One of you could always break the mould, you know. Whip up breakfast then go on your merry way, spreading French toast and joy wherever you went."

Daniel stopped what he was doing to rest his hip against the counter, contemplating her. "There's usually a pay-off for that kind of in-house service," he drawled.

"True." And it'd been thoughts of 'pay-off' with Cam that had interfered with Shal's beauty sleep last night. "Down side, I'd get pudgy after a while with the high sugar content and wouldn't be able to fit into all my favourite clothes."

"Well, that puts paid to that idea then." Daniel looked at Shal a little too searchingly for her liking, reminding her very much of his mother and brother with his head cocked a little to one side.

"Though I think you'll find a Dante harder to shake than your usual garden-variety bloke," he added slightly ominously.

Harder to shake. That was Shal's point exactly. Cam was on the search for his next long term thing, so he clearly wasn't put on this earth for her.

"I don't doubt you," she finally answered, trying to keep it light and ambiguous. "And it's such a shame, because that's possibly the best French toast I've ever had." Putting her chin in her hands, she watched Daniel clean down the bench.

"Cam makes a mean oven-baked muesli with honey and oats," Daniel stated candidly, his eyes twinkling with merriment. "Packed full of seeds and dried fruit."

He'd seen straight through her, and the realisation was a little galling.

"So?" Shal attempted to feign disinterest.

"Just saying. Healthier option." Daniel nudged one eyebrow up in query. "Fruit smoothies are another one of his specialties. You strike me as a fruit smoothie kind of girl."

"Hmm." She gave Daniel a non-committal response, but her mouth remained in the flat line of the 'm' long after the sound had passed.

Fruit smoothies and Cam for breakfast, a very palatable duo.

She gazed out at the courtyard for some time before changing tack. "What was Poppy angry about last night?" When Daniel's mother had been talking to Adele, the younger woman seemed to be putting a lot of effort into soothing her aunt's ruffled feathers.

"Nothing much. She had some things to get off her chest but I think I'm back in her good books now."

"What did you do to torment her?"

"Torment is a strong word." Daniel scratched at his morning stubble.

"Piss her off, then."

He laughed. "Her old family farm came back on the market a while back, so I bought it."

"What's wrong with that?"

Daniel turned back from putting the eggs away. "Ghosts she'd laid to rest, I guess. And it happens to be in Wānaka."

"Oh, right. She wants her boys home in Ōtepoti."

"Yes and no. We've come to an agreement."

Shal snorted. Poppy was a wily negotiator. "Does it involve the sacrifice of your firstborn?"

"Nooo." Daniel drew the word out, before jokingly adding, "Though the mention of grandchildren comes up way too frequently, now. The heat was off there for a while when Cam and... uh..."

To Shal's surprise, embarrassment suffused Daniel's face, rising up from his neck in a faint wash of red.

"But that didn't work out, so..." Daniel busied himself drying his hands on the tea towel, eyes averted.

"What didn't work out?"

"Cam and Jody."

"They were that serious?" Shal leant forward, eager to get more information on the Jody front.

But all she got from Daniel was a grim nod.

Of course they would've talked about children, they were engaged. And Cam would be the obvious choice if you were the kind of woman who was looking to have kids. Kind, generous, and honest.

Nice smelling, too. He was definitely that.

17

"Two days—two days—two days," Saffy chanted, skipping down the wide hallway as Adele removed the coat from her four-year-old moving target and hung it to drip-dry on the bannister. Shal smiled, remembering last night it'd been, 'Three days—three days—three days.'

The countdown was on everyone's mind.

Shal took the plastic sheathed flower girl and bridesmaid's dresses upstairs and hid them in her wardrobe next to Katie's wedding gown, as far from sticky hands as possible. It had been stressful at the dressmaker's with Saffy wanting to touch everything.

She checked the time and panicked, remembering to grab her jacket again before heading back downstairs.

Cramming as much as she could into the last couple of days, her usually meticulous schedule was now in hyperdrive. Overstretched with the timing of Links and Aroha's pickup, she was still loath to pass the errand off to someone else. Aroha had asked her specifically, and that had never happened before.

Shal needn't have worried. Ōtepoti traffic, rather than Te Whanganui-a-Tara, meant the road out to the airport was practically deserted. Consequently, she arrived a full five minutes before the couple landed—more than enough time to buy a couple of Otago postcards at the kiosk to send to the U.S. side of her family. One a picture of the old Railway Station, and the other an aerial view of Sandfly Bay.

Shal had an old photo of Aroha and Links taken at the same beach on the shelf in her Te Whanganui-a-Tara apartment, along with others from the same year. She'd snapped the high school sweethearts on a picnic rug, Links sporting an easy grin, Aroha a little more suspicious of both camera and photographer.

Links had run like a greyhound back then. Built for speed, his body was long-limbed and gangly, all ribs, knees, and elbows. He also had a large heart, soft enough to cushion any of Aroha's unintentionally sharp edges.

Aroha and Katie were firm friends, their connection going back decades, but Shal had come on the scene a lot later. Aroha had shown little interest in forming a connection, and Shal had honoured that. She knew she wasn't everyone's cup of tea. Instead, they held an uneasy sort of amnesty in respect for their mutual friends.

When Links strode across the tarmac and into the baggage pickup area of the small airport, both of Shal's hands flew to her mouth to hold in her exclamation. She knew he'd been fitted with new fitness prosthetics recently, because Aroha had told her on the phone, but watching them in action was something else. It was the first time she'd seen Links move like an athlete in eight years, and the confidence and pride on his face said it all.

Unaware a tear had sneaked out to slide down her face, she started when Aroha handed her a little plastic-wrapped packet of tissues.

"I had the same reaction the first time," Aroha conceded, though her mouth was pursed tight like the pull string on a kid's swimming bag.

"Oh, my God! Links, you look amazing! You move so—"

"Just like he used to."

"*Yes*! Do the others know?"

"Not yet." Links grinned from his full height. "Let's go and show these off, shall we?"

The old crowd were meeting for a fish'n'chip night at the Dundas Street house to celebrate Links and Aroha's homecoming. It also became a celebration of Links' return to form. He'd been in touch with his high school sprint coach and was back on the track— cautiously optimistic about how far he could go on the Para athletics scene.

Along with the scent of deep-fried food and tomato sauce, the air was warm with the banter between long missed friends.

New to the group was Mackenzie, Rue's brother. A younger, blonder version of the Englishman, he'd made the long haul from Sussex to stand as Rue's best man.

Rue seemed to naturally unwind around Mac, smiling more easily and talking with more animation. It made his English reserve appear much less pronounced.

Adele seemed calmer too, as Rosa had come to pick up Saffy for 'granny-time,' which involved an overnight stay.

Aroha was explaining the payout battle with the insurance company covering her and Links' earthquake-damaged house, and how it was finally over. The couple were planning to return home to Ōtepoti soon, with a much larger nest egg than they'd ever dared hope.

Partway through the evening, Shal pulled Adele up on the nicknames she kept using for Cameron and Daniel: Camry and Datsun.

"Why car names?" she wondered aloud.

Daniel, overhearing the question, jokingly clamped a hand over his cousin's mouth as if to mute the story, piquing Shal's curiosity even further.

Katie obligingly picked up as narrator instead.

In high school, Cam had lost his tender young heart (and judging by the innuendo, his virginity) to a senior named Amy-Marie Stirling.

According to Katie, Amy-Marie had golden hair down to her waist and soft doe-brown eyes. All the boys had fawned over her, including the Dante brothers.

Amy-Marie's sole parent had owned a Toyota Camry which the

teen was allowed to drive. Handy, as Cam hadn't gotten his full licence yet. They'd parked up on Tomahawk headland for their first date, overlooking the Pacific at the local park-and-shag, and the rest was history.

Coincidentally, Daniel had purchased *his* first car (a beaten up old Datsun Sunny) at around the same time, and unbeknownst to Cameron, had been seeing the same girl.

Amy-Marie had driven Camry up to the lookout one Friday night, and test-driven his older brother, Datsun, the following Saturday.

When the truth had eventually bubbled over, it culminated in hot fury between the brothers and ended with a trip to A&E. Apparently Poppy had coined the nicknames that night while the three of them had sat stonily in the after-hours, waiting for the surgeon to reset Daniel's nose.

Shal stared at Daniel. His nose *was* a little crooked now she took note. Most would assume an old rugby injury, but now she knew better.

Cam had done that over a girl?

The primitiveness of the act didn't quite fit in with her perception of his level-headed nature.

Katie drew Adele, Shal, and Aroha aside after the take-out remains had been cleared away. Aroha had missed the fitting for her bridesmaid's dress, and although the dressmaker had worked to a full set of her measurements, the woman was standing by to make any last minute adjustments tomorrow.

Aroha attached the stick-on bra under sufferance, but it was evident she approved of the dress and the overall effect once she was in it. Katie caught Shal's eye and they puffed out a unified breath of relief.

Aroha on-board was highly preferable to Aroha against.

Swishing from side to side in the full-length mirror, Aroha put one hand on her hip and struck a pose. The halter neck showed off her toned shoulders and the deep teal complemented her dark colouring.

She was much less enamoured with the strappy heels when Shal brought them out.

"Shit! How am I supposed to walk in these?"

"Practice," Shal cajoled, kneeling to do up the tiny buckles.

"Check out how they sex up your legs," Adele enthused, trying to sell the concept by strutting about in matching heels, minus the dress.

Adele was taller than Katie but just as curvy, and they were unmistakably related due to both colouring and features. The younger of the two, Adele had lush corkscrew curls in strawberry blonde and looked like a near-naked Celtic warrior. In heels.

"Put some clothes on, you old tart," Katie hassled her sister, sitting on the bed watching her three bridesmaids preen.

"If *I'm* old, then you've got one foot in the grave," Adele shot back.

Shal and Adele helped each other into their gowns until finally all three were standing in front of Katie. The bride-to-be stood slowly, holding her cheeks in both hands as if to hold all her emotion in.

"Wow. Just… *wow!*" Katie was grinning, even though her eyes were moist. "Aroha, you're gonna have to suck-it-up on the shoe front. The three of you look *amazing*."

"Katie says you actually have *two* sisters." Adele turned to Shal. They were back in the lounge, and due to the lack of seats available had perched themselves on the opposing arms of Katie's armchair.

"Yes, I do." Shal leaned her back against the wall and pulled one knee up to her chest. "Half-sisters. Bianca's about to turn fifteen and lives in Te Whanganui-a-Tara, so I see quite a bit of her."

Bianca had been so cute when she was little, but was now obsessed with surpassing Shal in height; insisting on going back-to-back every time they met.

"And the other one?"

"Eliza was born a few days shy of my nineteenth birthday. She's nine now. We all share the same father. There was talk of an older brother at one stage, but we haven't been able to find him." With a touch of discomfort Shal re-positioned her shoulders, realising she'd just disclosed too much information to the suddenly silent room. "My father likes to spread himself around," she quipped, lightening her tone to bely how much strife he'd put them all through. "David is…"

She studied her manicure instead of finishing her sentence. It was hard to think of the best way to sum her father up.

"A man-slut," Aroha finished bluntly from her position on the sofa.

Telling it painfully straight, as always.

"Yeah, I guess so," Shal agreed, though there was a touch of reluctance in her, and she did not look up to meet anyone's gaze.

David was self-absorbed. An opportunist. Always in search of the next shiny new thing to fill the whopping great void in his life. Shal chewed on her inner cheek, all too aware of the comparisons that could so easily be drawn to herself.

Cam sat next to Aroha, soaking in the conversation without adding to it or making his presence obvious. But Shal could feel his eyes on her, like they had been all night.

Aroha thankfully switched topics, extolling Links' current form and staunchly boasting that her long-standing partner could whip anyone's ass at the beach on Sunday if they dared challenge him. Shal didn't doubt it, though Mason had been the only one in the group who'd ever been cocky enough to think he could beat Links.

Finally composed enough to raise her head and scan the laughing faces around her, Shal had the distinct feeling someone was missing.

Links was the only one who wasn't smiling. Their solemn gazes caught and held, and Shal realised with sudden clarity just how much Links must miss Mason—how much he probably always would.

Grief was a strange and confusing emotion.

Links had lost his mate, his drinking buddy, his brother-from-another-mother… The one who'd stolen his ability to run, and almost stripped him of his life.

Daniel had a previous engagement with some rugby connections, so got up to leave part-way through the evening. Shal followed him down the hall to the front door. She needed to ask if

Links, Aroha, Saffy, and herself could get a lift to the ceremony practice with him tomorrow, as Adele needed to borrow her car.

Adele's husband, James, was supposedly arriving in the morning, and Shal had the distinct impression the couple had things to discuss in private.

Shal leaned her back against the front door as she explained, effectively blocking Daniel's way out.

"You'd let Adele drive your Alfa Romeo?" Daniel didn't try to mask his surprise.

"Sure." Shal wondered at his tone. "She's got her license, hasn't she?"

"I assume so."

"Oh, well then." She shrugged, pushing her hair behind her ear and stepping aside. "That's fine. If we can tag along with you, I won't need it."

Cam watched Shal as she followed Daniel out of the lounge and disappeared, the green, leafy scent of her lingering a moment after she'd moved past him on the sofa.

She was wearing a casual knitted sweater in deep blue that hugged her figure and grazed the top of her shoulders in a wide neck. He hadn't been able to take his eyes off her all evening, her finely turned collarbones and the honey sheen on her skin.

In contrast, Shal had appeared to spend a lot of *her* time studying Daniel, and right now she was out there alone with him...

The take-out food no longer felt settled in Cam's stomach, and once again he was longing to be anywhere but here.

Tonight was supposed to be all about Links and Aroha though, and it was still early. He'd have to grin-and-bear-it a little longer.

Using coffee as his excuse, Cam removed himself from the others and went out to boil the kettle, his blood simmering along with the water.

Jealousy—the worst emotion.

Anger—an easier one to get a handle on, and definitely the more familiar of the two.

"You read my mind," Shal mused from the kitchen doorway, her surprise at finding someone else in the room sliding into trepidation as Cam turned to glare at her.

She kicked herself for walking in on him when he'd obviously come in here to be alone. Their interactions had been weird all evening, and now her hankering for a cup of tea had landed her in the hot water she'd been trying to avoid.

"What's got your goat?" she muttered in a half-baked attempt at levity.

"What's got my goat?" Cam countered. "You've got to be kidding, asking me that right now."

Shal had a reputation for being obtuse where Cam was concerned, but she knew fury when she saw it, and Cam was holding onto the tail of that emotion right now. She blinked across at him, not understanding where this latest bout of distemper had come from.

"You'd better get out of here," he growled.

Taking an unconscious step backwards, her shoulder met with the door jam and suddenly Cam was striding towards her.

Shal squeaked and made an unbidden flinch to the side as his hand came up to rest against the wood and block her exit.

"You think I'd hit you, Shal? Do you even know me at all?" Cam's voice dipped low in disappointment, and Shal's breath caught.

Perhaps she didn't.

It wouldn't be the first time she'd completely misread a member of the male species. So maybe, just maybe, she didn't know Cameron Dante in the slightest.

Shal closed her eyes against the thought, and the face she didn't quite recognise as her old flatmate's—so close to hers but holding no trace of its usual affection.

"Your confidence in my character is heart-warming." Cam was being sarcastic, but Shal's fear had resolutely poked a hole through his black mood and registered. He could recognise her fight or flight reflex attempting to kick in.

It was with sinking sobriety he realised he'd actually frightened her, so *he* was the asshole in this scenario. Slowly removing his arm, he used that hand to drag across his tired eyes.

"I'm sorry," he muttered. "I didn't mean to scare you. Go." He flicked his head to indicate the door to the lounge, thankfully still closed on all the curious eyes.

Shal stood her ground, chin rising slightly in defiance.

Fight, then. Not flight.

Figured.

"No." Shal spoke the word distinctly, though it wasn't particularly confident in its delivery.

"You won't go?"

"No. I'm not afraid of you." But the statement was more likely said to convince herself, not him.

Cam reached for her then, his heart lurching sickeningly when Shal initially flinched backward. But with his hands gentle on her shoulders, he drew her inexorably towards him until her front was lined up against his—like two sides of a sandwich.

After a long moment, Shal's arms slid tentatively around his waist and she was holding him, too.

"Why are you so angry with me?" she murmured into his chest.

Why? Because of the two, she'd choose his brother. And if Cam was being honest, there was no one to blame for that but himself.

Shal felt the tension slowly ebb from Cam as their breathing evened out. Her forehead still fitted perfectly against his neck if she laid her head a certain way on his shoulder. From there, she could watch the thick pulse throb at the base of his neck above his pounamu, and smell the familiar, comforting scent of wood on him.

Cam brought his thumb under her chin, lifting and angling her face to study her, and suddenly this wasn't remotely like the hugs they'd shared in the past. With that single assessing look, Shal became acutely aware of every inch that Cam had pressed up against her.

Muscle and sinew—a hint of softness over an uncompromising framework.

She could see his intent well before he moved, but didn't try to pull away as Cam dipped his head and kissed her eyelids, one by one, then her cheeks.

It took him an age to reach her waiting mouth.

"Because I want you, Shal. I've always wanted you to be with me," Cam whispered across her lips before delving to taste her again, and again.

Each sliding kiss grew more forceful, taking more from her and asking for more in return. The silky touch of Cam's tongue slid across hers, awakening another calibre of need as his hand cradled the back of her neck. She moaned, opened, invited him in, and they careened together into the rising heat.

Both were breathing as heavily as if they'd been running races on the sand when Cam pulled back to stare at her.

The raw edge of his emotive state still shone in his eyes, close to the surface, but it no longer scared her. Rather, it heightened her own. What Cam exuded was so much deeper than anything she was used to, and just like in the half-finished kitchen up on Park Street, pure excitement flowed through her veins every time their lips sought each other and connected.

Then Cam was cradling her close to his chest again, the heavy thud of his blood-flow shuddering beneath her ear. He stroked her back with one long, languid movement before stepping away.

"I'm sorry," he said again, this time shrugging one shoulder towards his ear as his mouth formed a wry little twist. His eyes were soft and dark, lips still reddened by the pressure of her own. "I didn't intend to do that. It just kills me to see you with Daniel."

"With Daniel?" Her eyes widened. What the hell was he on about? "I'm not with Daniel."

"No?" Cam studied her watchfully.

"No!" The word exploded out of her mouth. "Look, just because I came on to you, doesn't make it okay to act like I'm doing the rounds. You turned me down, I might add, nulling and voiding your input." Her cheeks, already warm from making out, now burned with affront.

"I still want to be with you, Shal. That won't change. If you'd agree to see me seriously. Exclusively." Cam touched his index finger to her top lip. "Just you and me. No one else in the picture."

"No," she whispered against Cam's work-roughened fingertip, panicked by the steady sureness of his gaze.

"Okay, then." Cam nodded sagely, but at the same time he was taking a full step back from her, and not just physically. She could see by his shuttered expression just how deeply he'd felt the cut of rejection.

"Don't act all affronted." Her backhand was purely defensive; a direct reaction to the sad eyes Cam had just played. "I know you've got your fingers in another pie." It wasn't until the words were out of her mouth that Shal realised how crude the saying came across when used in this context. "So to speak," she added hastily.

Cam looked vaguely confused, then spoke slowly, as if to someone he suspected was a few biscuits short of a packet. "I'm single."

"*Right*, except when you have company up in the boutique apartment." She could be sarcastic too. "You don't have to lie about it Cam. It's not like we're going out."

"I'm being totally honest." And Shal knew he was, as a general rule. "I'm not seeing anyone right now."

Cam was either a decent actor or he was telling the truth. He looked feasibly confused and suitably frustrated.

"Except whoever you had upstairs the other night," Shal pressed, still unsure.

"I was alone at the boutique. Pieta—"

"I *knew* it!" God. She felt sick.

"Let me finish." Cam's exasperation was now coming through loud and clear. "Pieta called, and I had to leave to meet her at the studio."

"Oh, I get it, at the *studio*." Shal attempted to roll her eyes, but the movement only made her feel more nauseous.

"Christ! What is this?" Cam threw his hands up and glared at her.

This? Shal wasn't sure, but it felt frighteningly similar to possessiveness, and scarily close to jealousy.

"Nothing. We have absolutely nothing." She renounced the emotions bubbling up in her just as quickly as they'd appeared. "I offered you pretzels because that's all I have right now, and you said 'no.' You don't want my pretzels. Then you do. You accuse me of seeing Daniel. I'm not. You're with Pieta, or you aren't. Whatever. It's absolutely none of my business."

Cam grabbed her by the rough of the neck and brought his lips back down on hers. Hard. It was a kiss of desperate need, a kiss of heat and frustration, and she returned it with every fibre of her being; one leg sliding up to hook around his and pull him that little bit closer.

"Of course I want your bloody pretzels. I'm in love with you, you idiot," Cam ground out, pushing her back against the doorframe and kissing her once more for good measure.

"Stop *saying* that!" Shal jutted her chin up, nudging him off when he would've kissed her again.

"Saying what? You're an idiot? Or I love you?"

"Both." Shal shoved him in the chest. "Forget what I said in the bloody note. I've changed my mind."

"Note? What note?"

"With the flat pack," she snapped.

Cam may as well have been blindfolded, stumbling through this mash-up with Shal in semi-darkness, without a working torch. He kept bumbling into conversational obstacles that had no apparent connection to what they'd been talking about.

Fingers in a pie—Pieta—a flat pack—a note.

"The shelving unit?"

"No." Shal rolled her eyes at him again, reminding him of her nineteen-year-old self. "The table."

Oh, right. He knew the pack she meant, now. He'd been up at the boutique at Jonno's request a couple of nights ago with every intention of whipping together the simple dining table and chairs.

Then Pieta had interrupted, calling about a second layer of backing vocals on the ballad they were working on.

Urgent, as usual.

The singer had talked him into dropping his evening plans to meet her at the studio. Even when he'd switched her to speakerphone, he hadn't been able to concentrate enough on the flat pack to make much headway. He'd only completed one chair in the ten minutes he'd been up there.

Cam couldn't see the connection between that and a note. Had he missed something?

"I didn't finish it," he admitted slowly.

"Then don't. I'll do it myself." Shal had retreated back to huffy, her lips in a childish pout and her perfectly straight nose all out of joint.

Daniel wasn't back by the time the three women headed off to bed. Katie and Rue ferried a jet-lagged Mackenzie home to get an early night, so it was just Links and Cam who sat in the lounge, talking.

Cam had missed his old flatmate and the ease of their friendship.

"Katie said there are numerous music offers coming in due to the Pieta thing." Links clearly wanted to know more.

"One or two. Sticking with Pieta is my best option right now, though." Cam managed to neatly sidestep the larger conversation about career choice, which every one of his friends seemed to have an opinion on.

He could hear the shower running in the master ensuite, and what was going on up there was paramount in his thoughts, so he missed Links' next question.

When he looked back from the ceiling, his fingers steepled in thought, he caught his friend's expectant look.

"Sorry, what was that?"

"I said, what are you going to do about it?"

"About what?"

Links tapped his own temple, as if thinking deeply. "The conflict in Timbuktu." Leaning forward, he eased one prosthetic off, rubbing at the nub below his knee before beginning to work on the other leg. The view of Links' amputation sites had become a normalised event. It'd been a long time since Cam had felt the raw jolt of discomfort that'd affected him in the early days. He wondered if it was the same for Links?

"Shal, of course. What are you going to do about Shal?" As the old house settled around them with the odd creak, Links re-asked the question Cam had been rolling over in the back of his mind all evening. All fortnight. Ever since he'd known she was coming back down for the wedding, if he was being honest.

"I wasn't planning on doing anything right now." No matter how epic that would be. The ensuite shower was still running and Cam couldn't shake the picture in his head, Shal wrapping her leg around his like she had in the kitchen…

"Reason being?"

He shrugged. "She's a friend. I'd like it to be more, of course, but she's just looking for a fuck buddy right now." He picked up his coffee mug and looked into its empty depths, as if they might hold the answers to his best way forward.

"Shal *said* that?" Links' eyes were round with incredulity when Cam glanced up.

"Not in so many words, but, yeah. She's happy to sleep together as long as there are no strings attached."

"*Jeee*-sus! So, back up a minute, you turned her down?"

Cam nodded in the affirmative, not feeling particularly great about it.

"What the hell, Cam? You've always wanted her!" Links exploded. "I've had to listen to you moon on and on about her for years! Playing hard to get *now* isn't going to get you anywhere."

"I'm not playing hard to get. I want more." He attempted to explain.

"Dude. Take it from me, we *all* want more. But being handed something you've always hankered after, on a platter for chrissakes, and then quibbling about the condiments? That's just plain rude. When life hands you something, you need to fuckin' grab it. You think you got handed a lemon? Find the chick with the vodka and have a damn party."

"It'll kill me," Cam decided aloud, his voice lower and grimmer than he'd intended as he ran a hand over his face. "Shal keeps her relationships open—sees other people. I couldn't deal with that. You know I'm in love with her."

"Every man and his dog knows you're in love with her. You may as well have it tattooed on your forehead," Links muttered unhelpfully, using his hands to edge himself forward. "Shal's been screwed around, it's not rocket science she'd be skittish about getting tied into something serious. And knowing you, you probably got into this love crap straight off the bat—told her you're her forever guy."

Cam blinked, then nodded slowly as he measured the weight of Links' words. That's exactly what he'd done. Twice now.

"So, you freaked her out." Links whooshed out a long breath as he lay back on the upright sofa cushions. "Granted, she's likely to rip your heart out and stomp down hard on the bleeding organ. It's got slam-dunk written all over it. But she's interested in *you*, mate. You!" Links lifted his head long enough to point his finger in jesting accusation. He relaxed back to gaze up at the freshly painted ceiling, hands behind his head. "That's worth something. And if you don't do as you're asked and service the nice lady, I don't think we can be mates anymore."

"Service what nice lady?"

Cam and Links turned in unison towards the polite inquiry from the doorway, so engrossed in conversation they'd both missed the sound of someone entering.

"Jesus, Dan, you scared the shit out of me!" Cam spluttered.

"Who are you considering bumping uglies with to keep Links on as a Facebook friend?" Daniel prodded.

"Who do *you* think?" Links' sarcasm dripped as he pointed to the level above them.

"Ah, the lovely Shalom." Daniel settled himself into one of the armchairs, one socked foot on his opposing knee as he rubbed at his old operation site absently.

"Knee giving you shit, old man?" Links razzed, not particularly unkindly.

"Fuckin' oath it is," Daniel assured him before turning back to Cam. "Not worried you're punching above your weight with this one, little bro?" Copying Link's action, he pointed to the ceiling.

"Contract's under offer," Cam stated darkly, pissed off his sibling could so accurately pinpoint his own misgivings.

"Really? *Interesting.* So why are you…" Daniel gestured to the ground floor. "And not…" Again, he pointed in the vague direction of the master bedroom.

"He's fussing about the long term forecast, like a true Nana,"

Links interjected before Cam could answer. "Deciding whether he might get more rainfall than sunshine, in the long run."

Daniel took some time to consider that, searching first one face, then the other. "Just because it's on offer today, doesn't mean it will be tomorrow," he finally decided, scratching at his chin thoughtfully. "In my experience, when a woman thinks you're not interested she's likely to move on. The best way to look at this is a one-day-only sale."

"One-day-only sale? Gee, that's not the least bit insulting." Cam was starting to get riled, which was understandable considering the other two occupants of the room seemed to be nudging him there on purpose.

"If you're not considering buying, I could always—" Daniel tried another tack and hit the mother-load dead on.

"Don't you fuckin' dare!" Cam was up and over in Daniel's face before his brother even had time to get out of his chair.

Daniel raised his palms in a gesture of surrender. "I guess you've got this one, then," he placated calmly.

"Yeah, too right I've got this one!" Cam thundered, furious. "You even sniff in her direction and I'll break your nose!"

"Point taken."

"I mean it." He narrowed his eyes.

"Yours, not mine. Got it." Daniel eased up out of the armchair and made a show of stretching. "I'm off to bed." Cam continued to scowl at him, not trusting the smirk. "*Mine*, not hers."

Cam was in the process of looking away when he caught Daniel sending Links a large wink. If he wasn't very much mistaken by the returned grin, he'd just played that round directly into their hands.

"You asshole." He punched Daniel on the shoulder as his brother tried to slip past.

"*Ow*, shit. What was that for?"

"For being an asshole," he muttered.

Cam remained standing after Daniel climbed the stairs. He was exhausted in every way and knew if he sat back down on the sofa he'd end up sleeping on it.

He automatically reached one foot out to act as a stabilising wheel-brake as Links flipped himself expertly upwards and sideways into his waiting wheelchair, then saw Cam to the front door.

"What was our university motto?" Links wisecracked as he held the door open with one narrow wheel.

"*Sapere aude.*" Cam turned to look at his old friend. "Dare to be wise," he translated quietly, and the Latin of the university motto rang strangely prophetic.

They'd known each other since preschool, and even through the loss of his limbs and his God-given-talent for track and field, Links really hadn't changed all that much over the years. Cam knew his mate just wanted the best for him.

He thought about it all the way home, parking in the driveway and killing the lights. Rather than going in, he began to mull on the confused altercation he'd had with Shal in the kitchen at Dundas Street.

He'd been in the wrong—had no business being angry with her. She could choose to be with whomever she chose. He had absolutely no jurisdiction over her. None at all.

Her mouth had tasted delicious, velvet soft like sun-ripened fruit. Once he'd started kissing her, it had been incredibly hard to stop. Cam shook his head to clear the memory.

What the hell had she been going on about? Pieta at the boutique. Something about the flat pack, and a note.

He leant down to check the keys on his key ring. The boutique ones were still threaded on next to his Dundas Street set. Starting the engine again, he was backing out of the driveway before his brain had fully caught up with his actions.

18

Listening to...
Venus - James Reid
From the album: Supersystem - The Feelers

Cam woke to a grey day, and on a whim took the morning off to go surfing. Driving out to the peninsula without a clear destination in his head, Sandfly Bay drew him in as if by magnetic force.

It wasn't hard to go back eight years and see himself at twenty—twenty-one. Links was right, he'd always wanted Shal. He'd expected to snap out of it. Move on from it. The all consuming, crushing nature of it had certainly eased when she'd been out of his direct vicinity for all those years.

He'd been dating other women, some casual, some serious, never considering what would happen if Shal ever showed an interest, because she never had.

Cam had been dead serious about Jody. They would've been married by now if it had all gone to original plan. Married and struggling, probably. He still had some hurt there, heavily discordant in his chest, but he knew deep down he'd dodged a bullet.

A particularly fine, platinum bullet.

He'd loved her, but sometimes that wasn't enough. Jody

would've been a hard person to live with, a tricky personality to support. 'High maintenance,' to coin Katie's words.

A victim of her own insecurities, Jody had been constantly seeking confirmation from others. It hadn't taken long for Cam's regard to mean less. He was old news. She'd sought approval from a veritable queue, but it had been her infatuation with Daniel that'd pushed their relationship to breaking point.

Pushed both relationships to breaking point.

Cam stopped at the lookout and found he'd been unconsciously rubbing the bridge of his nose as he thought about his brother. Jody hadn't been the first female to cause a disagreement. The wrestling and scuffling of the brothers' childhood play had escalated into an all out brawl over the girl who'd played them both when they were just teens.

Amy-Marie Stirling, the little vixen.

Cam had thought, at the time, the brown-eyed blonde had been sent to him from heaven above. His mother held an entirely different view, and still referred to her as 'the wily little witch.'

Poppy had kicked both boys out of the house to 'finish each other off' after they'd shattered her coffee table. But when they were all spent, she'd driven them both to the after-hours surgery in relative calmness.

Cam had a split to his jaw that needed stitches, a black eye, and a suspected concussion, whereas Daniel was sporting a broken nose and blood all down the front of his shirt.

It was strange, the love you had for a brother. Like considering your own hand, or foot. Something that had always been there; part of yourself you relied on without realising you were. A best mate, an enemy, and the person you most looked up to, all rolled into a fierce knuckle sandwich. Someone who knew you better than you sometimes knew yourself.

When Daniel had first come to confront Cam about Jody, he'd brushed his brother off.

Too busy to talk right now. It's just in your head. Forget about it.

When Dan tried a second time, Cam had responded with anger. Who did Daniel think he was? Big-headed bastard. It wasn't always about Dante fuckin' D.

But his brother hadn't given up. He'd come back with the big guns, and Katie had a way of laying out the business so you had to take note and listen. Together they'd made Cam see the big picture, and it wasn't one he was willing to hang on his living room wall for the rest of his life.

Sandfly Bay was dressed in a sombre, overcast cloak until the cloud cover split, sending beams of ethereal light down onto the deep water and turning it into a beckoning pool of gold. Cam sighed, and time passed, easing the heaviness off his sternum. How many times had he stood at this lookout? He couldn't even begin to count.

An extreme, alien landscape lay far below. Vast swathes of desert-like dunes petered down to a half-moon bay, arcing towards the rocky headland before breaking off in chunky outcrops.

They'd come here in a group to surf once, long ago, but it'd been sunny—warmer than usual for March—the day of the mako.

Shal hadn't been down south very long, just a few weeks. She'd been quiet the whole trip out to the peninsula, silent until she'd seen the view from this lookout and breathed out a reverent, "Holy *cow*."

The others, immune to the bay's beauty after so many visits, had largely ignored it.

"Last one down's a rotten egg!" Links had thrown the taunt over his shoulder as he'd careened off down the rain-rutted trail.

Mason had whooped and taken up the challenge, thundering after the leggy runner with his surfboard flapping wildly under one arm like an oversized wing. Even with the shoulder straps fully extended, the kids batman backpack he always wore was ridiculously small for him.

Shal had eased off the main path to the lookout point, letting Katie and Aroha past as well, and Cam had waited a step behind her. Resting his board on its tail and shading his eyes, he'd checked out the surf.

"There's a hell of a rip in the middle of this bay."

"Out from that waterway?" Shal had pointed to the seemingly dried up stream, peeping from between sandhills.

"Yep." Leaning his board on the railing and moving forward to take her finger carefully between thumb and forefinger, he'd aimed it at the corresponding flat section of surf, checking she got the picture.

"Right. Got it."

"I'm liking the look of *this* break." He'd re-angled Shal's arm, still outstretched, and squinted down it as if sighting a rifle. Flicking a forefinger across her elbow, he'd mimed pulling the trigger. *Pow*.

Shal had smiled down at him goofing off and he'd immediately stepped back into his own space, the want for her kicking like a mule.

"Don't fight the rip, just ride it out. It spits you out past the breakers. Keep your wits about you, but we use it as a quick paddle out."

Shal had looked so pretty, all wide eyed and shy with her hair pulled back.

They'd strolled down the rest of the way in silence, single file and comfortable with the lull.

Cam and Links hadn't been sure what to expect when Mason's long-distance girlfriend from Tāmaki-makau-rau had crashed their lease, but all in all, it had worked out okay. The only discomfort being the giant crush Cam had been fighting.

Cam sighed again. Just a crush. No biggie at all. Except eight years later, Shal still affected him the same way. Worse, because rather than diminish, his feelings were expanding to unmanageable proportions.

Like an idiot, he'd actually fallen in love with her. How the hell was he supposed to get her out of his head now?

He rolled that thought over as he padded down the well-worn pathway.

Cam hitched a ride out on the rip, and in very little time was out back, sitting astride his board and facing the open ocean. The clouds were struggling to contain the sun and every now and again Rā broke through and beamed that crazy light down on the water.

Sapere aude. Dare to be wise. *Audeamus*. Dare.

He'd forever regret it if he didn't.

There was no point trying to get Shal out of his head when she kept naturally popping in there, brightening his day like the sunshine easing past the clouds. Her smile and goofy laugh, the way she saw design in every little quirk of nature, and the way she blithely helped herself to the world as if it was her own living room.

Why had he turned Shal down instead of scrabbling to take any morsel she was willing to offer? Why had he been so unwilling to give up on the pipe-dream in exchange for a potential few months with Shalom Ericsson Hoffner?

Fucked in the head, clearly.

It looked like a good day to give in; one hell of a perfect day to sell his soul to the Gypsy Queen.

Cam eased himself into the water; into the deep.

"Tēnā koe, Moana. Ko Cameron tōku ingoa."

He re-introduced himself quietly to the sea, as his father always had. It seemed only polite when he was about to be so intimate. He waited a beat before stating who his father was, the man the ocean had claimed as her own and never relinquished. "Ko Graham Dante tōku matua."

His father, Gray. Gone but never forgotten.

Out past the line-up, the waves weren't churning the water. It was a lot clearer, and clarity was exactly what he needed. Deliberately going against the one thing every surfer had drummed into them from the get-go, Cam detached his leg rope and abandoned his board.

Diving without a weight belt wasn't easy, but he swam hard against the buoyancy of the wetsuit, down and down until the pressure on his head was snug and tight. Turning to face the light at the surface, he could just make out the dark silhouette of his board far above him. Completely alone.

I miss you, Dad... we all do.

Daniel had always been the faster swimmer, but Cam could hold his breath for longer. His father had maintained it was his sheer bloody determination to win—to beat his older brother. But Cam disagreed. It was a matter of being able to quieten his mind and blank out everything else.

Down deep it was calm. Down deep it was still. Down deep everything was clear.

Cam had found Shal's note last night on a large scrap of cardboard, tucked between the flat pack components. 'If you change your mind,' she'd written.

If he changed his mind...

Time was precious and life came with no guarantees. Love and honesty were the only cards he had left to play.

By the time Cam broke the surface again his lungs were screaming for release. Taking it easy for a minute, he flipped onto his back to suck down deep gulps of beautiful air, blinking up at the slate grey cloud.

After re-orienting himself, he swam a lazy freestyle to where his board had drifted, checked his dive watch and smiled. Still time for one good set before he had to head back to the city for the ceremony practice.

Turning away from the open sea, he said a short karakia for his father before beginning the long paddle back to the break he'd spotted from the lookout, what seemed like aeons ago.

"Oh, here he is!" Katie skipped up and grabbed Cam's hand, dragging him into position to the right of the altar, between Rue's brother and his own. "You missed the bridal party coming up the aisle, but you just stand here for that bit, anyway."

"Sweet." As ever, his eyes were automatically seeking Shal.

She was on the opposite side with Aroha and Adele, fresh in the summer dress that flowed and swung across her long boots. She wore a denim jacket and looked so young with her hair down.

Glancing his way once in query, she seemed determined not to catch his eye again.

Still mad at him, and rightly so. He'd have to work on that.

As Katie moved back to the centre position with Rue and the celebrant, Cam surreptitiously switched places with Daniel; edging to the outer position so he'd eventually be paired with Shal.

Dan raised an eyebrow, but let the change-up slide, silently taking the step needed to fill the gap between himself and Mackenzie.

Halfway through the ceremony practice, Shal gave up trying to ignore Cam staring at her. She turned and poked her tongue out childishly and he grinned back at her, knowing he'd won that round. He'd noticed something else too, something that gave him hope. In the top buttonhole of Shal's jacket was a single pink rosebud.

That had to be a good sign.

It wasn't until they were practicing 'pair up and move to sign the register' that Katie noticed he was in the wrong spot. "Cam, you're supposed to be in the middle."

"Really? But I like it here." He'd already met Shal at the top of the aisle, and although she still wouldn't acknowledge him, on the celebrant's instruction she'd had to take his arm.

Katie flustered, "You're paired with Aroha."

"But she'll have much more fun with Dan. Besides, I'm the shortest, so I should go on the end."

"On the end? Do you think so?" Katie turned to Rue, who shrugged.

Rue probably didn't care if they were sitting on a bus during the ceremony, as long as he got to marry his girl tomorrow, but the Englishman eyed Cam thoughtfully.

"Mackenzie and I are about the same height." Rue indicated towards his brother next to him. "Daniel's almost as tall, and Cam's the shortest—so that works."

Aroha turned away to hide her smirk, and Links barked a single laugh from where he, Saffy, Rosa, and Amos were watching avidly from the front pew.

Never happier to be of average height, Cam turned back to Katie.

"Oh, *alright.*" Katie gave in, then as an afterthought turned to her bridesmaid. "Is that okay with you, Shal?

———

All eyes turned to Shal.

"Well, I guess so." Then the devil in her had another idea, and she smirked as she quipped, "I *was* kind of looking forward to walking down the aisle with an international rugby star, though."

She'd meant it as a joke, and had even turned to wink at Daniel when she felt Cam's arm go rigid. Out of the corner of her eye, she saw Katie bring one hand up to press her fingertips to her lips.

The church was suddenly eerily quiet.

Open mouth—insert foot.

Cam started to step aside, his face unreadable, and Shal knew she'd hurt him as sure as if she'd just shanked him with a stiletto. That hadn't been her intention, had it?

Admittedly, she was still a bit sore at him. He'd bruised her ego more than once, but to sting him back like that...?

She turned back to Daniel, silently pleading for help. The stillness was unbearable.

"You sure about that, Shal? Rugby guys tend to stink of old socks, mud, liniment, sweat." Daniel slid the self-condemning list in lightly, bless him.

"Eeew, gross." Shal wrinkled up her nose in distaste without having to drum up much pretence. "On second thoughts I'd much prefer a partner who smells of the ocean." She took the step now separating her from Cam. "Salt, fresh air..." Sliding her hand firmly back onto his arm, she looked up and gave his bicep a quick squeeze in apology.

Cam offered her the ghost of a smile. "Sure. I can be of service, then." He played along, but his voice was hollow.

Shal found herself alone with Katie after the ceremony practice, not realising she'd been wrangled into a car-ride-intervention until Katie started directly in on the topic of Cam's engagement.

"I never told you what happened with Jody." That was Katie's idea of preamble, cutting straight to the chase with her usual speed and efficiency.

"Oh!" It took a minute for Shal to blink and change gears in her head. "Um, no." She wondered if Katie's conversational dexterity was due to growing up in an extended family of such size and vivacity, with multiple discussions going on at once. "You didn't. I hadn't realised they were engaged until the other day."

"No? Well it was pretty short-lived. Things went downhill fast after the ring was on her finger."

"Why? What happened?"

Katie frowned, reaching up to manoeuvre the visor and block an annoying sun-flare. "Long story short, Jody made a play for Daniel, though I gather she only ever saw him as Dante D."

"No!" Shal winced. "For real?"

No wonder Cam had jumped to conclusions about herself and Daniel last night. She'd cold shouldered him at the ceremony practice too, but was only now beginning to realise the full implications of what she'd actually said.

"I think the tart was hedging her bets; seeing if Dante D would go for it before she signed on the dotted line."

Oh, *God*.

"That's awful… The 'rugby star' call. I'm sorry." Not for the first time, Shal wished she'd learned to keep her big mouth well and truly shut.

"Yeah, well." Katie glanced across at her, then back to the road. "You weren't to know. I only mention it…" It seemed unnatural for the redhead to hesitate when she usually barged forward. "Well, because of Camry and Datsun. I figured if you knew the full story you'd be better armed to deal with the punchline."

"What's the punchline?"

Katie scratched a single fingernail across the steering wheel, backwards and forwards. "Dante D gets the girl Cameron wants, sometimes without even meaning to."

Shal picked that apart in her head for a while.

Why would Daniel get the girl over Cam? Because of his fame? Or the corresponding wealth? Daniel was nice. He was lovely, but his younger brother had something really special. A spark, a warmth…

Maybe the women Katie was talking about hadn't heard Cam sing, or play guitar… Or taken the time to open their bloody eyes? Had they never had a conversation with the man, or made him laugh?

"You assumed I was going to make a play for Daniel," Shal stated, tone as flat as a pancake.

Katie and Cam had *both* assumed, which said something about Shal, not them. She'd been misread often and told that her communication style was flirtatious, when she was only trying to be friendly.

"Aren't you?"

There was so much concern in Katie's voice, Shal had to bite back the bubble of hysteria that threatened. Had she led Daniel on? No. There hadn't been a hint of spark between her and Cam's brother. Perhaps strangely, considering the big guy's credentials and the reputation preceding him, the atmosphere between the two of them had been purely platonic.

"Absolutely not."

"Really? No?" Relief was written all over Katie's face.

"No more than I've been thinking about making a play for Adele." Shal snorted.

"Well, she *is* attractive." Katie loosened up enough to smile. "It's only, you seem to get on so well with D. He isn't always relaxed meeting new people. And I wasn't the only one to notice you went out to say goodnight to him last night." She glanced Shal's way again, then back to the road.

"It wasn't like *that*. I needed a lift to the ceremony practice today so Adele could have my car to pick up James."

"Oh, right." Katie's knuckles whitened with her grip on the wheel. "Actually, he didn't show."

"James didn't fly in this morning?" He hadn't been at the ceremony practice, but Shal had assumed he'd just been tired from his flight.

"No. Adele says he can't spare the time off work, like that's all fine and dandy." Katie sniffed. "She's all clammed up. Not talking to me." She flicked another look Shal's way, concern as obvious as the freckles on her nose. "I'm so worried about her."

The pre-match dinner function in the evening was an early potluck at Rosa and Amos' house. Rosa had invited all family, plus the bridal party, so it was a huge, rambling affair.

Shal and Katie arrived directly from the ceremony practice at four, and the place was already full of people. The trestle tables lining one wall were groaning under the weight of all the food. Rosa must've known it would be an early-to-bed night, but she was never one to turn down a good excuse for a party.

The rain that had threatened all day held off, and the guests were able to spill outside onto the lawn as the evening darkened. Fairy lights sprang up through the trees like fireflies, and Shal sighed with the pure romance of it.

"Where *were* you today, Cam?" Aroha turned to Cam as they stood together near the veggie patch, Shal perched beside them on a raised garden box with her paper plate balanced on her lap. "For a minute there I thought we'd have to go on without you."

Cam grinned. "Surfing. But don't tell Katie." He glanced over his shoulder as if his cousin might still catch him at it.

"That much was easy to guess." Aroha cuffed some of the salt out of his temples.

"St Clair?" Shal wondered aloud with a slight pang of envy.

"No." Cam shuffled his feet. "Sandfly Bay."

"*What*?" Aroha's head snapped up. "Mako Bay?" She reverted to the name the group had re-christened it with, after their encounter there.

Shark Bay.

Shal had only been there once—bunking a Shakespeare lecture to tag along with her new group of friends to surf. She'd freaked out when Cam, kneeling on his board, had formed a triangle with his arms above his head in the shape of a fin.

Heart in her throat, she'd scanned the waves, yelling until Katie had joined her in the shallows. Then they'd watched helplessly from the beach as Cam had paddled out towards Mason.

Although the shark was a hundred metres away, the women had been able to see the dorsal fin distinctly. Shal had made a low moan of distress, watching it b-line for Mason, then Cam.

Kneeling, with his hand to his mouth, Cam's high-pitched whistle had been drowned in the roar of the surf. But Mason's head had turned towards it—just a speck of white in the vast blue.

'*Get the hell out!*' Shal's mind had screamed the words, but no sound came out of her mouth as the fin had disappeared under Cam's board.

Was it Mason or Cam she'd been so terrified of losing?

Shal swallowed the shadow of fear that always rose with the memory. "Who did you go with?"

"Ahh…" Cam could probably already see how this was going to go down, but he carried on with the truth, regardless. "No one."

"*Alone*?" Aroha pushed at Cam's chest as if she was in the schoolyard picking a fight, shoving him hard enough to nudge him back a half-step. "What are you, mental? Don't ever do that again!"

Shal was in total agreement with the gnarly little brunette, for once.

Alone. In Mako Bay.

A shiver ran clear down her back. The first and last time she'd ever seen a shark in its wild habitat, and her skin still quivered with the thought of sharing the ocean with it.

"Why would you do that?" Her thought escaped, little more than a reedy whisper.

Cam turned to her. "I needed to think," he offered with honest eyes. "And the water helps."

"Masochist," Aroha muttered, shooting Cam one last dirty look before leaving the pair to go and top up her plate.

Although Saffy arrived periodically on her dancing feet, skipping happily from group to group with a trail of children following, Shal realised this was the closest she'd get to speak to Cam alone. Placing her plate aside, she moved to stand beside him.

"I never thanked you for making up the shelving unit, Cam." She fingered the rosebud in her buttonhole with nervy fingers. The stem was a little droopy but the petals were still intact. "That was really thoughtful of you."

"Least I could do." Cam was watching her face carefully, no doubt searching for grounding. They were tiptoeing around on eggshells, being oh-so-polite. "And you did thank me. I got your note last night."

Shal turned to him in surprise. "Last night?"

"I went up to the boutique apartment and made up the dining table and chairs." Cam placed his empty plate atop hers on the planter box.

A little sound of distress came from deep in her throat. "You didn't have to do that!" She wished he hadn't. She couldn't remember exactly what she'd written on the damned thing.

"I was too riled up to sleep, and flat packs calm me down, so..." Cam shrugged, then slid his hands into his pockets.

"They calm you *down*?" Shal laughed outright, the shadow of a snort sneaking out by accident. "You *are* a masochist, Cameron Dante."

The lights were back dancing in Cam's eyes as he smiled across at her, and some of the tension between them abated.

"Yeah." Cam caught her hand as she mimed a loop-de-loop next to his temple. But instead of just holding it, he straightened the fingers carefully and laid her palm down on the contoured planes of his chest, slightly to the left. "I'm crazy," he said, his words as soft as the evening breeze.

Shal could feel the steady thump of Cam's heart under her hand, just as he must be able to feel the flutter of her own pulse where he was still holding her wrist. His eyes were deeply serious, even though a smile tugged at one corner of his mouth, teasing the bracketing dimple.

Saffy again arrived at Cam's elbow, breathless and bouncy. "Shal lets me play games on her phone sometimes," she informed her cousin cheerfully.

"Lucky." Cam nodded.

"There's a picture of your naked nipples on there," Saffy added matter-of-factly before skipping away.

Oh, for Heaven's sake. Was privacy an unknown factor within this extended family?

"Lucky," Cam repeated a little more slowly and with an upward bent, like a question.

Shal's face was instantly warm—probably beetroot. Yes, she'd sneaked a couple of pics on her phone of her favourite shots from Katie's album. Not exactly a crime, but neither was it something she was looking to advertise considering the subject matter of one of them.

"Just to let you know," she blurted, more than happy to change the subject. "I'm not interested in Daniel in that way."

Cam lifted one eyebrow expressively. "No?"

"No."

He still had her hand captive and she felt the warmth on her cheeks bloom as Cam's grin expanded.

How could Cam have forgotten how prettily Shal blushed? Her cheeks were rosy under the olive tone of her skin, and she lowered her chin to look up at him through her lashes.

He was more than likely looking flushed himself, ridiculously pleased with her statement. The Daniel thing had been eating at him insidiously. He was elated, not only because Shal had said it, but because she appeared to genuinely mean it.

"Just to let you know," he copied her words with careful diction. "Pieta and I have never hooked up." He held up his free hand and wiggled his digits. "No fingers. No pies. I just work with her."

Shal laughed a little nervously and pulled at her hand, so Cam let her go, but not before bringing her knuckles up to his lips like the seal on a promise.

"I'm glad you didn't get eaten by a shark, Cam," Shal whispered, not entirely steadily.

"Yeah," he laughingly replied. "You and me both, e hoa."

19

Listening to...
Be Mine Tonight - Dave Dobbyn, Ian Morris
From the album: Right First Time - Th' Dudes

Katie's wedding day dawned damp and cold, and by the time the bride arrived at Dundas Street at nine she was soundly pissed off about it. Shal could see Katie bordered on tears a few times there during the morning, but she pushed on through.

Amos had driven Katie over from Roseneath, and he was the only male not to have been chased off the premises. The elderly townhouse had morphed into an epic beauty parlour. The makeup artist and her apprentice were upstairs in Shal's room, while the hairdressers had claimed the dining room, their paraphernalia spread out across the table.

Decked out like a florist's market, the lounge had cellophane lidded boxes of bouquets and buttonholes on every available surface. The English roses, in clotted cream, contrasted beautifully against the wired-in scotch thistles.

Everyone calmed down when one of the photographers arrived, armed with soothing platitudes and enthusiasm for the beautiful 'flat' lighting of the overcast morning. The woman also brought with her a solid forecast for improving afternoon weather.

It was easy to forget the photographer was even there, she worked so quietly and efficiently behind the scenes, occasionally manoeuvring them into better light or more flattering angles. The initial nerves about being in front of the camera began to dissipate, and Shal started to really enjoy the morning for what it was—an all out pamper session.

"*Saffron*..." Rosa warned her granddaughter in a low tone for the umpteenth time. The little girl's hand was once more reaching out to touch the lace and pearl detailing of the wedding dress, laid out across the queen bed. "Look, but don't touch."

Saffy was gorgeous in her flower girl dress, her dark skin contrasting prettily against the pale turquoise and little pearls worked into her tight Dutch braids.

"Come and sit with me, Saffy," Shal called from her position on the chaise. "I have a gift for you."

"You don't have to keep spending money on Saffy." Adele clucked like a mother hen with her feathers all ruffled. "I appreciate the generosity, but—"

"Oh, it's not from me." Shal cut Adele off with a smile. "It's a present from Rue. A 'thank you' for supporting his bride with so much enthusiasm."

"What?" Katie's head snapped around and she narrowly missed getting a mascara brush through the pupil. The makeup artist eyed her client warily. "Sorry," Katie muttered, chastised by a single look.

When Shal pulled a slim jewellery case out of a large gift bag with aplomb, she suddenly had the attention of every woman in the room. Adele, Rosa, and Aroha all descended on Saffy to coo over the single pearl-drop on a fine silver chain.

"Could you...?" Shal turned to the photographer after securing the chain behind Saffy's neck, but the woman was already snapping off shots as Shal handed each of the bridal party attendants their simple matching gifts from the bridegroom.

"Oh, my God. I'm really going to cry now." Katie looked with desperation towards her makeup artist.

"Don't you dare," the woman mock-growled, looking a touch misty-eyed herself when she reached across and grabbed a tissue to save her work.

Cam slipped back into position next to Daniel after his information foray into the front of the church. He took his eyes off the nervy Englishman at the altar and glanced back to the whispering congregation.

Full house. Almost time. And not a moment too soon...

Rue wiped his hands down the back of his dress pants once again, and Mac leaned towards his brother to whisper, "Alright?"

"Yes. Think so." Rue cleared his throat. "Bloody hell. Is it hot in here, or is it just me?"

It wasn't particularly hot, no. Rue's temperature gauge must've been rising along with his nervous tension.

"Katie's arrived." Better late than never. Cam smiled encouragingly at the groom, who was looking more and more unfocused by the minute.

Rue turned to blink owlishly at him. "She's here?" The relief in his voice was unmistakable. Had he actually begun to think she wouldn't show? The woman was crazy about him.

"With bells on. Just you and her now, Rupert."

"Eyes on the ball," Daniel added as he leaned behind Mac to clap Rue on the shoulder.

Similar concept, though the terminology was a touch less than romantic.

Daniel must've thought so too. "Just focus on Katie," he reiterated.

All four of them straightened as the music began, and the pew occupants hushed expectantly.

The groomsmen needn't have worried. As soon as Rue had his eyes on the ball he was right as rain.

Cam had his eyes on the ball too. An entirely different one with ebony hair tied back in a mass of pinned curls down her nape. Shal's eyes looked enormous when they were made up like that, and Cam's mouth went dry. She met his gaze unwaveringly as she walked down the aisle towards him, only breaking it to slide gracefully into position next to Aroha.

God, she was stunning.

He smiled, sending Shal a wink. She returned it with interest, grinning back at him like a little kid in her best dress ups.

Oh, *no*.

Shal gripped Cam's arm as they followed the others past the small alcove where Cam's guitar sat waiting, and moved to sign the register. It was her turn at the table first, carefully scribing her signature above the line the celebrant indicated, before handing the pen to Cam.

Nerves jumped around willy-nilly in her guts.

The ceremony had gone off without a hitch, but now she was supposed to *sing*.

Cam caught her eye. "Gonna throw up?" he whispered as he signed his initials with a quick flourish.

Shal nodded mutely, horrified she'd been unable to quell the familiar nervous flutter. Desperate not to cause a scene at the most important ceremony of her friend's life, she searched around furtively for the nearest escape route.

The instant the focus moved back to the bridal couple, Cam took her arm and stepped her back behind the pillars. Shal was beside herself with relief to realise there was a door half-hidden between the stone effigies, and it was ajar.

Cam motioned her through the clergyman's office, then towards the small bathroom at the back, closing the door behind them.

"I've got you." Grabbing the hand towel, he slung it across her front and stood behind her.

Shal heaved twice over the porcelain bowl. When she was able to breathe again, she choked back a sob.

Oh, *shit*. The dress.

Looking down, she realised that must've been Cam's reasoning behind the hand towel. Her bridesmaid dress would be no worse for wear.

"All done?" Cam shuffled her towards the sink when she nodded shakily. "Good job," he commended her matter-of-factly. Handing her a chipped mug with cool water to sluice her mouth out, he then calmly flushed the loo and all evidence of her nerves.

If it'd been anyone else Shal would've been mortified to have them as an audience during that little performance. But this was Cam, and he'd pulled her through much worse in the past.

Shal got on with tidying up her eye makeup as quickly and efficiently as she could with dampened tissue, thanking her stars her hair was safe in its up-do. She was about done when she caught Cam's eye in the mirror.

"Thanks," she whispered.

"All part of the service." Cam routed around in his jacket pocket for something as he spoke. "I have something for you." He waved a tiny packet aloft.

A laugh of pure surprise slipped out. The bloody Boy Scout knew her so well!

"You're an absolute gem!" Shal crowed, turning to grab the hotel toothbrush and mini toothpaste pack. Unwrapping them, she hastily scrubbed at her teeth and tongue, knowing she had minimal time.

"Don't panic," Cam soothed. "Rue's covering for you."

"Wha' da ya 'ean?" Her mouth was full of toothpaste and the words came out wrong. She spat and rinsed. "What do you mean?"

"If we disappeared at any stage, he's prepared to stall." Cam handed her some fresh tissue. "Do you want me to do this first song solo?"

"No." Shal hesitated, checking in with herself as she dabbed her lips. "I'm okay now." That was the absolute truth as she met Cam's eyes in the antiquated mirror and shared a conspiratorial smile with him.

The Englishman didn't acknowledge he'd seen Shal and Cam slink back to the congregation side of the pillars, he just finished up his conversation with the celebrant and signed his name calmly on the dotted line.

After so much angst on Shal's part, the song she performed in the church with Cam went off without a hitch.

"Just sing it to me," Cam had murmured, angling his chair towards her and smiling encouragement as they set up. His eyes never left her and it was easy to imagine it was just the two of them, practicing.

Listening to Cam play the intro put her at ease, made her fall in love with the music and the fun of it instead of focusing negatively on who was listening, and what their opinion might be.

Katie took Rue's arm, and as a laughing, legally married pair, they strolled down the aisle to Shal and Cam's upbeat rendition of Brooke Fraser's love song.

After a slightly pitchy start, it was even easier onstage at the reception venue. Partly because Katie and Rue's first dance was a slower number Shal knew well, and partly because she had a mic stand to hide behind. It also helped to know all eyes were on the bride and groom, not the musicians.

The only couple on the dance floor, Katie and Rue danced as if there wasn't another living being in the room. Katie was grinning, Cheshire style, her arms wrapped around Rue's neck while still holding her half-full champagne flute.

Rue also looked to be cruising in a state of absolute calm, now the stressful part was over and Katie was finally his wife.

Shal grabbed a quick hug from Cam and thanked him before slipping down offstage to find Adele. Cam was staying up to do a few more songs with the band, and she knew the music would be good to dance to.

Adele shared Shal's love of boogying, and she could always rely on the strawberry blonde to join her on the dance floor. Though Adele had been underage the year Shal lived in Ōtepoti, it hadn't deterred the group from sneaking her into bars to dance.

The women removed their heels and stoles after the first song, hot, clammy, and laughing. Adele turned to Shal, blinking in disbelief as the band started a new number.

"Hey! Isn't this...?" The first few bars of the old Stagger song were unmistakable.

Links whooped from somewhere else in the room, clearly approving.

"*Bohemian*!" they exclaimed together.

Cam had written the lyrics, and Links had come up with the walking bass riff that gave the song such a distinctive lead in. The women turned in unison to stare at Cam, who'd been watching for their reaction. He flashed a broad grin before sliding in with the vocal.

"*You don't care less what they say about you…*"

Shal did a little run-on-the-spot out of pure happiness. "I *love* this song."

"So you should." Adele turned to fix her with an arch look. "Being the one to've inspired it."

"I did not!" She laughed openly at the other woman. "It's about Cam's bass guitar."

"*Is* it, though?"

There was something in Adele's droll tone and expression, above and beyond her usual sarcastic streak, that urged Shal to take notice.

She did a double take, gripping Adele's arm fiercely.

"*Bohemian* is about me?"

"Of course it is, dipstick." Adele's tone softened.

Cam was sliding into the second verse and the band was well on board. With the drummer on Djembe, the rhythm was lazy jungle funk.

"*If you're longing to, you need only ask me. I'd give it all for you, Bohemian…*"

When Cam stepped down off the stage on a light performance buzz, Shal was waiting there for him. Cool and sleek in her silky dress, her hair was still tied up in fancy scallops.

He'd seen her ditch the fur when dancing with Adele, and her smooth-skinned shoulders were now unadorned. Shal smiled and grabbed him around the midriff, shattering the untouchable image as her eyes warmed with sweetness.

"You were amazing, as always. I really enjoy watching you play." Then she was walking in front, dragging him by his belt buckle. "Come and dance with me."

There was no shyness in Shal. She knew he'd follow. The back of her dress was practically non-existent, which was a shock to his already overloaded senses.

"Is *Bohemian* about your bass guitar?" Shal shot the question at him when they'd reached her chosen spot on the dance floor.

"Ah, yeah. Acoustic bass. The one I have hanging on the wall."

"And…?" Shal coaxed, waiting expectantly.

Cam's mouth went dry and he bought himself some time by looking around the room. Links and Aroha were sitting at a nearby table, engrossed in conversation, but Adele was watching him from the bar, Saffy hoisted up on her hip.

His cousin nodded, almost imperceptibly.

Cam had made a pact with himself at Mako Bay to give Shal honesty. Both of them deserved that.

"You," he conceded.

"Thank you." Shal breathed the words out on an exhale. "It's my favourite." She reached up on tiptoe and kissed him softly on one cheek, then the other.

Staying close, one of her hands slid up behind his head, fingers playing through his freshly cropped hair as she studied him. If he'd been a cat, he would've rolled over and purred.

"I like your new haircut, it's very suave," she murmured.

They danced, close enough to make Cam ache. For once in his life he had no memory of what song played, what the lyrics were, or what the next verse would be. He was totally absorbed in the woman in his arms.

In an instrumental break, another Stagger song came to him, and it seemed like the most natural thing in the world to lean forward and brush Shal's earlobe with his lips, singing the lyrics for her ears alone.

They'd been written for her, after all.

"You walked in, looking like you do…"

Shal laughed when he left the chorus hanging, then finished the lines for him, clearly remembering the song. *"Brought me to my knees, my knees, my knees."*

God. She did that. Brought him to his knees in every way.

Shal smiled sunnily into his face with her head tilted to the side. "I take it that means you approve of the dress?" She put him at arm's length and coyly swished from side to side, then turned with her back to him, looking over her shoulder in askance.

"Very much." Did they take girls aside some time in high school and give them pointers on how to weaken a guy? Sucker punch to the gut with just one look.

Heaven help him, Shal seemed very much aware he was pretty much out of self-control. Flirting, knowing he didn't have a shit-show in hell against it.

Cam drew Shal slowly back in, hands fitting snugly around her waist. "I have another song for you." He stared at her for a long minute.

When he leant in again, Shal shivered as his cheek brushed hers.

"You, look what you've done to me. You lit me, you bit me, I'm rapt..."

He pulled back so he could gauge Shal's expression, not a hundred percent sure how she'd take it.

"Be mine. Be mine tonight," Shal finished in a whisper, her eyes widening.

It was an old Dudes song, beautiful in its simplicity. The world stopped spinning as he watched the magnitude of what he was asking sink in.

They'd stopped moving as if by mutual consent, standing just off centre on the dance floor and contemplating each other while couples and children swirled round them.

"Is that what you want?" Shal was still whispering, her voice barely audible above the noise of a hundred people in one room, the band, the children laughing, the thumping of his own blood in his ears.

"More than anything else."

"On my terms, or yours?"

"Yours. No strings attached. If that's what you need?"

"Are you..." Shal cleared her throat. "Are you *sure*?"

"Very."

"Oh." Shal looked a bit gobsmacked at first, but a slow smile began to form. "In that case, yes, please."

Placing one hand on either side of Cam's face, Shal stepped forward to kiss him full on the mouth, her lips soft and welcoming. They broke apart only when jostled by another pair of exuberant dancers, and Shal's eyes were dark with the promise of what was to come, her breathing coming hard and fast.

The party was winding down. Cam nursed his last beer for the night and Shal held a glass of flat champagne, though he noted she was playing with the flute rather than drinking it, running her fingers up and down the stem. They sat at one of the large round tables, surrounded by people but a little apart from the other guests.

Katie and Rue had left, amidst shouted well wishes and drunken innuendo about consummating their nuptials. The tin cans tied to their bumper had clunked loudly in the midnight air, 'Just Married' scribed in toothpaste on the back window as if penned by a semi-literate child.

"You know I'm in love with you, Shal." The words slipped out, in direct contradiction to the orders Cam had given himself *not* to freak her out.

"Shhh. Let's not use the 'L' word, okay?" Shal said it gently, laying a finger against his lips, but he heard the weight behind her words. The fear in her eyes was unmistakable.

"*Arghhh*," he groaned, turning his head into her shoulder. "Not saying it doesn't make me feel any less. What am I supposed to do with all of this if I can't tell you?"

"I don't know, write it down or something. It might sound harsh, but it feels like a collar to me."

"A *collar*?" Way to throw cold water on a guy.

"Something to hold me with. Or worse. Something for me to choke you with."

"It doesn't have to be like that, I need you to know—"

"*Shhh*," Shal interrupted again, more urgently this time, and once more laid her finger across his lips. "You said *my* terms. It's not what you say, it's what I hear." Her mouth took on a little downturn. "I may be intrinsically flawed, but when you bring love to the table, I hear alarm bells. I don't want to hurt you Cam. I... I care for you. A great deal."

"Okay." He watched her fingers skitter nervously over the pearl at her throat. "I'll take that." Sliding her free hand into his, he turned it until it was palm-up and planted a hot kiss in the centre, meeting her gaze at the same time. "I care for you a great deal, too."

Shal and Cam squeezed into the already-full wedding shuttle and got it to drop them at the base of the hill, telling the driver they wanted to walk the last bit.

Aroha and Links were heading back to Dundas Street in the same van-load, and Aroha squeezed Shal's shoulder to get her attention as Cam was getting out. Shal turned and received a twitchy, out of character smile from the brunette, along with a whisper.

"Be safe, and be happy."

Be *happy*? Shal blinked first at Aroha, then a grinning Links. The fun and heady sweetness of the night filled her, and she smiled back at both of them.

"We will. Don't wait up!"

It was possibly the nicest, girliest exchange they'd ever had, and Shal felt the shift in temperature distinctly.

Aroha had never particularly warmed to Shal arriving on the scene, and Shal understood. Enter the clueless Aucklander, monopolising Katie's time and screwing up Links' chance to win B-of-B.

Not that Aroha had ever actually said anything along those lines to Shal's face.

According to Katie, Aroha had long assumed Shal had turned her nose up at Cam, too. Which wouldn't have helped.

Aroha had probably needed someone to blame after the accident, and Shal had been more than accepting of the responsibility at that stage. If she'd stayed with Mason, Links wouldn't have been in the car in the first place. Though why they'd been driving up in the port hills on a wet Wednesday, drunk as skunks, no one knew.

Links had told police he had no recollection of the hours leading up to the accident; the whole day had been wiped clean off his memory.

Deep down, Shal knew loading the guilt on herself was unfair. No one deserved to be treated like a discarded toy. Aroha would never have stuck with a guy like that, either.

20

Listening to…
Caught - Shona Laing
From the album: South

Cam and Shal held off until the shuttle was out of sight to kiss, and
it took Cam a moment or two to reorient his thoughts afterwards.

"Um… Your place?" he quizzed.

"No. Too many people. Yours," Shal countered. "Though to be
fair, they're actually *both* yours."

"Park Street's pretty rudimentary."

"Do you have a bed?"

"Yes."

Shal wrapped her arms around his waist. "Then take me home."

With those sweet words, Cam was relieved to remember he'd
finally heeded Jonno's advice and changed the sheets.

"As you wish," he answered, channeling Shal's long ago
favourite movie. If she wouldn't let him say how he felt, he'd find
other ways. As many other ways as possible.

Shal's eyelids flickered, but she withheld comment.

Happy to get away with it, Cam leaned in to kiss her again. It
was proving to be a highly addictive practice. The sweetest cupid's

bow dipped into Shal's top lip, and tonight she tasted of strawberries and champagne.

"I hope you don't expect me to walk after that," Shal muttered. "My knees have turned to liquid."

Taking her face in both hands, Cam planted his lips on hers again, and this time there was no playfulness or tenderness left, just pent up need and heat.

Shal soaked up Cam's warmth, his taste, his scent, and plastered her body against him with her arms around his neck. She loved the way his fresh haircut flicked crisply between her fingers. All the sun-bleached tips had been removed, leaving Cam darker, more distinguished, and a little unfamiliar.

A car cruised past down the main drag, horn blasting. Cheers and whoops erupted from the raucous Saturday night occupants as they clocked the couple wrapped up in each other on the corner of George and Saint David.

Shal grinned against Cam's lips as he bent to slide one arm under her knees, and the other under her shoulders, lifting her up against his chest.

"Now you can stop your bloody complaining, woman," he teased.

Cosy, she snuggled into Cam's neck and began to nuzzle there.

Being carried held a certain kind of caveman charm.

"Mm, you smell so good," Shal murmured as he walked, taking a little nip or two as they crossed the street. "I can't wait to have you inside me, Cameron Dante."

Cam's steps didn't falter, but his breathing did, which made the game a ton more fun.

"I want you." She slid one hand down his chest, searching for his nipple beneath his jacket. "So bad."

"*Christ*, Shal."

Cam dumped her unceremoniously back on her heels on the footpath, turning her shoulders to face him. He was breathing hard, and she could see from the look in his eyes it wasn't only the effort of carrying her that was causing him oxygen issues.

"You started it," Shal stated baldly.

"No, I'm pretty sure you did. One more block to go, okay?" Cam gave her shoulders an extra squeeze. "But you've gotta stop that. Right? Or we won't make it and you'll end up naked on someone's front porch."

Shal issued a slow smile, trailing fingers down the cords of Cam's neck to the tell-tale pulse jumping around above his collar, then sliding still lower to fit snugly into the cleft of his chest. Looking up at him, she took in the hair she'd mussed up herself and the barely controlled wild in his eyes.

"Oh, Cam. I don't care *where*, you big doofus."

"Christ, Shal," Cam said again, but softly this time. He huffed out a breath and ran one hand through his hair, scruffing it up even further. "Well, I do. It's fuckin' freezing for starters, not to mention…" He looked around himself as if just noticing his whereabouts for the first time. "A bit public," he finished apologetically. Placing slightly shaky hands on either side of her face, Cam looked at her solemnly before firmly kissing her forehead. "I'll piggyback you the last bit." Turning, he took a step in front. "Jump up," he offered.

Shal shimmied her dress high up her thighs.

"Your back is just as beautiful as your front." She stretched her arms over Cam's jacketed shoulders as he hefted her upwards.

Getting a good grip under her knees, Cam started up the incline with measured strides.

"You know what, Surfer Girl? Right back at you," Cam growled. "That dress is something else."

Shal laughed, knowing exactly what he meant. There were classier design tricks to sex up a dress than the obvious cleavage and thigh cuts, and the bare shoulders and low-slung back of this particular piece were classic flatterers.

Park Street was still a building site, but all the essentials were there. Roof, walls, and bed. Cam was keenly aware it wasn't a particularly romantic setting for this stunning woman, dressed to the nines.

"Excuse the shambles." He moved a random drop sheet into the front room.

"I don't care where you live, Cam. I'm just happy to get you alone." Propped against the doorframe, Shal held her strappy high-heels in one hand as the other began to work her hair out of its constraining pins.

"I can help you with that." He stood behind her to pull the wiry U-bends from the arrangement of loops and curls, his fingers shaking. "Wily little buggers. God. How many are there?"

"She had to use a whole pack on me, my hair's so determined to be straight. I think that's the bulk of them, now." Shal turned to face him as her hair tumbled around her shoulders in wide, open curls instead of its usual slick curtain. The bare bulb behind her threw her face into shadow as she took the pins from his slack hand.

"So, ah…" At a loss, Cam took her shoes and placed them inanely by the door. They looked ridiculously frivolous next to a pair of his crusty work boots.

Steel-capped roughness next to classy and bejewelled—just like Shal and himself. Returning to where she stood, Cam pondered the uncertainty of his footing as he took her hand in his, brushing his lips across her knuckles.

"You call the shots from here, e hoa. I don't want to stomp on your ground rules," he murmured.

***

Shal shimmied closer to Cam, placing the hand holding hers firmly onto her left butt cheek. Reaching to take his other hand, she latched it just as securely on her right breast. "With pleasure. Do you have a shower that works?"

"Um, yep." Cam swallowed audibly.

"How about we get naked and set the ground rules in there?"

Going by the immediate escalation of heat in Cam's eyes, he liked that idea. Smiling, Shal began to shuffle him backwards through the open bedroom door, figuring she had quite a few ideas Cameron Dante was going to like.

"Am I allowed to compliment you?" Cam asked.

They'd made it a few steps into his room and Shal laughed,

throwing him a look over her shoulder as she dumped the hairpins on a narrow set of drawers. Taking off her stole, she flung it carelessly onto the back of the wooden chair that was acting as a bedside table. With her back exposed, she flicked open the pearl drop buttons holding the halter neck together at her nape.

"Compliments are *always* allowed." The silky fabric of her dress slid in a water-like sheen to the floor and she was suddenly naked, bar a baby-blue thong. Keeping her back to Cam, Shal watched his reaction over her shoulder.

If she wasn't mistaken, Cam lost the power of speech entirely for a minute there, which was gratifying. Slowly turning, she shifted the weight of her hair over one shoulder.

"You make it hard to breathe, Shal. I've never seen anything I wanted more," Cam rasped out.

"Why, thank you, Cam," Shal returned lightly, though his seriousness shook her, bringing with it a moment of pure panic.

Was this fair?

She didn't want to hurt this man, he was incredibly special to her. But the building need in her was matched by the longing she could see in his dark eyes. Shal pushed aside the flicker of trepidation. Something that felt this right surely couldn't be wrong.

Crooking her finger, she motioned Cam forward. "Come over here and say that."

Cam walked as if in a dream and stood before her, oh-so-close, but still not touching. He looked only into her eyes, though his words proved him intensely aware of her nakedness.

"I've never seen anything so beautiful in all my life." It came out as a raw whisper this time. "Shalom…"

Cam may've been fully clothed, but Shal was acutely aware he'd just stripped himself bare in other ways. His vulnerability hit her square in the solar plexus.

She took the step that separated them, crooning to him as she stroked her hands up his chest and over broad shoulders, sliding his charcoal jacket off with one smooth movement.

"Shush, now. Stay still and let me do this for you."

As Cam toed off his dress shoes and socks, Shal's nimble fingers worked to undo button after button on his shirt. Lifting each hand, she carefully removed his father's silver and greenstone cufflinks, putting them aside on the bedside chair. Then she surprised him by placing a gentle kiss on each inner wrist in turn.

His pulse must have been thundering against Shal's lips, belying the stillness of the stance he was trying to maintain as he let her undress him.

Cam had expected the sex to be hot and fast. Unanticipated was this tenderness from Shal—excruciating in its bitter-sweetness.

Sweet, because it felt like Shal was giving it in love. Bitter, because he knew she wasn't.

A symphony of grace and beauty, Shal was all long, lithe lines with sweetly curved breasts and lavish, dark areolae. The single pearl pendant glowed warm and high on her sternum, and her hair cascaded over one shoulder in a mass of gypsy ribbons. She looked timeless and achingly lovely.

And she was unbuttoning his pants.

"You smell incredible." It was hard to keep control of his voice— keep it even. His body was taking over and he shuddered. "I want to touch you."

How was that for understatement of the millennium?

"Stay still," Shal soothed, catching the hand that rose to stroke her hair and placing it back down by Cam's side. "Just a little longer." She slid his dress pants down over his hips and made short work of his boxers. "I want to look at you, too."

Cam was unashamedly aroused—stunning in his masculinity. There wasn't an ounce of extra weight on his slim, muscular frame, and his broad shoulders tapered from hard worked torso to narrow hips.

"You're lovely." Shal breathed the words out, sliding one hand up to fit her thumb into the cleft of his chest. Her new favourite spot. The muscle in Cam's jaw was working overtime as his hands slowly clenched and unclenched at his sides in a fight for control.

Nothing made her feel more feminine than the comparison of the undeniably masculine, and Cam was one-hundred percent male.

But oh-so-serious.

Katie's old taunt came to mind, and Shal couldn't help teasing him with it. "Careful though." She used the same soothing tone she'd undressed him with. "Don't break a tooth."

She grinned as Cam's eyes widened in surprise.

"You little..." There was one beat of stillness before Cam snapped into action.

Squealing, Shal tried to jump out of reach as his hand snaked around to smack her bum. She skipped over the low bed in her bare feet with Cam right on her tail, slap-tackling her ankles. Barely managing to stay upright, she was laughing as she vaulted towards the bathroom door.

"Minx!" Cam caught her as she turned, reaching the ensuite door, and his momentum shoved her back against it. A broad grin split his previously grim face.

"Minx," he repeated, but neither of them were laughing anymore, they were panting. Skin against skin, mouth against mouth—then finally, heat against wet heat.

"Shal, don't go to sleep." Cam was gently shaking her shoulder. "You should go pee."

"What?" Shal's head shot up, suddenly wide-awake.

"Go. Pee." Cam's voice showed he was close to sleep too; groggy, but still resolutely pushing her to the edge of the bed and making her get out of the cosy warm spot alongside him. "So you don't get a U.T.I."

Shal snorted in disbelief. "Who *are* you, actually?"

Cam pushed up on his elbows and blinked sleepily up at her from where she was now perched on the side of his low, futon-style bed. The sheet slid down across his hips, the curve of his back and shoulder sculptural in the low light from the open bathroom door. Reaching out, Shal trailed her fingers lightly down Cam's shark tattoo from tail to head, watching a soft smile play at one corner of his mouth.

It hadn't been long after their shared experience at Mako Bay that Cam had gotten the black mako inked on his shoulder blade. With koru designs on the fins, and matau on the tail curving across the back of his upper arm. The finer detailed markings of his late, great-grandmother's facial moko were incorporated on the head.

Cam had sworn the mako knew him, passing on a message from his tipuna it was time to stand up and be proud of his Māori heritage.

"Uh, didn't I introduce myself? That was rude of me. I'm the pretzel guy. Cameron Rimutaka Dante, at your service." Cam eased his face back down into the pillow, so the next part came out a bit muffled. "And you seem to forget I flatted with you for a year and know all about you. Now, are you going to go pee, or do I have to carry you in there?"

"I'm going, I'm going." Shal laughed.

When she returned Cam was fast asleep, one hand fisted under his chin, hair tousled, and face relaxed.

Peaceful.

She took her time studying him, absorbing all the details you didn't usually get the chance to notice when you were looking at another person. Not if you were being polite.

Even a very dear and familiar face could seem like a stranger's.

The curved edge of Cam's ear settled neatly into freshly cropped hair, and from this angle the thin scar running along his jawline was easily discernible. A brush of surprisingly dark eyelashes rested on high boned cheeks and a smattering of freckles darkened his temple. Shal knew Cam so well, and yet suddenly she hardly recognised him.

She loved him, and was clear on that. But Cam maintained he was *in* love with her, a much more frightening concept. She wasn't sure she was worthy.

'If you're longing to, you need only ask me. I'd give it all for you, Bohemian.'

Certainly not worthy of *that*.

Shal tiptoed back to the bathroom, and with her finger as a toothbrush used a small bauble of toothpaste to rub around her teeth. Picking up Cam's bottle of aftershave from the vanity unit, she sniffed it.

Nice, though strangely lacking potency without the person wearing it. When Cam wore the scent, it was warmer, more approachable—sexy.

Super sexy.

They hadn't made it to the shower that first time. Hard and fast against the bathroom door hadn't exactly been the plan, but it'd been deliciously wanton, and raging hot. If Cam hadn't grappled for a condom before pushing the blue lace aside, Shal might've gone ahead without fully protecting herself.

She frowned at herself in the mirror. That wasn't the least bit smart.

The hard, flat planes of wood had impressed on her back and butt as the contoured lines of Cam's divine body had pressed her forcefully against it. Sliding one hand under her knee, he'd lifted her leg, opening her, and any trace of remaining inhibition had fled when he'd paused there, eyes seeking confirmation.

"I want this. I want you," she'd promised, her voice ragged.

Cam had braced himself with his left hand on the door beside her head, and her eyes had closed with that first hedonistic thrust. She'd slid her arms around his shoulders to hold her balance and given him still more of her weight to bear.

He hadn't complained. Cam had groaned and called her name when she kissed his neck, but he certainly *hadn't* complained. Even when she'd sunk her teeth into his taut skin, when the sparks of pleasure had lit and fizzed behind her closed eyelids, he'd asked for more, not less.

She'd bitten him instead of crying out when the spiralling intensity of it had taken her by surprise—when the waves of warmth and need had become too much to hold inside.

I love this. I love you.

Shal hadn't wanted to take, and give again like this. Cam had awoken something lying dormant in her for the longest time. Something tired of hiding. But she knew it could just as easily fade, dissolve like salt in the ocean. It wasn't fair to feel it, or give it, or *say* it, only to take it away.

So she'd held the words back.

They'd managed to make it to the shower afterwards, and Cam

had insisted on lazily washing every inch of her with his wickedly clever hands, slowly building her up again with his slick fingers.

Shal's body kicked back into arousal just thinking about it.

With the slippery soap as a catalyst between them, skin had glided over skin as he'd rinsed her off, until he'd knelt to get better access to her body and brought his mouth to replace the water.

Cam had pushed Shal over the edge of reason, shuddering as she came. She would've fallen to pieces if she hadn't been gripping Cam's shoulders, and if his hands hadn't been rock steady on her hips. He'd held her up against the tiles as her knees turned to liquid, her cries swallowed by the rush of flowing water.

Cheeks flushed with memory, and suddenly very aware of her nakedness, Shal found one of Cam's clean t-shirts in the set of drawers and enveloped herself in it.

Tripping on something soft and furry in the low light on her way back to bed, her heart skipped a beat.

Rat?

But when she bent to investigate gingerly—heart in throat—her eyes met with those of a plush toy, not a rodent. Surprised and a bit confused to find something so frivolous in Cam's spartan room, she picked it up.

Not a toy, but an enormous slipper in the shape of a scorpion, with pincers stitched onto the front and a curved stinger on the heel.

What the…?

Oh, right. Poppy's idea of a joke. Scorpio and Pisces were both water signs—no doubt a favourable zodiac match.

Shal smiled, replacing the slipper before climbing back into bed to face Cam's sleeping form.

Once again, much more slowly, Cam had moved over her when they'd finally made it back into the bedroom. Discovering the nuances of her body with secreted somethings murmured against her skin, he'd pushed her into a frenzy, finding the tender points with his mouth that drove her mad.

Inner elbow. Ankle. Collar bone.

Holding himself back, Cam had made her writhe and moan for him before moving to get another condom, taking his weight on his arms and easing into her.

She'd wrapped her legs around Cam's hips, welcoming the

rhythm and release, inviting him deeper, faster, harder. Unable to get enough of kissing him when their bodies were joined, she'd gotten drunk off his groans and grunts of pleasure, and accepted every sweet thing he'd said to her without any thought of censorship.

Shal was too close to being overcome by the depth of emotion their intimacy had brought on. The fact Cam was generous in bed shouldn't have been a surprise. He was, after all, a generous man. But it had been so much more than that.

It was so strange how easy that shift had been from friend to lover. She could use that term, couldn't she? In the privacy of her own head.

There was no use trying to fool herself that Cam didn't feel anything for her. Their connection was all wrapped confusingly in friendship, and the past, and the intensity in his eyes when he'd made love.

Because that's what Cam had done. Made love.

Shal could ask him not to say it, and set ground rules until she was blue in the face. But she'd be lacking all her senses if she couldn't feel the difference between casual sex and what had just happened between them.

Not for the first time, Shal was acutely aware she was in way over her head, and sinking fast.

When Cam had his hands on her…

It'd be smart to leave now while Cam was sleeping—head back to the other house and her own bed. She should set her usual precedent of not sleeping over. Keep it casual.

But she didn't want to.

Lying on her side, Shal continued to watch Cam sleep. His face was not exactly symmetrical. If you took his right side and mirror-imaged it, he'd look more serious—more like his brother. There was a softness, a generosity around Cam's mouth, perhaps from his father's side. Even in sleep he looked ready to smile. It was an extremely attractive quality.

She wondered idly if Cam would pass that on to his children. Boys or girls? Would they have tawny hair like their father, or darker, like his ancestors? She was drifting to sleep with the image of a little boy reaching for her hand. He had Cam's full lower lip and an olive complexion, dark, almost raven hair, and familiar blue-green eyes.

Scorpio and Pisces, combined.

If she'd been more awake, Shal might've recognised the first faint 'ping' of her proverbial ovaries waking up from a very long sleep.

That would have freaked her out—big time.

21

Listening to...
While you Sleep - Don McGlashan
From the album: Envy of Angels - The Mutton Birds

The morning light glowed warmly through the drop sheet slung up as a makeshift curtain, and Shal's first conscious thought was one of relief.

No rain.

Katie and Rue's after-match function would be kicking off at the beach at one o'clock, giving the wedding revellers time to sleep off the beer and champagne from last night with a lazy morning in bed.

Her second thought was much more self-serving. Cam was spooning her from behind, and although his breathing proclaimed him fast asleep, one part of his anatomy was very much awake.

Cam woke with a soft moan, mid-way through a steamy dream. It took a few moments to realise Shal's naked ass really *was* rocking erotically against him.

Finding Shal's hips under the vaguely familiar t-shirt she was wearing, he drew her body hard against himself. Caught up in the lush scent of her hair, the memory of the night before came back with sweet intensity.

"Mōrena. Make yourself at home," he groaned.

"Waste not, want not." Shal smiled sleepily over her shoulder, and her mussed up, tousled look undid him. "Do you always wake up with a hard on, pretzel guy?"

"Always." He gave her a slow grin.

"Mm... No wonder you were always so perky before breakfast." Shal twisted, pushing his shoulder down until he was flat on his back. Climbing astride his midriff, she smiled into his eyes with her hair a wild mane around her shoulders. "Perhaps mornings aren't so bad after all." She began to rock her pelvis, stroking herself along him as she stripped the T-shirt off in one fluid motion. "I could grow to like them."

"Holy *shit*." Cam breathed the words out on a huff, sliding his hands up to hold Shal's hips and concentrating hard on not embarrassing himself. "Condom." He remembered, grappling one hand down next to the bed in a blind search for the foil.

Focus.

But it wasn't easy to be anywhere but in the moment. Shal's hands were busy exploring his chest, and her body was in every way exquisite.

By the time they'd finished what Shal had started in bed, showered, and begun the stroll down to Dundas Street, it was already past eleven. Cam's high was knocked down a notch when he went to hold Shal's hand, and she wouldn't have a bar of it.

A minor blip on his radar, although the words that went with it were terse.

"Please, don't hold onto me."

"Don't hold your hand?"

"No, I... I really don't like it. Especially when I'm walking." Shal seemed to struggle to find an explanation, testily folding her arms across her chest. "It's claustrophobic. Makes me feel like I'm on a leash," she finally muttered what Cam had to assume was an honest answer.

"Okay." Holding both hands up in surrender, he reassessed his observations. A few champagnes in Shal last night and some of her walls had tumbled down, but they were well and truly up again this morning. Throw in a dash of regular dating stuff and she got damn skittish.

They walked on in silence.

Shal was fresh faced, but back in her bridesmaid dress. She'd pulled a borrowed T-shirt and hoodie overtop, her furry shoulder-cover-thing from yesterday hanging off Cam's wrist in a supermarket bag.

Claustrophobia made sense. Shal hated being trapped in, tied up, or held onto, and Cam remembered her panicking when she'd been stuck in Links' car once, too agitated to figure out the unfamiliar door lock.

Collar. Leash. Not exactly encouraging words for him to have triggered at the onset.

"I have an idea."

"What?" Turning to look at him rather than concentrating on the footpath, Shal scraped a heel on the steep downward slope, but resolutely ignored the hand he held out to steady her.

The woman was purely exasperating in her bloody-minded stubbornness.

Cam crooked his elbow like an old-fashioned gent, turning to face straight ahead. "*Mademoiselle...*" He tipped the brim of his imaginary hat with his other hand. "I'm going to walk like this, so you can hold onto me if you want. You're in control."

He could feel, rather than see, Shal eyeballing his profile.

"No, I—"

"No harm in giving it a try."

Shal began to walk again, ignoring his elbow until he slid it a little closer to nudge her in the ribs.

"Oh, all *right*!" Shal relented, unfolding her arms to place a tentative hand in the crook of his arm.

As they walked, Cam slowly lowered the angle of his elbow, sliding his hand into his front pocket. Eventually Shal was bumping up next to him with her arm threaded around his, holding him and laughing about the wedding yesterday; the happy people, crazy nerves, entertaining speeches, and all important music.

Cam's mood shot back up to exceptional, but he held back the whistle itching to burst forth, not willing to push his luck.

They let themselves in the front door of Dundas Street, and Shal scooted upstairs as Cam wandered down the hall to meet the houseload of people he could hear gathered in the kitchen.

Daniel was at the stove, his usual morning position, flipping pancakes and generally making a mess with splatters of hastily thrown together ingredients.

"Cam! Nice of you to drop by. What could possibly bring you to this neck of the woods?" Aroha asked ever-so sweetly.

Cam weathered the inevitable ribbing as his due, putting the kettle on before securing himself a seat at the breakfast bar.

"My feet. I walked."

"You look chipper this morning. Could that grin get any bigger?" Aroha continued to dig, obviously in a good mood herself.

Cam couldn't have wiped it off his face if he was paid to.

"I'll have whatever he's having." Links turned to Daniel as if placing an order at the bar, and laughed when Aroha poked her tongue out at him.

"On my pancake?" Cam purposefully misunderstood. "I was thinking lemon and sugar, thanks, Dan."

"You're next in line. Need to keep your stamina up to counteract the energy expenditure." Daniel stepped back and looked Cam up and down overtly. "Because, man, it looks like you've been working out some." He laughed as he yanked up one of Cam's T-shirt sleeves, squeezing a large hand around his brother's bicep.

Adele sauntered over, all rosy from sleep, and slid her fingers over Cam's shoulder. "Don't listen to them, Camry." She beckoned him forward as if about to impart a secret, then added in a loud stage whisper, "I won't tell anyone, but it looks like you've got one hell of a hickey there, tiger." Making a big show of it, she pulled his sleeve back down, covering the distinctive bruising.

When Shal came downstairs ten minutes later, in casual jeans and a white V-neck, Cam had already downed two pancakes and a strong cup of coffee. He'd also timed her cup of tea perfectly, having heard her close the bedroom door and start down.

He handed her the steaming cup as she walked in.

"Great service." Shal smiled at Cam before becoming aware all eyes were on her, and recognising the silence to mean she'd just been the topic of conversation.

"I'm sorry." Links coughed dramatically. "Did you say you'd just been *serviced*?" Aroha gave a bark of laughter, even as she pinched her partner's forearm in reprimand.

Shal's cheeks may've coloured, but she was still able to meet Links' stare unfazed. She even managed to raise her eyebrows in his direction.

"Fully, thank you."

Adele stuck her fingers in her ears like a child, blocking out any details of her cousin's bedroom antics with a chanting, and somewhat desperate, "*La-la-la-la-la.*"

"You'll need a pancake, then," offered Daniel, deadpan.

"Absolutely. No arguments there." Shal turned to him gratefully. "Is there any maple syrup left?"

"You stayed *over*?" Cam caught Katie's whispered words over Shal's shoulder, probably not meant for his ears. Yesterday's bride was getting up to speed by snatching pieces of private conversation within a very social beach picnic.

Shal rose languidly, her dark tresses restless around her shoulders, and reached for Katie's hand.

"Let's walk." Shal slid Katie a tentative smile, flicking a telling glance in Cam's direction before moving off.

Cam watched the exchange from his comfortable position on the picnic rug, his aunts' chatter burbling around him like sea foam. Shal didn't mind holding Katie's hand, he noted, trying to imagine the dialogue as Katie and Shal strolled away from the group towards the headland. Both women were barefoot but wrapped in jackets against the wind.

Katie would hunt him out next. He knew it as sure as he knew the smug looks his mother was sending his way were fully informed ones.

Cam settled his head back on a rogue towel, aiming to catch up on a snippet of lost sleep. Today, life was better than good. The sun seemed brighter, the sea more beautiful, and if his body were any more relaxed he'd be on his way to comatose.

"No promises, no commitment, no strings—" Katie repeated the list Shal had just outlined. The ones Cam had loosely agreed to last night.

She didn't sound at all impressed, concern etched into the lines between her brows.

She wasn't the only one panicking, either.

Shal fished a rogue hair out of her mouth and tucked it back under her jacket collar, wishing she'd thought to bring a hair tie. Though the sun shone hot, the wind buffeted.

"I'd find it insulting if someone I cared for stipulated those terms. It's like asking him to be your friend-with-benefits until something better comes along." It was clear from Katie's tone she was offended on Cam's behalf.

Shal's smile slipped a smidgen when she remembered she'd used those those exact words when she'd first propositioned Cam, and originally he *had* been offended.

On the wet sand, feet sunk in and left an impression in the golden granules. Shal turned to walk backwards for a moment, the wind behind her rather than exfoliating her face. Their wavering, slightly erratic trail of footprints were the only ones clearly visible, following the scalloped edge where the ocean lapped at the shore.

"There is no one better," she assured Katie. "But we *are* friends, and this *is* an added benefit. It wasn't meant as an insult. We're adults. We fancy each other. But I'm not confident I'm capable of anything serious or long term, and this way Cam isn't tied into anything he can't get out of. So, friends-with-benefits is a pretty honest depiction."

"*You're* not looking for anything serious." Katie's voice wavered between anxious and snitchy. "Think about that for a minute. We're talking about Cam here. *He's* the one who's going to get hurt in this. He's as monogamous as they come," she added in a mutter.

Shal tried to smile, though the same thought had been haunting her. "Nobody's going to get hurt."

She turned her face towards the eastern horizon to hide her emotions from a perceptive pair of blue eyes, and prayed to the puff-topped clouds that statement was true. Because no matter how much she tried to fool herself, she couldn't honestly say she believed it.

Not after last night.

Cam had one more night with Shal before she was scheduled to drive back up to Te Whanganui-a-Tara, taking Aroha and Links with her as far as Ōtautahi.

There was already a sense of finality in the air.

Shal spent the late afternoon packing while he sat on the chaise lounge watching her—feet still bare from the beach and guitar in hand.

Every song that came out of the acoustic was morose.

Cam would miss having Links and Aroha around, Daniel would be on his way back to Wānaka first thing tomorrow, and Katie and Rue would be on their honeymoon soon. But Cam's true agitation lay elsewhere.

There was already an ominous black hole forming where Shal should be.

She'd methodically emptied the wardrobe, clearing the decks into her waiting suitcases. Cam wasn't aware exactly when she'd flipped the lid down on the final piece of clothing, but he couldn't fail to notice when she strolled over to him and placed one hand around the neck of the guitar, effectively blocking the music.

"Enough wallowing." Shal placed the instrument against the wall and swung one leg over both of his. "I have a *much* better idea." She sat on his lap, hugging his hips with her knees and roving her fingers all up in his hair. Drawing his head to the side, she took a light nip out of his neck and trailed kisses to his shoulder, pulling the fabric of his T-shirt aside as she went.

"What's this muscle called?"

"Ah, trapezoid? No... trapezius." His voice sounded thick and sluggish to his own ears.

"I really like how muscular you are." Shal used her tongue along his collarbone.

Cam's breath caught and he bought his hands up to hold Shal's waist, grounding himself with the feel of her.

Flesh and blood—not fantasy.

Shal stretched the neck of his shirt further, but instead of carrying on she stopped stock-still.

"Oh!"

"What?" He strained to see what Shal was staring at on his shoulder with such a serious frown, but whatever she'd found was too close to his line of vision.

"Did I hurt you?" Shal placed two fingers to her lips then pressed them to his shoulder, transferring a kiss. "I bit you." She turned back to him.

"No." Cam relaxed again, deciding not to mention the other marks Adele had discovered on his upper arm. "You bit me. I ate you. I'd say we're about even."

Shal snorted a laugh, looked slightly embarrassed about it, then brought her face in close, forehead to forehead. "I didn't mean to hurt you, though. I would never intentionally—"

"You didn't," he interrupted, answering honestly. "There's nothing about last night or this morning I didn't like. If you want to bite me, be my guest. You'll get no complaints from me."

"Mm..." Shal's eyes took on a contemplative look. "*Any*where?"

"Maybe not *any*where," he revised hurriedly, and Shal chuckled again.

Her lips hovered above his, but she didn't kiss him.

"Not these?" Shal raked her fingernails lightly down his chest and over his nipples, waiting until she had him groaning before finally kissing his mouth. "Or this?" Breathless from the kiss, she slid her open palm between them, down the centre of his stomach until she reached the bulge in his jeans.

"Oh! You're...?" Shal raised her head in comic surprise when she realised he was fully hard.

Laughing at her wide eyes, Cam moved quickly to upend her

while she was off her guard, flipping her onto her back on the chaise lounge. He pushed her arms up above her head on the cushioning so he had full access to her body, but didn't attempt to keep hold of her wrists.

Collar. Leash. Claustrophobia. He wouldn't do anything to compound those fears.

For a moment he remained perfectly still, looking down at Shal and drinking his fill. Her smile was beautiful, her body addictive, but it was her eyes that mesmerised him.

He missed her already.

"I think you'll find I'm never far from ready when you're around, my sweet, sweet e hoa."

A faint frown flickered between Shal's brows. "Wait, e hoa means friend, right?"

Cam held back a smile. "Sometimes," he murmured. "Now, where was I?" He brought his lips down on hers.

There were eight of them for dinner that evening. The restaurant was cosy, and the service friendly, but it was hard to shake the feeling things were coming to an end. Shal's appetite had all but left by the time her food arrived, and she pushed her salmon around on the plate.

"Are you finished killing that?" Links asked sardonically.

She silently handed her meal over, knowing from experience it was her ex-flatmate's not-so-subtle way of angling for her leftovers.

Shal and Cam were the only ones subdued in the group, the others were all exhibiting varying degrees of excitement and anticipation. For the newlyweds, it was their long awaited European honeymoon next, and Katie could hardly contain herself. Links and Aroha were pushing Cam for more information on the Dundas Street property, which was about to be listed. And at the end of the table, Adele was animatedly discussing Wānaka as an option for herself and Saffy with Daniel, who knew the area best.

There didn't appear to be any inclusion of Adele's absent husband, James, in the plan.

Shal was attempting to have a private conversation with Rue about her degree, but they kept getting interrupted. "It just feels unfinished. I don't like leaving it half done." She sighed.

"What feels unfinished?" Katie invited herself into the discussion.

"Shal's English degree." Rue turned to Katie and raised his wine glass for a top-up from the bottle she was brandishing. "She was just saying she's considering Otago. I'm thinking three to four years, part-time."

"I've been debating what to do about it for a while now. Ever since we decided to expand 2-PEAS down south. Wondering if Ōtepoti would be a good option, for the warmer months, anyway."

"To live? For *real*? You never mentioned..." Katie spluttered. "Well, from a purely selfish perspective, you definitely should."

"I agree. Good for the boutique too." Rue's gaze slid towards Cam, sitting too far away to hear. "Best way to get your business off the ground would be to baby it."

"It's hypothetical, of course." Shal back-pedalled.

"Oh, of *course*." Katie's solicitous tone struck a raw nerve.

"I haven't decided yet," Shal warned, wishing she hadn't brought it up. "I could just as easily consider Tāmaki-makau-rau. Or Massey."

Though neither of those options included Cam

Cam stayed over, and waking next to Shal's soft, sleeping body in the master bedroom of Dundas Street was a little too close to dream-like for comfort. Light streamed through the crack they'd inadvertently left in the curtains in their haste to get into bed the night before, causing the dust motes to dance.

He turned his head to take in the rest of the view, careful not to wake the principal occupant. Shal slept with the white coverlet snuggled tightly around her ears and fisted up to her chin, looking as innocent as the driven snow.

The faint scent of fig and honey soap teased his senses as she shifted and re-settled in her sleep, and he added another acute memory to his growing pile.

All too soon she'd be gone.

An hour later, Dundas Street was a frenzy of last minute showers, packing, and attempts to jigsaw puzzle multiple suitcases into Shal's compact car. Aroha and Links travelled light, which was fortunate considering Shal didn't have any skill in that department.

There wasn't time for long goodbyes or privacy, so when Shal purposefully cornered him in the lounge and shut the door, Cam raised his eyebrows at her. She wore an intent expression, leaning her butt up against the door to keep him in and the others out.

"Looking for a goodbye quickie?" he teased to cover his unease.

Shal laughed a little nervously. "Not exactly." She folded her arms across herself, eyes skittering away rather than meeting his for any longer than a moment. "I just wanted to make sure you're, um… clear on where we stand with this long distance thing. We'll be so far away from each other, Cam. It doesn't make sense to keep it exclusive. I think you should see other people."

———

Shal had never had qualms about discussing the terms of engagement before. But with Cam? Her palms were sweaty and the words too cold in comparison to what they'd shared. Up-front and honest was essential, but facing Cam's carefully expressionless face, the concept seemed all too mercenary.

"I don't want to see other people."

"But, you know you can, if you change your mind?" she double-checked, needing him to have the freedom to choose, though the idea was becoming less palatable by the second.

Cam edged her backwards until she was pressed firmly against the door by his body. He bent to kiss the tender skin just below her ear, and her breath quickened. The memory of how it'd felt to be naked with Cam in this position, not that long ago in the ensuite shower, was still fresh in her mind, and she released a soft moan as he slid both hands down her body in a slow stroke.

"I won't change my mind." Cam's hands stilled their languid travels, resting on her hips as his eyes met hers. She could see resignation there, and an unnerving sadness she knew she'd put there herself.

"I know your a loyal person, but I'm trying to tell you there's no need. You're not tied to me, Cam." Shal had to remind herself to breathe in and out between the difficult sentences. "You're free to do whatever you want. Just let me know if the foundation shifts and you start getting, you know, serious about someone." The idea of Cam seeing other people was fast becoming her number one ick. "When I'm back in Te Whanganui-a-Tara..." she trailed off.

What? When she was back in Te Whanganui-a-Tara she would be missing him over and over again. It wasn't smart. It wasn't in the plan. But she had no way of switching the feelings off, and no spreadsheet capable of tidying this kind of mess.

———

Cam couldn't help but pull back from Shal. The idea of her returning to the ins and outs of her former life and liaisons up north made his skin crawl. He hadn't assumed anything had changed, but the reality of hearing the words come out of her mouth after what he'd felt for her over the past couple of days was noxious.

Shal would see other people, and he had to come to terms with that. He'd love to take a leaf out of Adele's book, put his fingers in his ears and chant *la, la, la*. He did the next best thing, laying a finger over Shal's lips to silence her, just as she had to him at Katie's wedding.

"Don't." He could take only so much, and this was the limit. "That's your prerogative, see whoever you like, but don't tell me. I don't want to know. If I can't use the L-word, it's only fair I have a stipulation too. Deal?"

"Deal." Her agreement was quietly spoken, and she stepped deftly to the side, hand on the doorknob. "It's been so lovely, Cam. Thank you...' Her voice wavered. "For everything."

Then she kissed him on the cheek and was gone.

That's when Cam's own stupidity hit him squarely in the jaw, standing alone in the godforsaken lounge. Why had he bought into this? It felt bloody awful. Mad about Shal, while she blithely tripped off to be with someone else.

*Any*one else.

To add to that, she'd just made it clear she wouldn't give a stuff if he found another person to love.

If he hadn't gibbed and plastered this wall with his own two hands, it would've been tempting to put a fist through it.

22

Listening to…
Victoria - Jordan Luck
From the album: Prayers Be Answered - Dance Exponents

It seemed like months since Shal had been in her Te Whanganui-a-Tara apartment, not a mere fortnight. The place was eerily quiet after all the hubbub of Dundas Street, and nowhere near as inviting as she'd expected.

Shal made a vague attempt to unpack before she fell asleep on her feet, taking her toiletries to the bathroom and replacing her framed photo on the shelf with the others. She hesitated before taking down the image usually sitting next to it, the one of Katie and Cam at the Chinese Gardens in Ōtepoti.

There wasn't a lot to tie the cousins' youthful faces together as family, apart from the happy light in their eyes as they smiled for the camera—smiled for Shal. She'd always loved this particular shot, but now she could look at it through new eyes.

Cam had feelings for her then. And Katie knew but didn't tell.

Maybe if Shal had hooked up with Cam eight years ago, she could've trusted herself more with whatever this connection was morphing into. Maybe she would've had more to give, more to offer?

The photo and the thought made her miss Cam in a wave of feeling very like homesickness.

Too tired to fully analyse her screwy emotive state, Shal rummaged in her suitcases to find one of Cam's old sweatshirts to sleep in before crawling into bed.

She hadn't given any of Cam's loaned clothing back, and this particular one was from their first surf-day at St Clair almost two weeks ago. It was soft and baggy, and with the arms folded up, was likely to become her new favourite sleepwear.

There was a lot of admin work to catch up on. Shal loved being busy, but paperwork wasn't her favourite and it had been banking up during the two weeks she'd been down south.

Ōtepoti's staff contracts and tax details all needed to be formally filed, too.

Taking a break one evening, and checking her watch, Shal figured the time difference loosely and video-called Katie in England. It was the third time she'd tried in as many days, but this time the link went through.

"Hello!" The image was choppy at first, and the sound glitched, but suddenly Katie was there, grinning.

"Hi! I'm so glad I caught you. I can't get my head around the daytime-nighttime thing. Is it nine a.m. over there?"

"Eight." Katie held up a thickset mug. "I'm on my second cup, and Rue's just headed for a shower."

It was good to see her friend looking so relaxed and happy. "Tell me everything," Shal ordered.

Katie filled her in on London; excited about one of the live shows they were heading to later, the markets, and the shopping—holding up some items she'd bought. She laughed at her own lack of prowess converting pounds to dollars, and complained that Rue's accent had gained another plumb the instant they'd landed at Heathrow.

"But that's enough about me. How's it going between you and Cam?" Katie finally probed, her tone more serious.

"Well, ah… It's been busy, but we've texted and talked once or twice on the phone." Shal sidestepped a phone-sex reference at the last minute in consideration for cousin-dom (and the *la-la-la* factor).

"I talked to him last night," Katie informed her airily. "Sounds like he's juggling too much work. Building, on top of recording with Pieta. He's at The Den all hours. Those two are really hitting it off." Katie hesitated for a moment too long before adding, "Professionally."

Frost settled around Shal's rib cage as she absorbed that unwelcome morsel of information.

Cam hadn't mentioned Pieta. Not once.

"You're angling for the two of them to get together?"

"No. Not *angling*," Katie placated quickly. "I know it's Cam's work, but it could potentially shift into something else. I mean, they have so much in common. Music. Friends. Proximity. Pieta's a complete sweetheart, Shal. You'd like her."

There was a pregnant pause, where Shal wondered if it was reasonable to loathe someone you'd never met.

"Sorry if I've trodden on your toes there?" Katie added with a softness that hadn't been there before. "I was under the impression you and Cam were seeing other people."

There was no good reason why Shal should feel a chilly blast towards Katie, or a wave of hot jealousy towards Pieta. She'd made this bed herself and deserved the discomfort of having to lie on it.

It was exactly what she'd wanted, right? What she'd requested.

"No, you're right. He's free to see whoever he likes." Shal spoke as breezily as she could through the tension suddenly underpinning her jaw. "We've been really up front about that." Though she had no inclination to sing and dance about it right now.

The idea of Cam seeing Pieta, the 'complete sweetheart,' was very unsettling. It was totally unreasonable to feel so frustrated about it, but the self-realisation in no way curbed Shal's gut response.

"Boutique opens next Friday." She moved the conversation to safer topics before she said something she couldn't take back.

Jac and herself had staggered flights back down to Ōtepoti to set it up. A mere seven days after that, and she'd be off to Asia for a fortnight of supply-and-buy.

Beginning to feel the strain of not being in one place for more than a heartbeat, she complained to Katie about her roots being tugged on.

The quintessential gypsy within her was finally slowing down, longing to collect a little moss. They were able to laugh about it before they disconnected their call.

"What the hell happened to you?" Shal exclaimed when Cam picked her up from Ōtepoti airport. The black eye and grazes along Cam's cheekbone were painfully obvious, and her heart flew to her throat at the sight.

"Would you believe me if I told you I had a tussle with Dan over a pretty face?"

"Nooo…?" Shal drew the word out, not entirely sure Cam was joking until she caught the glint of self-deprecating humour in his eyes. Her hand reached out, stopping just before touching the multi-coloured skin, and she winced at the extent of the bruising. "Work accident?"

Cam hesitated, easing her suitcases onto a trolley with some care before answering. "Remember I told you we had that break-in up at the Park Street site? The garage?" He left the words hanging so she had to fill in the blanks by herself.

It took her a minute.

"You were *out* there?" First, Shal's hand flew to cover her mouth, then conversely, it curled into a fist and thumped him on the arm. "You were assaulted?"

Cam rubbed his arm absently, then raised his hand to stroke her loose hair over her shoulder and draw her closer. "Just a bit."

Then Cam was kissing her, his hands holding her steady, and Shal forgot everything except she'd missed him every day, and every night since she'd driven away last week.

"How do you assault someone 'just a bit?' " Shal managed to ask later, when her brain was back to functioning on all cylinders.

"You decide to use your fist instead of a crowbar," Cam quipped.

"Don't joke about this. I can't believe you didn't tell me!"

"I did tell you. Sort of. Look, I'm okay, and I knew you had a lot on your plate this past week."

Shal folded her arms across her chest in a gesture of censure.

"I was just in the wrong place at the wrong time." Cam shrugged.

"You said the break in was at Park Street before sunrise." She pursed her lips tightly.

"Mm," he conceded, looking slightly caught out.

"So, you were at *home*, in the middle of the *night*."

Shal wasn't happy about Cam's subterfuge on the break in, that much was clear. He thought back to the cold, dark morning four days ago. If he'd called the cops when he'd heard someone trying to jimmy the roller door, it would've been fine. But he'd assumed it was Jonno, coming in early and having trouble with the old lock.

Cam had gone out to help, and to tell Jonno to shut the hell up.

Only it hadn't been Jonno.

He hadn't taken much notice of the unfamiliar van in the drive, and was sleepy enough to have missed the shadow of the second guy behind him when he'd confronted the first.

Cam hadn't been joking about the crowbar, either. The guy in full view had been using one to wrench the lock on the garage, but opted to drop it and use his fist when the second man had grabbed Cam's arms behind his back. He'd taken one or two solid punches to the head, and from what they could gather at A&E, a couple of body kicks when he'd gone down.

Could've been much worse.

"I surprised them. They weren't expecting anyone onsite." He rubbed his jaw. "My ute was in at the shop, so the place would've looked like an easy target."

Cam accepted the resulting flack as his due. He'd had it from all sides this week and knew his actions that morning hadn't been the smartest he'd ever made.

Shal insisted on driving due to his swollen eye, and he told her to head to Poppy's. At the first stretch of straight road she leant over and scrabbled around in the glovebox until her fingers closed over his old iPod, which she then lobbed lightly into his lap.

"Shal's Playlist, please." She placed her request as if she'd never had anyone say no to her before, making Cam laugh.

The movement jolted his ribs and he swallowed a grunt of surprise pain. Surreptitiously readjusting the pressure-strapping under his T-shirt, he redistributed the load.

"You okay?" Shal glanced his way.

"Sure. Just be warned there might be a few unfamiliar ones on it," he sidestepped the question. "I've added to it every now and again."

He was surprised Shal handled the ute so confidently, and said so. The column-change could be tricky.

"I drive the work van in Te Whanganui-a-Tara, moving stock," Shal explained. "It's pretty much the same setup." She waved her hand around the cab vaguely.

It struck Cam he didn't know much about the everyday ins and outs of her business, so he asked a scree of questions on the way to St Clair to rectify that. It took some of the heat off him on the assault issue, and gave him an excuse to watch Shal while she talked about something she was passionate about.

She was a damn good view, and one week apart had been far too long.

Cam's mother was away in Wānaka looking after Dan's farmhouse for a spell, so the timing hadn't worked out too bad. He didn't want Shal anywhere near the Park Street property, although it was nearing completion. The cops had some leads on the break-in and assault, but no one had been arrested. The garage door had been replaced by a more robust version and was now alarmed, but there was no guarantee the thieves wouldn't return to finish the job.

Cam and Jonno had their own ideas about who'd be robbing them, and unfortunately, the disgruntled paint crew they'd replaced at the end of last year fit the description and the bill a little too perfectly.

Punches were likely par for the course, but the steel-toed boot to the ribs had sure felt personal.

In order to set the table for omelettes and salad for their evening meal, Shal had to move a collection of plans and papers aside to make space. Cam's next project was obviously a new build.

"Is this the one you're building from scratch?" Shal studied a surveyor's map of the hill site, not recognising it as the one she'd seen recently.

Was it a touch smaller?

"Yeah. I've got a meeting with the architect and engineer tomorrow to finalise."

"I thought you'd got building consent already?" She looked up in surprise.

"No, not for this one." Cam didn't elaborate, just took the papers from her hand and rolled them up.

He was a little on the quiet side this evening; less forthcoming than he would've normally been about a new project, and Shal caught him rubbing at his temple more than once.

"Headache?"

"Yeah. Bit of a killer, actually."

Shal rummaged through Poppy's medicine cabinet and arrived back at the kitchen table with a glass of water and some paracetamol, getting a good look at the damage on Cam's face under the unforgiving light.

"Bastards. I hope they get what's coming to them," she murmured, putting a hand under his chin to lift it for a better angle.

Cam moved back, away from her touch and out of the direct light, distancing himself.

Shal couldn't quite put her finger on what had changed, but when they climbed into bed together, Cam didn't make any attempt to hold her until she took matters into her own hands. She'd missed the contact, and judging from Cam's physical response, so had he. Their lovemaking was almost desperate, the need for each other a tangible static that left Shal clinging, trying to catch her breath.

Afterwards, Cam was downright melancholy.

It wasn't a mood Shal would normally attribute to him, but it could've been the residual headache and soreness chasing away his smile and sense of fun. She'd noticed some solid bruising along his ribcage when he'd been naked under her, and he'd flinched when she'd tried to touch.

When Shal woke in the darkness of the small hours, Cam was no longer in the bed next to her and the space where he should've been was cold. Sitting up abruptly, she pulled the blankets with her, disoriented by the unfamiliar room and disturbed by a vague sense of disquiet.

He'd gone. Left.

"Cam?" she whispered into the unfriendly darkness.

"I'm here."

His voice came from over by the window, and Shal could make out the shadowed outline of his body in the old armchair. He'd drawn the corner of the curtain back so he could see the ocean.

She let out a long sigh of relief. "Will you come back to bed?"

"Bad dream?"

"No. Just cold without you. Come and be my hot-water-bottle."

Cam padded back to the bed and slid under the covers, keeping his chilled feet away from her and spooning from behind. It reminded her of the week following Mason's death. Cam had held her so she could sleep.

"You used to hold me like this," she murmured, warming immediately with their combined heat.

"Yeah."

"So, you fancied me, even then?" At her worst.

"Of course. I've fancied you forever."

Shal turned, trying to catch Cam's expression. But his face was guarded by the deep shadows.

"Weren't you tempted to try it on?"

Cam laughed. "That wouldn't have been very gentlemanly." He took a long, deep sniff of the hair at her nape. "A: my mother was in the next room, and B: you needed a friend, not a randy dread-head with a hard-on."

"Oh, I don't know." Cam's mouth was tickling Shal's sensitive skin as she spoke, making her shiver. "A hard-on might've been quite useful to take my mind off everything else, looking back." She was only half joking.

"Tell me that *now*," Cam admonished. "Jesus, I had to run bloody rugby scores through my head."

Shal melted back into him.

This was a more familiar side of Cam—relaxed and joking. Shal was almost dreaming when he spoke again, his voice low and soft. "Do you still have the nightmares?"

"Sometimes. Not so often, now." she murmured.

Cam's arm tightened across her midriff for a moment, then took on the heavy weight of sleep.

23

Listening to…
Renegade Fighter - Nathan King, Ben Campbell
From the album: Silencer - Zed

When Shal met Pieta for the first time, she wasn't expecting to like her. Cam had set up the mid-week meeting at the boutique, but he couldn't be there to introduce the women or mediate in any way.

Perhaps for the best.

Shal would've been happy to let Jac cover the celebrity dressing by herself, but the other designer was adamant they should present a united front.

"We need to wow Pieta, stroke her ego if necessary, and build a solid working relationship," Jac maintained. "Let's face it, she's a Grammy just waiting to happen, and it makes total sense to secure her as a 2-PEAS advocate before she steps anywhere near that red carpet. We scratch her back, and she advertises the hell out of ours. It's win-win."

It was a good plan, in theory.

Contrary to Shal's predictions, Pieta came across as both sincere and humble during her fitting. She also got on Jac's good side immediately, which deserved a medal in itself and made Shal wonder if Cam had armed the songstress with a couple of tips.

One part star-struck, and the other on the defensive, Shal had been half-hoping the other woman would be a total diva behind the scenes. It would've been so much easier to hate her.

But if anything, Pieta seemed a little shy, evading the majority of the attention and bringing the focus back to the quality of the clothing, again and again.

Waif-like, with a heart shaped face and pale colouring, the woman would've looked good in a sack.

Jac opted to dress her in the silk shift, instead. Killjoy.

A one-off in pastel pink with maroon daisies, it was a romantic choice, and the plunge neckline suited Pieta's form. Her breasts were dainty—definitely pert enough to carry it off.

It was understandable the conversation would turn to Cam, their common connection. But as the informal dressing progressed, Shal got the distinct impression Jac and herself were being gently pumped for information.

Disconcerting, considering she'd been angling to do the same to Pieta. It made Shal's skin prickle uncomfortably.

"He's great, isn't he? We've been friends for years, but just started seeing each other recently," Shal finally stated. Was that innocuous enough? She didn't owe anyone an explanation, least of all Pieta.

"Which tie?" Cam moved behind Shal so she could see him in the bathroom mirror while she did her hair.

He held up one tie—his preferred choice—then the other against his black dress shirt.

"Um…" Shal's hands stopped moving as she considered the options. "Neither." She turned to adjust his collar, opening first one button, then a second. "It looks better without."

"Are you sure?" He wasn't convinced. "I could change the shirt."

Shal put her head to the side and looked him up and down. "No, that's perfect."

Cam caught his own reflection in the mirror and frowned. The black eye was still prominent. Nothing he could do about it, but he remained apologetic. He felt bad letting the side down accompanying Shal anywhere, let alone to her 2-PEAS launch.

She wore an asymmetric gold evening dress with one shoulder bare. When her hair was tied up, it showed off her high cheekbones and made-up eyes. Gone was the tousled, barefoot beach-nymph, with salt in her hair and sand in her ears.

She was barely recognisable.

As Cam turned to leave the bathroom, Shal called him back. Aiming for a much more open, less judgemental approach this time, she re-opened the Pieta pie.

"I was surprised when I met Pieta. She's not what I expected. She seems very, um… very sweet."

"Can be, when she wants to be." Cam was watchful, but his eyes promised honesty, catching and holding hers in the reflection. "She can also be a right pain in the ass, but she has something special. She's a natural."

"Right." Shal hesitated, not entirely sure if she was game to continue. "I know you told me you hadn't, um…" She waggled her fingers to prompt Cam's memory about their pie conversation. "Only, I got the impression that Pieta's very fond of you."

To her surprise, Cam threw back his head and laughed. "Ha! She's 'fond' of me because I totally saved her bacon. Super-Cam to the rescue, remember?"

"When you stepped in on guitar?"

"Yeah." Cam was leaning on the doorframe behind her and Shal could smell the faint scent of his aftershave as his eyes returned to hers in the mirror, shafting her with a double dose of pure sexuality. His features in humour were already heart-stoppingly attractive.

Cam's magnetism had a raw ferocity to it, and Shal felt the responding clench deep in her core. He always looked good, but tonight he was freshly shaven and had an unseasonably warm tone to his skin from the exterior work he'd been doing. The purpling eye and grazed cheekbone gave his boy-down-the-hall look an edgier, more dangerous vibe, which suited his black shirt and recently trimmed hair.

"She was in the shit, dumping her guitarist before they'd finished recording this album. But I'm not complaining." Cam shrugged.

"Right." Shal touched a finger to her tooth, removing a tiny trace of lipstick. "To be honest I got the impression Pieta had a different agenda, but she's being polite. Holding back because of what you and I are up to."

Cam stopped smiling. "And what is it you and I are up to, exactly?"

His quiet tone should've alerted Shal to his mood change, but she missed it, leaning forward to apply a layer of gloss over her lips.

"You know, fooling around. Making pretzels." Catching Cam's cooling expression in the mirror, she hurried on a little more uneasily, "If you wanted to tell her we aren't actually long-term…"

Merely saying the words aloud smarted, like an unexpected paper cut.

Shal slid the gloss dipper back into its sticky scabbard and screwed it shut before turning to face Cam. "Katie thought you might consider it." As soon as the words were out, embarrassment slid in.

That particular opinion wasn't hers to air, and she'd had no right to share it.

"It's none of Katie's fuckin' business." Cam spoke roughly, a touch of fire in his eyes. "I won't do that." His hand was clenching and unclenching on the doorframe above his head. "I *don't* do that. You're free to do whatever, of course," he muttered.

"You hate it." Shal could see the absolute truth of that statement, and turned away on the pretext of checking her hair one last time, gulping. "The whole idea of an open—"

"I don't have to like it. Those are the terms I agreed to." Again, their eyes met in the mirror.

"I'm trying to give you your freedom, not trying to hurt you," Shal whispered, caught in Cam's haunted expression.

The direct opposite to Mason, Cam didn't seem to see any of this as a liberty, he saw it as a sub-standard way to conduct a relationship. He saw it as pain.

No one had even come close to touching Shal emotionally since Mason, she'd made sure to of it. But there was a heady excitement and undeniable potential to this blossoming connection with Cam, one she hadn't ever felt ever before, with very dangerous levels of hope. Was there a guarantee the burgeoning bubble wouldn't pop? No, of course not. The law of averages was adamantly against it. And what was the point of promising future love if you had no expectation of ever being able to sustain it? *Zero* point. Hollow proclamations were the *worst*.

Yet couples did it. Over and over again they did it.

Cam rubbed the back of his arm across his forehead. "I knew the deal when I signed up, but that doesn't mean it doesn't bite."

He turned to leave.

"Cam." Shal halted him again, this time with a hand on his sleeve, urgent for him to understand. "I really care for you. I... I really care. But I don't think I'm capable of what you're asking."

"I'm not asking *anything* of you," Cam countered, eyes flashing. "I'm being bloody careful not to put *any* pressure on you about *any damn thing*."

True. So true, and their connection was suffering due to the unreasonable restraints she'd put on him.

"Please, can we not argue? Tonight's really important to me," she pleaded. "I'm sorry I brought it up. This is new territory for me, and I'm doing the best I can."

"I'm not arguing." The touch on her cheek was fleeting, as was Cam's sad smile. "Just disagreeing impolitely. I'll see you downstairs."

Shal stared at the space he'd left in the doorway. Would it be so bad to carry on as they were, long distance, and not see other people? Together for a few nights, then maybe apart for months? Why was the word 'exclusive' so freaky?

Perhaps because while one of them was falling in, heels and all, the other might well be falling out.

***

Cam knew he was several breeds of idiot. He was a sucker for Shal's big pleading eyes and always had been. He'd been writing everything he wasn't supposed to say to her on a pad of lined paper he kept with the St. Clair plans, like some lovesick high school student. The L-word was prevalent there, and it was looking more like a sprawling manuscript than the odd admission.

Once more, Shal had stood in front of him reiterating their lack of foundation and longevity. Hell, she was going a step further and choosing likely candidates for him now. He should hate the insensitivity, but in her own kooky way, Shal was actually trying to look out for him.

He'd noticed Pieta, of course. You'd have to be a cyborg not to. But by the time he figured she may've been noticing him back, he'd already been with Shal.

Cam didn't overlap, and had no intention of seeing anyone else. No doubt Shal would twist that and see it as some kind of trap, but he just wasn't built that way.

Pieta didn't make his soul sing, it was as simple as that. She didn't keep him awake nights, and he'd never been tempted to haul the woman over his shoulder and run away with her.

Purposefully, though it knotted in his gut, Cam was choosing not to ask Shal about her own love life. He slept better not knowing.

The fact Pieta and her social entourage were attending the launch party was the hook the media ran with, and Shal was grateful for the extra hype. 2-PEAS was well covered on that front, and through the ensuing interest they had no trouble filling the small boutique and upstairs apartment with potential clients.

That's not to say there weren't hiccups.

A day earlier, Jonno had put his shoulder through the glass-panelled door when helping move boxes of stock, and the shattered glass had coincided unhelpfully with Pieta's fitting. Following that was an incomplete knitwear delivery in the morning, couriered to Ōtautahi by mistake. And the caterer had gone ahead and substituted club-sandwiches for sushi due to a lack of available avocado, without bothering to consult Shal.

Although stressful, everything eventually fell into place, and half an hour before the opening party the boutique looked better than good. It looked amazing.

Cam stepped over to Shal and handed her his iPad.

Assuming it was something to do with stock, it took Shal a moment to recognise the couple beaming on the screen, and a moment more to realise it was a live feed, not a photo.

"*Hej, min älskling*!" Henke boomed. "*Hur går det*? Lookin' good!" He whistled long and low.

Ulrika squeezed her cheek in next to the large Swede, their combined faces filling the screen. Through a jumble of words and exclamations, everyone burbled at once, Swedish and English weaving into each other. 'Swinglish,' Ulrika laughingly called it, congratulating Shal on the new boutique and wanting to be 'shown around.'

Shal was over the moon to have her uncle and aunt see the boutique and share in her excitement. It also took care of the queasy knot of trepidation building in her gut. This Otago move was a big deal for 2-PEAS. They couldn't afford to fail.

Henke, though trying to be surreptitious about it, asked in Swedish if Shal's 'nice young man' was a boxer, played ice hockey, or rugby—referring to Cam's black eye without mentioning it. Her uncle wasn't an aggressive man, and clearly didn't want his niece with one.

"Cam's one of the gentlest people I know. You'll absolutely adore him." Shal assured her protective uncle and aunt in Swedish. Knowing it to be the truth because *she* absolutely adored him.

She pushed the thought away, leaving the last part unsaid. It wasn't fair to do that to Cam. She was already hurting him, a point made clear today by their bathroom discussion. Bringing words like love into the equation would only raise the stakes.

When Henke and Ulrika finally rung off, Shal wallowed in the emptiness for a moment, wishing more than anything she could've had them physically present.

She turned to Cam. "Did you arrange that?"

His eyes were watchful, picking up on her emotions like a well-tuned antenna. "No, Mum did." He took the iPad from her limp fingers and gave her shoulders a sideways squeeze. "You okay?"

"Yes, better than okay. That was just what I needed."

Mindful of not messing up her makeup, Cam kissed Shal's forehead.

"Who's Fred?" He'd caught the name flying backwards and forwards between Ulrika and Henke. They were excited about Fred coming to Hong Kong. When Fred came, they were going to do this, eat here, and go there.

Shal laughed. Tipping her head to study his face. "Why, jealous?"

"Of another man in your life? Absolutely. Always will be," he answered, dead serious.

"Me." Shal spoke with her lips still curved into a smile.

"You're Fred?"

"Short for *Fredslilja*. It means peace lily. It's been my Swedish nickname since… Well, since forever."

"Freds-lil-ya." He tried to get his mouth around the strange pronunciation, touching his fingers to her cheek.

"They're toxic," Shal cautioned, pulling away from him.

Cam laughed at her suddenly wooden demeanour. "Bit late to warn me off now, don't you think?"

"It's never too late," Shal answered in the same, flat tone.

"So, if you're Fred…" Cam floundered, suddenly making the connection. "Does that mean you're heading to Hong Kong?"

Hell, Te Whanganui-a-Tara had seemed far enough away. Now Shal was disappearing off to Asia?

"Next week."

She'd caught him by surprise and he blinked at her, stunned. How the hell was he going to play this now? Follow her across the globe?

Sure. Why not? The voice in his head answered glibly.

"Just a short buying trip," Shal added, and Cam consciously schooled the tension in his face back to relaxed and easy-going. "Possibly one of my last. We can't really justify the carbon footprint anymore. Not in the current climate. We're looking to work more with what's available locally as we move forward."

Well, thank the gods for that.

The 2-PEAS Ōtepoti opening was a blast, and Shal was over the moon to be experiencing it with Cam by her side. Potential customers and advocates of the boutique rubbed shoulders with the models hired to showcase the winter line. Each model had a blurb explaining the source and sustainability of the garments they wore, and were excelling on the promo side of it.

The polished, recycled copper change rooms were in constant use and the till chimed merrily.

Pieta wore the silk shift, and looked stunning in it.

Shal experienced a shimmer of guilt on chatting to the songwriter briefly. Was she holding one of her best friends back from someone who was essentially better suited to him?

An even more perplexing question kept surfacing. Was she actually falling for Cam, or was she just in love with the very idea of being in love? The newness of it, the intoxication…

People pretended, or became blinded. And love could be as fleeting as fashion. Experiencing one glorious season only to be cast off, never to be worn again.

Shal tried to slide back into enjoying the moment, sipping her Kiwi knock-off champagne and smiling, regardless of the morose twist her mood had just taken.

Katie, though absent herself, was well represented by her extended family. Snug in their eclectic support, Shal could liken it to a loud, patchwork blanket. The aunties were there, along with Rosa and Amos, who chatted and laughed, working the room as a single entity.

The opposite of a single season, Katie's parents were an ageless style. A vintage, but classic pairing. Like a Chanel suit, or a pair of well-used Louis Vuitton suitcases.

Timeless.

Awe inspiring, really.

How did they do it?

Jonno entered late with a date who looked half his age, and vaguely familiar. It took Shal a moment to recognise the young woman from the CD store. She wore a leather waistcoat and must've been freezing in tailored shorts, showcasing her mile-long legs.

Ōtepoti was like that, everyone knew everyone—zero degrees of separation.

With sordid interest, Shal watched Jac execute the meet-and-greet with much less grace than she was capable of. Whatever Jac said to Jonno before she stalked off, it left the builder looking like he'd just been clobbered over the head with a brick.

Slipping away from Cam, and remembering Jonno saying he didn't drink, Shal offered the newcomers flutes of virgin punch and an apologetic smile. She'd invited Jonno and his plus one, and by the looks of it Jac had just done her best to make them both feel unwelcome.

It took two days to come down off the high of the opening. The public response had been fantastic, initial sales were better than projected, and the new manager they'd brought down from Te Whanganui-a-Tara had surpassed all expectations.

With stock well-ordered and staff ticking all the boxes, Shal found herself looking at Jac over the dark wood of the cashier counter with nothing left to do.

"I thought we'd be snowed under." Shal held up both hands.

Jac grinned. "But they don't need either of us, let alone both. The staff might be young, but they're incredibly efficient." She sneaked a look around to check they were still alone, then lowered her voice. "Take a couple of days off with Cam. See if he can get some free time while you're down here."

"Are you going all romantic on me?"

"Shal, if somebody looked at me the way Cam looks at you I'd go romantic all the way," Jac returned with a straight face.

"You're joking."

Jac was the quintessential stand-alone woman.

Shal waited for a smirk, or some sign the other designer was amused, but there wasn't a twitch.

"I'm not," Jac returned quietly. "I'm probably not the best person to advise you, am I? I'm no relationship guru, but I've never seen you like this with anyone and I have to wonder..." She reached across the counter to touch Shal's fingers. "How long you've been in love with him?"

"What?" Shal pulled her hand back and glanced around testily.

"How long, Shal?"

"I've loved Cam forever, he's one of my closest friends."

"That's not what I meant and you know it," Jac countered matter-of-factly. "Was this going on when you two were flatmates?"

"No!"

"Oh." Jac hesitated. "Are you sure? Because—"

"No."

"*Riiiight*." With all the inflection Jac loaded on the single word, she might as well have said, 'you're so full of shit.' "Have you slept with anyone else since you two started up?"

"Of course not! But I don't see what that has to do with it. I—"

"Just answer the damn question," Jac snapped, and Shal blinked at her.

"Okay, no," she admitted. "But I was, you know, planning on having an open relationship."

"Planning on doesn't count." Jac slid in her signature twist of sarcasm. "And how would you feel if Cam made use of that little clause? You'd be happy if he had a bit on the side, would you? Pieta, for instance?"

Shal shook her head.

"Sorry?" Jac hassled, bringing a hand up to her ear as if she was hard of hearing.

"No," Shal groaned. "I keep telling him he can if he wants, but the thought of it is just *awful*. She's so lovely, but part of me—a very dark part—would like to scratch her eyes out."

"Catty," Jac chided. "What about sleeping over? Are you waking up with him?"

Jac appeared to take Shal's mulish silence as assent, nodding with a self-satisfied little smirk. "Mmm-hmm. That's what I thought. And how does it feel?" she probed further, leaning forward to catch Shal's answer.

Shal hesitated before answering. It somehow made it more real to say it aloud.

"Wonderful," she whispered.

"I get that you don't want to see it, but those are big steps for you. It's not exactly romantic, but it shows a certain degree of trust, and I've heard relationships are built on that."

"What if I'm just a magpie, collecting shiny new things?" Shal rubbed at her temple. "This feels really precious, but what if I can't keep it up? I can't tell Cam how much I feel, because I don't know if I can promise anything for the long term."

"No one can."

"But they do! They promise to love, and honour. They stand in front of a holy person and sign it all away *for the rest of their lives*. Who's to say I don't see the next bright thing—"

"You're no different, or any less capable of loving long-term than anyone else," Jac interrupted, more gently this time. "You're not your father, and you're not your mother. I know this is freaking you out, but don't write it off before it's hardly even started. *That* would be a true travesty. Cam's genuine. He makes you laugh, keeps you honest, and you're *yourself* around him. That's why you've loved him forever. And if you're up for it, you could make it work, long distance or otherwise. I know you could. You just have to want to."

"But 2-PEAS—"

"If it came down to it, I could hold down 2-PEAS Te Whanganui-a-Tara on my own. We're both taking a professional risk by expanding down south. No guarantees it'll work. Just hard slog, determination, and a bit of luck gaining roots here." Jac threw an arm wide, the gesture encompassing the boutique and all their carefully colour co-ordinated stock. "What's the difference between you taking a punt on this new branch and taking a risk in your personal life?"

Shal put her head in her hands.

"What if I'm keeping him away from his forever person," she moaned, laying her biggest fear on the counter to contemplate, feeling both the pressure and the guilt.

"Oh, Shal. What if you *are* his forever person, you big ninny?"

On the drive out to the peninsula, Cam explained the history of the marae; the people who'd come first, and those who'd come after.

Shal, hungry for information, asked him questions until he seemed to be out of answers.

"My whakapapa is all mixed up with whalers and warriors. Miriama's one of my second-cousins from dad's side—she'll meet us there and knows more. The best storyteller in the whānau; a keeper of the oral tradition. "

"And then you've got diehard Scots on Poppy's side," Shal mused. What a fierce combination. "Makes for an interesting mihi."

"Do you want to hear it in English, or Te Reo Māori?" Cam joked.

"Ooh!" Shal rubbed her hands together, excited about their impromptu trip and learning more about Cam's family history. "Both."

"Really?"

"Yes, really," she assured him, turning in her seat so she could watch him.

Cam had never done much more than touch on his Māori heritage with her when he was younger, and they'd talked about all manner of things when they'd shared a flat.

He sighed and shifted in his seat, but did as she'd asked. After a welcome and an acknowledgment to her listening, Cam named his mountain, his moana, and the ancestors connected to him.

When he moved onto the Māori version, it was longer and more elaborate, with richly deepened vowels. Shal heard her own name, along with Poppy, Daniel, and Cam's father, Gray.

"What does takoo-art-something mean?" She tried not to butcher the pronunciation too badly.

"Ko Shal te tau o tāku ate. Shal's my sweetheart."

"You put me in your mihi as your sweetheart?" she squeaked.

"Yes, I did." Cam glanced across at her as if daring her to challenge him, before swinging his eyes back to the road.

"That's... That's lovely of you," Shal murmured, realising she meant it. She wouldn't want another woman's name slotted into that spot, and felt a great hollowness when she considered that perhaps one day, one could be.

"I could call you e hoa wahine if you liked that better?"

"Your female friend?"

Cam cleared his throat. "Ah, no. It's not always a literal translation. It comes across more like... wife."

"Oh! Then maybe you'd better stick with the other one."

She sneaked a look at his profile to check she hadn't offended, but he was grinning. Teasing her.

Shal relaxed a little more.

"I've never heard you speak Te Reo before."

"I only got serious about learning a few years back, and I'm nowhere near what you'd call fluent. A work in progress, I guess."

"It's beautiful." *He* was beautiful. "Did your Dad...?"

"Speak it? Yeah. Some. Though it wasn't encouraged when he was a kid. Actively discouraged, unfortunately." Cam sighed. "It's one of the only things we ever really fought about. My lack of interest, and the fact I took the opportunity to learn for granted. When he was alive, I didn't take the connection to ancestors seriously."

"He'd be proud of you. Of what you're doing."

Cam shrugged. "I hope so."

"Any parent would be." Surely Cam had to know that? "What did you say at the end about a waka; a boat?"

Cam grinned. "That was one of Dad's favourite proverbs: He waka eke noa; we're in this boat together." He rapped his knuckles on the dashboard and chuckled. "Literally."

<hr />

They spent a lot of time just talking out on the marae, but Miriama also helped Shal flesh out her own sketchy high school-learned mihi, and made her practice it until the story of her lineage was a lilting song in her head.

The easy parts were her ancestry and birthplace in the introduction. The mountain she was born under, and the river laid out like a ribbon below it. Much harder was explaining the ties she felt as an adult.

"Let's switch out Ākarana, and use the name Tāmaki-makau-rau instead," Miriama suggested, sitting across from Shal at one of the dining tables in the hall. "It's the more widely used name for Auckland now. Much prettier."

Shal guessed Miriama to be somewhere near Amos in age. Sixty-ish? The older woman's sense of humour was as dry as burnt toast, and she had a way of flatlining most of Cam's levity with a deadpan expression, refusing to find him at all funny. It kept Cam trying, and Shal on her toes, because every now and again Miriama would give in—cracking up and walloping Cam on the shoulder.

"Aww, you're just saying that because of your misspent youth, Whaea Miri," Cam teased his distant cousin. "I've heard all about the many North Island hearts breaking in your wake."

Shal looked from one to the other as Miriama giggled like a schoolgirl, and Cam grinned.

"Tāmaki-makau-rau means desired by many, or many lovers," Cam informed Shal as an aside.

"Oh?" Shal considered Miriama in a slightly different light. With her high cheekbones and deep set eyes, she was very striking.

"Right. Back to business," Miriama hustled, straightening her face back into strict lines. "Where's home for you now?"

Shal baulked.

Perhaps sensing her rising discord, Miriama reached out and touched her arm. "Where are your *people*?" The older woman asked pointedly.

"All over," Shal answered hopelessly. Looking into Miriama's deep brown eyes, she was reminded of little Saffy.

She thought of Cam, Katie, Links and Poppy, telling her there would always be a home in Ōtipoti for her. She thought of Rosa and Amos, with their open-door dinner policy.

"Here?" she whispered, somewhat surprised.

Miriama smiled serenely, as if she'd been waiting for the penny to drop. "Ka pai, Shal. Here," she agreed. "Not your ancestors, but your close ones. Let's add that in, shall we? The elders will be more interested in your genealogical connections, but in more informal settings these lines will be useful." She waited until Cam moved away, taking their cups with him into the kitchen, before adding quietly, "You nabbed a good one, there."

Shal laughed along, hoping Miriama didn't notice the touch of hysteria rising.

Afterwards, Miriama showed her the photographs at the front of the wharenui; pointing out and introducing which tīpuna Cameron and Daniel were connected to.

Shal recognised Gray from Cam's photos, snapped fishing somewhere off the coast, and the facial tattoo on one of the elderly women. It matched the moko on Cam's shark tattoo.

The elder had been Cam's great grandmother, Miriama explained, and she'd been a very influential woman on the marae in her time.

"And you share this ancestor?"

"We do." Miriama smiled. "Sometimes family's a gift, and sometimes it's chosen." Her expression willed Shal to take heed. "But always it's an honour."

"Yes," Shal answered slowly, thinking she was beginning to understand Miriama's point.

"I have something to ask you." Shal took a measured breath in, then released it back out again slowly.

"Mm?" Cam was concentrating on the road home, but his mind was still swimming with the details Shal had chosen for her mihi, and the St. Clair property he'd just bought.

"If you don't have anything else on today, and you don't mind... I mean, I don't want you to feel you *have* to—"

"Spit it out, e hoa." He found Shal's dogged independence amusing. She rarely asked for help, but when she did, she tended to offer him the out before she gave him the deal.

"I know it's not exactly on the way, but I need to go to Mason's memorial and I promised Katie I wouldn't go on my own."

Cam understood the sentiment, because he felt it himself on occasion. Shal felt a need to go, not a desire to.

"Yeah. Let's do that. It'd be good to have some company up there."

"You go, sometimes?"

"I do." He slid his hand across the centre console in invitation, palm up, and Shal grabbed hold of it.

"Thank you, Cam," Shal whispered, bringing his hand up to rub the knuckles down her soft cheek.

Did she do that for her own comfort, or his?

Shal's nerves began to show as they got closer, winding their way slowly around the peninsula road and through Broad Bay before turning to climb the inland road.

"Ants in your pants," he noted.

"God. I feel sick." Shal wound down her window and cool air filled the cab. "I don't know if I can do this."

"You can. I'm here with you."

"Got a toothbrush in your pocket, Boy Scout?" Shal quipped.

"Not this time, no." He smiled in apology. "But I've got some chewing gum and a bottle of water if you need it. And possibly a rubber band that could pass as a hair-tie." He gestured towards the accumulation of junk in the centre console.

"Not bad. Not bad at all, considering you had very little notice."

"Give me half a chance and I could become indispensable," he joked, trying to keep Shal's mind off where they were headed.

Perhaps not a good time to tell her he'd felt pretty wretched himself the first time he'd come up here after the accident. The white cross hadn't been erected yet, but the evidence of the crash had still been pretty graphic. The temporary road cones had done little to hide the fact a vehicle had left the road at high speed on the bend, mangling the guardrail and meeting with solid trees and rock below.

Shal made a sound of distress as Cam pulled into a safe lay-by. "We can walk from here," he soothed, noting how white she'd gone. "Or we can just sit for a while, then turn around and head home. Entirely your choice."

Shal turned to stare at him. A possum caught in the headlights, her indecision clear.

"If it makes you feel any better, Matua Teddie came up here after the funeral and blessed the site."

"He did?"

"He did." Struck by a sudden impulse, Cam reached up and loosened his pounamu, sliding it easily over his head and settling it around Shal's neck instead. "This might help. A mere, for the strength of a warrior, but the koru..." He touched the furled carving at the wider end. "That's for new beginnings." Tightening the roped cord for her, conflicting emotion surged to see the carving he'd worn for years settled against Shal's skin.

His own throat felt strangely vulnerable.

"Thank you," Shal breathed, stroking the smooth pendant before holding it in a light fist for a moment.

Appearing to win the struggle with herself, she climbed out of the passenger side and pulled her jacket firmly around herself.

Mason's flatmates and friends had become Shal's by association, and no matter what else he'd thrown at her, on that point she'd be forever grateful. Her ex-boyfriend had inadvertently handed her the support group she'd need in his wake.

Their flat had been filled with music, cheap alcohol, and fun. Studying, playing cards and watching movies when the weather was bad, they'd also surfed and hung out on the beach together whenever they could.

Shal clung to those carefree times as she crunched along on the dry gravel, gripping onto Cam's arm as they approached the white cross. Her free hand reached up to touch the familiar greenstone pendant again and again.

Strength, and new beginnings.

If it hadn't been for Mason she would never have met Cam. So maybe, just maybe, she owed Mason everything.

24

Listening to...
Tears - The Crocodiles
From the album: Tears

It was hardly surprising Shal's dream came that night. Like a replay of the weeks following Mason's death, the only words Cam could hear clearly were "*No*, Mason," and Shal repeated them over and over in a low moan.

It killed Cam a little inside, the hold the dead drummer still had over her. Strong enough to make her whimper and cry out in her sleep.

He stroked her hair back off her forehead.

"Shh... It's just a dream, Shal." But he knew, just as she did, it wasn't a dream.

Sleep was elusive after that. Cam lay on his back with his arms folded under his head, trying in vain to find a comfortable position for his ribs, and waiting for the dawn light to creep across the ceiling and release the dark's stronghold.

Pō mārie—a peaceful night, though Cam felt anything but at peace in it.

Maybe given time, the pieces would adjust so he wasn't the third point in this triangle, forced to stare across at Mason's damn ghost and everything the bastard had done to destroy Shal's faith in relationships. But time was a commodity Shal seemed eager to restrict.

Cam was in love with her—crazily, stupidly in love with her. His hopeless crush from years ago had expanded and grown into a full-blown tree of feeling; a forest of emotion. This woman was tied intricately into branches of his family, his music, and his memories.

Shal was all he wanted, which posed a serious problem, as he couldn't honestly say he expected the sentiment to ever be mutual.

But it wouldn't be so bad. If what they were ever-so-tentatively building together now all fell apart like a house of cards, he'd take some leave, set Jonno up with a stand-in and go wherever the music took him.

The memory of his father would draw him back to Otago before too long, though. Inevitably, the need to be close always drew him back.

He'd worked the cruise ship scene for three seasons in a jazz quartet, but never re-signed for the more lucrative northern hemisphere route, opting to head home for the winter instead.

Why?

Poppy had plenty of family around, she didn't need him here, and it wasn't as if Gray's remains would ever be found. The family would never have the closure of an actual resting place, just the Pacific in all her beauty.

But what was Cam if he wasn't anchored by Gray?

Driftwood.

Long after Shal's breathing had returned to deepness; long after Cam was sure she'd fallen back to sleep, her hand slid over his bare chest, seeking reassurance. He took it and drew it slightly to the left where his heartbeat pulsed warm, regular, and true.

When Shal sighed in her sleep and snuggled closer, Cam finally found the clarity he'd been looking for.

He was exactly where he was supposed to be, and so was she.

Shal loved him. He knew it. Whether she'd let herself say so or not, whether she'd let herself believe it or not. It clearly scared the living daylights out of her, but she felt it nonetheless.

He'd be a fool to believe she'd allow this long distance

arrangement to go on any longer than a few months, and he'd be an even bigger idiot if he let her get away with that.

Somehow, Cam had to make it impossible for Shal to say goodbye. And in order to do that, he needed to get his shit together.

Cam was unsure about showing Shal the St. Clair property for two reasons. One, it would confirm to her just how deeply rooted he was in Ōtepoti, and two, the site was in a shambolic state. On the drive over there, reason three became apparent. It was beginning to mean far too much too him what Shal thought of the place.

Originally the extensive front garden for the property above, the steep section was overflowing with car wrecks and engine parts due to the past owner's penchant for iron. After twenty years worth of collecting it was an absolute eyesore, still needing a shit-ton of elbow grease just to clear the rubbish off for the foundation work.

The view that went with the now subdivided property made up for everything else, though, and he hoped Shal would be able to see past the car skeletons to its potential. Hands deep in his pockets, he viewed the quarter acre with Shal from the top boundary, nervous as a two-by-four within cooee of a nail gun.

"Stunning view," Shal breathed the words out in a reverent tone.

"Yeah, the best," he agreed, tension unwinding a little. "The lounge, dining, and two main bedrooms will all face this, with a wide deck off the front." He swept his arm across the ocean view, offering a teasing glimpse of the city centre to the left. "The lower level will have more of a native forest feel—views of the lower hill and trees."

"Who are you building for?"

"Ah, myself, actually."

"Oh!" Shal sounded truly surprised, and he felt, rather than saw her turn to stare at his profile. "I thought you were going to build in Roslyn?"

"We are. Well, the team will be. It's going to be mental if we try to juggle both of them at once. But the Roslyn one? That was Jody's dream, not mine, so it's Jonno's baby now."

"Jonno's?" Shal echoed.

263

"Yep. He's keen to move up on the hill into a bigger space."

"So are you, by the looks of things." Shal perused the steep site up and down.

"Well, yeah. At some stage." He felt himself reddening and scuffed his work boot over the long ryegrass, allowing himself to imagine living in this house with Shal.

"I'll come back to visit one day and you'll be married with two or three kids." Shal pointed to a flatter section of grass off to the right. "Trampoline over there." She angled her arm down towards the large ngaio. "Tree hut."

Shal attempted a tight smile, but Cam didn't bother trying to return it.

"Don't even joke about it," he growled, giving his head a single shake.

"One day you might have a real e hoa wahine, Cam," Shal whispered, and it was apparent she didn't like the idea much.

Chewing on her lip, she looked away again.

"Don't go there, either," he muttered. "I have what I want, and it's more than real." He slid his hand across the small of her back and she didn't pull away.

"I don't think I'd make a good mother," she disclosed without any outward show of emotion. "I wouldn't know how."

Did that worry her because her own mother had shown a distinct lack of maternal care?

"No one knows how to parent in the beginning," he assured her. "They figure it out as they go along, for better or worse. But nobody's pushing you to have children if you don't want them."

"You want them, though. Right?" She turned to stare for a moment before turning and making her way back to the ute, not waiting for an answer.

Cam stayed where he was a while longer, standing on the edge of the lot.

Yes, he'd always assumed he'd have children. But there was a deep hopelessness in Shal slotting another woman in the place he'd reserved for her in his head, merely because she wasn't sure if she wanted kids.

She didn't think she was ready for *any* kind of commitment, and was trying to give Cam a clear reminder how temporary she saw their connection.

He'd worked incredibly hard for the privilege of being able to build this house for himself. The mortgage would be substantial, but worth it to settle here—close to where his dad had been swept off the rocks all those years ago. The only place Cam knew he fitted. The only whenua that called to him.

If he needed to up and move, it wouldn't be any trouble to rent this property out. Or sell it. It would hurt to give up on the dream though; hurt to lose that link.

He strolled back to the ute and swung himself into the drivers seat, picking up on their conversation as if there hadn't been an awkward pause.

"Actually, I was thinking more along the lines of a hot tub in that flat area, with a deck running across to the lower den. Outdoor shower." He gestured, seeing it all fall into place in his head. "Brazier pit, and maybe some built in seating between, with native planting through the boulders."

Shal thought about Cam's St Clair property as he drove her back out to the airport.

From the section's high vantage point the water had beckoned to the east like turquoise silk. Cam would be able to stroll down to his favourite beach with his rugby-team of kids in tow, then take a spa with them all overlooking the ocean.

She turned to study his profile as he manoeuvred them through the urban sprawl and out to open farmland. He was creating a lifestyle far removed from the rat-race she'd wrapped herself in.

Though Shal had a choice, too. She could choose this, or something similar.

On Rue's advice, she'd talked it over with the staff in the Otago University Enrolment Office. If she loosened her hold on 2-PEAS, stepped back from store management and buying for a couple of years—if she focussed purely on the design and sustainability side the business again—she'd have time to complete her degree. And if she moved into the apartment above the boutique while she studied, her overheads would be low enough to allow her to leave for a decent break over the winter.

Cam would be within reach.

Shal tried not to think about, or read too much into the dream she'd had last night. For a while, scribing dreams in her journal had been an everyday occurrence, so it was pure habit that had made her note it down.

Dreamt Cam died in car. Mason driving. No seatbelt. I know *Cam always wears his seatbelt. Saw accident site yesterday. Maybe too close.*

Whether she'd gotten too close to the accident site or too close to Cam was a debate Shal had been having with herself all day. She'd been fending off intense flashbacks to the nightmare; the impact, the screeching of metal, and the sickening tug of gravity, dragging Cam to the base of the ravine.

Then blood. Copious amounts of blood.

The tension in the ute built as they neared the airport terminal. Shal wasn't looking forward to saying goodbye, nor was she sure how to handle it.

"You could just drop me here," she decided as Cam cruised past the five-minute parking zone.

Short and sweet was probably best.

She kissed Cam's cheek as he slid the suitcases out of the ute deck, but Cam held her wrist captive and wouldn't allow the casual goodbye, pulling her in for a long, heated kiss that melted her knees.

"Take care, e hoa. I'll be missing you every minute of every day," Cam murmured into her hair as he released her from his arms, his voice raw with emotion.

"Bye," she returned tightly, trying not to let the hurt in Cam's eyes or the flapping of her own heart get to her. "Thanks for the lift."

Walk fast, and don't look back.

Shal struggled to handle her suitcases. Though they were both on wheels, the two seemed to be heading in opposite directions.

Hold it together, and don't bloody cry.

(Hiccup).

The tears were already running rivulets down her cheeks when she heard the footfall behind her, then Cam's hand was covering one of hers on the suitcase handle, stopping her forward motion.

"Shal—"

She turned and buried her face in his chest, wrapping her arms tightly around his warm, comforting frame.

"I'll miss you too! So bloody much!" she wailed, underprepared for just how deeply it would cut to say goodbye and not know when she'd be seeing him again. She had at least three weeks of solid work lined up. One in Te Whanganui-a-Tara, and two in Asia. "You're too fa—*(hiccup)*... too far *away*."

"Shh. I know," Cam crooned into her hair, holding her close and stroking the back of her head. "Shh. It's okay. I'll figure something out."

Shal still had twenty minutes to spare after she'd checked in her suitcases. She cleaned up her face as best she could in the public basins, taking some deep breaths before heading to the airport coffee shop for a reviving pot of tea.

In the midst of choosing a table, order number in hand, she noticed a woman approaching. Well dressed in a pastel designer suit and expensive jewellery, she was too thin to be healthy. Her porcelain skin had an unearthly sheen to it, as if she'd spent too much time indoors.

The woman appeared to know her, so Shal smiled back politely. There *was* something vaguely familiar about her face. A client? One of Katie's more distant relatives from the wedding?

It wasn't until the woman spoke that Shal was brought back to a distinct time and place with a rude thud.

"Shalom Hoffner! It *is* you! I saw you come in and couldn't believe my eyes. It's been years!"

Shal was air-kissed on both sides as the woman spoke, giving her some time to settle the initial surge of panic. She couldn't have spoken now, even if she'd wanted to.

"Well, you look stunning, as always. Are you visiting your university friends down here? The last time I bumped into your mother, I heard you were in Wellington doing your designer thing, but that was some time ago now. I'm just down for the weekend myself—arrived a few minutes ago, but I can't stand the taste of the tap-water down here, so..." She was holding up a bottle of mineral water to explain her foray into the coffee shop.

Shal swallowed, realising it was her time to speak.

She couldn't remain mute to Mason's mother, the woman she'd once naïvely thought of as her future mother-in-law.

"Lynette. Lovely to see you," she lied with as much calm as she could muster. "Yes. It has been a long time."

Eight years.

Lynette Knox had lost weight. She'd never been this fragile before, and Shal wondered if she'd been ill.

"Please, sit down. How's Robert?" Scrabbling for some semblance of normality, Shal asked after Mason's father.

"Oh, he's gone, darling." Lynette settled primly on the edge of the chair opposite. "Heart attack. Three years ago, now." She fiddled with the rings swimming on her bony hands.

"Oh! God. I'm so sorry." Of all the questions she could've asked, she had to have chosen that one.

"Well, you weren't to know." Lynette straightened her back. "It was very hard, of course. Unexpected. Too young. *Far* too young." Shal was unsure if Lynette was still talking about her husband, or referring to her son. Maybe both? Her eyes had taken on a faraway look. "I'm able to come down here quite often now, to visit family," Mason's socialite mother continued, waving vaguely in the direction of the main entrance.

"How lovely. I didn't know you had family in Ōtepoti." Shal aimed for mindless small-talk, anything to remove herself from sitting in a tiny airport discussing early death with Lynette Knox, of all people.

Mrs Knox got decidedly more agitated, shifting her minimal weight.

"Well, to be completely honest, I didn't know I did either. Not until a couple of years ago." Lynette took a fortifying breath, then met Shal's eyes directly. "I'm a little unsure how to approach this Shalom, but I feel you should know. When you were with Mason, I'm afraid it appears he was unfaithful." Lynette must've been able to register the shock on Shal's face, because when she continued

268

there was a definite weight of responsibility in her tone. "I'm so very sorry."

"Oh, Lynette. That was a long time ago," Shal managed to choke out, surprised beyond belief.

Not only did Lynette appear to know about Mason's sexcapades, she'd actually brought them up in general conversation. Mrs Knox had always been one to keep up appearances, and this disclosure didn't allow Mason to look good at all.

"Yes, well." Lynette studied Shal for an uncomfortably long moment. "The thing is, there was a child."

"Pardon?"

What the hell did she mean, a *child*?

"My grandson. Matthew." Lynette couldn't completely veil the pride in her voice. "His mother contacted me out of the blue a couple of years ago when he started school and began asking questions about his father."

His *father*.

Shal's hand moved involuntarily, bumping into the pot of tea that had arrived, unnoticed, at her elbow. The knock jostled a shot of tea out of the narrow spout and onto the Formica, and she stared at the brown staining liquid as it trickled to the edge of the table and slid over the precipice.

Mason was a dad?

"My plane was a little early," Lynette continued doggedly. "But Mattie and his mother will be meeting me outside in..." She checked her dainty gold watch. "About five minutes. I know it's a lot to take in. It took me some time to believe it myself. But the first time I saw Matthew? Well, he's just the spitting image of Mason at the same age. Those blue eyes, they couldn't have come from anywhere else. He's a Knox, even if he doesn't carry the name."

Lynette let the silence settle, and Shal was grateful for the halt in information. Her mouth was as dry as a box of Weet-bix, but she eventually found the ability to respond.

"Well, that's a... a shock, Lynette."

"Yes, I can see that." The older woman rose, gathered her bag, and placed light fingers on Shal's shoulder. "I'll let you drink your tea, but it was lovely to see you. Really. If you're ever in

Auckland..." Leaving her business card and a faint hint of white musk, Lynette Knox walked away.

Shal tried to imagine the family scene unfolding somewhere outside, beyond the double doors. She automatically poured her tea, but when she left the table to meet her gate call ten minutes later, her cup remained untouched.

Autopilot had kicked in for the most basic of functions, but some of her systems hadn't fully rebooted yet.

25

Shal attempted to go through the motions, sliding back into her everyday role of designer, manager, and boss; a cog in the retail wheel.

It wasn't a particularly smooth transition.

If the Whanganui-a-Tara staff noticed her empty, somewhat robotic state, they didn't mention it. Jac was less polite and attempted to dig out answers. Confrontation was the redhead's natural state of being, but that didn't mean she got any closer to what was bugging her co-worker.

On the contrary, Shal clammed up a little more each time Jac niggled at her.

She avoided Bianca and Carmel, too. Telling her half-sister she was too busy to come over for a meal, and that sometime after her trip to Asia would work better.

It was sort of the truth.

With only a few days to touch base in her own apartment, Shal got on with the mundane business of washing, dry-cleaning, and packing her clothes. Confirming her flights and meetings, she emailed Henke the details and set up her standard out-of-office email reply. But all the while her thoughts were elsewhere.

She'd intended to study in Tāmaki-makau-rau after high school, to catch up with Mason each holiday and build on their relationship from there. But sometimes life decided on its own little twists and turns without the participant's consent.

Mason hadn't batted an eyelash when she'd called him, distraught and displaced after her parents' sudden split, asking how he'd feel about her coming down south and moving in with him.

She hadn't realised Mason had already moved on. She'd never asked, and he'd never said. He was her first serious boyfriend, so she'd been doggedly serious about him, and he was the only guy who'd ever elicited that response in her.

Until now.

When Mason's sleeping around had come to light, Shal had finally been forced to question their connection; where they were headed and how he felt about her.

They'd been mid-confrontation when Mason had shouted, "You're so needy, Shal! So constricting. Can't you see you're suffocating me with all your promises, and every bloody string attached? I never asked for this commitment! Why are you so concreted down to the idea of exclusive rights? Let me *live*, for Christ's sake!"

Unknowingly, she'd become an increasing weight around Mason's neck. So heavy, she was cutting off his airway. She understood it so much better now than she had at the time. If only they'd talked about it earlier; Mason's longing for space, his need to be single and free, sowing his wild oats. Granted, it would've hurt to call it quits, but she could've borne that so much easier than the deceit.

She'd vowed at the time to never ask another partner for commitment, and never to give or expect full loyalty. And that had pretty much worked up until now.

There was a little kid somewhere in Ōtepoti; a boy called Matthew who had his daddy's eyes.

Who was his mother? Had Mason been aware of her pregnancy? Was that part of the reason he'd sunk himself so deep in alcohol, as a means of escape?

Shal had a lot more questions than answers. But despite that, and with no way of knowing if there was any real justification, the guilt sitting heavy on her shoulders for so long had readjusted slightly.

There was an old storage box on the highest shelf in Shal's wardrobe. She was unsure exactly why she needed to go through Mason's things until her hand connected with his Batman backpack.

His son should have that.

Taking her time, she sifted through all the remaining keepsakes. Mason's dive watch and a couple of well-worn Rip Curl T-shirts. A bunch of photographs, a Nixon cap, and a set of drumsticks. It hurt less to handle his things than she'd expected, and she even found herself laughing at Mason's antics in the photographs.

Shal divided the pictures into two piles with regards to their child-appropriateness. One stack she kept aside for Links: Mason drinking, smoking, eyes red rimmed and dancing shirtless, making a 'fuck you' sign with his fingers and slitting his tongue between them.

The other stack of photos was for the little boy. His father on the beach with the afternoon sun burning his hair white-blonde, practicing on his drum kit with a bandana soaking up the sweat, and walking with his skateboard under his arm. A final one taken at uni completed the set: Mason with his iconic Batman backpack slung over one shoulder and his surf cap on backwards.

Shal kept the images with herself in them aside, staring for a long time at a selfie of her and Mason sitting together on the front step of their shared flat.

Cam was right. They'd been so young, and so very inexperienced. Green as grass.

One of Mason's arms was held across his forehead in the photo to shade the glare of the sun, and the other lay heavy around Shal's neck.

After years of feeling that pressure, the weight had begun to lift —taking the pain with it.

"I loved you," Shal murmured, finding the need to use past tense. "And I forgive you." Realising the truth of that statement, she laid her fingers to her lips and transferred the kiss to Mason's image.

Shal slotted everything for Mason's son carefully back into the backpack for the last time. Writing a quick cover note to go with the envelope of photos, she double-checked Lynnette Knox's current business address before leaving for the post office.

A thought niggled as she walked, chilling her blood slightly.

The others probably knew Mason had a child. Did they consider her too fragile to handle the truth?

Shal stewed on that, grateful her Asian trip would soon be upon her and she could immerse herself in flights, transfers, and meetings. She wouldn't have time to think.

"You went underground!" Katie admonished the instant Shal picked up her end of the phone. "I've been trying to reach you for days."

"I flew back from Hong Kong late last night," Shal moved out of customer earshot by sneaking into the 2-PEAS Te Whanganui-a-Tara storeroom. "I'm relying on the caffeine in my tea to prop my eyes open."

Katie's phone manner resembled a verbal essay on travelling in Britain rather than a conversation, which suited Shal just fine. She was so out of whack from the time shift it was a relief to just listen.

As always, her ears perked up when the subject moved to Cam, though. Katie had distinctly said 'hospital' before mentioning a disagreement with Jonno, then alluding to Cam packing up tools.

"What the hell's he doing, closing up shop? Jonno says Cam's put a blanket hold on the St Clair build, too, and Poppy thinks he might even consider *selling* it. His dream plot! What's that about? If he's turned down the tour, I don't understand why he's going up to this album promotion thing this weekend. Has he told you what his plans are? If it wasn't for Jonno I'd have *no* idea what was going on," Katie ranted.

Shal's confusion at the beginning of Katie's spiel had begun to morph into a general sense of foreboding.

"Who's in hospital? What tour?"

"Pieta's Oceania tour. Cam was discharged ages ago," Katie breezed.

Cam? Shal's head began to spin.

What had he said in his texts? Their communication had been stilted by the interruption of her trip to Hong Kong, but she was pretty sure she'd remember a hospital reference.

Shal sat down abruptly, and with very little grace, on a large cardboard box full of winter stock.

"Cam never said anything about a hospital, or a tour." She was positive about that.

"They kept him in for observation after he got knocked out."

Shal's free hand flew to her chest. "Wait, *what*? Cam got knocked out?"

There was a small hesitation from Katie. "Weeks ago. You knew about the break in, didn't you?"

"The assault? Yes. He had a black eye at the boutique opening. Cam actually got *knocked out*? He joked about it." An image of Cam popped into her head, as still and lifeless as he'd been in her nightmares. "I didn't know it was serious."

"He's fine, health-wise," Katie placated. "He was supposed to slow down, but a concussion and a couple of cracked ribs couldn't keep him off work."

"They broke his *ribs*?" Shal yelped.

"*Yeees*." Katie drew the word out, long and slow. "You saw him after that though, right?"

"Right, but he didn't say…" Cam hadn't said anything about his ribs, had he? Shal's memory was sluggish with the jet lag, but she didn't think so. They were bruised, that's all she knew.

"No. Well, we're in the same boat there. He hasn't been telling me shit, either. When you see him this weekend, can you talk him into calling me back? He's ignoring my messages and I'm on the other side of the frickin' planet."

"What's happening this weekend?"

Katie paused and the moment dragged.

Or maybe they'd been disconnected?

"Katie?"

Katie cleared her throat with a little 'ahem,' before asking mildly, "Cam hasn't made any plans with you this weekend?"

"Ah, no?"

"Crap… Sorry. I just assumed you'd touch base while he was up in Te Whanganui-a-Tara with Pieta. Did you two have a falling out?"

"Cam's in Te Whanganui-a-Tara?" With *Pieta?*

"Not yet, but the band has their first promo event this weekend."

"Are you sure? That's this week?" Shal leaned forward to scrabble for her iPad on the cluttered office desk. "I don't have anything in my diary."

Squeezing her phone between shoulder and ear, she flicked backwards and forwards distractedly through her e-calendar.

The weekend loomed empty.

"Friday through to Monday. They're staying at the Grand Chancellor."

"Cam's staying at a hotel? Why isn't he staying with me?"

"I don't know. Maybe a band-bonding thing? More likely he couldn't get hold of you last minute or didn't want to cramp your style. You might've had plans, you know… With someone else."

"With someone *else*?" Shal fumed. "What would I be doing with someone else? I'm with *Cam*." It took her a moment to realise it wasn't a crackle on the line, it was Katie chuckling softly.

"Ah, so you're wide awake now, are you? Welcome to Planet Serious, Shal. You're with Cam, and he's with you, and that's how it was always meant to be, you goose."

Shal took a deep breath before muttering, "Don't say I told you so."

"I *told* you so!" Katie crowed.

The first thing Shal did when she got off the phone was plough through three weeks worth of text messages from Cam.

There were quite a few.

Most, Shal had sent short replies to, and some had prompted a return phone call. Some were sweet, some informative, and one just described what the surf was doing on that particular day.

She had missed one text from him this morning.

Hey Surfer Girl. I'll be up your way for the weekend on a promotional thing, so if you're back from Hong Kong and want to catch up, that'd be sweet.

276

Not once had Cam ever mentioned a hospital, having a fallout with Jonno, or finishing work. Nor had he said anything about changing his plans for the St Clair property, or a tour with Pieta. None of his texts asked Shal for any concrete plans, which was hardly surprising, considering he'd been trying so hard not to put any pressure on her.

Shal's first instinct was to call, but when Cam's phone clicked immediately through to messages she hung up. Answering machine monologues were the worst form of torture.

Sinking her head into her hands, she sat like that for a few minutes.

She'd shut Cam out. Deliberately and purposefully cut him off. Over and over again.

Because deep in her bones she knew she was in love with him, and the reality scared her stupid. Worse than stupid.

She'd just spent two weeks in Asia, mostly on her own. Plenty of time to sort out the mish-mash of emotions swirling around inside her head. Her aunt and uncle had helped, listening to her sort through the tangle verbally, and giving some sage relationship advice.

It had made her realise she had a veritable treasure trove of friends and family to look to for answers and call on for help. Take Rosa and Amos, for example; the quintessential Luis-Vuitton-suitcase couple. Thirty-five years together and counting. How did they make it work so seamlessly?

On a phone call that began as a 'thank you' for all their hospitality surrounding the wedding, Rosa, when asked, had cited holding hands and dancing together every week. Amos had sworn by saying sorry for things that weren't necessarily your fault, and gifting gardening tools on every possible occasion. They'd both agreed on open communication and trust.

All in all, a very different picture of a long-term relationship than the one Shal had been shown by her parents while growing up.

New York Nana had said a couple that laughed together had no reason to go looking elsewhere for fun, and maintained a friends-to-lovers scenario had the most favourable odds. She'd also said that when the sexy had gone, and you were both wrinkly and worn, a shared sense of humour was worth its weight in platinum.

Henke had said compromising on the small things that mattered to the other person was an easy way to gain brownie points, and Ulrika had snorted, then agreed.

Shal had emerged from Hong Kong clear-headed and open to change, recognising the recurring patterns in her relationships that had been screwing her up for years. They were her own property and she was willing to front up and move on. It had taken Katie's phone call to slap her fully awake, though, and she hadn't spoken to Cam about any of this yet...

The omission loomed particularly ominously and she thumb-typed a quick affirmative.

Just opened this. Yes! I'm back! About to go sleep for 100 hours to shake off this jet-lag though... Would love to see you tomorrow! S x

Unsure of her next step, Shal tapped her phone lightly against her temple in agitation before bringing it down to stare at it, blinking.

There was someone she hadn't called to ask advice from. Someone who could perhaps help her understand the most glaring relationship deficit in her life.

Scrolling through her contacts, she took some time to bolster herself up before connecting.

Nothing ventured, nothing gained...

"*Hej* Mum? It's me, Shal. Do you have a moment to talk?"

26

Listening to...
Dark Child - Marlon Williams
From the album: Marlon Williams

"Hey!" Cam raised one hand in bewilderment, jolted to recognise Shal among the smattering of people waiting at the arrivals gate in Te Whanganui-a-Tara airport.

He hadn't sent Shal his flight details, unsure when he'd be catching up with her while he was in the capital, if at all. She'd texted she'd love to see him, then nothing more, and he hadn't wanted to call due to the jet-lag factor. She'd need her sleep.

To be honest, things had been a bit off since she'd left Ōtepoti after the 2-PEAS launch, and he'd gotten the message to back off.

It was Friday, so Shal was in full designer mode, probably having come straight from the boutique. The heels on her boots were high, as was the hem of her cinch-waisted dress. Bracelets jangled on her arm as she manoeuvred confidently towards him through the suitcase brigade. Her hair breezed behind her and a welcoming smile lit up her face like a surprise sunburst, threatening to steal his breath away.

Cam wasn't the only one in the lobby to have noticed her. Heads turned to watch Shal move and he couldn't blame any one of them. She was simply stunning.

"You didn't have to come out. I was going to catch a cab—" That was all he managed to get out before Shal was right up against him, fingers in his hair and lips on his.

Cam dropped his inflight bag, took her sweet face in his hands, and kissed her back for all he was worth.

The last three weeks had seemed like an age without this woman in his arms.

"I missed you," Shal murmured against his lips.

God, he'd missed her too.

"How did you know what flight I was coming in on?" Cam knew damn well he had to be grinning like a jerk, but was unable to wipe the smile off his face. Until Shal had kissed him senseless just now he hadn't been a hundred percent sure whether the 'benefits' part of their relationship was already done and dusted.

Picking up his bag and slinging it over one shoulder, Cam offered Shal his other arm—the old fashioned way.

She took it, smiling.

"Poppy." Shal gave up the name of her informant nonchalantly, sliding her hand around his bicep and leaning in to walk with her head against his shoulder. "I've got a meeting at eleven-thirty I couldn't get out of, but after that, would you be free to have lunch with me?"

"Sure. Love to. My first deadline isn't until four o'clock at the hotel." He looped his thumbs into his front pockets.

"The Grand Chancellor, right?"

"Right. How did you...?"

"Katie."

"Your various sources." He laughed.

"You have *no* idea." Shal's eyes twinkled with undisclosed secrets. "Do you have much check-in luggage?"

"Nope, this is it."

Shal stopped in her tracks, staring at him in open-mouthed disbelief. The fact he'd boggled her mind simply by limiting his baggage made him laugh out loud.

"My guitars are coming up in the van with all the other

instruments." Along with a few other essentials he didn't want to get into right now. "How was Hong Kong?"

"Hot. Busy. But productive. 2-PEAS has a new silk deal, and I signed a contract with a button manufacturer who's using recycled aluminium from soda cans. I also had three nights with Henke and Ulrika, which was absolutely fantastic. I only wish it had been longer."

Shal shifted, and Cam could feel her looking at his profile as they walked. He held his breath as her fingers slid naturally down his forearm and into his palm.

Keeping his thumb looped in his jeans and holding her hand lightly, he turned to meet her eyes, not wanting her to become aware of what she was doing and pull away. "You picked up a tan," he mused.

Shal had always moved from light honey to maple syrup with any hint of sun.

"My hotel in Singapore had a rooftop pool. Did you get the photos I sent through?"

"I did." Shal on a sun-lounger looking delicious in a teeny-tiny bikini and a huge floppy hat. "Crazy height to have so much water. The engineering that went into that must've been really something."

Shal gave his hand another light squeeze. "I wish you could've been there." Was that a sigh? It had sounded like one, which could well be wishful thinking on his part. "Tell me what you've been up to."

Cam filled her in on his weekend in Wānaka, celebrating Daniel and Saffy's combined birthday party, and glossed over some slightly heavier stuff. They'd hopefully have time to address all that later.

"Would you like me to drop you at your hotel for an hour or so?" Shal checked her phone as they reached her car. A lot cleaner than the last time he'd seen it; unmistakably top-of-the-range European now the grime had been removed. "Or come and be my whānau support at a very boring, but hopefully short Hoffner Trust meeting?"

Shal offered the option lightly, like it didn't matter to her either way, but Cam knew her well enough to realise the implications of an invitation involving her disjointed family.

It struck him as an opportunity to get some insight into the slick Hoffner machine Shal still struggled against.

"Sure, take me with you. That'll be easier." Heaving his carry-on into the boot, he removed a slim, book-sized package before shutting it.

He could read relief on Shal's face, but there were still some nerves there. She fidgeted with the crossover neckline of her dress and the small, unfamiliar show of timidity stabbed him right under the ribcage.

Lifting her fingers, he brushed her knuckles with his lips.

"Your legs look incredible in that dress," he stated, dead serious as he turned her hand over and nipped his teeth against the sweet, fleshy base of her thumb. "I missed the taste of you."

"Did you, now?"

As he'd expected, Shal's tone slid towards sultry with the compliment and the spark of sexual tension.

Confidence sat much more naturally on her than anxiety.

"I wasn't sure if you'd be around this trip, so I was going to post this if I didn't catch up with you." He raised his head and placed the small courier pack in Shal's hand.

She blinked at her own name and address, printed in blue biro.

"It's not my birthday."

"No, but I know you'd like a hardcopy of this and I happened to come across one."

He'd been trolling the buy-sell pages for weeks. It was out of production, so he'd had to wait for a second-hand copy to pop up out of the woodwork.

Shal picked carefully at the heavy plastic, to the point Cam almost lost patience, itching to rip the wrapper off. But she finally made a hole big enough to pull out The Princess Bride DVD.

They'd watched it together in their Ōtepoti flat, years ago, with Shal hogging the closest seat to the fire and Links wolfing down the lion's share of microwave popcorn.

Shal loved the gift. She said so politely, but Cam was confident she really did by the way she gripped it close to her chest for a moment when she realised what it was.

Cam insisted on paying for the Airport parking, which they both agreed was daylight robbery. Still, it was a little insulting when Shal fretted aloud about how twenty bucks might affect his cash-flow for the weekend.

"Despite my hobo existence, I've been far from destitute for a number of years now," he assured her.

"Of course! I mean… That's not what I meant." Shal got a bit huffy, like it hadn't been her assumption at all.

When they drove under the awning to feed the parking chit into the machine, Cam caught his reflection in the darkened passenger window. Pretty low key in his old leather jacket and faded Shihad T-shirt, he drew a hand up to rasp across his two-day stubble.

"I can get changed if you like, before your meeting?" he offered.

"Why?" Shal turned to study him as they waited for the arm to rise and release them from the carpark, and he was glad he wasn't sporting a black eye this time.

"I'm a bit on the grunge side." He smiled with what he hoped was an apologetic bent, leaning forward to turn up the Marlon Williams track that had just come on Radio Active.

Shal laughed as she merged into the outward traffic. "You look like yourself. Don't change. You'll add some sweet Dante flavour to the sour Hoffner table." Her mouth lost all hint of humour and she added more seriously, "I really appreciate you coming with me."

"Anytime." He shrugged. "Are you free for dinner tomorrow night? The band's getting together for a bit of a celebration. I know it's short notice and you might have plans."

"I'd love to."

"Really?" He couldn't keep the surprise out of his voice, and Shal peeled her eyes off the road to glance at him.

"Really." The hint of a smile was back, teasing the corners of her mouth upward. "I haven't been going out a lot. Too much travelling recently." The silence sat a little uneasily between them, and Shal cleared her throat before adding, "And I don't have any other plans this weekend, so I'm all yours if you have any free time."

"Oh, right. Sweet." More than sweet, superb. "I won't wear jeans," he added in an undertone, more as a reminder to himself.

Shal reached across to rest her hand on his denim-clad thigh, bracelets clinking.

"Cam, I'm a solid-gold fan of your southern ass in jeans. Seriously. Go ahead and wear them wherever you like, you won't get any complaints from me. In fact, I stole a snap of you from Katie's album wearing *just* jeans. It kept me warm at night when you weren't around to do the job yourself."

"Is that right?" He turned to stare at Shal and gauge if she was joking. She didn't appear to be. Was that what Saffy had meant by 'naked nipples?' "Okay, so maybe now would be a good time to ask if you'd be interested in seeing a bit more of each other? I mean, I could fly up weekends or set myself up in Te Whanganui-a-Tara if that works for you? Keep you warm in person." He felt Shal's start of surprise, but carried on stoically. "I could get my own place so I wouldn't be in your face."

"Is that why you're staying in a hotel this weekend? So you won't be in my face?"

Cam hadn't presumed he'd be welcome to stay with Shal. Why would he? He had no way of knowing what her plans were for the weekend and wasn't sure where they stood, relationship-wise.

"I'm in no rush to crowd you. I'm happy to grab a room at the hotel." He didn't particularly want to be in Shal's apartment, either, where he imagined she might spend time with other people. "You know you're always welcome to stay wherever I am if you're…" Free? Wrong word. She wasn't free. "If you'd like to," he amended.

The past three weeks had been full-throttle, tying up loose ends in Ōtepoti and trying to keep his mind off Shal traveling safe.

Pieta's album was done. Finished. Cut. There was just spit and polish on the promotional photos and videos to negotiate through before the tour prep began. The album was set to be released next month, and not only was he proud of the guitar work, Pieta had also chosen to add a recording of one of his own songs, *Crush*.

That was a significant shift from sessional musician to contributing artist, and he was pretty excited about how the track had come together with Pieta's unique vocals.

***

Shal waited for Cam to mention Pieta's upcoming tour, but he didn't.

If Jonno was to be believed, Cam might even try to forgo working the tour in order to spend more time with her. The idea could be seen as flattering, but to borrow Jonno's phrasing, was also completely insane.

Yesterday's phone conversation with her mother had been the most open they'd ever had, and it had gotten Shal on a roll.

Poppy had been a fabulous source of information, and Links and Daniel were also helpful in their own avenues. But not surprisingly, as they worked so closely together, the most illuminating phone conversation Shal had stirred up on the topic of Cameron Dante was with Jonno.

The builder had been honest and straightforward, only too happy to give Shal his observations and opinions—some of which had been hard truths.

Jonno didn't entirely trust her intentions at first, and it had taken a bit of explaining before she could get him fully onboard. But once they'd established they shared a mutual aim, Shal shot Jonno quick fire questions and let the builder's answers construct an almost complete picture.

She planned to pull Cam up about the points he was keeping hidden from her over lunch, but right now she was just happy to be sitting in the car next to him.

She'd longed for him more than she'd ever longed for anyone, and for the first time on one of her overseas buying trips hadn't relished the alone time. The rawness of separation and irritation of leaving things uncertain and unsaid had dogged her the entire trip.

Shal sneaked another look at him when they stopped at the lights. His face had healed well and there was no longer any outward sign of the assault.

She was grateful for that. It had hurt to see him hurting.

David Hoffner never engaged in small talk when it came to money, and to Shal's relief her father got straight down to business. Maybe she could get Cam out of this glass monstrosity of an office earlier, rather than later.

But as the solicitor passed Shal forms and papers to sign, and Cam (since he was conveniently there) to witness, David broke with protocol.

"You're not planning to get married in the near future? Maybe to Mr Dante, here?" David didn't bother to keep his voice down and waved a hand nonchalantly in Cam's direction as if redirecting an annoying fly. "If so, it'd pay to get a prenup drawn up while you're here."

Shal's ire rose both at the lack of respect shown and the insinuation. Her father's habit of talking about Cam as if he wasn't present in the room had been going on throughout the meeting, and she was beginning to wonder if David was baiting him on purpose.

Or baiting her? More likely.

It made sense David would try to gauge how upset she got, and therefore figure out how she felt about Cam. Her father was probably desperate to know where Cam fitted into the overall picture, purely because it was out of his control and none of his goddamn business.

"No. I'm not marrying anyone," she intoned, aiming to get David off Cam's case by feigning disinterest.

If anyone knew the pitfalls of marriage it would be her father.

Shame it was a glass table top, or she would've slid her hand onto Cam's thigh in a show of solidarity.

David smiled and seemed to relax with the information. "No, of course not, my pearl. Keeping your options open and looking out for number one is your best option. You take after me in that respect."

Shal's father couldn't have insulted her more if he'd slapped her across the face.

"Like *you*?" She was unable to keep the distaste out of her voice. "I'm not anything like you."

"Well, of course you are!" David chuckled, unmistakably amused rather than offended. "The pomegranate doesn't fall far from the tree." He turned towards the closed office door as if sensing someone approaching. "You have a cool ruthlessness about you that serves you well," he added, as if commending her on her exemplary freestyle stroke, or strong tooth enamel.

Shal's fury began to bubble.

What was the point of all this civility if it merely smoothed over David's offences? Had her silence on certain topics been seen as condoning his behaviour? Stroking the rabid bear?

If David wanted ruthless, she'd show him ruthless. Because as of today she refused to be complicit in this soul destroying charade.

She was done.

Cam had been conscious of the family likeness immediately, but while Shal's hair fell in straight dark ribbons her father's curled crisply at the neck and was liberally sprinkled with silver.

He was relieved that although the setting was similar, David Hoffner's eyes weren't the same colour as Shal's. They were brown. It would've been disconcerting to find those ocean eyes on such a selfish man.

Cam knew the history of David's constructed truths and how they'd affected Shal in the past, so he'd approached the Hoffner Trust meeting with as much caution as interest.

David was a slick talker and a controlling bastard. He spoke to Shal less like a daughter and more like a possession he was trying to mould into the image of himself; a pawn to be manoeuvred at his will. He was also stalling the proceedings for some reason, and kept glancing at his Rolex.

The American's vigilance was rewarded by a solid knock at the door.

"Ah, that will be Asher." David turned to look at Shal pointedly before commanding, "Come in!"

The man who entered was taller than Cam, but not by much, and of a similar age. Though dressed in a well-fitted suit, he had a barely controlled energy about him that seemed to emanate from his wiry dark hair and cat-like eyes. There was something very familiar about the guy's bone structure, and Cam tried to place him.

Had they met before?

Standing in the doorway for a moment, the man's eyes roved around the room before alighting on Shal and staying there. A flicker of recognition passed between the pigeon pair.

Cam began to rise slowly at the same time as Shal's chair scraped backwards and forcefully hit the tiled floor. She was standing, gripping the bevelled table edge with both hands.

"Asher, I'd like you to meet your sister, Shalom."

The air in the room flicked instantly to supercharged.

"You bastard!" Shal hissed, turning on her father, her face stricken and breath coming too fast. "You absolute bastard!" Her hands shook as she bent to gather her bag from where her chair had flung it to the marble. Then she stalked around to where David Hoffner stood, calmly contemplating his daughter's reaction.

His arms were folded across his chest, the only hint at his unnerved emotive state in the slight twitch of his lips.

"I confronted you. I asked you directly, and you *denied...*" Poking an aggressive finger towards David's chest, Shal turned to take a long look at what had to be her American half-brother.

Cam knew Shal and Bianca had searched for him, but they'd had very little to go on other than an old rumour within the New York side of the family.

"I tried to find you." The words came out as a plea, before Shal's voice strengthened with resolve. "David told me you never existed; that you were a figment of Nana's imagination." Taking a quick step back from her father she moved swiftly to the open door, disgust clear.

"Shalom," David intervened with authority as she reached the exit, obviously expecting to still wield control.

Shal turned back to point an accusatory finger at her nemesis.

"*Don't* call me Shalom, I hate it. I'm so over keeping the peace for you. And I'm *not* your pearl, you bloody liar!" Shal coated each word with more savagery than Cam had imagined was in her, the strength of her fury reverberating off the walls. "Mum was raw when she met you, shattered. But did you help put her back together? No! Did you show her how much she was worth? No! Right from the beginning, you lied and you cheated and you *crushed* her. Did you even love her at all? Any one of us?"

As far as Cam knew, Shal had never confronted her father before. She was blinking rapidly and he found himself waiting for the inevitable jarring hiccup in the super-charged silence.

It never came.

"You crushed *me*, David." Shal's voice had taken on a calmness that cut more sharply than her anger had. "I loved you more than I've ever loved anyone. Unconditionally. Absolutely. And you threw that away with your lies. I will never forgive you for that. Not ever.

You taught me how to distrust myself; distrust every relationship I entered into." Her gaze flicked to Cam, then away just as quickly. "Even the most trustworthy ones," she whispered.

Turning swiftly, Shal high-tailed it down the wide minimalist hall, faster and with more poise than seemed logistically possible in those heels.

The three men left standing sized each other up across the large glass table while the still seated solicitor pointedly cleaned his bifocals.

Asher's face was as readable as David's was closed, and Cam felt sorry for Shal's half-brother, who'd clearly just suffered a shock. Whether Asher knew of Shal's existence or not, the guy hadn't been expecting to meet her in this boardroom today, Cam was sure of it.

Shal's spitfire nature had come out to play, and whatever David had hoped to prove by lining up his offspring for a showdown, his daughter had absolutely refused to participate.

Cam slowly moved his chair back into position then plucked Shal's from the floor to replace it as well. Taking two business cards out of his wallet, he slid one across the table in front of the solicitor then walked purposefully around to where Asher stood, still rooted to the spot.

He offered his hand. "Pleasure to meet you, Asher. Cameron Dante." They shook hands firmly. "I'm a close friend of Shal's." He passed over the second card. "She's had a shock, just now, but I know she'd very much like to meet you." Looking around coolly, he included both Shal's father and the solicitor in his next comment. "At a more appropriate time and place. Are you in town long?"

"Another week," Asher replied, looking him over with undisguised curiosity.

Cam nodded. "Call tomorrow morning if you're able to. Not early though. She doesn't cope well with early." He smiled to himself before turning back to the solicitor. "You can contact me if you need anything further from Ms. Hoffner. I'll arrange that it gets done for you." Then, without further acknowledging the fourth man in the room, he left.

Cam was relieved to see Shal waiting for him when he reached her car. He'd been running through scenarios in his head of where he'd go to find her if she'd scarpered, but didn't know Te

Whanganui-a-Tara that well. Noting her wired, nervous tension long before he reached her, he knew instinctively she wouldn't want to be touched.

"Shall I drive?" he offered.

Without a word, Shal handed over her keys with shaking fingers.

"Where to?" he asked calmly when they exited the claustrophobic parking building.

The little hatchback drove more like a sports car than a city runaround, responsive and gutsy.

"Take me to the water, please." And other than murmuring the occasional directions, that was all Shal said for the fifteen minutes it took them to get out of the slow-moving gridlock and onto Shelly Bay Road.

It was a strange area, where the industrial side of the city ground to a halt before falling into the wild harbour. And it totally suited the atmosphere Shal was emanating—right down to the gritty shingle.

27

Listening to…
Stuff and Nonsense - Tim Finn
From the album: Frenzy - Split Enz

Shal waited until she was on the shore before she let her emotions
bleed out, but the tears Cam was expecting never eventuated. She
threw stuff instead, picking up small stones from the embankment
and hurling them one by one into the grey heave of water.

She didn't have a bad arm on her, and Cam stood nearby passing
over handfuls of pebbles when it looked like she was nearing
empty.

The stones were the wrong shape to skim, needing a thousand
more years of bumping their way down a braided river to smooth
and wear. High lobs with the larger ones were much more
satisfying, landing with a solid 'plop.'

"He's a lying, manipulative asshole with an ego the size of Texas
and a bloody ridiculous needy-prick-addiction to younger women,"
Shal informed the horizon.

From the little Cam had seen of Shal's father, she wasn't far
wrong.

"I had a right to know about my own brother, goddamnit. How

does he live with himself? Getting me in that office to ambush me was a bastard move. Mum should've hightailed it back to Sweden when she realised what he was like. But she stayed, even though she admits it wasn't healthy for either of us. David played us off each other like rivals in a WWF match, and I don't think Mum was anywhere near ready to have another kid."

"After Seb?"

"After Seb," Shal agreed, accepting another offering of stones. "Henke and Ulrika offered to take me, but she refused. Because *David* refused. He was building some kind of Hoffner empire, and I was apparently an integral part." She took in a deep breath and huffed it out, turning to Cam for the first time since they'd reached the water. "Guess what my mother said to me on the phone?"

He shook his head, but Shal wasn't after an answer, she'd already turned back to the water.

"Jag älskar dig," She muttered darkly. "She told me she loved me. That's the first time I can remember those words coming out of her mouth, and she waits until I'm twenty-bloody-eight."

For real? The admission shook Cam, and shed a little more light on Shal's formative years.

If anything, Poppy poured too *much* love in. Cam couldn't go a week without her sticking her nose into every part of his private business and smothering him with affection as if he was a little kid with a scraped knee.

For once, he fully appreciated his mother for what she'd handed him every single day of his life. Unadulterated love and acceptance.

"David's right. I'm *so* like him. Selfish. Fickle. My brother was right there and I just let him slip through my fingers." Shal held up her hands, fingers widespread, and her voice wavered. "Asher. His name is Asher. Oh, God. Bianca won't forgive me. She won't."

Cam nudged Shal's shoulder with his own. "Gimme a break. I couldn't pick a person you're less like. Fickle? You're as predictable as I am." For the second time since they reached the small bay, Shal turned to face him. The look she gave him was both sad, and grateful.

"Not quite *that* predictable, surely."

"Organic oat milk. Dilmah. No sugar. Predictable."

"I'm not sure that's any more of a compliment than fickle," Shal muttered.

"It'll be okay, Shal. I gave Asher my number and he'll call tomorrow." Hoping he was right, Cam took the precaution of paraphrasing, "I'm pretty sure he'll call, after you've both had time to process."

"You did?" Shal caught hold of that piece of information along with his bicep, and the frown she'd been sporting began to flicker, then clear. "Thank you." She squeezed hard.

His ribs, still in recovery, complained about the sideways yank, but Cam didn't make a sound.

"My family's such a mess."

"Your Uncle Henke and Ulrika don't strike me as a mess. Your grandmother? Carmel and Bianca… Are they a mess?" he countered softly.

"No, but—"

"You don't have to take on the crap from your parents like some kind of legacy. They're just people in your history, and their choices are their responsibility, not yours. You get to choose your own path."

"It's not as easy as it sounds. This shit is *in* me, Cam. I wasn't kidding when I said peace lilies are toxic."

"Bullshit." He hurled the last of the stones himself, and they scattered as they fell. "You can either let your experiences rule you, or you can learn from them and twist them around to suit yourself. You've already done it, Shal. You're the only one who can't see it."

They both turned back to look out over the water.

"I haven't ever been able to hold down a regular relationship," Shal finally muttered towards the sea. "Not since Mason." It was embarrassing to admit that, even to Cam, who knew all the raw facts about her better than anyone.

"Ha!" Cam barked a laugh without much humour. "I wouldn't give Mason the credit of holding a regular relationship. But that one's on him, Shal, not you. Nothing you do is regular and I mean that in the best possible way. You've never let anyone push you into anything you didn't want. Not me, not anyone. I love that about you."

There it was. The L-word.

She turned and blinked at him. "I'm pretty angry with you, too." She dabbed at her nose with the back of her hand, feeling like a grubby child without a tissue.

"Yeah?" He moved his feet, as if uncomfortable standing still all of a sudden.

"Yeah. Tell me something honestly. Did you know Mason had a kid?"

"A kid?" Cam's brows drew together. "What, in Tāmaki-makau-rau? *How*?"

She could see Cam trying to work out the logistics in his head, just as she had. How could Mason have a child if he was dead?

"I'm assuming the usual way, and no. Not in Tāmaki-makau-rau. In Ōtepoti. She must've been pregnant when he died."

"*Who* was pregnant?"

Shal slumped her shoulders. "I don't know. I thought *you* did. I thought maybe you'd been keeping that from me along with everything else."

When Cam reached out for her, she held him off.

"Are you sure?" Cam tried to reason with her. "Maybe—"

"Of course I'm sure," her voice wobbled and she struggled to gain control of it. "Mason's mother told me. There is a little seven year old boy running around with half his DNA. Buggered if I know how to process that."

"When did you find this out?"

"Does it matter?"

"It does to me," Cam pressed.

"I bumped into Lynette after the 2-PEAS launch. She was at Ōtepoti airport when I left. She'd just arrived to see her grandson."

"Hell. That's rough, Shal. I'm sorry." Again Cam put a hand on her arm, and this time she let it rest. "But you know if I had information like that, I'd tell you. I wouldn't keep that from you."

"Like how you told me you had the hots for me?" she countered.

"That was different." Cam ran his other hand through his hair. "It wasn't relevant at the time."

"Not relevant? Was the fact you had a concussion also not relevant? You didn't tell me when I stayed with you the headaches could be something serious. Your hospital stay? The fact you'd had a couple of ribs kicked in… Not worth mentioning?"

"Shit." Cam swore softly, regarding her suspiciously as if she might explode again. "I didn't want to worry you. You were busy organising the launch thing, and it sounded much worse than it actually was."

"I hate being lied to, Cam. Out of everyone, you should know that."

"I didn't lie, I omitted. But you're right, maybe I should've been a bit more open about it. I was under the impression you wanted some distance from this." Cam indicated to himself, and then her. "And I thought telling you might complicate things. Make you feel, I don't know… Obligated." He looked so lost, she almost forgot she still had a bone to pick with him.

She *had* distanced herself—hiding her own feelings and insisting he muted his. Pushing him away.

"You mean like playing the sympathy card?"

"Something like that."

"Anything else you might want to tell me?" she prodded.

"Ah, no?"

"Had any job offers lately?"

"Oh, right." Cam hesitated, moving both hands into his front pockets. "I've been approached about making the guitar stuff with Pieta more of a permanent thing, and I've been looking at a couple of doer-uppers coming up for auction in Te Whanganui-a-Tara, just for a bit of a change of scene." He shrugged, kicking at the shingle-heavy sand. "All negotiable."

All negotiable? Like hell.

When Cam looked back up, Shal was staring at him, shaking her head. The prickle of despondency in her eyes bit at him.

"I don't think we can do this anymore, Cam," Shal stated evenly, indicating first to herself and then him—exactly as he had earlier.

He was incredulous, and suddenly furious. "You're quitting on me because Mason got some girl pregnant, and I thought about moving to the same city as you?"

Moving to the North Island hadn't been an off-the-cuff decision on his part. It'd taken a week of soul-searching to realise he was never going to lose his sense of place merely by shifting position. He would always belong. More than that, the fear of being somehow less if he didn't have Otago under his feet had been holding him back for years.

"No, I should quit because what we have is beginning to interfere with your career, Cam," Shal returned accusingly.

"My career? I've managed to avoid having one of those all my life and I don't intend to start one now. I can flip houses in Te Whanganui-a-Tara as well as anywhere else."

"Your *music* career Cam. This is a real opportunity and you're willing to push it aside? A frickin' tour! Why would you deliberately withhold something like that from me?"

He drew both hands through his hair in exasperation, liberally spreading the last of the grit from the stones but past caring how he scrubbed up.

Yeah, he'd been offered the tour. Three months through Australia and New Zealand.

Who'd told Shal? Jonno, of course.

"Jonno has no right to interfere. *No* right," he muttered.

"Were you even going to tell me?" Shal's tone bordered on defeated.

"Yes, of course. Eventually." He looped his thumbs in his back pockets and turned back to the sea.

Shal sighed, bringing two fingers up to rub circles on her temples. "You *need* to take this tour."

"There'll be other opportunities," he answered obtusely, unsure if he was trying to convince Shal the guitar work would keep coming, or himself.

"Not like this one—Pieta's first tour. That's phenomenal." Shal left a breathing space before quietly adding her coup de grace. "If you turn this offer down we're over with. Done."

"Ah, I see. You thought an ultimatum might sway me?"

"Don't push me, Cam. You have no idea how far I'll go if I don't get my own way," Shal bit back snarkily, looking like she would've liked to stamp her foot.

He could've feigned shock or resignation, but instead he allowed himself to smirk. "Oh, yes I do. You forget I've known you for a long time, Shal, and you're predictable, remember? I love you, warts and all, whether you like it or not. You think you can turn me on and off like some damn light switch, but you're wrong."

Shal glared at him. He was dropping the L-bombs now in every conversation and could see it was beginning to get to her.

"Just like the rest of my family, you're buzzed about the idea of a tour, and thought you could manipulate me into taking it," he continued, knowing he'd figured it right when Shal pushed her lips together into a tight little line.

She didn't want to say anything to implicate herself further, and clearly had no idea he'd already signed on the dotted line for Pieta's initial Oceania tour.

That gave him a bit of much needed leverage.

"But if I *do* go, you've got to give me something, too."

Granted, Shal had been bluffing with the whole 'we're done' thing. But how else was she supposed to make sure Cam didn't blow this incredible opportunity? Jonno and Poppy had both been adamant she pull out all the stops.

With her mind still ticking over furiously, it took Shal a moment to register Cam's movement. When she did her anger turned first to surprise, then real fear as he knelt on one knee before her in the shingle.

"Oh, *shit*, no," she muttered, taking a quick step backwards but pulling up short due to the fact Cam had her wrist encircled and wasn't letting go.

"Don't panic, Surfer Girl. I don't have any shackles in my back pocket and I'm not asking for anything that requires a prenup." Cam tried to smile but it came off a little shaky, and Shal could suddenly see his raw, underlying nerves. He pulled a fat envelope from the interior pocket of his leather jacket and handed it over. "I do have a different kind of proposal for you to consider though. This is *my* ultimatum, I guess."

———

Cam took a deep breath, aware this was the last ace up his sleeve and that it could just as easily shove Shal in the wrong direction. But the thought of her picking up with someone else whenever they were apart had been ripping him in two.

"*If* I take this tour, I'm asking you for six-months where it's just you and me. I don't see anyone else, you don't see anyone else, and we give this a real shot. I'll move up here, but won't invade your turf. I can flip a couple of houses in that time if I get a good team together—live on-site like usual."

Moving up would crowd Shal, and Cam had stressed over the claustrophobic nature of it. But he had to go after what he wanted. He had to prove how good it could be, and show Shal exactly what she was turning down.

Shal was staring at him, wide eyed. There was real fear in that look—she was all but drenched in it. A perfect replica of the look she'd given him as she'd handed him the pen at Katie's wedding.

The odds weren't looking too good, but Cam pushed on regardless, needing to get it said.

"You don't have to open it, but I did what you asked." He tapped the envelope she was gripping with white fingertips. "I wrote it all down so you didn't have to hear it coming out of my mouth, but that doesn't mean it's not *in* me, Shal." He bumped his fist lightly against his own chest. "It doesn't matter if you can't say it back. I've got enough in here to carry us both for that long."

"Just six months?" Shal rasped out.

"I know that's usually your outer limit, but if the tour all goes to plan I'd be out of your hair by five."

"You'd leave Otago?" Shal looked vaguely suspicious on that point, and had every right to be. In any conversation they'd ever had, he'd always planted his future firmly in Ōtepoti.

But that was before.

"I'll go anywhere with you. Name the place," Cam confirmed. "If this is too much, then we can try going back to being mates. Your choice. But either way I'll always have your back." He slid a hand over his jaw and rubbed at the stubble, self-depreciation paramount. "Turns out I can't share you after all. I tried, but it's just not in me to do it."

Shal opened her mouth and closed it again before finally whispering, "I stopped seeing other people after we hooked up. I didn't, you know…" She waved her hand around vaguely.

Didn't *what*?

"Make pretzels with anyone else?" he asked after a wash of hope when she didn't finish her sentence.

Shal snorted, then covered her mouth as she blushed faintly.

"No one makes pretzels but you, Cam. I was going to say date. No dating, no kissing." She smirked as she held up one hand and waggled all the digits. "No fingers. No pies."

Warmth flowed back into his limbs. "Well, no matter what happens between us from here on in, I love you for that." He smiled back, and for one minute, could see Shal had forgotten to be frightened. Just *one* minute before all the panic poured back into her eyes like a landslide.

Cam was pretty sure he could see Shal's answer written on her face as she began to gulp, and shake her head.

Slowly he released her wrist and eased himself down until he was sitting on the shore behind her.

"It's just love, Shal. It's the most natural thing in the world. I've tried to kill it but it just keeps living in me."

Shal made a sound of distress in her throat as she turned from him and moved back towards the water's edge, and Cam watched silently as the soul destroying distance grew between them.

He put his head in his hands and swore, wishing more than anything he could've found a way to drive this outcome in the opposite direction.

Shal walked off to stand alone, swallowing down raw emotion as she folded her arms to warm and steady herself. The water chopped and swelled, and she could totally relate.

Cam and herself had effectively been exclusive since they'd gotten together, and she couldn't imagine herself with anyone else.

He'd filled pages with what he loved about her, and that was no small feat. She certainly hadn't made it easy, or been particularly worthy of his affection. He'd tried *not* to love her because of her inability to return it in kind—a pretty hard truth to hear.

Ōtepoti felt like home; not just the land itself but due to the fact Cam was there, waiting for her. If she and Cam lived together, home would be wherever he was.

Shal had rolled that admission over and over in her head during her trip to Asia, testing its validity, so she knew it to be true. And though there was no doubt—she was absolutely sure—it didn't make it any less freaky.

She stayed by the water's edge and held tight to the precious envelope Cam had given her, eventually feeling him come to stand behind her. She appreciated the warmth and solidity of someone so trustworthy having her back. Had she ever returned the favour; giving Cam any indication she had *his* back?

Absolutely not. She'd been much too busy trying to prove she could stand on her own.

How small of her to withhold any real form of spoken affection in case she'd felt too much, or shown too much.

In trying to stop herself from becoming her father, spreading love only to take it away, she'd managed to morph into her chilly mother.

It would be laughable if it wasn't so damn distressing.

Shal reached a hand back in invitation and Cam took the step that separated them. He squeezed her fingers, then released them.

Turning towards him, she took in his tired, hollowed-out expression and loaded that onto herself as payment. Because this was her fault. She'd screwed it all up from the very beginning, good and proper.

Shal lifted a fingertip to run along Cam's familiar jawline. It soothed her raw nerves to find the faint nick at the beginning of his scar and trace the line all the way down to his chin.

"Contrary to popular belief, I didn't get that protecting a damsel in distress." It was so like Cam to ignore the intensity of their previous conversation and try to make light of himself. "It was a gift from Dan, via my mother's coffee table."

"I love this scar," Shal whispered softly, noting Cam's small start of surprise.

She'd never used the L-word with him—had avoided it like the plague.

"It's not commonly considered my best feature," Cam mocked himself before moving to step away.

"No. Well. You have so many." She followed him.

Cam laughed. "Yeah, right."

He didn't actually believe her. Cam thought she had to be mucking around to say something nice about him, and that twisted the knife a little deeper. Tears began to form and Shal turned back to the sea, closing her eyes against the wind and the gloriously stormy view.

She formed a picture of Cam in her mind; his steady dependability and trustworthy nature. His belief in her, and his love through adversity. His shaggy hair and hole-ridden jeans, and the sparkling eyes and laughter lines that told the story of how much smiling the man practiced.

"I love how when you're happy your eyes have golden lights in them. It's like there's a fire on the inside."

Cam gave her shoulders a quick squeeze from behind. "You don't have to do this, Shal." She could feel him shift in discomfort.

She let him take another deep breath in and release it slowly before she started again.

"I love how you hold me after I've had a bad dream. Until I feel safe again." The tears were rolling down her face now in a slow race to her chin, but it didn't feel like crying. It was just her eyes leaking after holding back so much, for so long. "I've always loved how you make me feel safe."

Cam's initial surprise at Shal's words morphed into a slow circling sadness, like the gulls lamenting above them in the slate sky.

He could guess what she was trying to do, and it filled him with emptiness. He didn't want her guilt or her pity, and it wasn't necessary to soften her choices with undesired compliments.

It almost hurt more to hear them.

"Shal," he warned.

The larger part of himself had been waiting for this breakup since they'd first gotten together, so she needn't draw it out. Better to rip the bandaid off—clean and fast.

"I love it!" Shal insisted.

"Don't do this." He tried to turn her shoulders so she was facing him, but she stubbornly and steadfastly faced forward, clearly not wanting him to look at her.

"I love how you put me first, even when you shouldn't—how you've been letting me make the rules, even when you don't like them." Shal spoke calmly and evenly. "I love how you look after your family and your friends; how you talk to Saffy like she's an important person, not just a kid who doesn't get any say. I love how you know what songs I love, and how you make music your own when you play it. And the look on your face... Like it's painful growing the wings you're flying away on."

"Cut it out, Shal." Cam pressed his fingers into the flesh of her shoulders to caution her in a last ditch attempt to protect his own soft parts.

"I love how you fix things, recycle things, build things, and how you look after a hard day's work with sawdust in your hair and paint in your eyebrows." Shal finally turned to face him, and he was surprised to see tear tracks down her face.

He gently wiped away the wetness, first with one thumb, then the other.

"I love how you make me laugh, and make me take myself less seriously. I love that you make me cups of tea just the way I like them. How you compromise and have the ute heater on *much* hotter than you'd like it yourself. I love how you make love to me, how you love my body like you'll never tire of it. *God*, I love how you kiss me. It's epic."

"That's enough, now." His voice was gruff.

"It's *not* enough. It won't ever be enough. I was so frightened when Katie told me you'd been in hospital," Shal whispered. "*So* frightened. I don't ever want to lose you, Cam."

His own throat felt raw with emotion and he didn't attempt to speak.

"I really love how you pull a three-sixty like you're taking a stroll in the park. I wish you'd teach me. You look so damn good in a wetsuit."

Cam chose the only point he felt he could lighten the mood with. "You think I could teach you anything about how to look good in a wetsuit? I'm pretty sure you've got that covered." He flinched in reflex as Shal mock-punched his arm. "I mean, you've clearly won first prize on that one."

"You're right, Cam. I *have* won first prize." Shal laid her palm on his chest—just above his heart, reminding him of when they'd stood under the fairy lights at Rosa's house. "Because I love how you love me," she whispered. "I love that you wrote it all down for me, even when I felt I couldn't give you anything in return."

He shrugged as if the one-sidedness didn't matter. "I think you gave a great deal of yourself, all that you could, and I wouldn't exchange one minute of the time we've had."

"I want to give you everything." She cleared her throat a little nervously. "Ko Cam te tau o tāku ate." Her pronunciation of the Māori words might have needed a bit of polish, but there was no pretence or humour in the way Shal spoke, and her eyes shone like paua. "*Jag älskar dig*… I love you, Cam."

He frowned as he held Shal by the upper arms, searching her face. She meant she loved him as an old friend. Either that or the benefits they'd been messing around with.

"What?"

"I said I love you, Cameron Rimutaka Dante. As clear as the nose on your face."

"Um, I'm pretty sure that's against the rules," he negated, still confused by the flip in Shal's vocabulary and the very deliberate way she'd just overstepped her own guidelines.

"I'm well aware of that." Shal sniffed loudly, then wiped her nose inelegantly on her own shoulder like a tradie. She held both hands out to him, palms up as he once had to her, and repeated the same lines to go with them. "I'm sorry. It was out of my hands."

"Out of your hands?" Heart thumping, he slid his fingers over hers.

"Yes. Apparently the fact you're a Scorpio and I'm a Pisces should've been my wake-up call." Shal smiled faintly. "Clearly I missed that signpost. I tried to see you as the pretzel guy—and don't get me wrong, I have no complaints on that front—but the other stuff just crept up on me insidiously. Like a viral infection. Like a disease."

Cam couldn't be sure, but he thought he could see the light breaking through the heavy cloud cover, and from where he was standing it had the warm glow of summer to it.

"Like chicken pox?" he prodded.

"Just like chicken pox," Shal whispered, stepping in to lay her head on his shoulder and turn her forehead into his neck.

He knew exactly how Shal's body would feel when he slipped his arms around her, how it would relax against him in trust, and how her hands would soon slide around his back.

"Rampant. One day you're clear, and the next, you're covered from head to toe." Shal sighed.

"Ah... So a bad case, then?"

"The worst there is, Cam. I'm crazy in love with you. How could I not be? You're the kind of guy who holds my hair back while I throw up, then calmly hands me a toothbrush. I'm in *way* deep."

Cam laughed, then turned to press a firm kiss to the top of her forehead, heart ratcheting painfully in his chest with the unbelievable joy of it. "Don't worry, I'll nurse you through it."

"I was kind of hoping you'd say that. Because the answer is 'yes.' "

"Yes to six months?"

It was like catching the seventh wave, when you'd timed it perfectly and the immense power behind the surge thrust you forward. That instant when you knew it was yours, and every nerve ending in your body sung with the pure elation of it.

"Yes, please," Shal murmured against his chest, the embrace apparently making her dopey. "Then, if you're still happy in six months time, you could ask me again."

"Ask you for another six?"

He wanted to whoop aloud when Shal nodded firmly into his neck, but hesitated before asking the question that was still nibbling at his gut.

304

"Under your terms, or mine?"

He found himself hanging onto her answer. Everything hinged on it.

"Your terms. Kind of. With some modifications, if you agree." Shal angled for a firm tone, but Cam's arms were cosy and soothing and it came out sounding a little on the dreamy side. "I'm up for fidelity and security with you, minus any talk of marriage. You know it doesn't sit well with me, due to... Well, due to David, I guess. And I don't think I will ever change my mind on that one. Is that okay with you?"

"Absolutely." The single word rumbled from Cam's chest.

"Good. But we're exclusive, so I get to kill anyone who puts their hands on you, and you're free to do the same."

Cam hummed in agreement, stroking her back up, then down in a slow sweep. "Mmm-hmm."

Shal remained silent, thinking about the past men in her life who'd either cheated, or gone the other way and tried to grip her too tightly. There were a few other sticking points she should mention.

"I'd keep my own name and career and we'd have separate bank accounts. Maybe *one* joint one, like our old flat kitty. I also think we should live together straight away. We've done it before and know it works, so there's no point waiting." An image popped into her head of the Park Street property, with tools and half completed walls all over the place. "As long as it's not on one of your building sites," she added swiftly.

Cam's laugh was deeply resonating, and he gave her an extra squeeze. "No worries, I'm sure we can arrange that."

"I can't live in a cage, Cam, but I'm ready to lean on your support trusses if you're willing to lean on mine." Shal pulled back to get a good look at his face, trying to gauge his reaction so far. "I might be a bit of an earthquake zone, though. I'm new to all this."

"We've been through some pretty gnarly stuff together. I'm sure we can handle the odd tremor," Cam assured her, eyes glinting.

"I actually prefer Ōtepoti to Te Whanganui-a-Tara, partly because I'd like to graduate from there."

"Really?"

"Yes. But I can't handle an entire winter that far south." She gave a mock shudder, making Cam smile. "I need to go somewhere hot and clammy to thaw out around June. Maybe we could tie that in with a trip to the States, or your music somehow, because if you're going on tour then I expect to be invited too."

Shal had a sudden thought, and pushed back a little further in the circle of Cam's arms to contemplate him more seriously. The wind had blown his hair into a crest on one side and she ran her fingers through it to soothe it back down.

"Also, if we ever *did* decide to have children, they'd have to take your surname. I won't be lumping another poor soul with Ericsson Hoffner."

"*Children*?" Cam blinked at her as if she'd grown two heads.

"Maybe?" She hesitated, still not sure on that point. "But we'd have to be really solid on family support, and I want to finish my degree first."

"Sure," Cam finally croaked, nodding. "Wait. We're still allowed to put in a bit of practice, right?" His twitch of a smile grew into a somewhat wicked smirk. "A *lot* of practice."

"Gladly," she smirked right back at him. "So you'll ask me again if you're still happy in six months time. And so on and so forth."

Cam cradled his hands gently around her face, raising her chin so she met his gaze. Her breath hitched in her throat when she saw the depth of fierce emotion in Cam's warm eyes, as if he was showing her his whole heart for the first time.

"I think out of everything you just said, and *a lot* just came out of your mouth," Cam teased. " 'And so on and so forth' might just be my favourite part." He kissed her forehead then moved his lips to the bridge of her nose. "I love you, e hoa," he whispered.

"Wait." Shal frowned. "What *does* e hoa mean, exactly? Friend, right?"

"Usually friend, but every area has a different dialect; slightly different uses or formalities for the same word. It can also mean partner, or spouse." He stroked both thumbs along her jawline and stared at her mouth. "You can take it to mean whatever you want it to mean."

She touched her tongue to her bottom lip, tucking her fat envelope full of love-notes under Cams's belt so she could slip both hands into his back pockets and watch the smoulder burn in his eyes.

"Partner is good," she decided.

"Partner is *superb*," Cam amended, and he was laughing.

By the time Cam finally lowered his head to kiss her full on the lips, both of them were grinning. With three weeks of banked-up kissandmakeup, and an ocean-full of love, it packed one hell of a punch.

THE END

WANT MORE?

Thank you for reading Mako Bay, book 1 in the Otago Waters series. I hope you enjoyed Cam and Shal's journey as much as I enjoyed writing it!

But what happened to Pieta?! If you're dying to know, you're welcome to download your own complimentary e-copy of Pieta's love story in the award-winning novella, Tinsel River, here: https://dl.bookfunnel.com/1prs3l2xrx. A gift from me to you.

You will find Daniel's full story in Ruby Island, and Adele's in Lake Taimana.

To discover more about my other books, and gain access to exclusive short stories and new releases, sign up for my newsletter at www.stephanie-ruth.com.

As an indie author, I hugely appreciate your help in spreading the word about my writing. Request my books at your local library, or leave a review on Amazon, Bookbub, Goodreads, or your own favourite book-lovers site.

Turn the page for an excerpt from Ruby Island,
book 2 in the Otago Waters series.

SNEAK PEEK - RUBY ISLAND
CHAPTER 1 - TWO MISTAKES

"There are only two mistakes
one can make along the road to truth;
not going all the way, and not starting."
- Buddha

Kanako Janssen had an hour to kill before her arranged meeting time and though she was habitually early, a full sixty minutes was just plain ridiculous.

The mechanised voice of the sat nav observed her deviation off-course in Japanese as she turned towards the lakefront.

"Put a sock in it," she muttered in response to the suggested U-turn, leaning across to switch the device to mute.

The unsealed off-road was flanked by slim-trunked silver birches and towering conifers, but it was the willows and poplars further along the shoreline that really drew her in. Already taking on the golden hues of early autumn, the trees blazed and shimmered in the late morning sun like a fresh kiln-load waiting to be unpacked.

A young family shared an early lunch of fish and chips on a picnic table, the newsprint wrapping flapping lazily in the breeze, and a man on the pebbled beach threw a large stick for his dog. His lobs arced high and long, the canine nothing more than a blur of black and white as it streaked along the shoreline.

Kana parked, re-checking on the exact location of the dog before climbing out of her SUV.

Simply deepening her breaths eased the majority of tension from the long drive.

The air was different this far south, like long, cool sips of mineral water. Her senses were waking, emerging from the ingrained pollution of the city.

A step towards something fresh, something new. Better to look at this upheaval as a beginning rather than an end.

Taking her thermos and regional-map book with her, she settled at a vacant picnic table to sip her green tea, the action and taste winging her thoughts to Honshu.

What would Obāchan be doing now?

Kana opened the multi-city app on her phone. In Hiroshima it wasn't yet eight o'clock.

Still too early to call.

She imagined herself in Obāchan's traditional farmhouse instead, enveloped by the scents and sounds she knew so well. If her grandmother was still sleeping, snow-white hair would be fanning across her *futon* like a heron's tail. But if she'd risen with the hens, her hair would already be tortured into a no-nonsense bun and there would be fresh eggs to crack over their morning *gohan*.

Kana sighed. Turning her face towards the sun, she lifted her sunglasses and closed her eyes. The daily ritual of missing her grandmother took on a physical ache, and the artist within her imagined it manifesting as a tangible gap under her ribcage.

Visible to casual observers? Probably not…

The dog's sharp bark startled Kana's eyes open.

So close.

Temporarily blinded by the glare of light off the water, she dropped her sunglasses back onto the bridge of her nose and spun around. She hadn't been paying attention and it took a moment to re-orient herself.

A friendly-faced animal could be just as dangerous as an openly hostile one, in her experience. Thank Buddha this one was now on a leash.

Man and beast had left the shore, heading directly past her towards the farm ute, and the dog had dropped its well-chewed stick near her foot before issuing a clear invitation. It crouched low and barked again, making her jump and upend her tea.

Kana scrabbled to right the thermos, splashing liquid over herself in the process.

"Sorry. Forgotten his manners. Are you alright?" The man removed the stick and chucked it back towards the beach, his sheepdog responding with a high-pitched whine, straining at the leash to go after it.

Kana nodded, eyes still glued to the animal and all those gleaming teeth.

Piping hot when she'd prepared it in Ōtepoti, her tea was now only tepid; lacking the heat to burn. Surreptitiously wiping the back of her hand off on her jeans, she tried to get her head together.

"Quiet. Heel." The soft commands took immediate effect, the border collie slinking against its master's jean-clad leg, silent.

The man had height, with a broadness about him that shouted RUGBY. The slightly crooked bridging of his nose—possibly an old break—helped cement the image, as did the black beanie pulled down low over his ears. He wore muddied work boots, well-worn denim, and a checked cotton shirt.

Tricky to place his age with a good week's worth of dark stubble. More than thirty, less than forty, give or take.

But he wasn't moving off, as she'd hoped.

"Ah..." Kana was unsure how to politely tell the man to bugger off, having been wary of dogs since childhood. Ridiculously frightened, even by the smallest of breeds, she certainly didn't want anything to do with this relatively large one—well behaved or not.

Sliding her sunglasses down her nose, she narrowed her eyes at the two of them.

"You're not from around here." It was a statement, not a question. The dog owner motioned to Kana's open map book, just shy of the tea-puddle. "Are you lost?"

Mild irritation snapped—enough to make Kana forget the canine for a moment. She was beyond sick of being mistaken for a tourist in her own country. It hadn't happened for a while, but seemed to be ingrained in the story of her life.

Pure force of habit had her slip into a dismissive, slightly barbed old high school trick.

She spoke in Japanese.

"Sumimasen, Eigo wa wakarimasen."

Erecting a language barrier was the perfect conversation killer for this occasion. Rugby's cue to smile, take his dog, and get lost.

That threw him.

Daniel had assumed the woman was a Kiwi, with some Eastern heritage thrown in. She looked in keeping; at peace with the landscape. Her almond eyes and colouring would be very unusual in Japan. Autumnal—glowing like the trees lining the lakefront.

It was also uncommon for a Japanese woman to travel on her own in Aotearoa, especially without a basic grasp of English. Those less linguistically inclined tended to travel within groups.

Safety in numbers.

Glancing around himself, Daniel took stock of the surrounding area and the distinct lack of anything resembling a tour.

He hadn't been expecting to hear anything other than English, so it took a moment to change gears. Reaching into his memory banks, he dragged his meagre Japanese to the forefront. Tenses, and the more difficult pronoun choices had always been an issue. Prepared speeches were fine, but some of the off-the-cuff conversations he'd attempted in the past had been disastrous.

"Gomen'nasai. Kiwi ja nai desu ka? Nihon-jin desu ka?" He was pretty sure that equated to 'My apologies. You're not a Kiwi? You're Japanese?' He then went on to ask if she was lost.

When he'd lived in Japan, the locals had fallen all over themselves to be helpful. The least he could do was try and reciprocate in some small way.

It had nothing to do with the fact this particular female was incredibly easy on the eye.

When she'd had her sunglasses on and was jumping out of her skin about the dog, he'd assumed she was younger. But though she was just a slip of a thing, this was a grown woman, not a girl.

A stunning woman.

Her eyes, though still appearing nervous, caught the light and radiated soft amber. Infused with a chilli-chocolate, the hair glossing over her shoulders was even more intriguing due to its sheer mass, making his fingers itch to reach out and measure the weight.

He introduced himself as Daniel, and established her name was Kanako, all the while searching for any sign of recognition on her part.

Nothing. Not a single flicker.

The relief of being incognito washed over him, as welcome as a cool breeze off the lake, making him realise how rarely he experienced either nowadays. It turned the tables, making him slightly uneasy in his own skin. He'd become obtuse to the signs, unable to get a clear reading on other people's gut responses to him.

If he was just a man—any man—how would this woman perceive him?

Could he actually charm, merely by being himself? Or was it all in his reputation; his notoriety?

Disconcertingly, when Kanako smiled up at him from her lower position, her face upturned, it was Daniel who felt vaguely weaker. Almost as if the wattage she was using to turn on her sweet magnetism was somehow connected to his power source.

An unsettling thought. One he didn't care to analyse.

Mr Rugby, or Daniel, as he'd introduced himself, was adept at *Nihongo*. Not exactly fluent, but quite capable, with a decent grasp of the correct pronunciation.

Kana was left gaping, more than a little embarrassed. Her little tongue-in-cheek snub had just backfired and bitten her firmly on the butt.

She squirmed.

Daniel was waiting for her to answer his latest halting question, and she was acutely aware she wasn't behaving as a Japanese tourist would; delighted one of the locals was well studied in her native tongue.

"I'm not lost, just taking in the view and having a break at the same time," Kana replied in the language of her mother, sticking to the simplest verbs and studying Daniel even more warily. He used his hands when he spoke and his eyes when he listened, concentrating fully on her lips and expression.

They were an honest hazel-green, which made her squirm all the more for being *dis*honest.

Daniel continued in Japanese, asking which part of *Nippon* she hailed from, and how long she'd been in New Zealand. He was an intriguing contradiction of a man, all burly and gruff but exhibiting impeccable manners.

"Hiroshima," she finally offered. Answering the where, if not the when, and remembering her own manners enough to ask which areas of Japan he'd travelled through.

Daniel had spent five years in Kansai. Osaka City. A huge industrial metropolis, topped only in size by Tokyo and swarming in rich trading history. Far too urban for her own taste.

He'd played rugby for one of the large corporation teams.

Kana gave herself a mental pat on the back for that. She'd called it at first sight.

Daniel now helped trial and coach new players, and drew in internationals for the top Japanese league. He must've been a decent player himself to gain such a position. Not that Kana followed rugby. It struck her as a needlessly violent game, but she politely withheld that particular opinion from the man standing in front of her.

She hadn't forgotten about the dog, or the fact Daniel was a total stranger, so didn't invite either to sit. But it did feel good to speak Japanese and to hear someone use her full given name.

No one called her Kanako now except Obāchan. It always got shortened to Kana, which she didn't mind exactly. It just seemed somehow... *less*.

When Daniel left, he gave a polite bow and said he'd enjoyed meeting her, then wished her safe travels around the South Island. He hesitated for a long moment before finally turning away, to the point Kana began to wonder if he wanted something more from her.

Something *other*?

His eyes said yes, but his actions, no.

After Rugby's dusty farm ute had left the layby, Kana let out a long, shaky breath.

The ridiculous situations she got herself into, honestly. Her father would be in stitches when she told him. Not due to the fact she was talking to strange men in laybys, but due to her innate ability to entangle herself in accidental muck.

Taking off her Ugg boots, Kana rolled up her jeans. No longer having a husband around to try and talk her out of it or call her nuts, she was going to brave a paddle in the shallows… Even if it froze her toes off.

Up to her calves, with the shore behind her, Kana soaked in the colours and wide-open sky, wondering who'd planted all of these beautiful European trees along the lakeside, and how ancient they were. She would have to read up on it.

How at home they looked. Strange when you considered how far they'd been removed from their original rootstock.

Just like herself.

"*In the sky, there is no distinction of east and west; people create distinctions out of their own minds then believe them to be true,*" Kana murmured one of Obāchan's favourite Buddhist quotes under her breath.

If she were to emulate these particular colours in glazes, the poplar leaves would be mid-fired Abbots Dune through to Rimu in their graduated golds. The wind across the lake was chopping up patches of silver Chun over a thinly applied blue… Perhaps her modified Celadon in a high firing? And the deep, glossy black of Tenmoku would best match the far mountain peaks, with an added measure of iron oxide to slide it into the brown hues of the lower slopes.

Kana found herself assigning the colours she used on her stoneware to almost every view. It was an unconscious action, but this particular palette had her enthused about the six month artist-in-residence gig she was about to embark on. The backdrop of Lake Wānaka, diamond of the south, was nothing if not inspiring.

It took some time and a bit of stamping to be able to feel all ten of her toes again afterwards, but the dip was definitely worth it. It suited her mood to baptise her travelling feet, uplifting the corners of her mouth.

Her hour was almost up, and she was more than ready to go and meet her patron.

Continue reading Ruby Island
www.stephanie-ruth.com

SHAL'S PLAYLIST
LISTENING TO...

Shal's Playlist is available on Spotify.

Ch. 1: *Welcome Home* - Dave Dobbyn. From the album: Available Light

Ch. 2: *Love Your Ways* - Salmonella Dub. From the album: Inside The Dub Plates

Ch. 3: *Fallen* - Lauren Wood. From the album: Pretty Woman, Movie Soundtrack

Ch. 4: *Maxine* - Sharon O'Neill. From the album: Foreign Affairs

Ch. 5: *Something in the Water* - Brooke Fraser. From the album: Flags

Ch. 6: *Creep* - Thom Yorke. From the album: Pablo Honey - Radiohead

Ch. 7: *Together Alone* - Neil Finn, Mark Hart and Ngapo 'Bub' Wehi. From the album: Together Alone - Crowded House

Ch. 8: *Sway* - Bic Runga. From the album: Drive

Ch. 9: *Monarch* - Shapeshifter. From the album: Delta

Ch. 10: *How Bizarre* - Alan Jansson, Pauly Fuemana. From the album: How Bizarre - OMC

Ch. 11: *Isabelle* - Greg Johnson. From the album: Everyday Distortions - The Greg Johnson Set

Ch. 12: *Modern Fables* - Julia Deans. From the album: Modern Fables

Ch. 13: *Down in Splendour* - Straitjacket Fits. From the album: Melt

Ch. 14: *The Sum of Us* - Ruth Carr. From the EP: The Sum of Us - Minuit

Ch. 15: *Wandering Eye* - Fat Freddy's Drop. From the album: Based on a True Story

Ch. 16: *Undone* - Boh Runga. From the album: Mix - Stellar

Ch. 17: *Pacifier* - Shihad. From the album: The General Electric

Ch. 18: *Venus* - James Reid From the album: Supersystem - The Feelers

Ch. 19: *Be Mine Tonight* - Dave Dobbyn, Ian Morris. From the album: Right First Time - Th' Dudes

Ch. 20: *Caught* - Shona Laing. From the album: South

Ch. 21: *While you Sleep* - Don McGlashan. From the album: Envy of Angels - The Mutton Birds

Ch. 22: *Victoria* - Jordan Luck. From the album: Prayers Be Answered - Dance Exponents

Ch. 23: *Renegade Fighter* - Nathan King, Ben Campbell. From the album: Silencer - Zed

Ch. 24: *Tears* - The Crocodiles. From the album: Tears

Ch. 25: *Maybe* - Jason Kerrison. From the album: Second Hand Planet - Opshop

Ch. 26: *Dark Child* - Marlon Williams. From the album: Marlon Williams

Ch. 27: *Stuff and Nonsense* - Tim Finn. From the album: Frenzy - Split Enz

ALSO MENTIONED:

Englishman In New York - Sting. From the album: Englishman in New York

Slice of Heaven - Dave Dobbyn and Herbs. From the movie soundtrack: Footrot Flats

Roll on Summer - Stevi Nixon. From the EP: Bohemian - Rosie Said

Crush - Stevi Nixon. From the single release: Crush - Rosie Said

Bohemian - Stevi Nixon. From the EP: Bohemian - Rosie Said

Elephant in the Room - Lyrics by Stevi Nixon

On My Knees - Lyrics by Stevi Nixon

ACKNOWLEDGMENTS

Aotearoa is a stunning backdrop, and I'm proud to call it home. However, the cultures here are as diverse as the people, and I can't claim them all as my own. Thank you to Fiona, Heperi, and Ranui, for your time and invaluable suggestions in Te Reo Māori. Thank you also to Ron Bull, for your insight, corrections, and connections with regards to Kai Tahu, and the Ōtākou region. Ngā mihi nui.

Also acknowledging Ōtākou Marae; ngā kōrero tuku iho, te mana whenua, ngā tāngata, me ēnei manaakiatnga. Tēnā koutou katoa.

Aaron and Mat (and Don, by proxy), I appreciate your building expertise and information, detailing (among other things) the specific nationalities of gib, plasterboard, and drywall.

To Mathew and Lauren, who both had the dubious pleasure of trying to teach me to surf, thank you, and my deepest apologies. I was clearly born to snowboard.

I couldn't have published this book without the input from my ground crew. Lyssa and Melissa, I'm so grateful to have met you both, and would've thrown in the towel well before now without your editing skills and support. Fiona and Megan, your unmitigated enthusiasm in everything I give you to read makes me believe I will absolutely find my readership. And last but definitely not least, Josie, alpha reader, Ōtepoti-an, and tuakana extraordinaire, aroha nui!

A great many people have helped steer my waka as I wrote Cam and Shal's story, but any errors remaining are mine, and mine alone.

ABOUT STEPHANIE RUTH

A multi award-winning contemporary romance novelist and short story writer, Stephanie Ruth lives in the South Island of Aotearoa, Te Waipounamu, with her husband, three children, and an ever-expanding array of animals. If it doesn't have a happy ending in some form, Stephanie's not writing it.

Mako Bay, winner of the Daphne Clair de Jong First Kiss Award and finalist in the Koru First Book Award of Excellence, is her debut novel, and first in the Otago Waters Series.

When she's not writing, you can usually find Stephanie beach-combing or dabbling in the arts (the messier the better), but sometimes she's laughing at cat videos and chatting with other bibliophiles on social media. TikTok and Instagram: stephanie_ruth_writes_nz, and Facebook stephanieruth.nz.

Sign up to her newsletter and receive exclusive access to short stories, bonus reads, new releases, and book sales on her website www.stephanie-ruth.com.

ALSO BY STEPHANIE RUTH

OTAGO WATERS SERIES

- novels -
Mako Bay
Ruby Island
Lake Taimana

- novella -
Tinsel River
The Ocean Between
Taniwha Creek

- short story anthology -
Add a Splash of Love

THE BOUTIQUE SERIES

- novel -
2 Peas

- novella -
Anti-Freeze

- short stories -
Gregory Anders Drives Me Nuts
Between Friends